Louise Penny is the *New York Times*-bestselling author of six previous Gamache novels, including *Still Life*, which won the CWA John Creasey Dagger in 2006. Recipient of virtually every existing award for crime fiction, she lives in a small village south of Montréal.

This book is to be returned on or before
the last date stamped below.

Cro

2/12

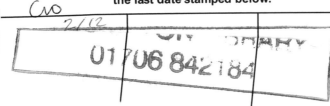

LOUISE
PENNY

A
Trick of the
Light

sphere

SPHERE

First published in the United States in 2011 by Minatour,
a division of St Martin's Press
First published in Great Britain in 2012 by Sphere

Printed and bound in Great Britain by
Clays Ltd, St Ives plc

Papers used by Sphere are from well-managed forests
and other responsible sources.

For Sharon, Margaret, Louise and all
the wonderful women who helped me find
a quiet place in the bright sunshine.

ONE

～

*O*h, *no, no, no*, thought Clara Morrow as she walked toward the closed doors.

She could see shadows, shapes, like wraiths moving back and forth, back and forth across the frosted glass. Appearing and disappearing. Distorted, but still human.

Still the dead one lay moaning.

The words had been going through her head all day, appearing and disappearing. A poem, half remembered. Words floating to the surface, then going under. The body of the poem beyond her grasp.

What was the rest of it?

It seemed important.

Oh, no no no.

The blurred figures at the far end of the long corridor seemed almost liquid, or smoke. There, but insubstantial. Fleeting. Fleeing.

As she wished she could.

This was it. The end of the journey. Not just that day's journey as she and her husband, Peter, had driven from their little Québec village into the Musée d'Art Contemporain in Montréal, a place they knew well. Intimately. How often had they come to the MAC to marvel at some new exhibition? To support a friend, a fellow artist? Or to just sit quietly in the middle of the sleek gallery, in the middle of a weekday, when the rest of the city was at work?

Art was their work. But it was more than that. It had to be. Otherwise, why put up with all those years of solitude? Of failure? Of silence from a baffled and even bemused art world?

She and Peter had worked away, every day, in their small studios in their small village, leading their tiny lives. Happy. But still yearning for more.

Clara took a few more steps down the long, long, white marble hallway.

This was the 'more'. Through those doors. Finally. The end point of everything she'd worked toward, walked toward, all her life.

Her first dream as a child, her last dream that morning, almost fifty years later, was at the far end of the hard white hallway.

They'd both expected Peter would be the first through those doors. He was by far the more successful artist, with his exquisite studies of life in close-up. So detailed, and so close that a piece of the natural world appeared distorted and abstract. Unrecognizable. Peter took what was natural and made it appear unnatural.

People ate it up. Thank God. It kept food on the table and the wolves, while constantly circling their little home in Three Pines, were kept from the door. Thanks to Peter and his art.

Clara glanced at him walking slightly ahead of her, a smile on his handsome face. She knew most people, on first meeting them, never took her for his wife. Instead they assumed some slim executive with a white wine in her elegant hand was his mate. An example of natural selection. Of like moving to like.

The distinguished artist with the head of graying hair and noble features could not possibly have chosen the woman with the beer in her boxing glove hands. And the pâté in her frizzy hair. And the studio full of sculptures made out of old tractor parts and paintings of cabbages with wings.

No. Peter Morrow could not have chosen her. That would have been unnatural.

And yet he had.

And she had chosen him.

Clara would have smiled had she not been fairly certain she was about to throw up.

Oh, no no no, she thought again as she watched Peter march purposefully toward the closed door and the art wraiths waiting to pass judgment. On her.

Clara's hands grew cold and numb as she moved slowly forward, propelled by an undeniable force, a rude mix of excitement and terror. She wanted to rush toward the doors, yank them open and yell, 'Here I am!'

But mostly she wanted to turn and flee, to hide.

To stumble back down the long, long, light-filled, art-filled, marble-filled hallway. To admit she'd made a mistake. Given the wrong answer when asked if she'd like a solo show. At the Musée. When asked if she'd like all her dreams to come true.

She'd given the wrong answer. She'd said yes. And this is where it led.

Someone had lied. Or hadn't told the whole truth. In her dream, her only dream, played over and over since childhood, she had a solo show at the Musée d'Art Contemporain. She walked down this corridor. Composed and collected. Beautiful and slim. Witty and popular.

Into the waiting arms of an adoring world.

There was no terror. No nausea. No creatures glimpsed through the frosted glass, waiting to devour her. Dissect her. Diminish her, and her creations.

Someone had lied. Had not told her something else might be waiting.

Failure.

Oh, no no no, thought Clara. *Still the dead one lay moaning.*

What was the rest of the poem? Why did it elude her?

Now, within feet of the end of her journey all she wanted to do was run away home to Three Pines. To open the wooden gate. To race up the path lined with apple trees in spring bloom. To slam their front door shut behind her. To lean against it. To lock it. To press her body against it, and keep the world out.

Now, too late, she knew who'd lied to her.

She had.

Clara's heart threw itself against her ribs, like something caged and terrified and desperate to escape. She realized she was holding her breath and wondered for how long. To make up for it she started breathing rapidly.

Peter was talking but his voice was muffled, far away. Drowned out by the shrieking in her head, and the pounding in her chest.

And the noise building behind the doors. As they got closer.

'This's going to be fun,' said Peter, with a reassuring smile.

Clara opened her hand and dropped her purse. It fell with a plop to the floor, since it was all but empty, containing simply a breath mint and the tiny paint brush from the first paint-by-number set her grandmother had given her.

Clara dropped to her knees, pretending to gather up invisible items and stuff them into her clutch. She lowered her head, trying to catch her breath, and wondered if she was about to pass out.

'Deep breath in,' she heard. 'Deep breath out.'

Clara stared from the purse on the gleaming marble floor to the man crouched across from her.

It wasn't Peter.

Instead, she saw her friend and neighbor from Three Pines, Olivier Brulé. He was kneeling beside her, watching, his kind eyes life preservers thrown to a drowning woman. She held them.

'Deep breath in,' he whispered. His voice was calm. This was their own private crisis. Their own private rescue.

She took a deep breath in.

'I don't think I can do it.' Clara leaned forward, feeling faint. She could feel the walls closing in, and see Peter's polished black leather shoes on the floor ahead. Where he'd finally stopped. Not missing her right away. Not noticing his wife was kneeling on the floor.

'I know,' whispered Olivier. 'But I also know you. Whether it's on your knees or on your feet, you're going through that door.' He nodded toward the end of the hall, his eyes never leaving hers. 'It might as well be on your feet.'

'But it's not too late.' Clara searched his face. Seeing his silky blond hair, and the lines only visible very close up. More lines than a thirty-eight-year-old man should have. 'I could leave. Go back home.'

Olivier's kindly face disappeared and she saw again her garden, as she'd seen it that morning, the mist not yet burned off. The dew heavy under her rubber boots. The early roses and late peonies damp and fragrant. She'd sat on the wooden bench in their backyard, with her morning coffee, and she'd thought about the day ahead.

Not once had she imagined herself collapsed on the floor. In terror. Longing to leave. To go back to the garden.

But Olivier was right. She wouldn't return. Not yet.

Oh, no no no. She'd have to go through those doors. They were the only way home now.

'Deep breath out,' Olivier whispered, with a smile.

Clara laughed, and exhaled. 'You'd make a good midwife.'

'What're you two doing down there?' Gabri asked as he watched Clara and his partner. 'I know what Olivier usually does in that position and I hope that isn't it.' He turned to Peter. 'Though that might explain the laughter.'

'Ready?' Olivier handed Clara her purse and they got to their feet.

Gabri, never far from Olivier's side, gave Clara a bear hug. 'You OK?' He examined her closely. He was big, though Gabri preferred to call himself 'burly', his face unscored by the worry lines of his partner.

'I'm fine,' said Clara.

'Fucked up, insecure, neurotic and egotistical?' asked Gabri.

'Exactly.'

'Great. So'm I. And so's everyone through there.' Gabri gestured toward the door. 'What they aren't is the fabulous artist with the solo show. So you're both fine and famous.'

'Coming?' asked Peter, waving toward Clara and smiling.

She hesitated, then taking Peter's hand, they walked together down the corridor, the sharp echoes of their feet not quite masking the merriment on the other side.

They're laughing, thought Clara. *They're laughing at my art.*

And in that instant the body of the poem surfaced. The rest of it was revealed.

Oh, no no no, thought Clara. *Still the dead one lay moaning.*
I was much too far out all my life
And not waving but drowning.

From far off Armand Gamache could hear the sound of children playing. He knew where it was coming from. The park across the way, though he couldn't see the children through the maple trees in late spring leaf. He sometimes liked to sit there and pretend the shouts and laughter came from his young grandchildren, Florence and Zora. He imagined his son Daniel and Roslyn were in the park, watching their children. And that soon they'd walk hand in hand across the quiet street in the very center of the great city, for dinner. Or he and Reine-Marie would join them. And play catch, or conkers.

He liked to pretend they weren't thousands of kilometers away in Paris.

But mostly he just listened to the shouts and shrieks and laughter of neighborhood children. And smiled. And relaxed.

Gamache reached for his beer and lowered the *L'Observateur* magazine to his knee. His wife, Reine-Marie, sat across from him on their balcony. She too had a cold beer on this unexpectedly warm day in mid-June. But her copy of *La Presse* was folded on the table and she stared into the distance.

'What're you thinking about?' he asked.

'My mind was just wandering.'

He was silent for a moment, watching her. Her hair was quite gray now, but then, so was his. She'd dyed it auburn for many years but just recently had stopped doing that. He was glad. Like him, she was in her mid-fifties. And this was what a couple of that age looked like. If they were lucky.

Not like models. No one would mistake them for that. Armand Gamache wasn't heavy, but solidly built. If a stranger visited this home he might think Monsieur Gamache a quiet academic, a professor of history or literature perhaps at the Université de Montréal.

But that too would be a mistake.

Books were everywhere in their large apartment. Histories, biographies, novels, studies on Québec antiques, poetry. Placed in orderly bookcases. Just about every table had at least one book on it, and often several magazines. And the weekend newspapers were scattered on the coffee table in the living room, in front of the fireplace. If a visitor was the observant type, and made it further into the apartment to Gamache's study, he might see the story the books in there told.

And he'd soon realize this was not the home of some retiring professor of French literature. The shelves were packed with case histories, with books on medicine and forensics, with tomes on Napoleonic and common law, fingerprinting, genetic coding, wounds and weapons.

Murder. Armand Gamache's study was filled with it.

But still, even among the death, space was made for books on philosophy and poetry.

Watching Reine-Marie as they sat on the balcony, Gamache was once again struck by the certainty he'd married above himself. Not socially. Not academically. But he could never shake the suspicion he had gotten very, very lucky.

Armand Gamache knew he'd had a great deal of luck in his life, but none more than having loved the same woman for thirty-five years. Unless it was the extraordinary stroke of luck that she should also love him.

Now she turned her blue eyes on him. 'Actually, I was thinking about Clara's *vernissage*.'

'Oh?'

'We should be going soon.'

'True.' He looked at his watch. It was five past five. The party to launch Clara Morrow's solo show started at the Musée at five and would end at seven. 'As soon as David arrives.'

Their son-in-law was half an hour late and Gamache glanced inside their apartment. He could just barely make out his daughter Annie sitting in the living room reading, and across from her was his second in command, Jean Guy Beauvoir. Kneading Henri's remarkable ears. The Gamaches' German shepherd could stay like that all day, a goofy grin on his young face.

Jean Guy and Annie were ignoring each other. Gamache smiled slightly. At least they weren't hurling insults, or worse, across the room.

'Would you like to leave?' Armand offered. 'We could call David on his cell and ask him to just meet us there.'

'Why don't we give him another couple of minutes.'

Gamache nodded and picked up the magazine, then he lowered it slowly.

'Is there something else?'

Reine-Marie hesitated then smiled. 'I was just wondering how you're feeling about going to the *vernissage*. And wondering if you're stalling.'

Armand raised his brow in surprise.

Jean Guy Beauvoir rubbed Henri's ears and stared at the young woman across from him. He'd known her for fifteen years, since he was a rookie on homicide and she was a teenager. Awkward, gawky, bossy.

He didn't like kids. Certainly didn't like smart-ass teenagers. But he'd tried to like Annie Gamache, if only because she was the boss's daughter.

He'd tried and he'd tried and he'd tried. And finally—

He'd succeeded.

And now he was nearing forty and she was nearing thirty. A lawyer. Married. Still awkward and gawky and bossy. But he'd tried so hard to like her he'd finally seen beyond that. He'd seen her laugh with real gaiety, seen her listen to very boring people as though they were riveting. She looked as though she was genuinely glad to see them. As though they were important. He'd seen her dance, arms flailing and head tilted back. Eyes shining.

And he'd felt her hand in his. Only once.

In the hospital. He'd come back up from very far away. Fought through the pain and the dark to that foreign but gentle touch. He knew it didn't belong to his wife, Enid. That bird-like grip he would not have come back for.

But this hand was large, and certain, and warm. And it invited him back.

He'd opened his eyes to see Annie Gamache staring at him with such concern. Why would she be there, he'd wondered. And then he knew why.

Because she had nowhere else to be. No other hospital bed to sit beside.

Because her father was dead. Killed by a gunman in the abandoned factory. Beauvoir had seen it happen. Seen Gamache hit. Seen him lifted off his feet and fall to the concrete floor.

And lie still.

And now Annie Gamache was holding his hand in the hospital, because the hand she really wanted to be holding was gone.

Jean Guy Beauvoir had pried his eyes open and seen Annie Gamache looking so sad. And his heart broke. Then he saw something else.

Joy.

No one had ever looked at him that way. With unconcealed and unbound joy.

Annie had looked at him like that, when he'd opened his eyes.

He'd tried to speak but couldn't. But she'd rightly guessed what he was trying to say.

She'd leaned in and whispered into his ear, and he could smell her fragrance. It was slightly citrony. Clean and fresh. Not Enid's clinging, full-bodied perfume. Annie smelled like a lemon grove in summer.

'Dad's alive.'

He'd embarrassed himself then. There were many humiliations waiting for him in the hospital. From bedpans and diapers to sponge baths. But none was more personal, more intimate, more of a betrayal than what his broken body did then.

He cried.

And Annie saw. And Annie never mentioned it from that day to this.

To Henri's bafflement, Jean Guy stopped rubbing the dog's ears and placed one hand on the other, in a gesture that had become habitual now.

That was how it had felt. Annie's hand on his.

This was all he'd ever have of her. His boss's married daughter.

'Your husband's late,' said Jean Guy, and could hear the accusation. The shove.

Very, very slowly Annie lowered her newspaper. And glared at him.

'What's your point?'

What was his point?

'We're going to be late because of him.'

'Then go. I don't care.'

He'd loaded the gun, pointed it at his head, and begged Annie to pull the trigger. And now he felt the words strike. Cut. Travel deep and explode.

I don't care.

It was almost comforting, he realized. The pain. Perhaps if he forced her to hurt him enough he'd stop feeling anything.

'Listen,' she said, leaning forward, her voice softening a bit. 'I'm sorry about you and Enid. Your separation.'

'Yeah, well, it happens. As a lawyer you should know that.'

She looked at him with searching eyes, like her father's. Then she nodded.

'It happens.' She grew quiet, still. 'Especially after what you've been through, I guess. It makes you think about your life. Would you like to talk about it?'

Talk about Enid with Annie? All the petty sordid squabbles, the tiny slights, the scarring and scabbing. The thought revolted him and he must have shown it. Annie pulled back and reddened as though he'd slapped her.

'Forget I said anything,' she snapped and lifted the paper to her face.

He searched for something to say, some small bridge, a jetty back to her. The minutes stretched by, elongating.

'The *vernissage*,' Beauvoir finally blurted out. It was the first thing that popped into his hollow head, like the Magic Eight Ball, that when it stopped being shaken produced a single word. '*Vernissage*,' in this case.

The newspaper lowered and Annie's stone face appeared.

'The people from Three Pines will be there, you know.'

Still her face was expressionless.

'That village, in the Eastern Townships,' he waved vaguely out the window. 'South of Montréal.'

'I know where the townships are,' she said.

'The show's for Clara Morrow, but they'll all be there I'm sure.'

She raised the newspaper again. The Canadian dollar was strong, he read from across the room. Winter potholes still unfixed, he read. An investigation into government corruption, he read.

Nothing new.

'One of them hates your father.'

The newspaper slowly dropped. 'What do you mean?'

'Well,' he realized by her expression he might have gone too far, 'not enough to harm him or anything.'

'Dad's talked about Three Pines and the people, but he never mentioned this.'

Now she was upset and he wished he hadn't said anything, but it at least did the trick. She was talking to him again. Her father was the bridge.

Annie dropped her paper onto the table and glanced beyond Beauvoir to her parents talking quietly on the balcony.

She suddenly looked like that teenager he'd first met. She was never going to be the most beautiful woman in the room. That much was obvious even then. Annie was not fine-boned or delicate. She was more athletic than graceful. She cared about clothes, but she also cared about comfort.

Opinionated, strong-willed, strong physically. He could beat her at arm-wrestling, he knew because they'd done it several times, but he actually had to try.

With Enid he would never consider trying. And she would never offer.

Annie Gamache had not only offered, but had fully expected to win.

Then had laughed when she hadn't.

Where other women, including Enid, were lovely, Annie Gamache was alive.

Late, too late, Jean Guy Beauvoir had come to appreciate how very important it was, how very attractive it was, how very rare it was, to be fully alive.

Annie looked back at Beauvoir. 'Why would one of them hate Dad?'

Beauvoir lowered his voice. 'OK, look. This's what happened.'

Annie leaned forward. They were a couple of feet apart and Beauvoir could just smell her scent. It was all he could do not to take her hands in his.

'There was a murder in Clara's village, Three Pines—'

'Yes, Dad has mentioned that. Seems like a cottage industry there.'

Despite himself, Beauvoir laughed. *'There is strong shadow where there is much light.'*

Annie's look of astonishment made Beauvoir laugh again.

'Let me guess,' she said. 'You didn't make that up.'

Beauvoir smiled and nodded. 'Some German guy said it. And then your father said it.'

'A few times?'

'Often enough that I wake up screaming it in the middle of the night.'

Annie smiled. 'I know. I was the only kid in school who quoted Leigh Hunt.' Her voice changed slightly as she remembered, *'But most he loved a happy human face.'*

Gamache smiled as he heard the laughter from the living room.

He cocked his head in their direction. 'Are they finally making peace, do you think?'

'Either that or it's a sign of the apocalypse,' said Reine-Marie. 'If four horsemen gallop out of the park you're on your own, monsieur.'

'It's good to hear him laugh,' said Gamache.

Since his separation from Enid, Jean Guy had seemed distant. Aloof. He'd never been exactly exuberant but Beauvoir was quieter than ever these days, as though his walls had grown and thickened. And his narrow drawbridge had been raised.

Armand Gamache knew no good ever came from putting up walls. What people mistook for safety was in fact captivity. And few things thrived in captivity.

'It'll take time,' said Reine-Marie.

'*Avec le temps*,' agreed Armand. But privately he wondered. He knew time could heal. But it could also do more damage. A forest fire, spread over time, would consume everything.

Gamache, with one last look at the two younger people, continued his conversation with Reine-Marie.

'Do you really think I don't want to go to the *vernissage*?' he asked.

She considered for a moment. 'I'm not sure. Let's just say you don't seem in a hurry to get there.'

Gamache nodded and thought for a moment. 'I know everyone will be there. I suppose it might be awkward.'

'You arrested one of them for a murder he didn't commit,' said Reine-Marie. It wasn't an accusation. In fact, it was said quietly and gently. Trying to tease the truth of her husband's feelings from him. Feelings he himself might not even be aware he had.

'And you consider that a social *faux pas*?' he asked with a smile.

'More than just a social *faux pas*, I'd say,' she laughed, relieved to see the genuine humor in his face. A face now clean-shaven. No more moustache. No more graying beard. Just Armand. He looked at her with his deep brown eyes. And as she held them she could almost forget the scar above his left temple.

After a moment his smile faded and he nodded again, taking a deep breath.

'It was a terrible thing to do to someone,' he said.

'You didn't do it on purpose, Armand.'

'True, but his time in prison wasn't more pleasant because of that.' Gamache thought for a moment, looking from the gentle face of his wife out into the trees of the park. A natural setting. He so yearned for that, since his days were filled with hunting the unnatural. Killers. People who took the lives of others. Often in gruesome and dreadful ways. Armand Gamache was the head of homicide for the famed Sûreté du Québec. He was very good at his job.

But he wasn't perfect.

He'd arrested Olivier Brulé for a murder he didn't commit.

'So what happened?' Annie asked.

'Well, you know most of it, don't you? It was in all the papers.'

'Of course I read the reports, and talked to Dad about it. But he never mentioned that someone involved might still hate him.'

'Well, as you know, it was almost a year ago,' said Jean Guy. 'A man was found dead in the bistro in Three Pines. We investigated and the evidence seemed overwhelming. We found fingerprints, the murder weapon, stuff stolen from the dead man's cabin in the woods. All of it hidden in the bistro. We arrested Olivier. He was tried and convicted.'

'Did you think he'd done it?'

Beauvoir nodded. 'I was sure of it. It wasn't just your father.'

'So how come you changed your mind? Did someone else confess?'

'No. You remember a few months ago, after that raid on the factory? When your father was recovering in Quebec City?'

Annie nodded.

'Well, he began to have his doubts, so he asked me to go back to Three Pines to investigate.'

'And you did.'

Jean Guy nodded. Of course he'd gone back. He'd do anything the Chief Inspector asked of him. Though he himself had no such doubts. He believed the right man was in prison. But he'd investigated, and discovered something that had truly shocked him.

The real murderer. And the real reason for the killing.

'But you've been back to Three Pines since you arrested Olivier,' said Reine-Marie. 'This won't be the first time you'll have seen them.'

She too had visited Three Pines and become friends with Clara and Peter and the others, though she hadn't seen them in quite a while. Not since all this had happened.

'That's true,' said Armand. 'Jean Guy and I took Olivier back after his release.'

'I can't even imagine how that felt for him.'

Gamache was quiet. Seeing the sun gleaming off snowbanks. Through the frosted panes of glass he could see the villagers gathered in the bistro. Warm and safe. The cheery fires lit. The mugs of beer and bowls of *café au lait*. The laughter.

And Olivier, stalled. Two feet from the closed door. Staring at it.

Jean Guy had gone to open it, but Gamache had lain a gloved hand on his arm. And together in the bitter cold they'd waited. Waited. For Olivier to make the move.

After what seemed an age, but was probably only a few heartbeats, Olivier reached out, paused for one more moment, then opened the door.

'I wish I could've seen Gabri's face,' said Reine-Marie, imagining the large, expressive man seeing his partner returned.

Gamache had described it all to Reine-Marie, when he'd returned home. But he knew that no matter how much ecstasy Reine-Marie imagined, the reality was even greater. At least on Gabri's part. The rest of the villagers were elated to see Olivier too. But—

'What is it?' Reine-Marie asked.

'Well, Olivier didn't kill the man, but as you know a lot of unpleasant things about him came out in the trial. Olivier had certainly stolen from the Hermit, taken advantage of their friendship and the man's frail state of mind. And it turned out that Olivier had used the stolen money to secretly buy up a lot of property in Three Pines. Gabri didn't even know about that.'

Reine-Marie was quiet, considering what she'd just heard.

'I wonder how his friends feel about that,' said Reine-Marie at last.

So did Gamache.

'Olivier is the one who hates my father?' asked Annie. 'But how could that be? Dad got him out of prison. He took him back to Three Pines.'

'Yes, but the way Olivier sees it, I got him out of prison. Your father put him in.'

Annie stared at Beauvoir, then shook her head.

Beauvoir went on. 'Your father apologized, you know. In front of everyone in the bistro. He told Olivier he was sorry for what he did.'

'And what did Olivier say?'

'That he couldn't forgive him. Not yet.'

Annie thought about that. 'How did Dad react?'

'He didn't seem surprised, or upset. In fact, I think he'd have been surprised had Olivier suddenly decided all was forgiven. He wouldn't have really meant it.'

Beauvoir knew the only thing worse than no apology was an insincere one.

Jean Guy had to give Olivier that. Instead of appearing to accept the apology, Olivier had finally told the truth. The hurt went too deep. He wasn't ready to forgive.

'And now?' asked Annie.

'I guess we'll see.'

TWO

—

'Remarkable, don't you think?'
Armand Gamache turned to the distinguished older man beside him.

'I do,' nodded the Chief Inspector. Both men were silent for a moment, contemplating the painting in front of them. All around was the hubbub of the party in full swing, talking, laughing, friends getting caught up, strangers being introduced.

But the two men seemed to have formed a separate peace, a quiet little *quartier*.

In front of them on the wall was, either intentionally or naturally, the centerpiece of Clara Morrow's solo show. Her works, mostly portraits, hung all around the white walls of the main gallery of the Musée d'Art Contemporain. Some were clustered close together, like a gathering. Some hung alone, isolated. Like this one.

The most modest of the portraits, on the largest of the walls.

Without competition, or company. An island nation. A sovereign portrait.

Alone.

'How do you feel when you look at it?' the man asked and turned his keen gaze on Gamache.

The Chief Inspector smiled. 'Well, it isn't the first time I've seen it. We're friends of the Morrows. I was there when she first brought it out of her studio.'

'Lucky man.'

Gamache took a sip of the very good red wine and agreed. Lucky man.

'François Marois.' The older man put out his hand.

'Armand Gamache.'

Now his companion looked more closely at the Chief and nodded.

'*Désolé*. I should have recognized you, Chief Inspector.'

'Not at all. I'm always happier when people don't,' smiled Gamache. 'Are you an artist?'

He looked, in fact, more like a banker. A collector, perhaps? The other end of the artistic chain. He'd be in his early seventies, Gamache guessed. Prosperous, in a tailored suit and silk tie. There was a hint of expensive cologne about the man. Very subtle. He was balding, with hair immaculately and newly cut, clean-shaven, with intelligent blue eyes. All this Chief Inspector Gamache took in quickly and instinctively. François Marois seemed both vibrant and contained. At home in this rarified, and quite artificial, setting.

Gamache glanced into the body of the room, packed with men and women milling about and chatting, juggling hors d'oeuvres and wine. A couple of stylized, uncomfortable benches were installed in the middle of the cavernous space. More form than function. He saw Reine-Marie chatting with a woman across the room. He found Annie. David had arrived and was taking off his coat, then he went to join her. Gamache's eyes swept the room until he found Gabri and Olivier, side-by-side. He wondered if he should go and speak with Olivier.

And do what? Apologize again?

Had Reine-Marie been right? Did he want forgiveness? Atonement? Did he want his mistake purged from his personal record? The one he kept deep inside, and wrote in each day.

The ledger.

Did he want that mistake stricken?

The fact was, he could live just fine without Olivier's forgiveness.

But now that he saw Olivier again he felt a slight *frisson* and wondered if he wanted that forgiveness. And he wondered if Olivier was ready to give it.

His eyes swept back to his companion.

It interested Gamache that while the best art reflected humanity and nature, human or otherwise, galleries themselves were often cold and austere. Neither inviting nor natural.

And yet, Monsieur Marois was comfortable. Marble and sharp edges appeared to be his natural habitat.

'No,' said Marois to Gamache's question. 'I'm not an artist.' He gave a little laugh. 'Sadly, I'm not creative. Like most of my colleagues I dabbled in art as a callow youth and immediately discovered a profound, almost mystical lack of talent. Quite shocking, really.'

Gamache laughed. 'So what brings you here?'

It was, as the Chief knew, a private cocktail party the night before the public opening of Clara's big show. Only the select were invited to a *vernissage*, especially at the famous Musée in Montréal. The monied, the influential, the artist's friends and family. And the artist. In that order.

Very little was expected of an artist at the *vernissage*. If they were clothed and sober most curators considered themselves fortunate. Gamache stole a glance at Clara, looking panicked and disheveled in a tailored power suit that had experienced a recent failure. The skirt was slightly twisted and the collar was riding high as though she'd tried to scratch the middle of her back.

'I'm an art dealer.' The man produced his card and Gamache took it, examining the cream background with the simple embossed black lettering. Just the man's name and a phone number. Nothing more. The paper was thick and textured. A fine-quality business card. No doubt for a fine-quality business.

'Do you know Clara's work?' Gamache asked, tucking the card into his breast pocket.

'Not at all, but I'm friends with the chief curator of the Musée and she slipped me one of the brochures. I was frankly astonished. The description says Madame Morrow has been living in Québec all her life and is almost fifty. And yet no one seems to know her. She came out of nowhere.'

'She came out of Three Pines,' said Gamache and at the blank look from his companion, he explained. 'It's a tiny village south of here. By the Vermont border. Not many people know it.'

'Or know her. An unknown artist in an anonymous village. And yet—'

Monsieur Marois opened his arms in an elegant and eloquent gesture, to indicate the surroundings and the event.

They both went back to gazing at the portrait in front of them. It showed the head and scrawny shoulders of a very old woman. A veined and arthritic hand clutched a rough blue shawl to her throat. It had slipped to reveal skin stretched over collarbone and sinew.

But it was her face that captivated the men.

She looked straight at them. Into the gathering, with the clink of glasses, the lively conversations, the merriment.

She was angry. Filled with contempt. Hating what she heard and saw. The happiness all around her. The laughter. Hating the world that had left her behind. Left her alone on this wall. To see, to watch and to never be included.

Like Prometheus Bound, here was a great spirit endlessly tormented. Grown bitter and petty.

Beside him Gamache heard a small gasp and knew what it was. The art dealer, François Marois, had understood the painting. Not the obvious rage, there for all to see, but something more complex and subtle. Marois had got it. What Clara had really created.

'Mon Dieu,' Monsieur Marois exhaled. 'My God.'

He looked from the painting to Gamache.

Across the room Clara nodded and smiled, and took in almost nothing.

There was a howl in her ears and a swirl before her eyes, her hands were numb. She was losing her senses.

Deep breath in, she repeated to herself. *Deep breath out.*

Peter had brought her a glass of wine and her friend Myrna had offered a plate of hors d'oeuvres, but Clara was shaking so badly she'd had to give them both back.

And now she concentrated on trying not to look demented. Her new suit itched and she realized she looked like an accountant. From the old Eastern Bloc. Or maybe a Maoist. A Maoist accountant.

It wasn't the look she'd been going for when she'd bought the suit at a swank boutique on rue St-Denis in Montréal. She'd wanted a change, something different from her usual billowy skirts and dresses. Something sharp and sleek. Something minimalist and coordinated.

And in the store she'd looked just great, smiling at the smiling saleswoman in the mirror and telling her all about the upcoming solo show. She told everyone about it. Cab drivers, waiters, the kid sitting next to her on the bus, plugged into his iPod and deaf. Clara hadn't cared. She'd told him anyway.

And now the day had finally arrived.

That morning, sitting in her garden in Three Pines, she'd dared to think this would be different. She'd imagined walking through those two huge, frosted glass doors at the end of the corridor to wild applause. Looking fabulous in her new suit. The art community would be dazzled. Critics and curators would rush over, anxious to spend a moment with her. Falling all over themselves to congratulate her. To find just the right words, *les mots justes*, to describe her paintings.

Formidable. Brilliant. Luminous. Genius.

Masterpieces, each and every one.

In her quiet garden that morning Clara had closed her eyes and tilted her face to the young sun, and smiled.

The dream come true.

Perfect strangers would hang on her every word. Some might

even take notes. Ask advice. They'd listen, rapt, as she talked about her vision, her philosophy, her insights into the art world. Where it was going, where it had been.

She'd be adored and respected. Smart and beautiful. Elegant women would ask where she'd bought her outfit. She would start a movement. A trend.

Instead, she felt like a messy bride at a wedding gone bad. Where the guests ignored her, concentrating instead on the food and drink. Where no one wanted to catch her bouquet or walk her down the aisle. Or dance with her. And she looked like a Maoist accountant.

She scratched her hip, and smoothed pâté into her hair. Then looked at her watch.

Dear God, another hour to go.

Oh, no no no, thought Clara. Now she was simply trying to survive. To keep her head above water. To not faint, or throw up, or pee. To remain conscious and continent was her new goal.

'At least you're not on fire.'

'I'm sorry?' Clara turned to the very large black woman in the bright green caftan standing beside her. It was her friend and neighbor, Myrna Landers. A retired psychologist from Montréal, she now owned the new and used bookstore in Three Pines.

'Right now,' said Myrna. 'You're not on fire.'

'Very true. And perceptive. Nor am I flying. There's quite a long list of things I'm not.'

'And a long list,' laughed Myrna, 'of things you are.'

'Are you going to be rude now?' asked Clara.

Myrna paused and considered Clara for a moment. Almost every day Clara came across to Myrna's bookstore to have a cup of tea and talk. Or Myrna would join Peter and Clara for dinner.

But today was like no other. No other day in Clara's life had ever been like this, and it was possible none would ever be again. Myrna knew Clara's fears, her failures, her disappointments. As Clara knew hers.

And they knew each other's dreams too.

'I know this is difficult for you,' said Myrna. She stood right in front of Clara, her bulk blotting out the room, so that what had been a crowd scene was suddenly very intimate. Her body was a perfect green orb, blocking out the sights and sounds. They were in their own world.

'I wanted it to be perfect,' said Clara in a whisper, hoping she wasn't about to cry. Where other little girls fantasized about their wedding day, Clara had dreamed of a solo art show. At the Musée. Here. She just hadn't seen it in quite this way.

'And who gets to decide? What would make it perfect?'

Clara thought about that for a moment. 'If I wasn't so afraid.'

'And what's the worst thing that can happen?' asked Myrna quietly.

'They'll hate my art, decide I'm talentless, ridiculous. Laughable. That a terrible mistake was made. The show'll be a failure and I'll be a laughingstock.'

'Exactly,' said Myrna, with a smile. 'All survivable. And then what'll you do?'

Clara thought for a moment. 'I'll get into the car with Peter and drive back to Three Pines.'

'And?'

'Have the party there, with friends tonight.'

'And?'

'I'll get up tomorrow morning . . .' Clara's voice petered out as she saw her life post-apocalypse. She'd wake up tomorrow to her quiet life in the tiny village. A return to a life of walking the dog, and drinks on the *terrasse*, of café au lait and croissants in front of the fireplace at the bistro. Of intimate dinners with friends. Of sitting in her garden. Reading, thinking.

Painting.

Nothing that happened here would ever change that.

'At least I'm not on fire,' she said, and grinned.

Myrna took both of Clara's hands in hers and held them for a moment. 'Most people would kill for this day. Don't let it go by without enjoying it. Your works are masterpieces, Clara.'

Clara squeezed her friend's hand. All those years, those months, those quiet days when no one else noticed or cared what Clara did in her studio, Myrna had been there. And into that silence she'd whispered.

'Your works are masterpieces.'

And Clara had dared to believe her. And dared to keep moving forward. Urged on by her dreams, and that gentle, reassuring voice.

Myrna stepped aside then, revealing a whole new room. One filled with people, not threats. People having fun, enjoying themselves. There to celebrate Clara Morrow's first solo show at the Musée.

'Merde,' shouted a man into the ear of the woman beside him, trying to raise his voice above the din of conversation. 'This stuff is shit. Can you believe Clara Morrow got a solo show?'

The woman beside him shook her head and grimaced. She wore a flowing skirt and a tight T-shirt with scarves wrapped around her neck and shoulders. Her earrings were hoops and each of her fingers held rings.

In another place and time she'd have been considered a gypsy. Here she was recognized for what she was. A mildly successful artist.

Beside her her husband, also an artist and dressed in cords and a worn jacket with a rakish scarf at the neck, turned back to the painting.

'Dreadful.'

'Poor Clara,' agreed his wife. 'The critics'll savage her.'

Jean Guy Beauvoir, who was standing beside the two artists, his back to the painting, turned to glance at it.

On the wall among a cluster of portraits was the largest piece. Three women, all very old, stood together in a group, laughing.

They looked at each other, and touched each other, holding each other's hands, or gripping an arm, tipping their heads together. Whatever had made them laugh, it was to each other they turned. As they equally would if something terrible had happened. As they naturally would whatever happened.

More than friendship, more than joy, more than even love this painting ached of intimacy.

Jean Guy quickly turned his back on it. Unable to look. He scanned the room until he found her again.

'Look at them,' the man was saying, dissecting the portrait. 'Not very attractive.'

Annie Gamache was across the crowded gallery, standing next to her husband, David. They were listening to an older man. David looked distracted, disinterested. But Annie's eyes were bright. Taking it in. Fascinated.

Beauvoir felt a flash of jealousy, wanting her to look at him that way.

Here, Beauvoir's mind commanded. *Look over here.*

'And they're laughing,' said the man behind Beauvoir, looking disapprovingly at Clara's portrait of the three old women. 'Not much nuance in that. Might as well paint clowns.'

The woman beside him snickered.

Across the room, Annie Gamache laid a hand on her husband's arm, but he seemed oblivious.

Beauvoir put his hand on his own arm, gently. That's what it would feel like.

'There you are, Clara,' said the chief curator of the Musée, taking her by the arm and leading her away from Myrna. 'Congratulations. It's a triumph!'

Clara had been around enough artistic people to know what they call 'a triumph' others might call simply an event. Still, it was better than a kick in the shins.

'Is it?'

'*Absolument*. People are loving it.' The woman gave Clara an enthusiastic hug. Her glasses were small rectangles over her eyes. Clara wondered if there was a permanent slash of frame across her world, like an astigmatism. Her hair was short and angular, as were her clothes. Her face was impossibly pale. She was a walking installation.

But she was kind, and Clara liked her.

'Very nice,' said the curator, stepping back to take in Clara's new look. 'I like it. Very retro, very chic. You look like …' She moved her hands around in a contained circle, trying to find the right name.

'Audrey Hepburn?'

'*C'est ça*,' clapped the curator and laughed. 'You're sure to start a trend.'

Clara laughed too, and fell in love just a little. Across the room she saw Olivier standing, as always, beside Gabri. But while Gabri was gabbing away to a complete stranger, Olivier was staring through the crowd.

Clara followed his sharp gaze. It ended at Armand Gamache.

'So,' said the curator, putting her arm around Clara's waist. 'Who do you know?'

Before Clara could answer, the woman was pointing out various people in the crowded room.

'You probably know them.' She nodded to the middle-aged couple behind Beauvoir. They seemed riveted by Clara's painting of the Three Graces. 'Husband and wife team. Normand and Paulette. He draws the works and she does the fine detailing.'

'Like the Renaissance masters, working as a team.'

'Sort of,' said the curator. 'More like Christo and Jeanne-Claude. Very rare to find a couple of artists so in sync. They're actually very good. And I see they adore your painting.'

Clara did know them, and suspected 'adore' wasn't the word they themselves would use.

'Who's that?' Clara asked, pointing to the distinguished man beside Gamache.

'François Marois.'

Clara's eyes widened and she looked around the crowded room. Why was there no stampede to speak to the prominent art dealer? Why was Armand Gamache, who wasn't even an artist, the only one speaking to Monsieur Marois? If these *vernissages* were for one thing it wasn't to celebrate the artist. It was to network. And there was no greater catch than François Marois. Then she realized few in the room probably even knew who he was.

'As you know, he almost never comes to shows, but I gave him one of the catalogs and he thought your works were fabulous.'

'Really?'

Even allowing for the translation from 'art' fabulous to 'normal people' fabulous, it was a compliment.

'François knows everyone with money and taste,' said the curator. 'This really is a coup. If he likes your works, you're made.' The curator peered more closely. 'I don't know the man he's talking to. Probably some professor of art history.'

Before Clara could say the man wasn't a professor she saw Marois turn from the portrait to Armand Gamache. A look of shock on his face.

Clara wondered what he'd just seen. And what it meant.

'Now,' said the curator, pointing Clara in the opposite direction. 'André Castonguay over there's another catch.' Across the room Clara saw a familiar figure on the Québec art scene. Where François Marois was private and retiring, André Castonguay was ever-present, the *éminence grise* of Québec art. Slightly younger than Marois, slightly taller, slightly heavier, Monsieur Castonguay was surrounded by rings of people. The inner circle was made up of critics from various powerful newspapers. Radiating out from there were rings of lesser gallery owners and critics. And finally, in the outer circle, were the artists.

They were the satellites and André Castonguay the sun.

'Let me introduce you.'

'Fabulous,' said Clara. In her head she translated that 'fabulous' into what she really meant. Oh *merde*.

*

Is it possible?' François Marois asked, searching Chief Inspector Gamache's face.

Gamache looked at the older man, and smiling slightly he nodded.

Marois turned back to the portrait.

The din in the gallery was almost deafening as more and more guests crowded into the *vernissage*.

But François Marois had eyes for only one face. The disappointed elderly woman on the wall. So full of censure and despair.

'It's Mary, isn't it?' asked Marois, almost in a whisper.

Chief Inspector Gamache wasn't sure the art dealer was talking to him, so he said nothing. Marois had seen what few others grasped.

Clara's portrait wasn't simply of an angry old woman. She'd in fact painted the Virgin Mary. Elderly. Abandoned by a world weary and wary of miracles. A world too busy to notice a stone rolled back. It had moved on to other wonders.

This was Mary in the final years. Forgotten. Alone.

Glaring out at a room filled with bright people sipping good wine. And walking right by her.

Except for François Marois, who now tore his eyes from the painting to look at Gamache once again.

'What has Clara done?' he asked quietly.

Gamache was silent for a moment, gathering his thoughts before answering.

Hello, numb nuts.' Ruth Zardo slipped a thin arm through Jean Guy Beauvoir's. 'Tell me how you are.'

It was a command. Few had the fortitude to ignore Ruth. But then, few were ever asked how they were, by Ruth.

'I'm doing well.'

'Bullshit,' said the old poet. 'You look like crap. Thin. Pale. Wrinkled.'

'You're describing yourself, you old drunk.'

Ruth Zardo cackled. 'True. You look like a bitter old woman. And that's not the compliment it might seem.'

Beauvoir smiled. He'd actually been looking forward to seeing Ruth again. He examined the tall, thin, elderly woman leaning on her cane. Ruth's hair was white and thin and cut close to her head, so that it looked like her skull was exposed. Which seemed to Beauvoir about right. Nothing inside Ruth's head was ever unexposed or unexpressed. It was her heart she kept hidden.

But it came out in her poetry. Somehow, and Beauvoir couldn't begin to guess how, Ruth Zardo had won the Governor General's Award for poetry. None of which he understood. Fortunately, Ruth in person was a lot easier to decode.

'Why're you here?' she demanded and fixed him with a steady look.

'Why're you? You can't tell me you came all the way from Three Pines to support Clara.'

Ruth looked at him as though he'd lost his mind. 'Of course not. I'm here for the same reason everyone else is. Free food and drink. But I've had my fill now. Are you coming back to the party in Three Pines later?'

'We were invited, but I don't think so.'

Ruth nodded. 'Good. More for me. I heard about your divorce. I suppose she cheated on you. Only natural.'

'Hag,' muttered Beauvoir.

'Dick-head,' said Ruth. Beauvoir's eyes had wandered and Ruth followed his stare. To the young woman across the room.

'You can do better than her,' said Ruth and felt the arm she was holding tense. Her companion was silent. She turned sharp eyes on him then looked once again at the woman Beauvoir was staring at.

Mid to late twenties, not fat, but not thin either. Not pretty, but not dirt ugly either. Not tall, but not short either.

She would appear to be completely average, completely unremarkable. Except for one thing.

The young woman radiated well-being.

As Ruth watched an older woman approached the group and put an arm around the younger woman's waist and kissed her.

Reine-Marie Gamache. Ruth had met her a few times.

Now the wizened old poet looked at Beauvoir with heightened interest.

Peter Morrow was chatting up a few gallery owners. Minor figures in the art world but best to keep them happy.

He knew André Castonguay, of the Galerie Castonguay, was there and Peter was dying to meet him. He'd also noticed the critics for the *New York Times* and *Le Figaro*. He glanced across the room and saw a photographer taking Clara's picture.

She looked away for a moment and caught his eye, shrugging. He lifted his wine in salute, and smiled.

Should he go over and introduce himself to Castonguay? But there was such a crowd around him, Peter didn't want to look pathetic. Hovering. Better to stay away, as though he didn't care, didn't need André Castonguay.

Peter brought his attention back to the owner of a small gallery, who was explaining they'd love to do a show for Peter, but were all booked.

Out of the corner of his eye he saw the rings around Castonguay part, and make way for Clara.

You asked how I feel when I see this painting,' said Armand Gamache. The two men were looking at the portrait. 'I feel calm. Comforted.'

François Marois looked at him with amazement.

'Comforted? But how? Happy maybe that you aren't so angry yourself? Does her own immense rage make yours more acceptable? What does Madame Morrow call this painting?' Marois removed his glasses and leaned into the description stenciled on the wall.

Then he stepped back, his face more perplexed than ever.

'It's called *Still Life*. I wonder why.'

As the art dealer concentrated on the portrait Gamache noticed Olivier across the room. Staring at him. The Chief Inspector smiled a greeting and wasn't surprised when Olivier turned away.

He at least had his answer.

Beside him Marois exhaled. 'I see.'

Gamache turned back to the art dealer. Marois was no longer surprised. His veneer of civility and sophistication had slipped, and a genuine smile broke through.

'It's in her eyes, isn't it.'

Gamache nodded.

Then Marois cocked his head to one side, looking not at the portrait but into the crowd. Puzzled. He looked back to the painting, then again into the crowd.

Gamache followed his gaze, and wasn't surprised to see it resting on the elderly woman speaking with Jean Guy Beauvoir.

Ruth Zardo.

Beauvoir was looking vexed, annoyed, as one so often does around Ruth. But Ruth herself was looking quite pleased.

'It's her, isn't it?' asked Marois, his voice excited and low as though not wanting to let anyone else in on their secret.

Gamache nodded. 'A neighbor of Clara's in Three Pines.'

Marois watched Ruth, fascinated. It was as though the painting had come alive. Then he and Gamache both turned back to the portrait.

Clara had painted her as the forgotten and belligerent Virgin Mary. Worn down by age and rage, by resentments real and manufactured. By friendships soured. By entitlements denied and love withheld. But there was something else. A vague suggestion in those weary eyes. Not even seen really. More a promise. A rumor in the distance.

Amid all the brush strokes, all the elements, all the color and nuance in the portrait, it came down to one tiny detail. A single white dot.

In her eyes.

Clara Morrow had painted the moment despair became hope.

François Marois stepped back half a pace and nodded gravely.

'It's remarkable. Beautiful.' He turned to Gamache then. 'Unless, of course, it's a ruse.'

'What do you mean?' asked Gamache.

'Maybe it isn't hope at all,' said Marois, 'but merely a trick of the light.'

THREE

—

The next morning Clara rose early. Putting on rubber boots and a sweater over her pajamas, she poured herself a coffee and sat in one of the Adirondack chairs in their back garden.

The caterers had cleaned up and there was no evidence of the huge barbecue and dance the night before.

She closed her eyes and could feel the young June sun on her upturned face and could hear birdcalls and the Rivière Bella Bella gurgling past at the end of the garden. Below that was the thrum of bumblebees climbing in and over and around the peonies. Getting lost.

Bumbling around.

It looked comical, ridiculous. But then so much did, unless you knew.

Clara Morrow held the warm mug in her hands and smelt coffee, and the fresh-mown grass. The lilacs and peonies and young, fragrant roses.

This was the village that had lived beneath the covers when Clara was a child. That was built behind the thin wooden door to her bedroom, where outside her parents argued. Her brothers ignored her. The phone rang, but not for her. Where eyes slid over and past her and through her. To someone else. Someone prettier. More interesting. Where people butted in as though she was invisible, and interrupted her as though she hadn't just spoken.

But when as a child she closed her eyes and pulled the sheets over her head, Clara saw the pretty little village in the valley. With the forests and flowers and kindly people.

Where bumbling was a virtue.

As far back as she could remember Clara wanted only one thing, even more than she'd wanted the solo show. It wasn't riches, it wasn't power, it wasn't even love.

Clara Morrow wanted to belong. And now, at almost fifty, she did.

Was the show a mistake? In accepting it had she separated herself from the rest?

As she sat, scenes from the night before came to mind. Her friends, other artists, Olivier catching her eye and nodding reassuringly. The excitement at meeting André Castonguay and others. The curator's happy face. The barbecue back in the village. The food and drink and fireworks. The live band and dancing. The laughter.

The relief.

But now, in the clear light of day, the anxiety had returned. Not the storm it had been at its worst, but a light mist that muted the sunshine.

And Clara knew why.

Peter and Olivier had gone to get the newspapers. To bring back the words she'd waited a lifetime to read. The reviews. The words of the critics.

Brilliant. Visionary. Masterful.

Dull. Derivative. Predictable.

Which would it be?

Clara sat, and sipped, and tried not to care. Tried not to notice the shadows lengthening, creeping toward her as the minutes passed.

A car door slammed and Clara spasmed in her chair, surprised out of her reverie.

'We're hoo-ome,' Peter sang.

She heard footsteps coming around the side of their cottage. She got up and turned to greet Peter and Olivier. But instead of the two men walking toward her, they were standing still. As though turned into large garden gnomes.

And instead of looking at her, they were staring into a bed of flowers.

'What is it?' Clara asked, walking toward them, picking up speed as their expressions registered. 'What's wrong?'

Peter turned and dropping the papers on the grass he stopped her from going further.

'Call the police,' said Olivier. He inched forward, toward a perennial bed planted with peonies and bleeding hearts and poppies.

And something else.

Chief Inspector Gamache straightened up and sighed.

There was no doubt. This was murder.

The woman at his feet had a broken neck. Had she been at the foot of a flight of stairs he might have thought it an accident. But she was lying face up beside a flower bed. On the soft grass.

Eyes open. Staring straight into the late morning sun.

Gamache almost expected her to blink.

He looked around the pleasant garden. The familiar garden. How often had he stood back there with Peter and Clara and others, beer in hand, barbecue fired up. Chatting.

But not today.

Peter and Clara, Olivier and Gabri were standing down by the river. Watching. Between Gamache and them was the yellow tape, the great divide. On one side the investigators and on the other, the investigated.

'White female,' the coroner, Dr Harris, said. She was kneeling over the victim, as was Agent Isabelle Lacoste. Inspector Jean Guy Beauvoir was directing the Scene of Crime team for the Sûreté du Québec. They were methodically going over the area. Collecting evidence. Photographing. Carefully, meticulously doing the forensics.

'Middle-aged,' the coroner's voice carried on. Clinical. Factual.

Chief Inspector Gamache listened as the information was reeled off. He, better than most, knew the power of facts. But he also knew few murderers were ever found in facts.

'Dyed blond hair, graying roots just showing. Slightly overweight. No ring on the ring finger.'

Facts were necessary. They pointed the way, and helped form the net. But the killer himself was tracked by following not only facts but feelings. The fetid emotions that had made a man into a murderer.

'Neck snapped at the second vertebra.'

Chief Inspector Gamache listened and watched. The routine familiar. But no less horrifying.

The taking of one life by another never failed to shock him, even after all these years as head of homicide for the storied Sûreté du Québec. After all these murders. All these murderers.

He was still amazed what one human could do to another.

Peter Morrow stared at the red shoes just poking out from behind the flower bed. They were attached to the dead woman's feet, which were attached to her body, which was lying on his grass. He couldn't see the body now. It was hidden by the tall flowers, but he could see the feet. He looked away. Tried to concentrate on something else. On the investigators, Gamache and his team, bending, bowing, murmuring, as though in common prayer. A dark ritual, in his garden.

Gamache never took a note, Peter noticed. He listened and nodded respectfully. Asked a few questions, his face thoughtful. He left the note-taking to others. In this case, Agent Lacoste.

Peter tried to look away, to focus on the beauty in his garden.

But his eyes kept being dragged back to the body in his garden.

Then, as Peter watched, Gamache suddenly and quite swiftly turned. And looked at him. And Peter immediately and instinctively dropped his eyes, as though he'd done something shameful.

He instantly regretted it and raised his eyes again, but by then the Chief Inspector was no longer staring at them. Instead, he was approaching them.

Peter considered turning away, in a casual manner. As though he'd heard a deer in the forest on the other side of the Rivière Bella Bella.

He started to turn, then stopped himself.

He didn't need to look away, he told himself. He'd done nothing wrong. Surely it was natural to watch the police.

Wasn't it?

But Peter Morrow, always so sure, felt the ground shifting beneath him. He no longer knew what was natural. No longer knew what to do with his hands, his eyes, his entire body. His life. His wife.

'Clara,' said Chief Inspector Gamache, extending his hand to her, then kissing Clara on both cheeks. If the other investigators found it odd that their Chief would kiss a suspect, they didn't show it. And Gamache clearly didn't care.

He went around the group, shaking hands with all of them. He came to Olivier last, obviously giving the younger man a chance to see it coming. Gamache extended his hand. And everyone watched. The body momentarily forgotten.

Olivier didn't hesitate. He shook Gamache's hand but couldn't quite look him in the eye.

Chief Inspector Gamache gave them a small almost apologetic smile, as though the body was his fault. Was that how dreadful things started? Peter wondered. Not with a thunder clap. Not with a shriek. Not with sirens, but with a smile? Something horrible come calling, wrapped in civility and good manners.

But the something horrible had already been, and gone. And had left a body behind.

'How are you doing?' asked Gamache, his eyes returning to Clara.

It wasn't a casual question. He looked genuinely concerned.

Peter could feel himself relax as the body was lifted from his shoulders. And given to this sturdy man.

Clara shook her head. 'Stunned,' she said at last, and glanced behind her. 'Who is she?'

'You don't know?'

He looked from Clara to Peter, then over to Gabri and finally Olivier. Everyone shook their heads.

'She wasn't a guest at your party?'

'She must have been, I suppose,' said Clara. 'But I didn't invite her.'

'Who is she?' asked Gabri.

'Did you get a look at her?' Gamache persisted, not quite ready to answer the question.

They nodded.

'After we called the police I went back into the garden, to look,' said Clara.

'Why?'

'I had to know if I knew her. See if she was a friend or neighbor.'

'She wasn't,' said Gabri. 'I was preparing breakfast for our B and B guests when Olivier called to tell me what had happened.'

'So you came over?' asked Gamache.

'Wouldn't you?' asked the large man.

'I'm a homicide detective,' said Gamache. 'I sort of have to. You don't.'

'I'm a nosy son-of-a-bitch,' said Gabri. 'I sort of have to too. And like Clara, I needed to see if we knew her.'

'Did you tell anyone else?' asked Gamache. 'Did anyone else come into the garden to look?'

They shook their heads.

'So you all took a good look, and none of you recognized her?'

'Who was she?' asked Clara again.

'We don't know,' admitted Gamache. 'She fell on her purse and Dr Harris doesn't want to move her yet. We'll find out soon enough.'

Gabri hesitated then turned to Olivier. 'Doesn't she remind you of something?'

Olivier was silent, but Peter wasn't.

'The witch is dead?'

'Peter,' said Clara quickly. 'The woman was killed and left in our garden. What a terrible thing to say.'

'I'm sorry,' said Peter, shocked at himself. 'But she does look like the Wicked Witch of the West, with her red shoes sticking out like that.'

'We're not saying she is,' Gabri hurried to say. 'But you can't deny in that get-up she doesn't look like anyone from Kansas.'

Clara rolled her eyes and shaking her head she muttered, 'Jesus.'

But Gamache had to admit, he and his team had talked about the same thing. Not that the dead woman reminded them of the Wicked Witch, but that she clearly was not dressed for a barbecue in the country.

'I didn't see her last night,' said Peter.

'And we'd remember,' said Olivier, speaking at last. 'She'd be hard to miss.'

Gamache nodded. He'd appreciated that as well. The dead woman would have stood out in that brilliant red dress. Everything about the woman screamed 'look at me'.

He looked back at her and searched his memory. Had he seen anyone in a bright red dress at the Musée last night? Perhaps she'd come straight from there, as presumably many guests did. But none came to mind. Most of the women, with the notable exception of Myrna, wore more muted colors.

Then he had a thought.

'Excusez-moi,' he said and walking swiftly back across the lawn he spoke to Beauvoir briefly then returned more slowly, thinking.

'I read the report on the drive down, but I'd like to hear from you myself how she was found.'

'Peter and Olivier saw her first,' said Clara. 'I was sitting in that chair.' She waved toward the yellow Adirondack chair, one of two. A coffee mug still sat on the wooden arm. 'While the guys went to Knowlton to pick up the papers. I was waiting for them.'

'Why?' asked the Chief Inspector.

'The reviews.'

'Ahh, of course. And that would explain . . .' He waved toward the stack of papers sitting on the grass, within the yellow police cordon.

Clara looked at them too. She wished she could say she'd forgotten all about the reviews in the shock of the discovery, but she hadn't. The *New York Times*, the Toronto *Globe and Mail* and the London *Times* were piled on the ground where Peter had dropped them.

Beyond her reach.

Gamache looked at Clara, puzzled. 'But if you were that anxious, why not just go online? The reviews would've been up hours ago, *non*?'

It was the same question Peter had asked her. And Olivier. How to explain it?

'Because I wanted to feel the newspaper in my hands,' she said. 'I wanted to read my reviews the same way I read reviews of all the artists I love. Holding the paper. Smelling it. Turning the pages. All my life I've dreamed of this. It seemed worth the extra hour's wait.'

'So you were alone in the garden for about an hour this morning?'

Clara nodded.

'From when to when?' Gamache asked.

'From around seven thirty this morning until they returned about eight thirty.' Clara looked at Peter.

'That's right,' said Peter.

'And when you got back, what did you see?' Gamache turned to Peter and Olivier.

'We got out of the car and since we knew Clara was in the garden we decided to just walk around there.' Peter pointed to the corner of the house, where an old lilac held on to the last flowers of the season.

42

'I was following Peter when he suddenly stopped,' said Olivier.

'I noticed something red on the ground as we came around the house,' Peter picked up the story. 'I think I assumed it was one of the poppies, fallen over. But it was too big. So I slowed down and looked over. That's when I saw it was a woman.'

'What did you do?'

'I thought it was one of the guests who might've had too much to drink and passed out,' said Peter. 'Slept it off in our garden. But then I could see that her eyes were open and her head—'

He tilted his, but of course he couldn't achieve that angle. No living person could. It was a feat reserved for the dead.

'And you?' Gamache asked Olivier.

'I asked Clara to call the police,' he said. 'Then I called Gabri.'

'You say you have guests?' Gamache asked. 'People from the party?'

Gabri nodded. 'A couple of the artists who came down from Montréal for the party decided to stay at the B and B. A few are also staying up at the inn and spa.'

'Was this a last-minute booking?'

'At the B and B it was. They made it sometime during the party.'

Gamache nodded and turning away he gestured toward Agent Isabelle Lacoste, who quickly joined him, listened as the Chief murmured instructions, then walked rapidly away. She spoke to two young Sûreté agents, who nodded and left.

It always fascinated Clara to see how easily Gamache took command, and how naturally people took his orders. Never barked, never shouted, never harsh. Always put in the most calm, even courteous manner. His orders were couched almost as requests. And yet not a person mistook them for that.

Gamache turned back to give the four friends his full attention. 'Did any of you touch the body?'

They looked at each other, shaking their heads, then back to the Chief.

'No,' said Peter. He was feeling more certain now. The ground had firmed up, filled in with facts. With straightforward questions and clear answers.

Nothing to be afraid of.

'Do you mind?' Gamache started walking toward the Adirondack. Even had they minded, it wouldn't have mattered. He was going there and they were welcome to join him.

'Before they came back, when you were sitting here alone, you didn't notice anything strange?' he asked as they walked. It seemed obvious that had Clara seen a body in her garden she'd have said something earlier. But it wasn't just the body he wanted to know about. This was Clara's garden, she knew it well, intimately. Perhaps something else was wrong. A plant broken, a shrub disturbed.

Some detail his investigators might miss. Something so subtle she herself might have missed it, until he asked her directly.

And, to her credit, she didn't come back with a smart-ass reply.

But Gabri did. 'Like the body?'

'No,' said the Chief, as they arrived at the chair. He turned and surveyed the garden from there. It was true that at this angle the dead woman was hidden by the flower beds. 'I mean something else.'

He turned thoughtful eyes on Clara.

'Is there anything unusual about your garden this morning?' He shot a warning glance at Gabri, who put a finger to his mouth. 'Anything small? Some detail off?'

Clara looked around. The back lawn was dotted with large flower beds. Some round, some oblong. Tall trees along the riverbank threw dappled shade, but most of it was in bright noonday sun. Clara scanned her garden, as did the others.

Was there something different? It was so hard to tell now, what with all the people, the newspapers, the activity, the yellow police tape. The newspapers. The body. The newspapers.

Everything was different.

She turned back to Gamache, her eyes asking for help.

Gamache hated to give it, hated to suggest in case he led her to see something that wasn't really there.

'It's possible the murderer hid back here,' he finally said. 'Waiting.'

He left it at that. And he could see Clara understood. She turned back to her garden. Had a man intent on murder waited here? In her private sanctuary?

Had he hidden himself in the flower beds? Crouching behind the tall peony? Had he peered out from the morning glory climbing the post? Had he knelt behind the growing phlox?

Waiting?

She looked at each and every perennial, each shrub. Looking for something knocked down, knocked askew, a limb twisted, a bud broken off.

But it was perfect. Myrna and Gabri had worked days on the garden, getting it immaculate for the party. And it was. Last night. And it was that morning.

Except for the police, like pests, crawling all over it. And the bright body. A blight.

'Do you see anything?' she asked Gabri.

'No,' he said. 'If the murderer hid back here it wasn't in one of the flower beds. Maybe behind a tree?' He waved toward the maples but Gamache shook his head.

'Too far away. It would take him too long to make it across the lawn and around the flower beds. She'd have seen him coming.'

'So where did he hide?' Olivier asked.

'He didn't,' said Gamache, sitting in the Adirondack chair. From there the body was also hidden. No, Clara couldn't see the dead woman.

The Chief Inspector hauled himself up. 'He didn't hide. He waited in plain sight.'

'And she walked right up to him?' Peter asked. 'She knew him?'

'Or he walked up to her,' said Gamache. 'Either way, she wasn't alarmed or frightened.'

'What was she doing back here?' Clara asked. 'The barbecue was out there,' she waved beyond their home. 'Everything was on the green. The food, the drinks, the music. The caterers set up all the tables and chairs out front.'

'But if people wanted to, they could walk into back yards?' Gamache asked, trying to get a picture of the event.

'Sure,' said Olivier. 'If they wanted. There weren't any fences or ropes up to stop them, but there was no need.'

'Well . . .' said Clara.

They turned to her.

'Well, I didn't come back here last night, but I have at other parties. To kind of escape for a few minutes, you know?'

To their surprise, Gabri nodded. 'I do the same thing, sometimes. Just to be quiet, get away from all the people.'

'Did you last night?' Gamache asked.

Gabri shook his head. 'Too much to do. We had caterers, but you still have to supervise.'

'So it's possible the dead woman came back here for a quiet moment,' said Gamache. 'She might not have known it was your home.' He looked at Clara and Peter. 'She just chose any place that was private, away from the crowds.'

They were silent then, for a moment. Imagining the woman in the bright red 'look at me' dress. Slipping around the side of the old brick home. Away from the music, and fireworks, from the people looking at her.

To find a few moments of peace and quiet.

'She doesn't seem the shy type,' said Gabri.

'Neither do you,' said Gamache with a small smile and surveyed the garden.

There was a problem. There were quite a few problems, actually, but the one that perplexed the Chief Inspector at the moment was that none of the four people with him now had seen the dead woman alive, at the party.

'*Bonjour.*'

Inspector Jean Guy Beauvoir approached. As he got closer Gabri broke into a smile and extended his hand.

'I'm beginning to think you're bad luck,' said Gabri. 'Every time you come to Three Pines there's a body.'

'And I think you provide them just for the pleasure of my company,' said Beauvoir, warmly shaking Gabri's hand, then accepting Olivier's.

They'd seen each other the evening before, at the *vernissage*. At that time they'd been in Peter and Clara's element. The gallery. But now they were in Beauvoir's habitat. A crime scene.

Art scared him. But pin a dead body to the wall and he was fine. Or, in this case, drop it into a garden. This he understood. It was simple. Always so simple.

Someone had hated the victim enough to kill her.

His job was to find that person and lock him up.

There was nothing subjective about it. No question of good and bad. It wasn't an issue of perspective or nuance. No shading. Nothing to understand. It just was.

Collect the facts. Put them in the right order. Find the killer.

Of course, while it was simple it wasn't always easy.

But he'd take a murder over a *vernissage* any day.

Though, like everyone else here, he suspected in this case the murder and the *vernissage* were one and the same. Inter-locked.

The thought dismayed him.

'Here're the pictures you asked for.' Beauvoir handed the Chief Inspector a photograph. Gamache studied them.

'*Merci. C'est parfait.*' He looked up at the four people watching him. 'I'd like you all to look at these photographs of the dead woman.'

'But we've already seen her,' said Gabri.

'I wonder if that's true. When I asked if you'd seen her at the party you all said she'd be hard to miss in her red dress. I thought the same thing. When I tried to remember if I'd seen her at your *vernissage* yesterday, Clara, what I was really doing was scouring my memory for a woman in bright red. I was focusing on the dress, not the woman.'

'So?' asked Gabri.

'So,' said Gamache. 'Suppose the red dress was recent. She might have been at the *vernissage*, but wearing something more conservative. She might have even been here—'

'And changed into the red dress mid-party?' asked Peter, incredulous. 'Why would someone do that?'

'Why would someone kill her?' asked Gamache. 'Why would a perfect stranger be at the party? There're all sorts of questions, and I'm not saying this is the answer, but it is a possibility. That you were all so impressed by the dress you didn't really concentrate on her face.'

He held up a photograph.

'This is what she looks like.'

He handed it to Clara first. The woman's eyes were now closed. She looked peaceful, if a little flaccid. Even in sleep there's some life in a face. This was an empty face. Blank. No more thoughts, or feelings.

Clara shook her head and passed the picture to Peter. Around the circle of friends the photo circulated, to the same reaction.

Nothing.

'The coroner's ready to move the body,' said Beauvoir.

Gamache nodded and placed the photo in his pocket. Beauvoir and Lacoste and the others would have their own copies, he knew. Excusing themselves they walked back to the body.

Two assistants stood by a stretcher, waiting to lift the woman onto it and take her to the waiting van. The photographer also waited. All looking at Chief Inspector Gamache. Waiting for him to give the order.

'Do you know how long she's been dead?' Beauvoir asked the coroner, who'd just stood up and was moving her stiff legs.

'Between twelve and fifteen hours,' said Dr Harris.

Gamache checked his watch and did the math. It was now eleven thirty on Sunday morning. That meant she was alive at eight thirty last night and dead by midnight. She never saw Sunday.

'No apparent sexual assault. No assault at all, except the broken neck,' said Dr Harris. 'Death would've been immediate. There was no struggle. I suspect he stood behind her and twisted her neck.'

'As simple as that, Dr Harris?' asked the Chief Inspector.

'I'm afraid so. Especially if the victim wasn't tensing. If she was relaxed and caught off guard there'd be no resistance. Just a quick twist. A snap.'

'But do most people know how to break someone's neck?' asked Agent Lacoste, brushing off her slacks. Like most Québécoise she was petite and managed a casual elegance even while dressed for the country.

'It doesn't take much, you know,' said Dr Harris. 'A twist. But it's possible the killer had a fall-back plan. To throttle her, if the twist didn't work.'

'You make it sound like a business plan,' said Lacoste.

'It might have been,' said the coroner. 'Cold, rational. It might not be physically hard to snap someone's neck, but believe me, it would be very difficult emotionally. That's why most people are killed with guns or a club to the head. Or even a knife. Let something else do the actual killing. But to do it with your own hands? Not in a fight but in a cold and calculated act? No.' Dr Harris turned back to the dead woman. 'It would take a very special person to do that.'

'And by "very special" you mean?' Gamache asked.

'You know what I mean, Chief Inspector.'

'But I want you to be clear.'

'Someone who either didn't care at all, was psychotic. Or someone who cared very, very deeply. Who wanted to do it with his bare hands. To literally take the life, himself.'

Dr Harris stared at Gamache, who nodded.

'*Merci.*'

He glanced at the coroner's assistants and at a signal they lifted the body onto a stretcher. A sheet was placed over the dead woman and she was carried away, never to be in the sun again.

The photographer started snapping pictures and the forensics team moved in. Collecting evidence from beneath the body. Including the clutch purse. The contents were carefully cataloged, tested, photographed, printed then brought to Beauvoir.

Lipstick, foundation, Kleenex, car keys, house keys and a wallet.

Beauvoir opened it and read the driver's license then handed it to the Chief Inspector.

'We have a name, Chief. And an address.'

Gamache glanced at the driver's license, then at the four villagers, watching him. He walked back across the lawn to join them.

'We know who the dead woman is.' Gamache consulted the driver's license. 'Lillian Dyson.'

'What?' exclaimed Clara. 'Lillian Dyson?'

Gamache turned to her. 'You know her?'

Clara stared at Gamache in disbelief then looked beyond her garden, across the meandering Rivière Bella Bella, and into the woods.

'Surely not,' she whispered.

'Who was she?' Gabri asked but Clara seemed to have fallen into a stupor, staring bewildered into the forest.

'Can I see her picture?' she finally asked.

Gamache handed her the driver's license. It wasn't the best photo, but certainly better than the one taken that morning. Clara examined it, then took a long, deep breath, and held it for a moment before exhaling.

'It could be her. The hair's different. Blond. And she's a lot older. Heavier. But it might be her.'

'Who?' demanded Gabri again.

'Lillian Dyson, of course,' said Olivier.

'Well I know that,' Gabri turned to, and on, his partner. 'But who's she?'

'Lillian was—'

Peter stopped as Gamache raised his hand. Not in a threat, but an instruction. To stop talking. And Peter did.

'I need to hear it from Clara first,' said the Chief Inspector. 'Would you like to speak in private?'

Clara thought for a moment, then nodded.

'What? Without us?' asked Gabri.

'I'm sorry, *mon beau* Gabri,' said Clara. 'But I'd rather speak to them quietly.'

Gabri looked hurt, but accepted. The two men left, walking around the corner of the home.

Gamache caught Agent Lacoste's eye and nodded then he looked at the two Adirondack chairs in front of them. 'Could we find two more chairs?'

With Peter's help two more Adirondack chairs were brought over and the four of them sat in a circle. Had there been a campfire in the center it might have felt like a ghost story.

And in a way, it was.

FOUR

—

Gabri and Olivier returned to the bistro in time for the lunch hour rush. The place was packed, but all conversation, all activity stopped when the two men entered.

'Well,' demanded Ruth into the silence. 'Who kakked?'

That broke the dam and a flood of questions followed.

'Was it someone we know?'

'I heard it was someone from the inn and spa.'

'A woman.'

'Must have been someone from the party. Did Clara know her?'

'Was it a villager?'

'Was it murder?' Ruth demanded.

And while she'd broken the silence, now she created it. All questions stopped and eyes swung from the old poet to the two owners of the bistro.

Gabri turned to Olivier.

'What should we say?'

Olivier shrugged. 'Gamache didn't tell us to be quiet.'

'Oh, for fuck's sake,' snapped Ruth, 'just tell us. And get me a drink. Better still, get me a drink, then tell us.'

There was a round of debate and Olivier raised his arms. 'OK, OK. We'll tell you what we know.'

And he did.

The body was a woman named Lillian Dyson. That was met with silence, then a small buzz as people compared notes. But there were no shrieks, no sudden faints, no rending of shirts.

No recognition.

She was found in the Morrows' garden, Olivier confirmed.

Murdered.

There was a long pause after the word.

'Must be something in the water,' muttered Ruth, who paused neither for life nor death. 'How was she killed?'

'Broken neck,' said Olivier.

'Who was this Lillian?' someone at the back of the crowded bistro asked.

'Clara seems to know her,' said Olivier. 'But she never mentioned her to me.'

He looked over at Gabri, who shook his head.

In doing that he noticed that someone else had slipped in after them and was standing quietly by the door.

Agent Isabelle Lacoste had been watching the whole thing, sent there by Chief Inspector Gamache, who understood that the two men would give away all they knew. And the Chief wanted to know whether someone in the bistro, on hearing it, would then give themselves away.

'Tell me,' said Gamache.

He was leaning forward in his chair, elbows resting on his knees. One hand held the other lightly. In a new, but necessary, gesture.

Beside him, Inspector Beauvoir had his notebook and pen out.

Clara sat back in the deep wooden chair and held on to the wide warm armrests, as though bracing herself. But instead of hurtling forward, she was plunging backward.

Back through the decades, out the door of their home and out of Three Pines. Back to Montréal. Into art college, into the classes, into the student shows. Clara Morrow slammed backward out of college and into high school, then elementary school. And nursery school.

Before skidding to a stop in front of the little girl with the shining red hair next door.

Lillian Dyson.

'Lillian was my best friend growing up,' said Clara. 'She lived next door and was two months older than me. We were inseparable. But were opposites, really. She grew fast and tall and I didn't. She was smart, clever in school. I kinda plodded along. I was good at some things, but sort of froze up in the classroom. I got nervous. Kids started picking on me early, but Lillian always protected me. Nobody messed with Lillian. She was a tough kid.'

Clara smiled at the memory of Lillian, her orange hair gleaming, staring down a bunch of girls who were being mean to Clara. Daring them. Clara standing behind her. Longing to stand beside her friend, but not having the courage. Not yet.

Lillian, the precious only child.

The precious friend.

Lillian the pretty one, Clara the character.

They were closer than sisters. Kindred spirits, they told each other in flowery notes they wrote back and forth. Friends forever. They made up codes and secret languages. They'd pricked their fingers and solemnly smeared their blood together. There, they'd declared. Sisters.

They loved the same boys from TV shows and kissed posters and cried when the Bay City Rollers broke up and *The Hardy Boys* was canceled.

All this she told Gamache and Beauvoir.

'What happened?' the Chief asked quietly.

'How do you know anything happened?'

'Because you didn't recognize her.'

Clara shook her head. What happened? How to explain it.

'Lillian was my best friend,' Clara repeated, as though needing to hear it again herself. 'She saved my childhood. It would've been miserable without her. I still don't know why she chose me as a friend. She could've had anyone. Everyone wanted to be Lillian's friend. At least, at first.'

The men waited. The midday sun beat down on them, making it increasingly uncomfortable. But still they waited.

'But there was a price for being Lillian's friend,' said Clara at last. 'It was a wonderful world she created. Fun and safe. But she always had to be right, and she always had to be first. That was the price. It seemed fair at first. She set the rules and I followed. I was pretty pathetic anyway, so it was never an issue. It never seemed to matter.'

Clara took a deep breath. And exhaled.

'And then, it did seem to matter. In high school things began to change. I didn't see it at first, but I'd call Lillian on Saturday night to see if she'd like to go out, to a movie or something, and she'd say she'd get back to me, but didn't. I'd call again, to find she'd gone out.'

Clara looked at the three men. She could see that while they were following the words they weren't necessarily following the emotions. How it felt. Especially that first time. To be left behind.

It sounded so small, so petty. But it was the first hairline fracture.

Clara hadn't realized it at the time. She thought maybe Lillian'd forgotten. And besides, she had a right to go out with other friends.

Then, one weekend, Clara had arranged to go out with a new friend herself.

And Lillian had gone ballistic.

'It took months for her to forgive me.'

Now she saw it in Jean Guy's face. A look of revulsion. For the way Lillian had treated her, or the way she'd taken it? How to explain it to him? How did she explain it to herself?

At the time it had seemed normal. She loved Lillian. Lillian loved her. Had saved her from the bullies. She'd never hurt Clara. Not on purpose.

If there was bad blood it must have been Clara's fault.

Then everything would shift. All was forgiven and Lillian and Clara would be best friends again. Clara was invited back into the shelter that was Lillian.

'When did you first suspect?' Gamache asked.

'Suspect what?'

'That Lillian was not your friend.'

It was the first time she'd heard the words out loud. Said so clearly, so simply. Their relationship had always seemed so complex, fraught. Clara the needy, clumsy one. Dropping their friendship, breaking it. Lillian the strong, self-reliant one. Forgiving her. Picking up the pieces.

Until, one day.

'It was near the end of high school. Most girls fell out over boys or cliques, or just misunderstandings. Hurt feelings. Teachers and parents think those classrooms and hallways are filled with students but they're not. They're filled with feelings. Bumping into each other. Hurting each other. It's horrible.'

Clara moved her arms off the Adirondack chair. They were baking in the sun. Now she folded them across her stomach.

'Things were going well for Lillian and me. There didn't seem the wild ups and downs anymore. Then one day in art class our favorite teacher complimented me on a piece I'd done. It was the only class I was any good in, the only one I really cared about, though I did quite well in English and history. But art was my passion. And Lillian's too. We'd bounce ideas off each other. I see now we were really muses for each other, though I didn't know the term then. I even remember the piece the teacher liked. It was a chair with a bird perched on it.'

Clara had turned to Lillian, happy. Eager to catch her friend's eye. It had been a small compliment. A tiny triumph. She'd wanted to share it with the only other person who'd understand.

And she had. But. But. In that instant before the smile appeared on Lillian's face Clara had caught something else. A wariness.

And then the supportive, happy smile. So fast Clara almost convinced herself her own insecurity had seen something not really there.

That once again, it was her fault.

But looking back, Clara knew that the fissure had widened. Some cracks let the light in. Some let the darkness out.

She'd had a brief glance at what was inside Lillian. And it wasn't nice.

'We went on to art college together and shared an apartment. But by then I'd learned to downplay any compliments I got about my work. And spent a lot of time telling Lillian how terrific her work was. And it was. Of course, like all of our stuff, it was evolving. We were experimenting. At least, I was. I sort of figured that was the point of art college. Not to get it right, but to see what was possible. To really be out there.'

Clara paused and looked down at her hands, fingers entwined.

'Lillian didn't like it. My stuff was too weird for her. She felt it reflected on her, and said people thought that if she was my muse then my paintings must be about her. And since my paintings and other pieces were so strange, then she must be strange.' Clara hesitated. 'She asked me to stop.'

For the first time she saw a reaction from Gamache. His eyes narrowed just a bit. And then his face and demeanor returned to normal. Neutral. Without judgment.

Apparently.

He said nothing. Just listened.

'And I did,' said Clara, her voice low, her head down. Speaking into her lap.

She took a ragged breath and exhaled, feeling her body deflate.

That was how it had felt back then too. As though there was a small tear and she was deflating.

'I told her time and again that some of the works were inspired by her, some were even a tribute to our friendship, but they weren't her. She said it didn't matter. If others thought they were that's all that mattered. If I cared about her, if I was her friend I'd stop making my art so strange. And make it attractive.

'So I did. I destroyed all the other stuff and started making things that people liked.'

Clara rushed ahead, not daring to look at the people listening.

'I actually got better grades too. And I convinced myself it was the right choice. That it would be wrong to trade a career for a friend.'

She looked up then, directly into Chief Inspector Gamache's eyes. And noted, again, the deep scar by his temple. And the steady, thoughtful gaze.

'It seemed a small sacrifice. Then came the student show. I had a few works in it, but Lillian didn't. Instead she decided to write a piece for credit in the art criticism course she was taking. She wrote a review for the campus paper. In it she praised a few of the student pieces but savaged my works. Said they were vacuous, empty of all feeling. Safe.'

Clara could still feel the quaking, the rumbling, volcanic fury.

Their friendship had been blown to smithereens. No piece large enough to even examine. Impossible to mend.

But what did rise from the rubble was a deep, deep enmity. A hatred. Mutual, it seemed.

Clara came to a stop, trembling even now. Peter reached out and unfastening her hand from its tight grip, he held it and smoothed it.

The sun continued to beat down and Gamache got up, indicating they should move the chairs into the shade. Clara rose, and flashing a quick smile at Peter she took her hand back. They each picked up their chair and walked to the edge of the river where it was cooler and shady.

'I think we should take a little break,' said Gamache. 'Would you like something to drink?'

Clara nodded, unable to speak just yet.

'Bon,' said Gamache, looking across to his forensics team. 'I'm sure they'd like something too. If you can arrange for sandwiches from the bistro,' he said to Beauvoir, 'Peter and I will make some drinks.'

Peter led the Chief toward the kitchen door while Beauvoir walked to the bistro and Clara wandered along the riverbank, alone with her thoughts.

'Did you know Lillian?' Gamache asked, once he and Peter were in the kitchen.

'I did.' Peter got out a couple of large pitchers and some glasses while Gamache took the bright pink lemonade from the freezer and slid the frozen concentrate into the pitchers. 'We all met at art college.'

'What did you think of her?'

Peter pursed his lips in concentration. 'She was very attractive, vivacious I think is the word. A strong personality.'

'Were you attracted to her?'

The two men were side-by-side at the kitchen counter, staring out the window. To the right they could see the homicide team scouring the scene and straight ahead they could see Clara skipping stones into the Rivière Bella Bella.

'There's something Clara doesn't know,' said Peter, turning away from looking at his wife, and meeting Gamache's eyes.

The Chief waited. He could see the struggle in Peter and Gamache let the silence stretch on. Better to wait a few minutes for the full truth than push him and risk getting only half.

Eventually Peter dropped his gaze to the sink and started filling the lemonade containers with water. He mumbled into the running water.

'I beg your pardon?' said Gamache, his voice calm and reasonable.

'I was the one who told Lillian that Clara's works were silly,' said Peter, raising his head and his voice. Angry now, at himself for doing it and Gamache for making him admit it. 'I said Clara's work was banal, superficial. Lillian's review was my fault.'

Gamache was surprised. Stunned in fact. When Peter had said there was something Clara didn't know, the Chief Inspector had assumed an affair. A short-lived student indiscretion between Peter and Lillian.

He hadn't expected this.

'I'd been to the student exhibit and seen Clara's works,' said Peter. 'I was standing beside Lillian and a bunch of others and they were snickering. Then they saw me and asked what I thought. Clara and I had begun dating and I think I could see even then that she was the real deal. Not pretending to be an artist, but a genuine one. She had a creative soul. Still does.'

Peter stopped. He didn't often speak of souls. But when he thought of Clara that was what came to mind. A soul.

'I don't know what came over me. It's like sometimes when it's very quiet I feel like screaming. And sometimes when I'm holding something delicate I feel like dropping it. I don't know why.'

He looked at the large, quiet man beside him. But Gamache continued to be silent. Listening.

Peter took a few short breaths. 'I think too I wanted to impress them, and it's easier to be clever when you criticize. So I said some not very nice things about Clara's show and they ended up in Lillian's review.'

'Clara knows none of this?'

Peter shook his head. 'She and Lillian barely spoke after that and she and I grew closer and closer. I even managed to forget that it happened, or that it mattered. In fact, I convinced myself I'd done Clara a favor. In breaking up with Lillian it freed Clara to do her own art. Try all the things she wanted. Really experiment. And look where it got her. A solo show at the Musée.'

'Are you taking credit for that?'

'I supported her all these years,' said Peter, a defensive note creeping into his voice. 'Where would she be without that?'

'Without you?' asked Gamache, turning now to look the angry man straight in the face. 'I have no idea. Have you?'

Peter made fists of his hands.

'What became of Lillian after art college?' the Chief asked.

'She wasn't much of an artist, but she was, as it turned out, a very good critic. She got a job at one of the weekly papers in Montréal and worked her way up until finally she was doing reviews in *La Presse*.'

Gamache raised his brows again. '*La Presse*? I read the reviews in there. I don't remember a Lillian Dyson by-line. Did she have a *nom de plume*?'

'No,' said Peter. 'She worked there years ago, decades ago now, when we were all starting out. This would've been twenty years ago or more.'

'And then what?'

'We didn't keep in touch,' said Peter. 'Only ever saw her at some *vernissages* and even then Clara and I avoided her. Were cordial when there was no option, but we preferred not to be around her.'

'But do you know what happened to her? You say she stopped working at *La Presse* twenty years ago. What did she do?'

'I heard she'd moved to New York. I think she realized the climate wasn't right for her here.'

'Too cold?'

Peter smiled. 'No. More a foul odor. By climate I mean the artistic climate. As a critic she hadn't made many friends.'

'I suppose that's the price of being a critic.'

'I suppose.'

But Peter sounded unconvinced.

'What is it?' the Chief pressed.

'There're lots of critics, most are respected by the community. They're fair, constructive. Very few are mean-spirited.'

'And Lillian Dyson?'

'She was mean-spirited. Her reviews could be clear, thoughtful, constructive and even glowing. But every now and then she'd let loose a real stinker. It was amusing at first, but grew less and less fun when it became clear her targets were random. And the attacks vicious. Like the one on Clara. Unfair.'

He seemed, Gamache noticed, to have already floated right past his own role in it.

'Did she ever review one of your shows?'

Peter nodded. 'But she liked it.' His cheeks reddened. 'I've always suspected she wrote a glowing review just to piss off Clara. Hoping to drive a wedge between us. She assumed since she was so petty and jealous Clara would be too.'

'She wasn't?'

'Clara? Don't get me wrong, she can be maddening. Annoying, impatient, sometimes insecure. But she's only ever happy for other people. Happy for me.'

'And are you happy for her?'

'Of course I am. She deserves all the success she gets.'

It was a lie. Not that she deserved her success. Gamache knew that to be true. As did Peter. But both men also knew he was far from happy about it.

Gamache had asked not because he didn't know the answer, but because he wanted to see if Peter would lie to him.

He had. And if he'd lie about that, what else had he lied about?

Gamache, Beauvoir and the Morrows sat down to lunch in the garden. The forensics team, on the other side of the tall perennial beds, were drinking lemonade and eating an assortment of sandwiches from the bistro, but Olivier had prepared something special for Beauvoir to take back for the four of them. And so the Inspector had returned with a chilled cucumber, soup with mint and melon, a sliced tomato and basil salad drizzled with balsamic, and cold poached salmon.

It was an idyllic setting disturbed every now and then by a homicide investigator walking by, or appearing in a nearby flower bed.

Gamache had placed Peter and Clara with their backs to the activity. Only he and Beauvoir could see, but he realized it was a conceit. The Morrows knew perfectly well that the gentle scene they looked upon, the river, the late spring flowers, the quiet forest, wasn't the whole picture.

And if they'd forgotten, the conversation would remind them.

'When was the last time you heard from Lillian?' Gamache asked, as he took a forkful of pink salmon and added a dab of mayonnaise. His voice was soft, his eyes thoughtful. His face kind.

But Clara wasn't fooled. Gamache might be courteous, might be kind, but he made a living looking for killers. And you don't do that by being just nice.

'Years ago,' said Clara.

She took a sip of the cold, refreshing soup. She wondered if she really should be quite this hungry. And, oddly, when the body had been an anonymous woman Clara had lost her appetite. Now that it was Lillian she was ravenous.

She took a hunk of baguette, twisted off a piece and smeared it with butter.

'Was it intentional, do you think?' she asked.

'Was what intentional?' Beauvoir asked. He picked at his food, not really hungry. Before lunch he'd gone into the bathroom and taken a painkiller. He didn't want the Chief to see him taking it. Didn't want him to know that he was still in pain, so many months after the shootings.

Now, sitting in the cool shade, he could feel the pain ease and the tension begin to slide away.

'What do you think?' asked Gamache.

'I can't believe it was a coincidence that Lillian was killed here,' said Clara.

She twisted in her chair and saw movement through the deep green leaves. Agents, trying to piece together what happened.

Lillian had come here. On the night of the party. And been murdered.

That much was beyond dispute.

Beauvoir watched Clara turn in her seat. He agreed with her. It was strange.

The only thing that seemed to fit was that Clara herself had killed the woman. It was her home, her party, and her former friend. She had motive and opportunity. But Beauvoir didn't know how many little pills he'd have to take to believe Clara was a killer. He knew most people were capable of murder. And, unlike Gamache who believed goodness existed, Beauvoir knew that was a temporary state. As long as the sun shone and there was poached salmon on the plate, people could be good.

But take that away, and see what happens. Take the food, the chairs, the flowers, the home. Take the friends, the supportive spouse, the income away, and see what happens.

The Chief believed if you sift through evil, at the very bottom you'll find good. He believed that evil has its limits. Beauvoir didn't. He believed that if you sift through good, you'll find evil. Without borders, without brakes, without limit.

And every day it frightened him that Gamache couldn't see that. That he was blind to it. Because out of blind spots terrible things appeared.

Someone had killed a woman not twenty feet from where they sat, having their genteel picnic. It was intentional, it was done with bare hands. And it was almost certainly no coincidence Lillian Dyson died here. In Clara Morrow's perfect garden.

'Can we get a list of guests at your *vernissage* and the barbecue afterward?' Gamache asked.

'Well, we can tell you who we invited, but you'll have to get the complete list from the Musée,' said Peter. 'As for the party here in Three Pines last night ...'

He looked at Clara, who grinned.

'We have no idea who came,' she admitted. 'The whole village was invited and most of the countryside. People were told to just come and go as they pleased.'

'But you said some people from the Montréal opening came down,' said Gamache.

'True,' said Clara. 'I can tell you who we invited. I'll make a list.'

'Not everyone at the *vernissage* was invited down?' asked Gamache. He and Reine-Marie had been, as had Beauvoir. They hadn't been able to make it, but he'd assumed it was an open invitation. Clearly it wasn't.

'No. A *vernissage* is for working, networking, schmoozing,' said Clara. 'We wanted this party to be more relaxed. A celebration.'

'Yeah, but . . .' said Peter.

'What?' asked Clara.

'André Castonguay?'

'Oh, him.'

'From the Galerie Castonguay?' asked Gamache. 'He was there?'

'And here,' said Peter.

Clara nodded. She hadn't admitted to Peter the only reason she'd invited Castonguay and some other dealers to the barbecue afterward was for him. In the hopes they'd give him a chance.

'I did invite a few big-wigs,' Clara said. 'And a few artists. It was a lot of fun.'

She'd even enjoyed herself. It was amazing to see Myrna chatting with François Marois and Ruth trading insults with a few drunken artist friends. To see Billy Williams and the local farmers laughing and talking with elegant gallery owners.

And by the time midnight sounded, everyone was dancing.

Except Lillian, who was lying in Clara's garden.

Ding, dong, thought Clara.

The witch is dead.

FIVE

—

Chief Inspector Gamache picked up the stack of papers just inside the yellow police cordon and handed them to Clara.

'I'm sure the critics loved your show,' he said.

'Why, oh why aren't you an art critic instead of wasting your time in such a trivial profession?' Clara asked.

'Dreadful waste of a life, I agree,' smiled the Chief.

'Well,' she looked down at the papers, 'I guess I can't count on another body showing up. I might just have to read these now.'

She looked around. Peter had gone inside and Clara wondered if she should too. To read the reviews in peace and quiet. In secret.

Instead, she thanked Gamache and walked toward the bistro, hugging the heavy papers to her chest. She could see Olivier out on the *terrasse*, serving drinks. Monsieur Beliveau sat at a table, with its blue and white sun umbrella, sipping a Cinzano and reading the Sunday newspapers.

Indeed all the tables were taken, filled with villagers and friends enjoying a lazy Sunday brunch. As she appeared most eyes turned to her.

Then looked away.

And she felt a stab of rage. Not at these people, but at Lillian. Who'd taken the biggest day of Clara's professional life and done this. So that instead of smiling and waving and commenting on the big celebrations, now people turned away. Clara's triumph stolen, yet again, by Lillian.

She looked at the grocer, Monsieur Beliveau, who quickly dropped his eyes.

As did Clara.

When she raised them again a moment later she almost leapt out of her skin. Olivier was standing within inches of her, holding two glasses.

'Shit,' she exhaled.

'Shandies,' he said. 'Made with ginger beer and pale ale, as you like them.'

Clara looked from him to the glasses then back to Olivier. A slight breeze picked at his thinning blond hair. Even with an apron around his slender body he managed to look sophisticated and relaxed. But Clara remembered the look they'd exchanged while kneeling in the corridor of the Musée d'Art Contemporain.

'That was fast,' she said.

'Well, they were actually meant for someone else, but I judged it was an emergency.'

'That obvious?' smiled Clara.

'Hard not to be, when a body appears at your place. I know.'

'Yes,' said Clara. 'You do know.'

Olivier indicated the bench on the village green and they walked over to it. Clara dropped the heavy newspapers and they hit the bench with a thump, as did she.

Clara accepted a shandy from Olivier and they sat side-by-side, their backs to the bistro, to the people, to the crime scene. To the searching eyes and averted eyes.

'How're you doing?' asked Olivier. He'd almost asked if she was all right, but of course she wasn't.

'I wish I could say. Lillian alive in our back garden would have been a shock, but Lillian dead is inconceivable.'

'Who was she?'

'A friend from long ago. But no longer a friend. We had a falling out.'

Clara didn't say more, and Olivier didn't ask. They sipped their drinks and sat in the shade of the three huge pine trees that soared over them, over the village.

'How was it seeing Gamache again?' asked Clara.

Olivier paused to consider, then he smiled. He looked boyish and young. Far younger than his thirty-eight years. 'Not very comfortable. Do you think he noticed?'

'I think it's just possible,' said Clara, and squeezed Olivier's hand. 'You haven't forgiven him?'

'Could you?'

Now it was Clara's turn to pause. Not to reflect on her answer. She knew it. But on whether she should say it.

'We forgave you,' she finally said and hoped her tone was gentle enough, soft enough. That the words wouldn't feel as barbed as they could. But still she felt Olivier stiffen, withdraw. Not physically, but there seemed an emotional step back.

'Have you?' he said at last. And his tone was soft too. It wasn't an accusation, more a wonderment. As though it was something he quietly asked himself every day.

Was he forgiven. Yet.

True, he hadn't murdered the Hermit. But he'd betrayed him. Stolen from him. Taken everything the delusional recluse had offered. And some he hadn't. Olivier had taken everything from the fragile old man. Including his freedom. Imprisoning him in the log cabin, with cruel words.

And when it had all come out, at his trial, he'd seen the looks on their faces.

As though they were suddenly staring at a stranger. A monster in their midst.

'What makes you think we haven't forgiven you?' asked Clara.

'Well, Ruth for one.'

'Oh, come on,' laughed Clara. 'She's always called you a dick-head.'

'True. But you know what she calls me now?'

'What?' she asked with a grin.

'Olivier.'

Clara's grin slowly faded.

'You know,' said Olivier, 'I thought prison would be the worst. The humiliations, the terror. It's amazing what you can get used to. Even now those memories are fading. No, not really fading, but they're more in my head now. Not so much here.' He pressed his hand to his chest. 'But you know what doesn't go away?'

Clara shook her head and steeled herself. 'Tell me.'

She didn't want what Olivier was offering. Some scalded memory. Of a gay man in prison. A good man, in prison. God knew, he was flawed. More than most, perhaps. But his punishment had far out-stripped the crime.

Clara didn't think she could stand to hear the best part of being in prison, and now she was about to hear the worst. But he had to tell it. And Clara had to listen.

'It's not the trial, not even prison.' Olivier looked at her with sad eyes. 'Do you know what wakes me up at two in the morning with a panic attack?'

Clara waited, feeling her own heart pounding.

'It was here. After I'd been released. It was walking from the car with Beauvoir and Gamache. That long walk across the snow to the bistro.'

Clara stared at her friend, not quite understanding. How could the memory of coming home to Three Pines possibly be more frightening than being locked behind bars?

She remembered that day clearly. It had been a Sunday afternoon in February. Another crisp, cold winter day. She and Myrna and Ruth and Peter and most of the village had been snug inside the bistro, having *café au laits* and talking. She'd been chatting with Myrna when she'd noticed Gabri had grown uncharacteristically quiet and was staring out the windows. Then she'd looked. Children were skating on the pond, playing a pick-up game of hockey. Other kids were tobogganing, having snowball fights, building forts. Down rue du Moulin she saw the familiar Volvo drive slowly into Three Pines. It parked by the village green. Three men, wrapped in heavy parkas, got out of the vehicle. They paused, then slowly walked the few paces to the bistro.

Gabri had stood up, almost knocking over his coffee mug. Then the entire bistro had grown quiet, as all eyes followed Gabri's stare. They watched the three figures. It was almost as though the pines had come alive and were approaching.

Clara said nothing and waited for Olivier to continue.

'I know it was just a few yards, really,' he finally said. 'But the bistro seemed so far away. It was freezing cold, the kind that goes right through your coat. Our boots on the snow sounded so loud, crunching and squealing, like we were stepping on something alive, and hurting it.'

Olivier paused, and narrowed his eyes again.

'I could see everyone inside. I could see the logs burning in the fireplace. I could see the frost on the windowpanes.'

As he spoke Clara could see them too, through his eyes.

'I haven't even told Gabri this, I didn't want to hurt him, didn't want him to take it the wrong way. When we were walking toward the bistro I almost stopped. Almost asked them to drive me somewhere else, anywhere else.'

'Why?' Clara's voice had dropped to a whisper.

'Because I was terrified. More afraid than I'd ever been in my life. More afraid even than in prison.'

'Afraid of what?'

Once again Olivier felt the bitter cold scraping his cheeks. Heard his feet shrieking on the hard snow. And saw the warm bistro through the mullioned windows. His friends and neighbors over drinks, talking. Laughing. The fire in the grate.

Safe and warm.

They on the inside. He on the outside, looking in.

And the closed door between him and everything he ever wanted.

He'd almost passed out from terror, and had he been able to find his voice he felt sure he'd have shouted at Gamache to take him back to Montréal. Drop him at some anonymous fleabag. Where he might not be accepted, but he wouldn't be rejected.

'I was afraid you wouldn't want me back. That I wouldn't belong anymore.'

Olivier sighed and dropped his head. His eyes stared at the ground, taking in each blade of grass.

'Oh, God, Olivier,' said Clara, dropping her shandy onto the newspapers, where it fell over, soaking the pages. 'Never.'

'Are you sure?' he asked, turning to her. Searching her face for reassurance.

'Absolutely. We really have let it go.'

He was quiet for a moment. They both watched as Ruth left her small cottage on the far side of the village green, opened her gate, and limped across to the other bench. Once there she looked at them and lifted her hand.

Please, thought Olivier. *Give me the finger. Say something rude. Call me a fag, a queer. Dick-head.*

'I know you say that, but I don't really think you have.' He watched Ruth, but spoke to Clara. 'Let it go, I mean.'

Ruth looked at Olivier. Hesitated. And waved.

Olivier paused, then nodded. Turning back to Clara he gave her a weary smile.

'Thank you for listening. If you ever want to talk about Lillian, or anything, you know where to find me.'

He waved, not toward the bistro, but toward Gabri, who was busy ignoring customers and chatting away with a friend. Olivier watched him with a smile.

Yes, thought Clara. *Gabri is his home.*

She picked up her sodden newspapers and began to walk across the village green when Olivier called after her. She turned and he caught up with her.

'Here. You spilled yours.' He held out his shandy.

'No, that's OK. I'll get something at Myrna's.'

'Please?' he asked.

She looked at the partly drunk shandy, then at him. His kind, beseeching eyes. And she took the glass.

'*Merci, mon beau* Olivier.'

As she approached the village shops she thought about what Olivier had said.

And wondered if he was right. Maybe they hadn't forgiven him.

Just then two men came out of the bistro and made their way slowly up rue du Moulin, toward the inn and spa at the top of the hill. She turned to watch them, surprised. That they were there. And that they were together.

Then her gaze shifted. To her own home. And a solitary figure standing by the corner of the house. Also watching the two men.

It was Chief Inspector Gamache.

Gamache watched François Marois and André Castonguay slowly make their way up the hill.

They didn't seem in conversation, but they did seem companionable. Comfortable.

Had it always been so? Gamache wondered. Or had it been different decades ago, when both were young turks just starting out. Fighting for territory, fighting for influence, fighting for artists.

Perhaps the two men had always liked and respected each other. But Gamache doubted that. They were both too powerful, too ambitious. Had too much ego. And too much was at stake. They could be civil, could even be gracious. But they almost certainly were not friends.

And yet here they were, like old combatants, climbing the hill together.

As he watched, Gamache became aware of a familiar scent. Turning slightly he saw he was standing beside a gnarled old lilac bush at the corner of Peter and Clara's home.

It looked delicate, fragile, but Gamache knew lilacs were in fact long lived. They survived storms and droughts, biting winters and late frosts. They flourished and bloomed where other more apparently robust plants died.

The village of Three Pines, he noticed, was dotted with lilac bushes. Not the new hybrids with double blooms and vibrant colors. These were the soft purples and whites of his grandmother's garden. When had they been young? Had doughboys returning from Vimy and Flanders and Passchendaele marched past these same bushes? Had they breathed in the scent and known, at last, they were home? At peace.

He looked back in time to see the two elderly men turn as one into the entrance to the inn and spa, and disappear inside.

'Chief.' Inspector Beauvoir walked toward him from Peter and Clara's back garden. 'The Crime Scene team's just finishing up and Lacoste's back from the bistro. As you thought, Gabri and Olivier weren't in the place thirty seconds before they announced what had happened.'

'And?'

'And nothing. Lacoste says everyone behaved as you'd expect. Curious, upset, worried for their own safety, but not personally upset. No one seemed to know the dead woman. Lacoste spent some time going from table to table after that, showing the photo of the dead woman and describing her. No one remembers seeing her at the barbecue.'

Gamache was disappointed but not surprised. He had a growing suspicion that this woman was not meant to be seen. Not alive, anyway.

'Lacoste's setting up the Incident Room in the old railway station.'

'*Bon.*' Gamache began walking across the village green and Beauvoir fell into step beside him. 'I wonder if we should make it a permanent detachment.'

Beauvoir laughed. 'Why not just move the whole homicide

department down here? By the way, we found Madame Dyson's car. Looks like she drove herself. It's just up there.' Beauvoir pointed up rue du Moulin. 'Want to see it?'

'*Absolument.*'

The two men changed direction and walked up the dirt road, in the footsteps of the two older men moments before. Once they'd crested the hill Gamache could see a gray Toyota parked on the side of the road a hundred yards further along.

'Long way from the Morrow house and the party,' said Gamache, feeling the warmth as the afternoon sun shone through the leaves.

'True, I imagine the place was packed with cars. This was probably as close as she could get.'

Gamache nodded slowly. 'Which would mean she wasn't among the first to arrive. Or, maybe she parked this far away on purpose.'

'Why would she do that?'

'Maybe she didn't want to be seen.'

'Then why wear neon red?'

Gamache smiled. It was a good point. 'Very annoying, having a smart second in command. I long for the days you used to just tug your forelock and agree with me.'

'And when were those?'

'Right again. This must stop.' He smiled to himself.

They came to a halt beside the car.

'It's been gone over, searched, swabbed, fingerprinted. But I wanted you to see it before we had it towed away.'

'*Merci.*'

Beauvoir unlocked it and the Chief Inspector climbed into the driver's seat, pushing the seat back to make room for his more substantial body.

The passenger's seat was covered with Cartes Routières du Québec. Maps.

Reaching across he opened the glove compartment. There was the usual assortment of stuff you think you'll use and forget is there. Napkins, elastics, Band-Aids, a double A battery. And some information on the car, with the insurance and registration slips. Gamache pulled it out and read. The car was five years old, but only bought by Lillian Dyson eight months ago. He closed the glove box and picked up the maps. Putting on his half-moon reading glasses he scanned them. They'd been imperfectly folded back together, in that haphazard way impatient people had with annoying maps.

One was for all of Québec. Not very helpful unless you were planning an invasion and just needed to know, roughly, where Montréal and Quebec City were. The other was for Les Canton de l'est. The Eastern Townships.

Lillian Dyson couldn't have known it when she bought them, but these maps were also useless. Just to be sure, he opened one and where Three Pines should have been there was the winding Bella Bella river, hills, a forest. And nothing else. As far as the official mapmakers were concerned Three Pines didn't exist.

It had never been surveyed. Never plotted. No GPS or sat nav system, no matter how sophisticated, would ever find the little village. It only appeared as though by accident over the edge of the hill. Suddenly. It could not be found unless you were lost.

Had Lillian Dyson been lost? Had she stumbled onto Three Pines and the party by mistake?

But no. That seemed too big a coincidence. She was dressed for a party. Dressed to impress. To be seen. To be noticed.

Then why hadn't she been?

'Why was Lillian here?' he asked, almost to himself.

'Did she even know it was Clara's home, do you think?' Beauvoir asked.

'I've wondered that,' admitted Gamache, taking off his reading glasses and getting out of the car.

'Either way,' said Beauvoir, 'she came.'

'But how.'

'By car,' said Beauvoir.

'Yes, I've managed to get that far,' said Gamache with a smile. 'But once in the car how'd she get here?'

'The maps?' asked Beauvoir, with infinite patience. But when he saw Gamache shaking his head he reconsidered. 'Not the maps?'

Gamache was silent, letting his second in command find the answer himself.

'She wouldn't have found Three Pines on those maps,' said Beauvoir, slowly. 'It isn't on them.' He paused, thinking. 'So how'd she find her way here?'

Gamache turned and started making his way back toward Three Pines, his pace measured.

Something else occurred to Beauvoir as he joined the Chief. 'How'd any of them get here? All those people from Montréal?'

'Clara and Peter sent directions with the invitation.'

'Well, there's your answer,' said Beauvoir. 'She had directions.'

'But she wasn't invited. And even if she somehow got her hands on an invitation, and the directions, where are they? Not in her handbag, not on her body. Not in the car.'

Beauvoir looked away, thinking. 'So, no maps and no directions. How'd she find the place?'

Gamache stopped opposite the inn and spa.

'I don't know,' he admitted. Then Gamache turned to look at the inn. It had once been a monstrosity. A rotting, rotten old place. A Victorian trophy home built more than a century ago of hubris and other men's sweat.

Meant to dominate the village below. But while Three Pines survived the recessions, the depressions, the wars, this turreted eyesore fell into disrepair, attracting only sorrow.

Instead of a trophy, when villagers looked up what they saw was a shadow, a sigh on the hill.

But no longer. Now it was an elegant and gleaming country inn.

But sometimes, at certain angles, in a certain light Gamache could still see the sorrow in the place. And just at dusk, in the breeze, he thought he could hear the sigh.

In Gamache's breast pocket was the list of guests Clara and Peter had invited from Montréal. Was the murderer's name among them?

Or was the murderer not a guest at all, but someone already here?

'Hello, there.'

Beside him Beauvoir gave a start. He tried not to show it, but this old home, despite the facelift, still gave Beauvoir a chill.

Dominique Gilbert appeared around the side of the inn. She was wearing jodhpurs and a black velvet riding hat. In her hand she carried a leather crop. She was about to either go for a ride, or direct a Mack Sennett short.

She smiled when she recognized them, and put out her hand.

'Chief Inspector.' She shook his hand then turned to Beauvoir and shook his. Then her smile faded.

'So it's true about the body in Clara's garden?'

She removed her hat to show brown hair flattened to her skull by perspiration. Dominique Gilbert was in her late forties, tall and slender. A refugee, along with her husband, Marc, from the city. They'd made their bundle and escaped.

Her fellow executives at the bank had predicted they wouldn't last a winter. But they were now into their second year and showed no sign of regretting their decision to buy the old wreck and turn it into an inviting inn and spa.

'It's true, I'm afraid,' said Gamache.

'May I use your phone?' Inspector Beauvoir asked. Despite knowing perfectly well it wouldn't work, he'd been trying to call the forensics team on his cell phone.

'*Merde*,' he'd muttered, 'it's like going back to the dark ages here.'

'Help yourself.' Dominique pointed into the house. 'You don't even have to wind it up anymore.'

But her humor was lost on the Inspector, who strode in, still punching re-dial on his cell.

'I hear some of the guests at the party stayed with you last night?' said Gamache, standing on the verandah.

'A few. Some booked, some were last minute.'

'A bit too much to drink?'

'Sloshed.'

'Are they still here?'

'They've been dragging themselves out of bed for the past couple of hours. Your agent asked them not to leave Three Pines, but most could barely leave their beds. They're not in any danger of fleeing. Crawling, perhaps, but not fleeing.'

'Where is my agent?' Gamache looked around. When he'd learned some of the guests had stayed over, he'd directed Agent Lacoste to send out two junior agents. One to guard the B and B, the other to come here.

'He's around back with the horses.'

'Is that right?' said Gamache. 'Guarding them?'

'As you know, Chief Inspector, our horses aren't exactly flight risks either.'

He did know. One of the first things Dominique had done when moving here was to buy horses. The fulfillment of a childhood dream.

But instead of Black Beauty, Flicka, Pegasus, Dominique had found four broken-down old plugs. Ruined animals, bound for the slaughterhouse.

Indeed, one looked more like a moose than a horse.

But such was the nature of dreams. They were not always recognizable, at first.

'They'll be right up to take the car away,' said Beauvoir, returning. Gamache noticed Beauvoir still held his cell phone in his hand. A pacifier.

'A few of the hardier guests wanted to go riding,' Dominique explained. 'I was just about to take them. Your agent said it would be OK. At first he was unsure but once he saw the horses he relented. I guess he realized they wouldn't exactly make for the border. I hope I haven't gotten him into trouble.'

'Not at all,' said Gamache but Beauvoir looked as though that wouldn't have been his answer.

As they walked across the grass toward the barn they could see people and animals inside. All in shadow, silhouettes cut and pasted there.

And among them the outline of a young Sûreté agent in uniform. Slender. Awkward, even at a distance.

Chief Inspector Gamache felt his heart suddenly pound and the blood rush to his core. In an instant he felt light-headed and he wondered if he might pass out. His hands went cold. He wondered if Jean Guy Beauvoir had noticed this sudden reaction, this unexpected spasm. As another young agent came to mind. Came to life. For an instant.

And then died again.

The shock was so great it threw Gamache off for a moment. He almost swayed on his feet but when it cleared he found his body still moving forward. His face still relaxed. Nothing to betray what had just happened. This *grand mal* of emotion.

Except a very, very slight tremor in his right hand, which he now closed into a fist.

The young agent's silhouette broke away from the rest and came into the sunshine. And became whole. Handsome face eager, and worried, he hurried over to them.

'Sir,' he said, and saluted the Chief Inspector, who waved him to drop the salute. 'I came to just see,' the agent blurted out. 'To make sure it would be OK if they rode the horses. I didn't mean to leave the place unguarded.'

The young agent had never met Chief Inspector Gamache before. He'd obviously seen him at a distance. As had most of the province. On news programs, in interviews, in photographs in the newspaper. In the televised funeral cortege for the agents who had died. Under Gamache's command, just six months earlier.

The agent had even attended one of the Chief's lectures at the academy.

But now, as he looked at the Chief Inspector, all those other images disappeared. To be replaced by a leaked video of that police action, where so many had died. No one should have ever seen those images, but millions had, as it went viral on the Internet. It was difficult to see the Chief Inspector now, with his jagged scar, and not also see that video.

But here was the man in person. The famed head of the famed homicide department. He was so close that the young agent could even smell the Chief Inspector's scent. A very slight hint of sandalwood and something else. Rose water. The agent looked into Gamache's deep brown eyes and realized they were unlike any he'd seen. He'd been stared at by many senior officers. In fact, everyone was senior to him. But he'd never had quite this experience before.

The Chief Inspector's gaze was intelligent, thoughtful, searching.

But where others were cynical and censorious at their center, Chief Inspector Gamache's eyes were something else.

They were kind.

Now, finally the agent was face-to-face with this famous man and where had the Chief found him? In a barn. Smelling of horse shit and feeding carrots to what looked like a moose. Saddling horses for murder suspects.

He waited for the wrath. For the curt correction.

But instead, Chief Inspector Gamache did the unthinkable.

He put out his hand.

The young agent stared at it for a moment. And noticed the very, very slight tremble. Then he took it and felt it strong and firm.

'Chief Inspector Gamache,' the large man said.

'*Oui, patron*. Agent Yves Rousseau of the Cowansville detachment.'

'All quiet here?'

'Yessir. I'm sorry. I probably shouldn't have allowed them to go riding.'

Gamache smiled. 'You have no right to stop them. Besides, I don't think they'll get far.'

The three Sûreté officers looked over at the two women and Dominique, each leading a clopping horse from the barn.

Gamache turned his gaze back to the agent in front of him. Young, eager.

'Did you get their names and addresses?'

'Yessir. And cross checked with their ID. I got everyone's information.'

He unclicked his pocket, to get at his notebook.

'Perhaps you can take it to the Incident Room,' said Gamache, 'and give it to Agent Lacoste.'

'Right,' said Rousseau, writing that down.

Jean Guy Beauvoir inwardly groaned. *Here we go again*, he thought. *He's going to invite this kid to join the investigation. Does he never learn?*

Armand Gamache smiled and nodded to Agent Rousseau, then turned and walked back toward the inn, leaving two surprised men behind him. Rousseau that he'd been spoken to so civilly and Beauvoir that Gamache hadn't done what he'd done on almost every investigation in the past. Invited one of the young, local agents to join them.

Beauvoir knew he should be happy. Relieved.

Then why did he feel so sad?

Once inside the inn and spa, Chief Inspector Gamache was again taken by how attractive it had become. Cool and calm. The old Victorian wreck had been lovingly restored. The stained-glass lintels cleaned and repaired, so that the sun shone emerald and ruby and sapphire on the polished black and white tiles of the entry hall. It was circular, with a wide mahogany stairway sweeping up.

A large floral arrangement of lilac and Solomon's Seal and apple boughs stood on the gleaming wood table in the center of the hall.

It felt fresh and light and welcoming.

'May I help you?' a young receptionist asked.

'We were looking for two of your guests. Messieurs Marois and Castonguay.'

'They're in the living room,' she said, smiling, and led them off to the right.

The two Sûreté officers knew perfectly well where it was, having been in it many times before. But they let the receptionist do her job.

After offering them coffee, which was declined, she left them at the door to the living room. Gamache took in the room. It too was open and bright with floor-to-ceiling windows looking down on the village below. A log fire was laid, but not lit and flowers sat in vases on occasional tables. The room was both modern in its furniture and traditional in details and design. They'd done a sympathetic job of bringing the grand old ruin into the twenty-first century.

'*Bonjour.*' François Marois rose from one of the Eames chairs and put down a copy of that day's *Le Devoir.*

André Castonguay looked over from the easy chair where he was reading the *New York Times*. He too rose as the two officers entered the room.

Gamache, of course, already knew Monsieur Marois, having spoken with him the night before at the *vernissage*. But the other man was a stranger to him, known only by reputation. Castonguay stood and Gamache saw a tall man, a little bleary perhaps from celebrating the night before. His face was puffy, and ruddy from tiny broken blood vessels in his nose and cheeks.

'I hadn't expected to see you here,' said Gamache, walking forward and shaking hands with Marois as though greeting a fellow guest.

'Nor I you,' said Marois. 'André, this is Chief Inspector Gamache, of the Sûreté du Québec. Do you know my colleague André Castonguay?'

'Only by reputation. A very good reputation. The Galerie Castonguay is renowned. You represent some fine artists.'

'I'm glad you think so, Chief Inspector,' said Castonguay.

Beauvoir was introduced. He bristled and took an immediate

dislike to the man. He'd in fact disliked the man before even hearing the dismissive remark made to the Chief. Any owner of a high-end art gallery was immediately suspect, of arrogance if not murder. Jean Guy Beauvoir had little tolerance for either.

But Gamache didn't seem put out. Indeed, he seemed almost pleased with André Castonguay's response. And Beauvoir noticed something else.

Castonguay had begun to relax, to grow more sure of himself. He'd pushed this police officer and he hadn't pushed back. Clearly Castonguay felt himself the better man.

Beauvoir smiled slightly and lowered his head so Castonguay wouldn't see.

'Your man took our names and addresses,' said Castonguay, taking the large easy chair by the fireplace. 'Our home addresses as well as business. Does this mean we're suspects?'

'*Mais, non, monsieur*,' said Gamache, sitting on the sofa opposite him. Beauvoir stood off to the side and Monsieur Marois took up a position at the mantelpiece. 'I hope we haven't inconvenienced you.'

Gamache looked concerned, contrite even. André Castonguay relaxed more. It was clear he was used to commanding a room. Getting his way.

Jean Guy Beauvoir watched as the Chief Inspector appeared to acquiesce to Castonguay. To bow before the stronger personality. Not mince, exactly. That would be too obviously a conceit. But to cede the space.

'*Bon*,' said Castonguay. 'I'm glad we got that straight. You didn't inconvenience us. We were planning to stay a few days anyway.'

We, thought Beauvoir and looked over at François Marois. The men would be about the same age, Beauvoir guessed. Castonguay's hair was thick and white. Marois was balding, gray and trimmed. Both men were well groomed and well dressed.

'Here's my card, Chief Inspector.' Castonguay handed Gamache a business card.

'Do you specialize in modern art?' Gamache asked, crossing his legs as though settling in for a nice chat.

Beauvoir, who knew Gamache better than most, watched with interest and some amusement. Castonguay was being wooed. And it was working. He clearly regarded Chief Inspector Gamache as one step up from the beasts. An evolved creature who walked upright but didn't have much of a frontal lobe. Beauvoir could guess what Castonguay thought of him. The missing link, if that.

He longed to say something intelligent, something clever and knowledgeable. Or, failing that, something so shockingly, violently rude this smug man would no longer believe he was in charge of anything.

But Beauvoir, with an effort, kept his mouth shut. Mostly because he couldn't think of anything intelligent to say about art.

Castonguay and the Chief Inspector were now discussing trends in modern art, with Castonguay lecturing and Gamache listening as though rapt.

And François Marois?

Jean Guy Beauvoir had all but forgotten him. He was so quiet. But now the Inspector shifted his eyes to Marois. And discovered the quiet, older man was also staring. But not at Castonguay.

François Marois was staring at Chief Inspector Gamache. Examining him. Closely. Then he shifted his gaze to Beauvoir. It wasn't a cold look. But it was clear and sharp.

It froze Beauvoir's blood.

The conversation between the Chief Inspector and Castonguay had segued back to the murder.

'Terrible,' said Castonguay, as though voicing a unique and insightful sentiment.

'Terrible,' agreed Gamache, sitting forward. 'We have a couple of photographs of the murdered woman. I wonder if you'd mind looking at them?'

Beauvoir handed the photos to François Marois first. He looked at them then passed them on to André Castonguay.

'I'm afraid I don't know her,' said Castonguay. To give him grudging credit, Beauvoir thought the man looked pained to see the woman dead. 'Who was she?'

'Monsieur Marois?' Gamache turned to the other man.

'No, I'm afraid she doesn't look familiar to me either. She was at the party?'

'That's what we're trying to find out. Did either of you see her there? As you can see in one of the pictures, she was wearing quite a remarkable red dress.'

The men glanced at each other, but shook their heads.

'*Désolé*,' said Castonguay. 'But I spent the evening speaking to friends I don't often see. She could've been there and I just didn't notice. Who was she?' he asked again.

The photos were handed back to Beauvoir.

'Her name was Lillian Dyson.'

There was no reaction to the name.

'Was she an artist?' Castonguay asked.

'What makes you ask?' said Gamache.

'Wearing red. Flamboyant. Artists are either complete bums, hardly wash, drunk and filthy most of the time, or they're well, that.' He waved toward the pictures in Beauvoir's hand. 'Over-the-top. Loud. "Look at me" types. Both are very tiring.'

'You don't seem to like artists,' said Gamache.

'I don't. I like the product, not the person. Artists are needy, crazy people who take up a lot of space and time. Exhausting. Like babies.'

'And yet, you were an artist once, I believe,' said François Marois.

The Sûreté agents looked over at the quiet man by the fireplace. Was there a satisfied look on his face?

'I was. Too sane to be a success.'

Marois laughed, and Castonguay looked annoyed. It wasn't meant as a joke.

'You were at the *vernissage* at the Musée yesterday, Monsieur Castonguay?' Gamache asked.

'Yes. The chief curator invited me. And of course Vanessa is a close friend. We dine together when I'm in London.'

'Vanessa Destin-Brown? The head of the Tate Modern?' asked Gamache, apparently impressed. 'She was there last night?'

'Oh yes, there and here. We had a long discussion of the future of figurative—'

'But she didn't stay? Or is she one of the guests at the inn?'

'No, she left early. I don't think burgers and fiddle music's her style.'

'But it is yours?'

Beauvoir wondered if André Castonguay had noticed the tide shifting?

'Not normally, but there were some people here I wanted to speak with.'

'Who?'

'Pardon?'

Chief Inspector Gamache was still cordial, still gracious. But he was also clearly in command. And always had been.

Once again Beauvoir shot a look over to François Marois. He suspected the shift came as no surprise to him.

'Who did you particularly want to speak to at the party here?' Gamache asked, patient, clear.

'Well, Clara Morrow for one. I wanted to thank her for her works.'

'Who else?'

'That's a private matter,' said Castonguay.

So he had noticed, thought Beauvoir. But too late. Chief Inspector Gamache was the tide and André Castonguay a twig. The best he could hope was to stay afloat.

'It might matter, monsieur. And if it doesn't I promise to keep it between us.'

'Well, I'd hoped to approach Peter Morrow. He's a fine artist.'

'But not as good as his wife.'

François Marois spoke quietly. Not much more than a whisper. But everyone turned to look at him.

'Is her work that good?' Chief Inspector Gamache asked.

Marois looked at Gamache for a moment. 'I'll be happy to answer that, but I'm curious to hear what you think. You were at the *vernissage*. You were the one who pointed out that remarkable portrait of the Virgin Mary.'

'The what?' asked Castonguay. 'There was no Virgin Mary painting.'

'There was if you looked,' Marois assured him before turning back to the Chief Inspector. 'You were one of the few people actually paying attention to her art.'

'As I may have mentioned last night, Clara and Peter Morrow are personal friends,' said Gamache.

This brought a look of surprise and suspicion from Castonguay.

'Is that allowed? That means you're investigating friends for murder, *n'est-ce pas*?'

Beauvoir stepped forward. 'In case you didn't know it, Chief Inspector Gamache—'

But the Chief put his hand up and Beauvoir managed to stop himself.

'It's a fair question.' Gamache turned back to André Castonguay. 'They are friends and yes, they're also suspects. In fact, I have a lot of friends in this village, and all of them are suspects as well. And I realize this could be interpreted as a disadvantage, but the fact is, I know these people. Well. Who better to find the murderer among them than someone who knows their weaknesses, their blind spots, their fears? Now,' Gamache leaned slowly forward, toward Castonguay, 'if you're thinking I might find the murderer and let him go ...'

The words were friendly, there was even a mild smile on the Chief Inspector's face. But even André Castonguay couldn't miss the gravity in the voice and eyes.

'No. I don't believe you'd do that.'

'I'm glad to hear it.' Gamache leaned back in his seat once again.

Beauvoir stared at Castonguay a moment longer, making certain he wasn't about to challenge the Chief again. Gamache might think it was natural and even healthy to challenge him, but Beauvoir didn't.

'You're wrong about the Morrow woman's art, you know,' said Castonguay, sullen. 'It's just a bunch of portraits of old women. There was nothing new there.'

'There's everything new, if you look below the surface,' said Marois, taking the easy chair beside Castonguay. 'Look again, *mon ami.*'

But it was clear they were not friends. Not, perhaps, enemies, but would they seek each other out for a friendly lunch at Leméac kafé bistro or a drink at the bar at L'Express in Montréal?

No. Castonguay might, but not Marois.

'And why are you here, monsieur?' Gamache asked Marois. There seemed no power struggle between the two men. There was no need. Each was confident in himself.

'I'm an art dealer, but not a gallery owner. As I told you last night, the curator gave me a catalog and I was taken with Madame Morrow's works. I wanted to see them myself. And,' he smiled ruefully, 'I'm afraid even at my age I'm a romantic.'

'Are you going to admit to a crush on Clara Morrow?' asked Gamache.

François Marois laughed. 'Not exactly, though after seeing her work it's hard not to like her. But it's more of a philosophical state, my romanticism.'

'How so?'

'I love that an artist could be plucked out of obscurity and discovered at the age of almost fifty. What artist doesn't dream of it? What artist doesn't believe, every morning, it will happen before bedtime? Remember Magritte? Belgian painter?'

'*Ceci n'est pas une pipe?*' asked Gamache, losing Beauvoir completely. He hoped the Chief hadn't just had a seizure and started spouting nonsense.

'That's the one. He worked away for years, decades. Living in squalor. Supported himself by painting fake Picassos and forging banknotes. When he did his own work Magritte was not only ignored by the galleries and collectors, he was mocked by other artists, who thought he was nuts. I have to say, it gets pretty bad when even other artists think you're nuts.'

Gamache laughed. 'And was he?'

'Well, perhaps. You've seen his works?'

'I have. I like them, but I'm not sure how I would have felt had someone not told me they were genius.'

'Exactly,' said Marois, suddenly sitting forward, more animated than Beauvoir had seen him. Excited even. 'That's what makes my job like Christmas every day. While every artist wakes up believing this is the day his genius will be discovered, every dealer wakes up believing this is the day he'll discover genius.'

'But who's to say?'

'That's what makes this all so thrilling.'

Beauvoir could see the man wasn't putting on an act. His eyes were gleaming, his hands were gesturing, not wildly, but with excitement.

'The portfolio I believe is brilliant someone else can look at and think is dull, derivative. Witness our reactions to Clara Morrow's paintings.'

'I still say they're just not interesting,' said Castonguay.

'And I say they are, and who's to say who's right? That's what drives artists and dealers crazy. It's so subjective.'

'I think they're born crazy,' mumbled Castonguay, and Beauvoir had to agree.

'So that explains you being at the *vernissage*,' said Gamache. 'Why come to Three Pines?'

Marois hesitated. Trying to decide how much to say, and not even trying to hide his indecision.

Gamache waited. Beauvoir, notebook and pen out, started to doodle. A stick figure and a horse. Or perhaps it was a moose. From the easy chair came the heavy sound of Castonguay breathing.

'I had a client once. Dead now, years ago. Lovely man. A commercial artist, but also a very fine creative artist. His home was full of these marvelous paintings. I discovered him when he was already quite old, though now that I think of it, he was younger than I am now.'

Marois smiled, as did Gamache. He knew that feeling.

'He was one of my first clients and he did quite well. He was thrilled, as was his wife. One day he asked a favor. Could his wife put in a few of her works into his next show. I was polite, but declined. But he was quite uncharacteristically insistent. I didn't know her well, and didn't know her art at all. I suspected she was putting pressure on the old man. But I could see how important it was to him, so I relented. Gave her a corner, and a hammer.'

He paused and his eyes flickered.

'I'm not very proud of it now. I should have either treated her with respect, or declined the show totally. But I was young, and had a lot to learn.'

He sighed. 'The evening of the *vernissage* was the first time I saw her works. I walked into the room and everyone was crowded into that corner. You can guess what happened.'

'All her paintings sold,' said Gamache.

Marois nodded. 'Every one, with people buying others she'd left in her home, sight unseen. There was even a bidding war for several of them. My client was a gifted artist. But she was better. Far better. A stunning find. A genuine Van Gogh's ear.'

'*Pardon?*' asked Gamache. 'A what?'

'What did the old man do?' Castonguay interrupted, now paying attention. 'He must've been furious.'

'No. He was a lovely man. Taught me how to be gracious. And he was. But it was her reaction I'll never forget.' He was quiet for a moment, clearly seeing the two elderly artists. 'She gave up painting. Not only never showed again, she never painted again. She saw the pain it had caused him, though he'd hidden it well. His happiness was more important to her than her own. Than her art.'

Chief Inspector Gamache knew this should have sounded like a love story. Of sacrifice, of selfless choices. But it only sounded like a tragedy to him.

'Is that why you're here?' Gamache asked the art dealer.

Marois nodded. 'I'm afraid.'

'Of what?' Castonguay demanded, losing the thread yet again.

'Did you not see how Clara Morrow looked at her husband yesterday?' asked Marois.

'And how he looked at her,' said Gamache.

The two men locked eyes.

'But Clara isn't that woman you're remembering,' said the Chief Inspector.

'True,' admitted François Marois. 'But Peter Morrow isn't my elderly client either.'

'Do you really think Clara might give up painting?' asked Gamache.

'To save her marriage? To save her husband?' asked Marois. 'Most wouldn't, but the woman who created those paintings just might.'

Armand Gamache had never thought that was a possibility, but now he considered it and realized François Marois might be right.

'Still,' he said. 'What could you hope to do about it?'

'Well,' said Marois, 'not much. But I at least wanted to see where she'd been hiding all these years. I was curious.'

'Is that all?'

'Have you never wanted to visit Giverny to see where Monet painted, or go to Winslow Homer's studio in Prouts Neck? Or see where Shakespeare and Victor Hugo wrote?'

'You're quite right,' admitted Gamache. 'Madame Gamache and I have visited the homes of many of our favorite artists and writers and poets.'

'Why?'

Gamache paused for a few moments, considering. 'Because they seem magical.'

André Castonguay snorted. Beauvoir bristled, embarrassed for the Chief Inspector. It was a ridiculous answer. Perhaps even weak. To admit to a murder suspect he might believe in magic.

But Marois sat still, staring at the Chief Inspector. Finally he nodded, slightly and slowly. It might have even been, Beauvoir thought, a slight tremble.

'*C'est ça*,' said Marois at last. 'Magic. I hadn't planned to come, but when I saw her works at the *vernissage* I wanted to see the village that had produced such magic.'

They talked for a few more minutes, about their movements. Who they saw, who they spoke to. But like everyone else, it was unremarkable.

Chief Inspector Gamache and Inspector Beauvoir left the two men sitting in the bright living room of the inn and spa and went looking for the other guests. Within an hour they'd interviewed them all.

None knew the dead woman. None saw anything suspicious or helpful.

As they walked back down the hill into Three Pines, Gamache thought of their interviews and what François Marois had said.

But there was more to Three Pines than magic. Something monstrous had roamed the village green, had eaten the food and danced among them. Something dark had joined the party that night.

And produced not magic but murder.

SIX

—

Out the window of her bookstore Myrna could see Armand Gamache and Jean Guy Beauvoir walking down the dirt road into the village.

Then she turned back to her shop, with its wooden shelves filled with new and used books, the wide plank pine floors. Sitting on the sofa beside the window and facing the woodstove was Clara.

She'd arrived a few minutes earlier clutching her haul of newspapers to her breasts, like an immigrant at Ellis Island clinging to something ragged and precious.

Myrna wondered if what Clara held was really that important.

She was under no illusion. Myrna knew exactly what was in those papers. The judgment of others. The views of the outside world. What they saw when they saw Clara's art.

And Myrna knew even more. She knew what those beer-sodden pages said.

She too had gotten up early that morning, dragged her weary ass out of bed, trudged to the bathroom. Showered, brushed her teeth, put on fresh clothes. And in the light of the new day she'd gotten into her car and driven to Knowlton.

For the papers. She could have simply downloaded them from the various websites, but if Clara wanted to read them as newspapers, then so did Myrna.

She didn't care how the world saw Clara's art. Myrna knew it was genius.

But she cared about Clara.

And now her friend sat like a lump on the sofa while she sat in the armchair facing her.

'Beer?' Myrna offered, pointing to the stack of newspapers.

'No thank you,' smiled Clara. 'I have my own.' She pointed to her sodden chest.

'You must be every man's dream,' laughed Myrna. 'Finally, a woman made entirely of beer and croissants.'

'A wet dream, certainly,' agreed Clara, smiling.

'Have you had a chance to read them?'

Myrna didn't need to point again to the reeking papers, they both knew what she meant.

'No. Something keeps getting in the way.'

'Something?' asked Myrna.

'Some fucking body,' said Clara, then tried to rein herself in. 'God, Myrna, I don't know what's wrong with me. I should be upset, devastated that this has happened. I should feel horrible for poor Lillian, but you know what I keep thinking? The only thing I keep thinking?'

'That she ruined your big day.' It was a statement. And it was true. She had. Lillian herself, it must be admitted, had not had a great day either. But that discussion would come later.

Clara stared at Myrna, searching for censure.

'What's wrong with me?'

'There's nothing wrong with you,' said Myrna, leaning toward her friend. 'I'd feel the same way. Everyone would. We just may not admit it.' She smiled. 'If it had been me lying back there—' But Myrna got no further. Clara burst in.

'Don't even think such a thing.'

Clara actually looked frightened, as though saying a thing made it more likely to happen, as though whatever God she believed in worked like that. But Myrna knew neither Clara's God nor hers was so chaotic and petty they needed or heeded such ridiculous suggestions.

'If it was me,' Myrna continued, 'you'd care.'

'Oh, God, I'd never recover.'

'These papers wouldn't matter,' said Myrna.

'Not at all. Never.'

'If it was Gabri or Peter or Ruth . . .'

Both women paused. It might have been a step too far.

'. . . anyway,' Myrna continued. 'If it was even a complete stranger you'd have cared.'

Clara nodded.

'But Lillian wasn't a stranger.'

'I wish she had been,' admitted Clara, quietly. 'I wish I'd never met her.'

'What was she?' Myrna asked. She'd heard the broad strokes, but now she wanted to hear the details.

And Clara told her everything. About the young Lillian, about the teenage Lillian. About the woman in her twenties. As she got further into the story Clara's voice dropped and dragged, lugging the words along.

And then she stopped, and Myrna was silent for a moment, staring at her friend.

'She sounds like an emotional vampire,' said Myrna, at last.

'A what?'

'I ran into quite a few in my practice. People who sucked others dry. We all know them. We're in their company and come away drained, for no apparent reason.'

Clara nodded. She did know a few, though no one in Three Pines. Not even Ruth. She only drained their liquor cabinet. But Clara, oddly, always felt refreshed, invigorated after a visit with the demented old poet.

But there were others who just sucked the life right out of her.

Lillian was one.

'But it wasn't always like that,' said Clara, trying to be fair. 'She was a friend once.'

'That's often the way too,' nodded Myrna. 'The frog in the frying pan.'

Clara wasn't at all sure how to respond to that. Were they still talking about Lillian, or had they somehow veered into some French cooking show?

'Do you mean the emotional vampire in the frying pan?' asked Clara, uttering a sentence she was pretty sure had never been said by another human. Or at least, she hoped not.

Myrna laughed and sitting back in her armchair she raised her legs onto the hassock.

'No, little one. Lillian's the emotional vampire. You're the frog.'

'Sounds like a rejected Grimm's fairy tale. "The Frog and the Emotional Vampire".'

Both women paused for a moment, imagining the illustrations.

Myrna came back to her senses first.

'The frog in the frying pan is a psychological term, a phenomenon,' she said. 'If you stick a frog into a sizzling hot frying pan what'll it do?'

'Jump out?' suggested Clara.

'Jump out. But if you put one into a pan at room temperature then slowly raise the heat, what happens?'

Clara thought about it. 'It'll jump out when it gets too hot?'

Myrna shook her head. 'No.' She took her feet off the hassock and leaned forward again, her eyes intense. 'The frog just sits there. It gets hotter and hotter but it never moves. It adjusts and adjusts. Never leaves.'

'Never?' asked Clara, quietly.

'Never. It stays there until it dies.'

Clara look a long, slow, deep breath, then exhaled.

'I saw it with my clients who'd been abused either physically or emotionally. The relationship never starts with a fist to the face, or an insult. If it did there'd be no second date. It always starts gently. Kindly. The other person draws you in. To trust them. To need them. And then they slowly turn. Little by little, increasing the heat. Until you're trapped.'

'But Lillian wasn't a lover, or a husband. She was just a friend.'

'Friends can be abusive. Friendships can turn, become foul,' said Myrna. 'She fed on your gratitude. Fed on your insecurities, on your love for her. But you did something she never expected.'

Clara waited.

'You stood up for yourself. For your art. You left. And she hated you for it.'

'But then why'd she come here?' asked Clara. 'I haven't seen her in more than twenty years. Why'd she come back? What did she want?'

Myrna shook her head. Didn't say what she suspected. That there was really only one reason for Lillian to return.

To ruin Clara's big day.

And she had. Only not, almost certainly, in the way Lillian had planned.

Which, of course, begged the question: Who had planned this?

'Can I say something to you?' Myrna asked.

Clara made a face. 'I hate it when people ask that. It means something awful's coming. What is it?'

'Hope takes its place among the modern masters.'

'I was wrong,' said Clara, perplexed and relieved. 'It's just nonsense. Is this a new game? Can I play? Wallpaper chair is often cows. Or,' Clara looked at Myrna with suspicion, 'have you been smoking your caftan again? I know they say hemp isn't really dope, but I still wonder.'

'Clara Morrow's art makes rejoicing cool again.'

'Ah, a conversation of non sequiturs,' said Clara. 'It's like talking to Ruth, only not as many fucking swear words.'

Myrna smiled. 'Do you know what I was just quoting?'

'Those were quotes?' asked Clara.

Myrna nodded and looked over at the damp and smelly newspapers. Clara's eyes followed her, then widened. Myrna rose and went upstairs, finding her own copies of the papers. Clean and dry. Clara reached out but her hands were trembling too hard and Myrna had to find the sections.

The portrait of Ruth, as the Virgin Mary, glared from the front page of the *New York Times* art section. Above it was a single word, 'Arisen'. And below it the headline HOPE TAKES ITS PLACE AMONG THE MODERN MASTERS.

Clara dropped the section and grabbed for the London *Times* art review. On the front page was a photo of a Maoist accountant at Clara's *vernissage*. And below it the quote, 'Clara Morrow Makes Rejoicing Cool Again.'

'They're raving, Clara,' said Myrna with a smile so wide it hurt.

The pages dropped from Clara's hand and she looked at her friend. The one who'd whispered into the silence.

Clara got up. Arisen, she thought. Arisen.

And she hugged Myrna.

Peter Morrow sat in his studio. Hiding from the ringing phone.

Ring. Ring. Ring.

He'd gone back into their home after lunch, hoping for some peace and quiet. Clara had taken the papers and gone off, presumably to read them by herself. So he had no idea what the critics had said. But as soon as he'd walked in the door the phone had started to ring, and had barely stopped since. All wanting to congratulate Clara.

There were messages from the curators at the Musée, thrilled with the reviews and the subsequent ticket sales. There was a message from Vanessa Destin-Browne, of the Tate Modern in London, thanking them for the party and congratulating Clara. And wondering if they might get together to discuss a show.

For Clara.

He'd eventually just let the phone ring and had gone to stand at the open door to her studio. From there he could see a few puppets, from the time she thought she might do a series on them.

'Perhaps too political,' Clara had said.

'Perhaps,' said Peter, but 'political' wasn't the word that had sprung to mind.

He could see the Warrior Uteruses stacked in the corner. Left there after another disastrous show.

'Perhaps ahead of its time,' Clara had said.

'Perhaps,' said Peter. But 'ahead of its time' wasn't what came to mind either.

And when she'd started in on the *Three Graces*, and even had the three elderly friends pose for her, he'd felt sorry for the women. Thought Clara was being selfish, expecting the old women to stand there for some painting that would never see the light of day.

But the women hadn't minded. Had seemed to have fun, judging by the laughter that disturbed his concentration.

And now that painting was hanging in the Musée d'Art Contemporain. While his meticulous works were on someone's stairway or perhaps, if he was lucky, above a fireplace.

Seen by a dozen people a year. And noticed as much as the wall-paper or curtains. Interior decoration in an affluent home.

How could Clara's portraits of unremarkable women possibly be masterpieces?

Peter turned his back on her studio, but not before he saw the afternoon sun catch Clara's huge fiberglass feet, marching across the back of her space.

'Perhaps too sophisticated,' Clara had said.

'Perhaps,' Peter had mumbled.

He closed the door and went back to his studio, the sound of the ringing phone in his ears.

Chief Inspector Gamache sat in the large living room of the bed and breakfast. The walls were painted a creamy linen, the furniture was handpicked by Gabri from Olivier's antiquing finds. But rather than heavy Victoriana he'd gone for comfort. Two large sofas faced each other across the stone fireplace and armchairs created quiet conversation areas around the room. Where Dominique's inn and spa gleamed and preened like a delightful gem on the hill, Gabri's bed and breakfast sat peacefully, cheerfully, a little shabbily in the valley. Like Grandma's house, if Grandma had been a large gay man.

Gabri and Olivier were over at the bistro still serving lunch, leaving the Sûreté officers alone with the B and B guests.

It had been a rocky start to the interviews, beginning before they'd even crossed the threshold. Beauvoir gingerly took the Chief aside just as they reached the porch of the B and B.

'There's something I think you should know.'

Armand Gamache looked at Beauvoir with amusement.

'What have you done?'

'What do you mean?'

'You sound exactly like Daniel when he was a teenager and had gotten into trouble.'

'I got Peggy Sue pregnant at the big dance,' said Beauvoir.

For just an instant Gamache looked surprised, then he smiled. 'What is it really?'

'I did something stupid.'

'Ahh, this does bring me back. Good times. Go on.'

'Well—'

'Monsieur Beauvoir, what a pleasure to see you again.'

The screen door opened and a woman in her late fifties greeted him.

Gamache turned to Beauvoir. 'What exactly have you done?'

'I hope you remember me,' she said with a coy smile. 'My name's Paulette. We met at the *vernissage* last night.'

The door swung open again and a middle-aged man appeared. Seeing Beauvoir, he beamed.

'It is you,' he said. 'I thought I saw you coming down the road just now. I looked at the barbecue last night but you weren't there.'

Gamache gave Beauvoir an inquiring gaze.

Beauvoir turned his back on the smiling artists. 'I told them I was the art critic for *Le Monde*.'

'And why would you do that?' the Chief Inspector asked.

'It's a long story,' said Beauvoir. But it wasn't so much long as embarrassing.

These were the two artists who'd insulted Clara Morrow's works. Mocking the Three Graces as clowns. And while Beauvoir didn't much like art, he did like Clara. And he'd known and admired the women who became the Three Graces.

So he'd turned to the smug artists and said he very much liked the work. Then he used some of the phrases he'd heard floating around the cocktail party. About perspective, and culture and pigment. The more he said the harder it was to stop himself. And he could see that the more ridiculous his statements the more these two paid attention.

Until he'd finally delivered his *coup de grâce*.

He trotted out a word he'd heard someone use that evening, a word he'd never heard before and had no idea what it meant. He'd turned to the painting of the Three Graces, the elderly and joyous old women, and said—

'The only word that comes to mind is, of course, "chiaroscuro".'

Not surprisingly, the artists had looked at him as though he was mad.

Which made him mad. So mad he said something he instantly regretted.

'I haven't introduced myself,' he said in his most refined French. 'I am Monsieur Beauvoir, the art critic for *Le Monde*.'

'Monsieur Beauvoir?' the man had asked, his eyes widening nicely.

'But of course. Just Monsieur Beauvoir. I find no need for a first name. Too bourgeois. Clutters up the page. You read my reviews, *bien sûr?*'

The rest of the evening had been quite pleasant, as word spread that the famous Parisian critic 'Monsieur Beauvoir' was there. And all agreed that Clara's works were a marvelous example of chiaroscuro.

He'd have to look it up, one of these days.

The two artists had in turn introduced themselves as simply 'Normand' and 'Paulette'.

'We use only our first names.'

He'd thought they were joking, but apparently not. And now here they were again.

Normand, in the same slacks, worn tweed jacket and scarf from the night before, and his partner Paulette, also in the same peasant-type skirt, blouse and scarves.

Now they were looking from him to Gamache, and back again.

'I have two pieces of bad news,' said Gamache, steering them inside. 'There's been a murder, and this is not Monsieur Beauvoir, the art critic for *Le Monde*, but Inspector Beauvoir, a homicide investigator with the Sûreté du Québec.'

The murder they already knew about, so it was the Beauvoir news they found most upsetting. Gamache watched with some amusement as they lit into the Inspector.

Beauvoir, noticing the Chief's grin, whispered, 'Just so you know, I also said you were Monsieur Gamache, the head curator at the Louvre. Enjoy.'

That, thought Gamache, would explain the unexpectedly large number of invitations to art shows he'd received at the *vernissage*. He made a note not to show up to any of them.

'When did you decide to stay overnight?' asked the Chief, once the vitriol had been exhausted.

'Well, we'd planned to head home after the party, but it was late and …' Paulette gave a shove of her head toward Normand, as though to indicate he'd had too many.

'The B and B owner gave us toiletries and bathrobes,' Normand explained. 'We're heading off to Cowansville in a few minutes to buy some clothes.'

'Not going back to Montréal?' asked Gamache.

'Not right away. We thought we'd stay for a day or so. Make a holiday of it.'

At Gamache's invitation they took seats in the comfortable living room, the artists sitting side-by-side on one sofa, Beauvoir and the Chief Inspector sitting opposite them on the other.

'So who was killed?' Paulette asked. 'It wasn't Clara, was it?'

She almost managed to hide her optimism.

'No,' said Beauvoir. 'Are you friends?' Though the answer seemed obvious.

This brought a snort of amusement from Normand.

'You clearly don't know artists, Inspector. We can be civil, friendly even. But friends? Better to make friends with a wolverine.'

'What brought you here then, if not friendship with Clara?' Beauvoir asked.

'Free food and drink. Lots of drink,' said Normand, smoothing the hair from his eyes. There was a sort of world-weary style about the man. As though he'd seen it all and was slightly amused and saddened by it.

'So it wasn't to celebrate her art?' Beauvoir asked.

'Her art isn't bad,' said Paulette. 'I like it better than what she was producing a decade ago.'

'Too much chiaroscuro,' said Normand, apparently forgetting who'd mentioned the word to begin with. 'Her show last night was an improvement,' Normand continued, 'though that wouldn't be hard. Who could forget her exhibition of massive feet?'

'But really, Normand,' said Paulette. 'Portraits? What self-respecting artist does portraits anymore?'

Normand nodded. 'Her art's derivative. Facile. Yes the subjects had character in their faces, and they were well executed, but not exactly breaking new ground. Nothing original or bold. There was nothing there we couldn't see in a second-rate provincial gallery in Slovenia.'

'Why would the Musée d'Art Contemporain give her a solo show if her art was so bad?' asked Beauvoir.

'Who knows,' said Normand. 'A favor. Politics. These big institutions aren't about real art, not about taking chances. They play it safe.'

Paulette was nodding vigorously.

'So if Clara Morrow wasn't a friend and if you thought her art was so crappy, why're you here?' Beauvoir asked Normand. 'I can see going to the *vernissage* for the free food and drink, but to come all the way here?'

He had the man, and they both knew it.

After a moment Normand answered. 'Because this was where the critics were. Where the gallery owners and dealers were. Destin-Browne from the Tate Modern. Castonguay, Fortin, Bishop from the Musée. *Vernissages* and art shows aren't about what's on the walls, they're about who's in the room. That's the real work. I came to network. I don't know how the Morrows did it, but it was an amazing group of critics and curators in one place.'

'Fortin?' asked Gamache, clearly surprised. 'Would that be Denis Fortin?'

Now it was Normand's turn to be surprised, that this rustic cop should know who Denis Fortin was.

'That's right,' he said. 'Of the Galerie Fortin.'

'Denis Fortin was at the *vernissage* in Montréal,' pressed Gamache, 'or here?'

'Both. I tried to speak to him but he was busy with others.'

There was a pause, and the world-weary artist seemed to sag. Dragged down by the great weight of irrelevance.

'Very surprising Fortin was here,' said Paulette, 'considering what he did to Clara.'

It was left hanging, begging a question. Paulette and Normand looked eagerly at the two investigators, like hungry children staring at a cake.

To Beauvoir's delight Chief Inspector Gamache chose to ignore the opening. Besides, they already knew what Denis Fortin had done to Clara. Which was why his presence at the party surprised them so much.

Beauvoir watched Normand and Paulette. They looked exhausted. But from what, the Inspector wondered. The long night of free food and drink? The longer night of desperate networking, disguised as a party? Or just plain tired of swimming so hard but still going under.

Chief Inspector Gamache took a photograph from his pocket. 'I have a picture of the dead woman. I'd like you to take a look please.'

He handed it to Normand, whose brows immediately rose.

'That's Lillian Dyson.'

'You're kidding,' said Paulette, moving closer and grabbing the picture. After a moment she nodded. 'That is her.'

Paulette's eyes rose to the Chief Inspector. It was a sharp look, clever. Not as immature as she'd first appeared. If she was child-like, thought Gamache, she was a cunning child.

'So you knew Madame Dyson?' Beauvoir asked.

'Well, didn't know, exactly,' said Normand. He seemed, Gamache thought, almost liquid. Certainly languid. Someone who adjusted to the currents.

'Then what, exactly?' asked Beauvoir.

'We knew her a long time ago, but hadn't seen her for a while. Then she showed up again this past winter at a couple of shows.'

'Art shows?' asked Beauvoir.

'Of course,' said Normand. 'What else?' As though no other form of culture existed, or mattered.

'I saw her too,' said Paulette, not wanting to be left behind. Gamache wondered at their partnership, and what creations came out of it. 'At a few shows. Didn't recognize her at first. She had to introduce herself. She'd dyed her hair. Used to be bright red, orange really. Now it's blond. She'd put on weight too.'

'Was she working again as a critic?' Gamache asked.

'Not that I know of. I have no idea what she was doing,' said Paulette.

Gamache looked at her for a moment. 'Were you friends?'

Paulette hesitated. 'Not now.'

'But back then, before she left?' asked the Chief.

'I thought we were,' said Paulette. 'I was getting my career going.

Had had some successes. Normand and I had just met and were trying to decide if we should collaborate. It's very unusual for two artists to work on the same painting.'

'You made the mistake of asking Lillian what she thought,' said Normand.

'And what did she think?' asked Beauvoir.

'I don't know what she thought, but I can tell you what she did,' said Paulette. There was no mistaking the anger now, in her voice and in her eyes. 'She told me Normand had bad-mouthed me at a recent *vernissage*. Joked about my art and said he'd rather collaborate with a chimp. Lillian said she was telling me as a friend, to warn me.'

'Lillian came to me shortly after that,' said Normand. 'Said Paulette had accused me of plagiarizing her works. Stealing her ideas. Lillian said she knew it wasn't true, but wanted me to know what Paulette was telling everyone.'

'What happened?' asked Gamache. The air around them suddenly seemed to sour, with old words and bitter thoughts.

'God help us,' said Paulette. 'We each believed her. We broke up. Took years for us to realize that Lillian had lied to both of us.'

'But now we're together.' Normand laid a hand softly on Paulette's and smiled at her. 'Despite the years wasted.'

Perhaps, thought Gamache as he watched, that was what exhausted Normand. Lugging around this memory.

Unlike Beauvoir, Chief Inspector Gamache had a great deal of respect for artists. They were sensitive. Often self-absorbed. Often not fit for polite society. Some, he suspected, were deeply unbalanced. It would not be an easy life. Living on the margins, often in poverty. Being ignored and even ridiculed. By society, by funding agencies, even by other artists.

François Marois's story of Magritte wasn't singular. The man and woman sitting here in the B and B were both Magrittes. Fighting hard to be heard and seen, respected and accepted.

A difficult life for anyone, never mind people as sensitive as artists.

He suspected living like that created fear. And fear begat anger and enough anger over enough time led to a dead woman in a garden.

Yes, Armand Gamache had a great deal of time for artists. But he was under no illusion about what they were capable of. Great creation, and great destruction.

'When did Lillian leave Montréal?' Beauvoir asked.

'I don't know and I don't care,' said Paulette.

'Did you care that she was back?' asked Beauvoir.

'Would you?' Paulette glared at Beauvoir. 'I kept my distance. We all knew what she'd done, what she was capable of. You don't want to be in those sights.'

'He's a natural, producing art like it's a bodily function,' said Normand.

'Pardon?' asked Beauvoir.

'It's a line from one of her critiques,' said Paulette. 'She's famous for it. It got picked up by the wire services and the review went international.'

'Who was she writing about?' Beauvoir asked.

'That's the funny thing,' said Paulette, 'everyone remembers the quote, but no one remembers the artist.'

Both Beauvoir and Gamache knew that wasn't true.

He's a natural, producing art like it's a bodily function.

Clever, almost a compliment. But then it veered into a scathing dismissal.

Someone would remember that review.

The artist himself.

SEVEN

⌐⌐

Armand Gamache and Jean Guy Beauvoir stepped down from the wide, sweeping verandah of the B and B onto the path.

It was a warm day and Beauvoir was thirsty.

'Drink?' he suggested to the Chief, knowing it was a pretty safe bet. But Gamache surprised him.

'In a few minutes. There's something I need to do first.' The two men paused at the dirt road. The day was going from warm to almost hot. Some of the early white irises in the flower beds around the village green had opened fully, and then some. Almost exploding, exposing their black centers.

It seemed to Beauvoir a confirmation. Inside every living thing, no matter how beautiful, if opened fully enough was darkness.

'I find it interesting that Normand and Paulette knew Lillian Dyson,' said Gamache.

'Why's that interesting?' asked Beauvoir. 'Isn't it what you'd expect? After all they hang around the same crowd. Did twenty-five years ago, and did a few months ago. It would've been surprising if they didn't know each other.'

'True. What I find interesting is that neither François Marois nor André Castonguay admitted to knowing her. How could Normand and Paulette know Lillian, but Marois and Castonguay not?'

'They probably didn't move in the same circles,' suggested Beauvoir.

They walked away from the B and B and toward the hill out of

Three Pines. Beauvoir took off his jacket, but the Chief kept his on. It would take more than a merely warm day to get him to walk around in his shirtsleeves.

'There aren't that many circles in the Québec art scene,' said Gamache. 'And while the dealers might not be personal friends with everyone, they'd be sure to at least be aware of them. If not today, then back twenty years, when Lillian was a critic.'

'So they were lying,' said Beauvoir.

'That's what I'm going to find out. I'd like you to check on progress at the Incident Room. Why don't we meet at the bistro,' Gamache looked at his watch, 'in about forty-five minutes.'

The two men parted, Beauvoir pausing to watch the Chief walk up the hill. His gait strong.

He himself made his way across the village green toward the Incident Room. As he walked across the grass he slowed, then veered off to his right. And sat on the bench.

'Hello, dick-head.'

'Hello, you old drunk.'

Ruth Zardo and Jean Guy Beauvoir sat side-by-side, a loaf of stale bread between them. Beauvoir took a piece, broke it up and threw it on the grass for the robins gathered there.

'What're you doing? That's my lunch.'

'We both know you haven't chewed lunch in years,' Beauvoir snapped. Ruth chuckled.

'That is true. Still, you owe me a meal now.'

'I'll buy you a beer later.'

'So what brings you back to Three Pines?' Ruth tossed more bread for the birds, or at the birds.

'The murder.'

'Oh, that.'

'Did you see her last night, at the party?' Beauvoir handed Ruth the photograph of the dead woman. She studied it then handed it back.

'Nope.'

'What was the party like?'

'The barbecue? Too many people. Too much noise.'

'But free booze,' said Beauvoir.

'It was free? *Merde*. I didn't have to sneak it after all. Still, more fun to steal it.'

'Nothing strange happened? No arguments, no raised voices? All that drinking and no one got belligerent?'

'Drinking? Lead to belligerence? Where'd you get that idea, numb nuts?'

'Absolutely nothing unusual happened last night?'

'Not that I saw.' Ruth tore off another piece of bread and tossed it at a fat robin. 'I'm sorry about your separation. Do you love her?'

'My wife?' Beauvoir wondered what prompted Ruth to ask. Was it caring or simply no sense of personal boundaries? 'I think—'

'No, not your wife. The other one. The plain one.'

Beauvoir felt his heart spasm and the blood pour from his face.

'You're drunk,' he said, getting to his feet.

'And belligerent,' she said. 'But I'm also right. I saw how you looked at her. And I think I know who she is. You're in trouble, young Mr Beauvoir.'

'You know nothing.'

He walked away. Trying not to break into a run. Willing himself to stay slow, steady. Left, right. Left, right.

Ahead he could see the bridge, and the Incident Room beyond. Where he'd be safe.

But young Mr Beauvoir was beginning to appreciate something.

There was no such place as 'safe'. Not anymore.

'Did you read this?' Clara asked, putting her empty beer glass on the table and handing the *Ottawa Star* over to Myrna. 'The *Star* hated the show.'

'You're kidding.' Myrna took the paper and scanned it. It was, she had to admit, not a glowing review.

'What was it they called me?' demanded Clara, sitting on the arm of Myrna's easy chair. 'Here it is.' Clara jabbed a finger and poked the newspaper. '*Clara Morrow is an old and tired parrot mimicking actual artists.*'

Myrna laughed.

'You find that funny?' Clara asked.

'You're not actually taking that comment seriously?'

'Why not? If I take the good ones seriously don't I have to take the bad too?'

'But look at them,' said Myrna, waving to the papers on the coffee table. 'The London *Times,* the *New York Times, Le Devoir,* all agree your art is new and exciting. Brilliant.'

'I hear the critic from *Le Monde* was there but he didn't even bother to write a review.'

Myrna stared at her friend. 'I'm sure he will, and he'll agree with everyone else. The show's a massive success.'

'*Her art, while nice, was neither visionary nor bold,*' Clara read over Myrna's shoulder. 'They don't think it's a massive success.'

'It's the *Ottawa Star,* for God's sake,' said Myrna. 'Someone was bound to dislike it, thank heaven it was them.'

Clara looked at the review then smiled. 'You're right.'

She walked back to her chair in the bookshop. 'Did anyone ever tell you that artists are nuts?'

'First I've heard of it.'

Out the window Myrna watched as Ruth pelted birds with hunks of bread. At the crest of the hill she saw Dominique Gilbert heading back to her barn, riding what looked like a moose. Outside the bistro, on the *terrasse,* Gabri was sitting at a customer's table, eating her dessert.

Not for the first time Three Pines struck Myrna as the equivalent of the Humane Society. Taking in the wounded, the unwanted. The mad, the sore.

This was a shelter. Though, clearly, not a no-kill shelter.

*

Dominique Gilbert curried Buttercup's rump. Around and around her hand went. It always reminded her of the scene in *The Karate Kid*. Wax goes on. Wax goes off. But instead of a shammy, this was a brush, and instead of a car, this was a horse. Sort of.

Buttercup was in the alley of the barn, outside his stall. Chester was watching this, doing his little dance as though he had a mariachi band in his head. Macaroni was in the field, having already been groomed, and was now rolling in the mud.

As she rubbed the caked and dried dirt off the huge horse, Dominique noticed the scabs, the scars, the patches of skin that would never grow horse hair, so deep were the wounds.

And yet, the massive horse let her touch him. Let her groom him. Let her ride him. As did Chester and Macaroni. If any creatures had earned the right to buck it was them. But instead, they chose to be the gentlest of beasts.

Outside now she could hear voices.

'You've already shown us the photograph.' It was one of her guests, and Dominique knew which one. André Castonguay. The gallery owner. Most of the guests had left but two remained. Messieurs Castonguay and Marois.

'I'd like you to look again.'

It was Chief Inspector Gamache, come back. She glanced out the square of light at the end of the barn, hiding slightly behind Buttercup's enormous bottom. She felt a little uneasy and wondered if she should make her presence known. They were standing in the sunshine, leaning against the fence rails. Surely they knew this wasn't a private place. Besides, she was there first. Besides, she wanted to hear.

So she said nothing, but continued to curry Buttercup, who couldn't believe his luck. The grooming was going on so much longer than usual. Though what appeared to be undue fondness for his rump was worrisome.

'Perhaps we should look again,' came François Marois's voice. He sounded reasonable. Friendly even.

There was a pause. Dominique could see Gamache hand a picture each to Marois and Castonguay. The men looked then exchanged photographs.

'You said you didn't know the dead woman,' said Gamache. He also sounded relaxed. A casual conversation with friends.

But Dominique wasn't fooled. She wondered if these two men were taken in. Castonguay, perhaps. But she doubted Marois was.

'I thought,' Gamache continued, 'you might have been surprised and needed another look.'

'I don't—' Castonguay began, but Marois laid a hand on his arm and he stopped.

'You're quite right, Chief Inspector. I don't know about André but I'm embarrassed to say I do know her. Lillian Dyson, right?'

'Well, I don't know her,' said Castonguay.

'I think you need to search your memory more thoroughly,' said Gamache. His voice, still friendly, carried a weight. It wasn't quite as light as a moment ago.

Behind Buttercup, Dominique found herself praying Castonguay would take the rope offered by the Chief Inspector. That he'd see it for what it was. A gift and not a trap.

Castonguay looked out into the field. All three did. Dominique couldn't see the field from where she stood, but she knew that view well. Looked at it every day. Often sat on the patio at the back of their home, private from the guests, with a gin and tonic at the end of the day. And stared. The way she'd once stared out the window of her corner office on the seventeenth floor of the bank tower.

The view from her windows now was more limited, but even more beautiful. Tall grasses, tender young wild flowers. Mountains and forests, and the broken-down old horses lumbering about in the fields.

In her view there was nothing more magnificent.

Dominique knew what the men were seeing, but not what they were thinking.

Though she could guess.

Chief Inspector Gamache had returned. To interview these two men again. Ask them the same questions he'd asked before. That much was clear. As was the conclusion.

They'd lied to him the first time.

François Marois opened his mouth to speak but Gamache silenced him with a movement.

No one would rescue Castonguay but himself.

'It's true,' the gallery owner said at last. 'I guess I do know her.'

'You guess, or you do?'

'I do, OK?'

Gamache gave him a stern look and replaced the photographs. 'Why did you lie?'

Castonguay sighed and shook his head. 'I didn't. I was tired, maybe a little hung-over. I didn't take a good enough look at the picture the first time, that's all. It wasn't deliberate.'

Gamache doubted that was true but decided not to press it. It would be a waste of time and only make the man more defensive. 'Did you know Lillian Dyson well?' he asked instead.

'Not well. I'd seen her at a few openings recently. She'd even approached me.' Castonguay said this as though she'd done something unsavory. 'Said she had a portfolio of work and could she show me.'

'And what did you say?'

Castonguay looked at Gamache with astonishment. 'I said no, of course. Do you have any idea how many artists send me their portfolios?'

Gamache remained silent, waiting for the haughty response.

'I get hundreds a month, from all over the world.'

'So you turned her down? But maybe her work was good,' suggested the Chief Inspector and was treated to another withering look.

'If she was any good I'd have heard of her by now. She wasn't exactly a bright young thing. Most artists, if they're going to do anything good, have done it by the time they're in their thirties.'

'But not always,' persisted Gamache. 'Clara Morrow's the same age as Madame Dyson, and she's only now being discovered.'

'Not by me. I still say her work stinks,' said Castonguay.

Gamache turned to François Marois. 'And you, monsieur? How well did you know Lillian Dyson?'

'Not well. I'd seen her at *vernissages* in the last few months and knew who she was.'

'How did you know?'

'It's a fairly small artistic community in Montréal. A lot of low-level, leisure artists. Quite a few of medium talent. Those who have the odd show. Who haven't made a splash but are good, journeymen artists. Like Peter Morrow. Then there are a very few great artists. Like Clara Morrow.'

'And where did Lillian Dyson fit in there?'

'I don't know,' admitted Marois. 'Like André, she asked me to look at her portfolio but I just couldn't agree. Too many other calls on my time.'

'Why did you decide to stay in Three Pines last night?' Gamache asked.

'As I told you before, it was a last-minute decision. I wanted to see where Clara creates her works.'

'Yes, you did,' said Gamache. 'But you didn't tell me to what end.'

'Does there have to be an end?' asked Marois. 'Isn't just seeing enough?'

'For most people, perhaps, but not for you, I suspect.'

Marois's sharp eyes held Gamache. None too pleased.

'Look, Clara Morrow's standing at a cross-roads,' said the art dealer. 'She has to make a decision. She was just handed a phenomenal opportunity, so far the critics adore her, but tomorrow they'll adore someone else. She needs someone to guide her. A mentor.'

Gamache looked bemused. 'A mentor?'

He left it hanging there.

There was a long, charged, silence.

'Yes,' said Marois, his gracious manner enveloping him again. 'I'm near the end of my career, I know that. I can guide one, perhaps two more remarkable artists. I need to choose carefully. I have no time to waste. I've spent the past year looking for that one artist, perhaps my last. Gone to hundreds of *vernissages* worldwide. Only to find Clara Morrow right here.'

The distinguished art dealer looked around. At the broken-down horse in the field, saved from slaughter. At the trees and at the forest.

'In my own backyard.'

'In the middle of nowhere, you mean,' said Castonguay, and went back to staring with displeasure at the scene.

'It's clear Clara's a remarkable artist,' said Marois, ignoring the gallery owner. 'But the very gifts that make her that also make her unable to navigate the art world.'

'You might be underestimating Clara Morrow,' said Gamache.

'I might, but you might be underestimating the art world. Don't be fooled by the veneer of civility and creativity. It's a vicious place, filled with insecure and greedy people. Fear and greed, that's what shows up at *vernissages*. There's a lot of money at stake. Fortunes. And a lot of egos involved. Volatile combination.'

Marois stole a quick glance at Castonguay, then back to the Chief Inspector.

'I know my way around. I can take them to the top.'

'Them?' asked Castonguay.

Gamache had assumed the gallery owner had lost interest and was barely listening, but he now realized Castonguay had been fol-lowing the conversation very closely. And Gamache quietly warned himself not to underestimate either the venality of the art world, or this haughty man.

Marois turned his full attention on Castonguay, clearly surprised as well that he'd been paying attention.

'Yes. Them.'

'What do you mean?' demanded Castonguay.

'I mean both the Morrows. I want to take them both on.'

Castonguay's eyes widened and his lips narrowed, and when he spoke his voice was raised. 'You talk about greed. Why would you take both? You don't even like his paintings.'

'And you do?'

'I think they're far better than his wife's. You can have Clara, and I'll take Peter.'

Gamache listened and wondered if this was how the Paris Peace Conference was negotiated after the Great War. When Europe was divided up by the winners. And Gamache wondered if this would have the same disastrous results.

'I don't want one,' said Marois. His voice was reasonable, silken, contained. 'I want both.'

'Fucking bastard,' said Castonguay, but Marois didn't seem to care. He turned back to the Chief Inspector as though Castonguay had just complimented him.

'At what point yesterday did you decide Clara Morrow was the one?' asked Gamache.

'You were with me, Chief Inspector. The moment I saw the light in the Virgin Mary's eye.'

Gamache was quiet, recalling that moment. 'As I remember you thought it might simply be a trick of the light.'

'I still do. But how remarkable is that? For Clara Morrow to, in essence, capture the human experience? One person's hope is another person's cruelty. Is it light, or a false promise?'

Gamache turned to André Castonguay, who seemed completely taken aback by their conversation, as though they'd been at different art shows.

'I want to get back to the dead woman,' said Gamache, and saw Castonguay looking lost for a moment. Murder eclipsed by greed. And fear.

'Were you surprised to see Lillian Dyson back in Montréal?' the Chief asked.

'Surprised?' asked Castonguay. 'I felt nothing either way. Didn't give her a second thought.'

'I'm afraid I felt the same way, Chief Inspector,' said Marois. 'Madame Dyson in Montréal or Madame Dyson in New York was all the same to me.'

Gamache looked at him with interest. 'How did you know she'd been in New York?'

For the first time Marois hesitated, his composure pierced.

'Someone must have mentioned it. The art world's full of gossips.'

The art world, thought Gamache, was full of something else he could mention. And this seemed a fine example. He stared at Marois until the dealer dropped his eyes and brushed an invisible hair off his immaculate shirt.

'I hear another of your colleagues was here at the party. Denis Fortin.'

'That's true,' said Marois. 'I was surprised to see him.'

'Now there's an understatement,' snorted Castonguay. 'After how he treated Clara Morrow. Did you hear about that?'

'Tell me,' said Gamache, though he knew the story perfectly well himself, and the two artists had also just taken pleasure in reminding him.

And so, with glee, André Castonguay related how Denis Fortin had signed Clara to a solo show only to change his mind and drop her.

'And not just drop her, but treated her like shit. Told everyone she was worthless. I actually agree, but can you imagine his surprise when the Musée of all places picked her up?'

It was a story that appealed to Castonguay, since it belittled both Clara and his competitor, Denis Fortin.

'Then why do you think he was here?' asked Gamache. Both men considered it.

'Not a clue,' admitted Castonguay.

'He had to have been invited,' said Marois, 'but I can't see him being on Clara Morrow's guest list.'

'Do people crash these parties?' asked Gamache.

'Some,' said Marois, 'but mostly artists looking to make connections.'

'Looking for free booze and food,' mumbled Castonguay.

'You said Madame Dyson asked you to look at her portfolio,' Gamache said to Castonguay, 'which you refused. But I was under the impression she was a critic, not an artist.'

'True,' said Castonguay. 'She'd written for *La Presse*, but that was many years ago. Then she vanished and someone else took over.'

He seemed barely polite, bored.

'Was she a good critic?'

'How d'you expect me to remember that?'

'The same way I expected you to remember her from the photo, monsieur.' Gamache eyed the art gallery owner steadily. Castonguay's already flushed face grew ruddier.

'I remember her reviews, Chief Inspector,' Marois said and turned to Castonguay. 'And so do you.'

'I do not.' Castonguay shot him a look of loathing.

'He's a natural, producing art like it's a bodily function.'

'No,' laughed Castonguay. 'Lillian Dyson wrote that? *Merde*. With that sort of bile she might've been a decent artist after all.'

'But who was the line written about?' Gamache asked both men.

'It can't have been anyone famous or we'd have remembered,' said Marois. 'Probably some poor artist who sank into oblivion.'

Tied to this rock of a review, thought Gamache.

'Does it matter?' asked Castonguay. 'It was twenty years ago or more. You think a review from decades ago has anything to do with her murder?'

'I think murder has a long memory.'

'If you'll excuse me, I have some phone calls to make,' said André Castonguay.

Marois and Gamache watched him walk off toward the inn and spa.

'You know what he's doing, don't you?' Marois turned back to his companion.

'He's calling the Morrows, to convince them to meet with him.'

Marois smiled. '*Exactement.*'

The two men strolled back toward the inn and spa themselves.

'Aren't you worried?'

'I'm never worried about André. He's no threat to me. If the Morrows are foolish enough to sign with him then he's welcome to them.'

But Gamache didn't believe it for a moment. François Marois's eyes were too sharp, too shrewd for that. His relaxed manner too studied.

No, this man cared a great deal. He was wealthy. He was powerful. So it wasn't about that.

Fear and greed. That was what drove the art world. And Gamache knew it was probably true. So if it wasn't greed on Marois's part, then the other must be true.

It was fear.

But what could this elderly, eminent dealer be afraid of?

'Will you join me, monsieur?' Armand Gamache extended his arm, inviting François Marois to walk with him. 'I'm going into the village.'

Marois, who had had no intention of walking down into Three Pines again, considered the invitation and recognized it for what it was. A polite request. Not quite a command, but close enough.

He took his place beside the Chief Inspector and both walked slowly down the slope and into the village.

'Very pretty,' said Marois. He stopped and surveyed Three Pines, a smile on his lips. 'I can see why Clara Morrow chose to live here. It is magical.'

'I sometimes wonder how important place is to an artist.' Gamache also looked out over the quiet village. 'So many choose the great cities. Paris, London, Venice. Cold water flats and lofts in Soho and Chelsea. Lillian Dyson moved to New York, for instance. But Clara didn't. The Morrows chose here. Does where they live affect what they create?'

'Oh, without a doubt. Where they live and who they spend time with. I don't think Clara's series of portraits could have been created any place other than here.'

'It's fascinating to me that some look at her work and see just nice portraits of mostly elderly women. Traditional, staid even. But you don't.'

'Neither do you, Chief Inspector, any more than when you and I look at Three Pines we see a village.'

'And what do you see, Monsieur Marois?'

'I see a painting.'

'A painting?'

'A beautiful one, to be sure. But all paintings, the most disturbing and the most exquisite, are made up of the same thing. The play of light and dark. That's what I see. A whole lot of light, but a whole lot of dark too. That's what people miss in Clara's works. The light is so obvious they get fooled by it. It takes some people a while to appreciate the shading. I think that's one of the things that makes her brilliant. She's very subtle, but very subversive. She has a lot to say, and takes her time revealing it.'

'*C'est intéressant, ça,*' Gamache nodded. It wasn't unlike what he'd been thinking about Three Pines. It too took a while to reveal itself. But Marois's analogy had its limits. A painting, no matter how spectacular, would only ever be two dimensional. Is that how Marois saw the world? Was there an entire dimension he missed?

They started walking again. On the village green they noticed Clara plunking down beside Ruth. They watched as Ruth fired chunks of stale bread at the birds. It was unclear if she was trying to feed them or kill them.

François Marois's eyes narrowed. 'That's the woman in Clara's portrait,' he said.

'It is. Ruth Zardo.'

'The poet? I thought she was dead.'

'It's a natural mistake,' said Gamache, waving at Ruth, who gave him the finger. 'Her brain seems fine, it's only her heart that's stopped.'

The afternoon sun was directly on François Marois, forcing the dealer to squint. But behind him there extended a long and definite shadow.

'Why do you want both Morrows,' Gamache asked, 'when you obviously prefer Clara's works? Do you even like Peter Morrow's paintings?'

'No, I don't. I find them very superficial. Calculated. He's a good artist, but I think he could be a great one, if he could use more instinct and less technique. He's a very good draftsman.'

It was said without malice, making the cold analysis all the more damning. And perhaps true.

'You said you had only so much time and energy left,' persisted Gamache. 'I can see why you'd choose Clara. But why Peter, an artist you don't even like?'

Marois hesitated. 'It's just easier to manage. We can make career decisions for both of them. I want Clara to be happy, and I think she's happiest if Peter is also looked after.'

Gamache looked at the art dealer. It was an astute observation. But it didn't go far enough. Marois had made it about Clara and Peter's happiness. Deflecting the question.

Then the Chief Inspector remembered the story Marois told, of his first client. The elderly artist whose wife overtook him. And, to protect her husband's fragile ego the woman had never painted again.

Was that what Marois was afraid of? Losing his final client, his final find, because Clara's love for Peter was greater than her love for art?

Or was it, again, even more personal? Did it have nothing to do with Clara, with Peter, with art? Was François Marois simply afraid of losing?

André Castonguay owned art. But François Marois owned the artists. Who was the more powerful? But also the more vulnerable?

Framed paintings couldn't get up and leave. But the artists could.

What was François Marois afraid of? Gamache asked himself again.

'Why are you here?'

Marois looked surprised. 'I've already told you, Chief Inspector. Twice. I'm here to try to sign Peter and Clara Morrow.'

'And yet you claim not to care if Monsieur Castonguay gets there first.'

'I can't control other people's stupidity,' smiled Marois.

Gamache considered the man, and as he did the art dealer's smile wavered.

'I'm late for drinks, monsieur,' said Gamache pleasantly. 'If we have nothing more to talk about I'll be going.'

He turned and walked toward the bistro.

'Bread?' Ruth offered Clara what looked and felt like a brick.

They each hacked off pieces. Ruth tossed them at the robins, who darted away. Clara just pelted the ground at her feet.

Thump, thump, thud.

'I hear the critics saw something in your paintings I sure don't see,' said Ruth.

'What d'you mean?'

'They liked them.'

Thud, thud, thud.

'Not all,' laughed Clara. 'The *Ottawa Star* said my art was nice, but neither visionary nor bold.'

'Ahh, the *Ottawa Star*. The journal of note. I remember the *Drummondville Post* once called my poetry both dull and uninteresting.' Ruth snorted. 'Look, get that one.' She pointed to a particularly bold blue jay. When Clara didn't move Ruth tossed a bread stone at him.

'Almost got him,' said Ruth, though Clara suspected if she'd wanted to hit the bird she wouldn't have missed.

'They called me an old and tired parrot mimicking actual artists,' said Clara.

'That's ridiculous,' said Ruth. 'Parrots don't mimic. Mynah birds mimic. Parrots learn the words and say them in their own way.'

'Fascinating,' mumbled Clara. 'I'll have to write a stern letter correcting them.'

'The *Kamloops Record* complained that my poetry doesn't rhyme,' said Ruth.

'Do you remember all your reviews?' asked Clara.

'Only the bad ones.'

'Why?'

Ruth turned to look at her directly. Her eyes weren't angry or cold, not filled with malice. They were filled with wonder.

'I don't know. Perhaps that's the price of poetry. And, apparently, art.'

'What d'you mean?'

'We get hurt into it. No pain, no product.'

'You believe that?' asked Clara.

'Don't you? What did the *New York Times* say about your art?'

Clara searched her brain. She knew it was good. Something about hope and rising up.

'Welcome to the bench,' said Ruth. 'You're early. I'd have thought it would take another ten years. But here you are.'

And for a moment Ruth looked exactly like Clara's portrait. Embittered, disappointed. Sitting in the sun but remembering, reviewing, replaying every insult. Every unkind word, bringing them out and examining them like disappointing birthday gifts.

Oh, no no no, thought Clara. *Still the dead one lay moaning.* Is this how it starts?

She watched as Ruth again pelted a bird with a chunk of inedible bread.

Clara got up to leave.

'Hope takes its place among the modern masters.'

Clara turned back to Ruth, looking at her, the sun just catching her rheumy eyes.

'That's what the *New York Times* said,' said Ruth. 'And the London *Times* said, *Clara Morrow's art makes rejoicing cool again*. Don't forget, Clara,' she whispered.

Ruth turned away again and sat ramrod straight, alone with her thoughts and her heavy, stone bread. Glancing, occasionally, into the empty sky.

EIGHT

—

Gabri put a lemonade in front of Beauvoir and a glass of iced tea in front of the Chief Inspector. A wedge of lemon sat on each rim and the glasses were already perspiring in the warm afternoon.

'Do you want to make a reservation at the B and B?' Gabri asked. 'There's plenty of room, if you'd like.'

'We'll discuss it. *Merci, patron,*' said Beauvoir with a small smile. He still didn't feel comfortable making friends with suspects, but he couldn't seem to help it. They got up his nose, to be sure. But they also got under his skin.

Gabri left and the men drank in silence for a moment.

Beauvoir had arrived at the bistro first and gone directly to the bathroom. He'd splashed cool water on his face and wished he could take a pill. But he'd promised himself to wait until bedtime for the next one, to help him sleep.

By the time he returned to the table the Chief was there.

'Any luck?' he asked Gamache.

'The dealers admitted they knew Lillian Dyson, though claim not to know her well.'

'Do you believe them?'

It was always the question. Who do you believe? And how do you decide?

Gamache thought about it, then shook his head. 'I don't know. I thought I knew the art world, but I realize now I only saw what they wanted me – what they want everyone – to see. The art. The galleries. But there's so much more going on behind.' Gamache leaned toward Beauvoir. 'For instance, André Castonguay owns a prestigious gallery. Shows artists' works. Represents artists. But François Marois? What does he have?'

Beauvoir was quiet, watching the Chief, taking in the gleam in his eye, the enthusiasm as he described what he'd found. Not the physical landscape, but the emotional. The intellectual.

Many might have thought the Chief Inspector was a hunter. He tracked down killers. But Jean Guy knew he wasn't that. Chief Inspector Gamache was an explorer by nature. He was never happier than when he was pushing the boundaries, exploring the internal terrain. Areas even the person themselves hadn't explored. Had never examined. Probably because it was too scary.

Gamache went there. To the end of the known world, and beyond. Into the dark, hidden places. He looked into the crevices, where the worst things hid.

And Jean Guy Beauvoir followed.

'What François Marois has,' Gamache continued, holding Beauvoir's eyes, 'is the artists. But even more than that, what he really has is information. He knows people. The buyers, the artists. He knows how to navigate a complex world of money and ego and perception. Marois hoards what he knows. I think he only lets it out when it either suits his purposes or he has no choice.'

'Or when he's trapped in a lie,' said Beauvoir. 'As you trapped him this afternoon.'

'But how much more does he know that he isn't telling?' asked Gamache, not expecting an answer from Beauvoir, and not getting one.

Beauvoir glanced at the menu but without interest.

'Have you chosen?' Gabri asked, his pen at the ready.

Beauvoir closed the menu and handed it to Gabri. 'Nothing, thanks.'

'I'm fine, *merci, patron,*' said the Chief, handing the menu back and watching Clara leave Ruth and walk toward Myrna's bookstore.

Clara hugged her friend and felt the thick rolls of Myrna under the brilliant yellow caftan.

Finally they pulled apart and Myrna looked at her friend.

'What brought that on?'

'I was just talking to Ruth—'

'Oh, dear,' said Myrna and gave Clara another hug. 'How many times have I told you to never speak to Ruth on your own? It's far too dangerous. You don't want to go wandering around in that head all alone.'

Clara laughed. 'You'll never believe it, but she helped me.'

'How?'

'She showed me my future, if I'm not careful.'

Myrna smiled, understanding. 'I've been thinking about what happened. The murder of your friend.'

'She wasn't a friend.'

Myrna nodded. 'What do you think about a ritual? Something to heal.'

'The garden?' It seemed a little late to heal Lillian, and privately Clara doubted she'd have wanted to bring her back to life anyway.

'Your garden. And whatever else might need healing.' Myrna looked at Clara with a melodramatic gaze.

'Me? You think finding a woman I hated dead in my garden might have screwed me up?'

'I hope it has,' said Myrna. 'We could do a smudging ritual to get rid of whatever bad energy and thoughts are still hanging around your garden.'

It sounded silly, Clara knew, said so boldly like that. As though wafting smoke over a place where murder had happened could have any effect. But they'd done smudging rituals before and it was very calming, very comforting. And Clara needed both right now.

'Great,' she said. 'I'll call Dominique—'

'—and I'll get the stuff.'

By the time Clara got off the phone Myrna was back down from her apartment above the bookshop. She carried a gnarled old stick, some ribbons and what looked like a huge cigar. Or something.

'I think I have smudge envy,' said Clara, pointing to the cigar.

'Here,' said Myrna, handing Clara the tree limb. 'Take this.'

'What is it? A stick?'

'Not just a stick. It's a prayer stick.'

'So I probably shouldn't beat the crap out of the critic for the *Ottawa Star* with it,' Clara said, following Myrna out of the bookshop.

'Perhaps not. And don't beat yourself with it either.'

'What makes it a prayer stick?'

'It's a prayer stick because I say it is,' Myrna said.

Dominique was coming down du Moulin and they waved to each other.

'Wait a second.' Clara veered off to speak to Ruth, still sitting on the bench. 'We're going into the back garden. Want to join us?'

Ruth looked at Clara holding the stick, then at Myrna with the cigar made of dried sage and sweetgrass.

'You're not going to do one of those profane witch ritual things are you?'

'We certainly are,' said Myrna from behind Clara.

'Count me in.' Ruth struggled to her feet.

The police were gone. The garden was empty. No one to even stand watch over the place where a life was lost. Where a life was taken. The yellow 'crime scene' tape fluttered and circled part of the lawn grass and one of the perennial beds.

'I've always thought this garden was a crime,' said Ruth.

'You have to admit, it's gotten better since Myrna started helping,' said Clara.

Ruth turned to Myrna. 'So that's who you are. I've been wondering. You're the gardener.'

'I'd plant you,' said Myrna, 'if you weren't a toxic waste site.'

Ruth laughed. *'Touché.'*

'Is this where the body was found?' Dominique asked, pointing to the circle.

'No, the tape is part of Clara's garden design,' snapped Ruth.

'Bitch,' said Myrna.

'Witch,' said Ruth.

They were beginning to like each other, Clara could see.

'Do you think we should cross it?' asked Myrna. She hadn't expected the yellow tape.

'No,' said Ruth, batting the tape down with her cane and stepping over it. She turned back to the others. 'Come on in, the water's fine.'

'Except it's very hot,' said Clara to Dominique.

'And there's a shark in it,' said Dominique.

The three women joined Ruth. If anyone could contaminate a site it was Ruth, and the damage was probably already done. Besides, they were there to decontaminate it.

'So what do we do?' Dominique asked as Clara planted the prayer stick into the flower bed beside where Lillian's body was found.

'We're going to do a ritual,' Myrna explained. 'It's called smudging. We light this,' Myrna held up the dried herbs, 'and then we walk around the garden with it.'

Ruth was staring at the cigar of herbs. 'Freud might have a little something to say about your ritual.'

'Sometimes a smudge stick is just a smudge stick,' said Clara.

'Why're we doing this?' Dominique asked. This was clearly a side to her neighbors she hadn't seen before and it didn't seem an improvement.

'To get rid of the bad spirits,' said Myrna. It did, when said so baldly, sound a little unlikely. But Myrna believed it, with all her considerable heart.

Dominique turned to Ruth. 'Well, I guess you're screwed.'

There was a pause and then Ruth snorted in laughter. Hearing that Clara wondered whether turning into Ruth Zardo would be such a bad thing.

'First, we form a circle,' said Myrna. And they did. Myrna lit the sage and sweetgrass and walked from Clara to Dominique to Ruth, wafting the perfumed smoke over each woman. For protection, for peace.

Clara inhaled and closed her eyes as the soft smoke swirled around her for a moment. Taking, said Myrna, all their negative energy. The bad spirits, outside and in. Absorbing them. And making room for healing.

Then they walked around the garden, not just the dreadful place Lillian had died, but the entire garden. They took turns drifting smoke into the trees, into the babbling Rivière Bella Bella, into the roses and peony and black-centered irises.

And finally they ended at the beginning. At the yellow tape. The hole in the garden where a life had disappeared.

'*Now here's a good one,*' Ruth quoted one of her own poems as she stared at the spot.

'*You're lying on your deathbed.*
You have one hour to live.
Who is it, exactly, you have needed
all these years to forgive?'

Myrna pulled bright ribbons from her pocket and gave one to each of them saying, 'We tie our ribbon to the prayer stick and send out good thoughts.'

They glanced at Ruth, waiting for the cynical comment. But none came. Dominique went first, fastening her pink ribbon to the gnarled stick.

Myrna went next, tying her purple ribbon and closing her eyes briefly to think good thoughts.

'Won't be the first time I've tied one on,' Ruth admitted with a smile. Then she fastened her red ribbon, pausing to rest her veined hand on the prayer stick, like a cane, and look to the sky.

Listening.

But there was only the sound of bees. Bumbling.

Finally, Clara tied on her green ribbon, knowing she should think kind thoughts of Lillian. Something, something. She searched inside, peering into dark corners, opening doors closed for years. Trying to find one nice thing to say about Lillian.

The other women waited while the moments went by.

Clara closed her eyes and reviewed her time with Lillian, so many years ago. It whipped past, the early, happy memories blighted by the horrible events later on.

Stop, Clara commanded her brain. This was the route to the park bench. With the inedible stone bread.

No. Good things did happen and she needed to remember that. If not to release Lillian's spirit, then to release her own.

Who is it, exactly, you have needed
all these years to forgive?

'You were kind to me, often. And you were a good friend. Once.'

The gem bright ribbons, the four female ribbons, fluttered and intertwined.

Myrna bent to pat the garden soil more firmly around the prayer stick.

'What's this?'

She stood up, holding something caked in dirt. Wiping it off, she showed it to the others. It was a coin, the size of an Old West silver dollar.

'That's mine,' said Ruth, reaching for it.

'Not so fast, Miss Kitty. Are you sure?' asked Myrna. Dominique and Clara took turns examining it. It was a coin, but not a silver dollar. In fact, it was coated in silver paint but it seemed plastic. And there was writing on it.

'What is it?' Dominique handed it back to Myrna.

'I think I know. And I'm pretty sure it isn't yours,' Myrna said to Ruth.

Agent Isabelle Lacoste had joined Chief Inspector Gamache and Inspector Beauvoir on the *terrasse*. She ordered a Diet Coke and gave them an update.

The Incident Room was up and running in the old railway station. Computers, phone lines, satellite links installed. Desks, swivel chairs, filing cabinets, all the hardware in place. It happened quickly, expertly. The homicide division of the Sûreté was used to going into remote communities to investigate murder. Like the Army Corps of Engineers, they knew time and precision counted.

'I've found out about Lillian Dyson's family.' Lacoste pulled her chair forward and opened her notebook. 'She'd divorced. No children. Her parents are both alive. They live on Harvard Ave in Notre-Dame-de-Grâce.'

'How old are they?' Gamache asked.

'He's eighty-three, she's eighty-two. Lillian was an only child.'

Gamache nodded. This was, of course, the worst part of any case. Telling the living about the death.

'Do they know?'

'Not yet,' said Lacoste. 'I wondered if you—'

'I'll go into Montréal this afternoon and speak to them.' Where possible he told the family himself. 'We should also search Madame Dyson's apartment.' Gamache took the guest list from his breast pocket. 'Can you get agents to interview everyone on this list? They were at the party last night or the *vernissage*, or both. I've marked the people we've already spoken to.'

Beauvoir put out his hand for the list.

It was his role, they knew, to coordinate the interviews, assemble the evidence, assign agents.

The Chief Inspector paused, then handed the list to Lacoste.

Effectively handing control of the investigation to her. Both agents looked surprised.

'I'd like you with me in Montréal,' he said to Beauvoir.

'Of course,' said Beauvoir, perplexed.

They all had delineated roles within the homicide division. It was one of the things the Chief insisted on. That there be no confusion, no cracks. No overlap. They all knew what their jobs were, knew what was expected. Worked as a team. No rivalry. No in-fighting.

Chief Inspector Gamache was the undisputed head of homicide.

Inspector Jean Guy Beauvoir was his second in command.

Agent Lacoste, up for promotion, was the senior agent. And below them were more than a hundred agents and investigators. And several hundred support staff.

The Chief made it clear. In confusion, in fractures, lay danger. Not just internal squabbles and politics, but something real and threatening. If they weren't clear and cohesive, if they didn't work together as a team, a violent criminal could escape. Or worse. Kill again.

Murderers hid in the tiniest of cracks. And Chief Inspector Gamache was damned if he was going to let his department provide one.

But now the Chief had broken one of his own cardinal rules. He handed the investigation, the day-to-day operations, over to Agent Isabelle Lacoste instead of Beauvoir.

Lacoste took the list, scanned it, and nodded. 'I'll get on it right away, Chief.'

Both men watched Agent Lacoste leave, then Beauvoir leaned forward.

'OK, *patron*. What's this about?' he whispered. But before Gamache could answer they saw four women heading their way. Myrna in the lead, with Clara, Dominique and Ruth in her wake.

Gamache rose and bowed slightly to the women. 'Would you like to join us?'

'We won't stay long, but we wanted to show you something. We found this in the flower bed by where the woman was killed.' Myrna handed him the coin.

'Really?' said Gamache, surprised. He looked down at the dirty coin in his palm. His people had done a thorough search of the whole garden, of the whole village. What could they have missed?

There was the image of a camel on the face of it, just visible beneath the smears.

'Who's touched this?' Beauvoir asked.

'We all did,' said Ruth, proudly.

'Do you not know what to do with evidence at a crime scene?'

'Do you not know how to collect evidence?' Ruth asked. 'If you did we wouldn't have found it.'

'This was just lying in the garden?' Gamache asked. With the tip of his finger, careful not to touch it more than necessary, he flipped it over.

'No,' said Myrna. 'It was buried.'

'Then how did you find it?'

'With the prayer stick,' said Ruth.

'What's a prayer stick?' Beauvoir asked, afraid of the answer.

'We can show you,' Dominique offered. 'We put it in the flower bed where the woman was murdered.'

'We were doing a ritual cleansing—' said Clara, before being cut off by Myrna.

'*Phhht.*' Myrna made a noise. 'Ix-nay on the leansing-cay.'

Beauvoir stared at the women. It wasn't enough that they were English and had a prayer stick, but now they'd lapsed into pig latin. It was no wonder there were so many murders here. The only mystery was how any got solved, with help like this.

'I bent down to mound dirt around the prayer stick and this thing appeared,' Myrna explained, as though this was a reasonable thing to be doing at a murder scene.

'Didn't you see the police tape?' Beauvoir demanded.

'Didn't you see the coin?' Ruth countered.

Gamache held up his hand and the two stopped bickering.

On the side now exposed there was writing. What looked like a poem.

Putting on his half-moon reading glasses he furrowed his brow, trying to read through the dirt.

No, not a poem.

A prayer.

NINE

‸

For the second time that day Armand Gamache stood from crouching beside this flower bed.

The first time he'd been staring at a dead woman, this time he'd been staring at a prayer stick. Its bright, cheerful ribbons fluttering in the slight breeze. Catching, according to Myrna, currents of good energy. If she was right, there was a lot around, as the ribbons flapped and danced.

He straightened up, brushing his knees. Beside him, Inspector Beauvoir was glowering at the spot where the coin had been found.

Where he'd missed it.

Beauvoir was in charge of the crime scene investigation, and had personally searched the area directly around the body.

'You found it just here?' the Chief pointed to the mounded earth.

Myrna and Clara had joined them. Beauvoir had called Agent Lacoste and she arrived that moment with a crime scene kit.

'That's right,' said Myrna. 'In the flower bed. It was buried and caked with dirt. Hard to see.'

'I'll take that,' said Beauvoir, grabbing the crime scene kit, annoyed at what he took to be a patronizing tone in Myrna's voice. As though she needed to make excuses for his failure. He bent down to examine the earth.

'Why didn't we find it before?' asked the Chief.

It wasn't a criticism of his team. Gamache was genuinely perplexed. They were professional and thorough. Still, mistakes happened. But not, he thought, missing a silver coin sitting in a flower bed two feet from the dead body.

'I know how it was missed,' said Myrna. 'Gabri could tell you too. Anyone who gardens could tell you. We'd weeded yesterday morning and mulched the earth in the beds so that it'd be fresh and dark and show off the flowers. Gardeners call it "fluffing" the garden. Making the earth soft. But when we do that the ground becomes very crumbly. I've lost whole tools in there. Laid them down and they sort of tumble into a crevice and get half buried.'

'This is a flower bed,' said Gamache, 'not the Himalayas. Could something really be swallowed up in there?'

'Try it.'

The Chief Inspector walked to the other side of the flower bed. 'Did you mulch here too?' he asked.

'Everywhere,' said Myrna. 'Go on. Try it.'

Gamache knelt and dropped a one dollar coin into the flower bed. It sat on top of the earth, clearly visible. Picking it back up, he rose and looked at Myrna.

'Any other suggestions?'

She gave the dirt a filthy look. 'It's probably settled now. If it was freshly turned it'd work.'

She got a trowel from Clara's shed and dug around, turning the earth, fluffing it up.

'OK, try it now.'

Gamache knelt again, and again dropped the coin into the flower bed. This time it slid over onto its side, down a small crevice.

'See,' said Myrna.

'Well, yes, I do see. I see the coin,' said Gamache. 'I'm afraid I'm not convinced. Could it have been there for a while? It might've fallen into the bed years ago. It's made of plastic so it wouldn't rust or age.'

'I doubt it,' said Clara. 'We would've found it long ago. They sure would've found it yesterday when they weeded and mulched, don't you think?'

'I've given up thinking,' said Myrna.

They walked back to where Beauvoir was working.

'Nothing more, Chief,' he said, standing abruptly and slapping his knees free of dirt. 'I can't believe we missed it the first time.'

'Well, we have it now.' Gamache looked at the coin in the evidence bag Lacoste was holding. It wasn't money, wasn't currency of any country. At first he'd wondered if it might be from the Middle East. What with the camel. After all, Canadian currency had a moose on it, why shouldn't Saudi currency have a camel?

But the words were English. And there was no mention of a denomination.

Just the camel on one side and the prayer on the other.

'You're sure it doesn't belong to you or Peter?' he asked Clara.

'I'm sure. Ruth briefly claimed it, but Myrna said it couldn't possibly belong to her.'

Gamache turned to the large, caftaned woman beside him, his brows raised.

'And how do you know that?'

'Because I know what it is and I know Ruth would never have one. I assumed you recognized it.'

'I have no idea what it is.' They all looked again at the coin sitting in the Baggie.

'May I?' Myrna asked and when Gamache nodded Lacoste handed her the bag. Myrna looked through the plastic.

'God,' she read. '*Grant me the serenity,*

To accept the things I cannot change,
Courage to change the things I can,
And wisdom to know the difference.'

'It's a beginner's chip,' she said. 'From Alcoholics Anonymous. It's given to people who're just getting sober.'

'How do you know that?' the Chief asked.

'Because when I was in practice I suggested a number of clients join AA. Some of them later showed me what they called their beginner's chip. Just like that.' She gestured to the bag back in Lacoste's hand. 'Whoever dropped it is a member of AA.'

'I see what you mean about Ruth,' said Beauvoir.

Gamache thanked them and watched as Clara and Myrna walked back to the house, to join the others.

Beauvoir and Agent Lacoste were talking, going over notes and findings. Inspector Beauvoir would be giving her some instructions, Gamache knew. Leads to follow while they were in Montréal.

He wandered around the garden. One mystery was solved. The coin was an AA beginner's chip.

But who dropped it? Lillian Dyson as she fell? But even if she did his experiment showed it would just sit on the earth. They'd have seen it right away.

Did her killer lose it? But, if he was going to break her neck with his bare hands he wouldn't be holding a coin. Besides, the same thing held true for the killer. If he dropped it, why didn't they find it? How did it get buried?

The Chief Inspector stood quietly in the warm, sunny garden and imagined a murder. Someone sneaking up behind Lillian Dyson in the dark. Grabbing her around the neck, and twisting. Quickly. Before she could call out, cry out. Struggle.

But she would have done something. She'd have flailed her arms out, even for a moment.

And he saw clearly that he'd made a mistake.

Walking back to the flower bed he called Beauvoir and Lacoste, who quickly joined him.

From his pocket he again brought out the one dollar coin. Then he tossed it into the air and watched as it fell to the freshly turned soil, sat briefly on top of a chunk of dirt, then slipped off to be buried by earth that crumbled in after it.

'My God, it did bury itself,' said Lacoste. 'Is that what happened?'

'I think so,' said the Chief, watching as Lacoste picked the coin back up and handed it to him. 'When I first tried it I was kneeling down, close to the dirt. But if it fell during the murder it would have dropped from a standing position. Higher up. With greater force. I think when the murderer grasped her neck her arms shot out, almost a spasm, and the coin was flung away from her body. It would have hit with enough impact to dislodge the loose earth.'

'That's how it got buried and how we missed it,' said Agent Lacoste.

'*Oui,*' said Gamache, turning to leave. 'And it means that Lillian Dyson had to have been holding it. Now, why would she be standing in this garden holding an AA beginner's chip?'

But Beauvoir suspected the Chief was also thinking something else. That Beauvoir had fucked up. He should have seen the coin and not have it found by four crazy women worshiping a stick. That wasn't going to sound good in court, for any of them.

The women had left, the Sûreté officers had left. Everyone had left and now Peter and Clara were finally alone.

Peter took Clara in his arms and hugging her tight he whispered, 'I've been waiting all day to do this. I heard about the reviews. They're fantastic. Congratulations.'

'They are good, aren't they,' said Clara. 'Yipppeee. Can you believe it?'

'Are you kidding?' asked Peter, breaking from the embrace and striding across the kitchen. 'I had no doubt.'

'Oh, come on,' laughed Clara, 'you don't even like my work.'

'I do.'

'And what do you like about them?' she teased.

'Well, they're pretty. And you covered up most of the numbers with the paint.' He'd been poking in the fridge and now he turned around, a bottle of champagne in his hand.

'My father gave this to me on my twenty-first birthday. He told me to open it when I'd had a huge personal success. To toast myself.' He unwrapped the foil around the cork. 'I put it in the fridge yesterday before we left, so we could toast you.'

'No wait, Peter,' said Clara. 'We should save that.'

'What? For my own solo show? We both know that won't happen.'

'But it will. If it happened for me, it—'

'—can happen for anyone?'

'You know what I mean. I really think we should wait—'

The cork popped.

'Too late,' said Peter with a huge smile. 'We had a call while you were out.'

He carefully poured their glasses.

'From who?'

'André Castonguay.' He handed her a glass. Time enough later to tell her about all the other calls.

'Really? What did he want?'

'Wanted to talk to you. To us. To both of us. *Santé.*'

He tipped his glass and clinked hers. 'And congratulations.'

'Thank you. Do you want to meet with him?'

Clara's glass hung in the air, not quite touching her lips. Her nose felt the giddy popping of the champagne bubbles. Finally released. Like her, they'd waited years and years, decades, for this moment.

'Only if you do,' said Peter.

'Can we wait? Let all of this settle down a bit?'

'Whatever you'd like.'

But she could hear the disappointment in his voice.

'If you feel strongly, Peter, we can meet with him. Why don't we? I mean, he's right here now. Might as well.'

'No, no, that's OK.' He smiled at her. 'If he's serious he'll wait. Honestly, Clara, this is your time to shine. And neither Lillian's death nor André Castonguay can take that away.'

More bubbles popped, and Clara wondered if they were popping on their own or had been pricked by tiny, almost invisible needles like the one Peter had just used. Reminding her, even as they toasted her success, of the death. The murder, in their own garden.

She tipped the glass up and felt the wine on her lips. But over the flute she was staring at Peter, who suddenly looked less substantial. A little hollow. A little like a bubble himself. Floating away.

I was much too far out all my life, she thought as she drank. *And not waving, but drowning.*

What were the lines just before that? Clara slowly lowered her glass to the counter. Peter had taken a long sip of the champagne. More of a swig, really. A deep, masculine, almost aggressive gulp.

Nobody heard him, the dead man,
But still he lay moaning.

Those were the lines, thought Clara, as she stared at Peter.

The champagne on her lips was sour, the wine turned years before. But Peter, who'd taken a huge gulp, was smiling.

As though nothing was wrong.

When had he died? Clara wondered. And why hadn't she noticed?

'No, I understand,' said Inspector Beauvoir.

Chief Inspector Gamache looked across at Beauvoir in the driver's seat. Eyes staring ahead at the traffic as they approached the Champlain Bridge into Montréal. Beauvoir's face was placid, relaxed. Noncommittal.

But his grip was tight on the wheel.

'If Agent Lacoste is going to be promoted to inspector I want to see how she'll handle the added responsibility,' said Gamache. 'So I gave the dossier to her.'

He knew he didn't have to explain his decisions. But he chose to. These weren't children he was working with, but thoughtful, intelligent adults. If he didn't want them to behave like children he'd better not treat them like that. He wanted independent thinkers. And he got them. Men and women who'd earned the right to know why a decision was taken.

'This is about giving Agent Lacoste more authority, that's all. It's still your investigation. She understands that, and I need you to understand that as well, so there's no confusion.'

'Got it,' said Beauvoir. 'I just wish you'd mentioned it to me beforehand.'

'You're right, I should have. I'm sorry. In fact, I've been thinking it makes sense for you to supervise Agent Lacoste. Act as a mentor. If she's going to be promoted to inspector and become your second in command you'll have to train her.'

Beauvoir nodded and his grip loosened on the wheel. They spent the next few minutes discussing the case and Lacoste's strengths and weaknesses before lapsing into silence.

As he watched the graceful span of the bridge across the St. Lawrence River approach, Gamache's mind turned elsewhere. To something he'd been considering for a while now.

'There is something else.'

'Oh?' Beauvoir glanced over to his boss.

Gamache had been planning to speak to Beauvoir about this quietly. Perhaps over dinner that night, or a walk on the mountain. Not when they were hurtling down the autoroute at 120 kilometers an hour.

Still, the opening was there. And Gamache took it.

'We need to talk about how you're doing. There's something wrong. You aren't getting better, are you.'

It was not a question.

'I'm sorry about the coin. It was stupid—'

'I'm not talking about the coin. That was just a mistake. It happens. God knows it's just possible I've made a few in my life.'

He saw Beauvoir smile.

'Then what are you talking about, sir?'

'The painkillers. Why're you still taking them?'

There was silence in the car as Québec whizzed by their windows.

'How'd you know about that?' asked Beauvoir, finally.

'I suspected. You carry them with you, in your jacket pocket.'

'Did you look?' asked Beauvoir, an edge to his voice.

'No. But I've watched you.' As he did now. His second in command had always been so lithe, so energetic. Cocky. He was full of life and full of himself. It could annoy Gamache. But mostly he'd watched Beauvoir's vitality with pleasure and some amusement, as Jean Guy threw himself headlong into life.

But now the young man seemed drained. Dour. As though every day was an effort. As though he was dragging an anvil behind him.

'I'll be fine,' said Beauvoir, and heard how empty that sounded. 'The doctor and therapists say I'm doing well. Every day I feel better.'

Armand Gamache didn't want to pursue it. But he had to.

'You're still in pain from your wounds.'

Again, this wasn't a question.

'It'll just take time,' said Beauvoir, glancing over to his Chief. 'I really am feeling much better, all the time.'

But he didn't look it. And Gamache was concerned.

The Chief Inspector was silent. He himself had never been in better shape, or at least, not for many, many years. He was walking more now, and the physiotherapy had brought back his strength and agility. He went to the gym at Sûreté Headquarters three times a week. At first it had been humiliating, as he'd struggled to lift weights about the size of honey-glazed doughnuts, and to stay on the elliptical for more than a few minutes.

But he'd kept at it, and kept at it. And slowly his strength had not just returned, but surpassed where he'd been before the attack.

There were still some residual effects, physically. His right hand trembled when he was tired or overstressed. And his body ached when he first woke up, or got up after sitting for too long. There were a few aches and pains. But not nearly as much as the emotional, which he struggled with every day.

Some days were very good. And some, like this, were not.

He'd suspected Jean Guy was struggling, and he knew recovery was never a straight line. But Beauvoir seemed to be slipping further and further back.

'Is there something I can do?' he asked. 'Do you need time off to focus on your health? I know Daniel and Roslyn would love to have you visit them in Paris. Maybe that would help.'

Beauvoir laughed. 'Are you trying to kill me?'

Gamache grinned. It would be hard to imagine what could ruin a trip to Paris, but a week in the small flat with his son, daughter-in-law and two young grandchildren sure took a run at it. He and Reine-Marie now rented a flat close-by when they visited.

'*Merci, patron.* I'd rather hunt cold-blooded killers.'

Gamache laughed. The skyline of Montréal was looming in the foreground now, across the river. And Mont Royal rose in the middle of the city. The huge cross on top of the mountain was invisible now, but every night it sprang to life, lit as a beacon to a population that no longer believed in the church, but believed in family and friends, culture and humanity.

The cross didn't seem to care. It glowed just as bright.

'The separation from Enid can't have helped,' said the Chief.

'Actually it did,' said Beauvoir, slowing for the traffic on the bridge. Beside him Gamache was gazing at the skyline. As he always did. But now the Chief turned to look at him.

'How'd it help?'

'It's a relief. I feel free. I'm sorry it hurt Enid, but it's one of the best things to come out of what happened.'

'How so?'

'I feel like I was given another chance. So many died, but when I didn't I took a look at my life and realized how unhappy I was. And it wasn't going to get better. It wasn't Enid's fault, but we were never really well suited. But I was afraid to change, to admit I made a mistake. Afraid to hurt her. But I just couldn't take it anymore. Surviving the raid gave me the courage to do what I should have done years ago.'

'The courage to change.'

'*Pardon?*'

'It was one of the lines from that prayer on the coin,' said Gamache.

'Yeah, I guess so. Whatever it was, I could just see my life stretching ahead getting worse and worse. Don't get me wrong, Enid's wonderful—'

'We've always liked her. A lot.'

'And she likes you, as you know. But she's not the one for me.'

'Do you know who is?'

'No.'

Beauvoir glanced at the Chief. Gamache was now looking out the windshield, his face thoughtful, then he turned to Beauvoir.

'You will,' said the Chief.

Beauvoir nodded, deep in thought. Then he finally spoke.

'What would you have done, sir? If you'd been married to someone else when you met Madame Gamache?'

Gamache looked at Beauvoir, his eyes keen. 'I thought you said you hadn't met the one for you.'

Beauvoir hesitated. He'd given the Chief the opening, and Gamache had taken it. And now looked at him. Waiting for an answer. And Beauvoir almost told him. Almost told the Chief everything. Longed to open his heart and expose it to this man. As he'd told Armand Gamache about everything else in his life. About his unhappiness with Enid. They'd talked about that, about his own family, about what he wanted, and what he didn't want.

Jean Guy Beauvoir trusted Gamache with his life.

He opened his mouth, the words hovering there, just at the

opening. As though a stone had rolled back and these miraculous words were about to emerge. Into the daylight.

I love your daughter. I love Annie.

Beside him Chief Inspector Gamache waited, as though he had all the time in the world. As though nothing could be more important than Beauvoir's personal life.

The city, with its invisible cross, got bigger and bigger. And then they were over the bridge.

'I haven't met anyone,' said Beauvoir. 'But I want to be ready. I can't be married. It wouldn't have been fair to Enid.'

Gamache was quiet for a moment. 'Nor would it be fair to your lover's husband.'

It wasn't a rebuke. Wasn't even a warning. And Beauvoir knew then if Chief Inspector Gamache had suspected he'd have said something. He'd not play games with Beauvoir. The way Beauvoir was with Gamache.

No, this wasn't a game. Nor was it a secret, really. It was just a feeling. Unfulfilled. Not acted upon.

I love your daughter, sir.

But those words were swallowed too. Returned to the dark to join all the other unsaid things.

They found the apartment block in the Notre-Dame-de-Grâce *quartier* of Montréal. Squat and gray, it might have been designed by Soviet architects in the 1960s.

The grass had been peed white by dogs, and lumps of poop sat on it. The flower beds were overgrown with strangled bushes and weeds. The concrete walk to the front door was cracked and heaved.

Inside, it smelled of urine and resonated with the distant echoes of doors slamming and people shouting at each other.

Monsieur and Madame Dyson lived on the top floor. The handrail on the concrete stairs was sticky and Beauvoir quickly took his hand off of it.

Up they walked. Three flights. Not pausing for breath but not racing either. They took measured steps. Once at the top they found the door to the Dyson apartment.

Chief Inspector Gamache raised his hand, and paused.

To give the Dysons one more second of peace before shattering their lives? Or to give himself one more moment before facing them?

Rap. Rap.

It opened a crack, a security chain across a fearful face.

'*Oui?*'

'Madame Dyson? My name is Armand Gamache. I'm with the Sûreté du Québec.' He already had his ID out and now showed it to her. Her eyes dropped to it, then back up to the Chief's face. 'This is my colleague Inspector Beauvoir. May we speak with you?'

The thin face was obviously relieved. How many times had she opened the door a crack, to see kids taunting her? To see the landlord demanding rent? To see unkindness take human form?

But not this time. These men were with the Sûreté. They wouldn't hurt her. She was of a generation who still believed that. It was written all over her worn face.

The door closed, the chain was lifted and the door swung open.

She was tiny. And in an armchair sat a man who looked like a puppet. Small, stiff, sunken. He struggled to get up, but Gamache walked swiftly over to him.

'No, please, Monsieur Dyson. *Je vous en prie.* Stay seated.'

They shook hands and he reintroduced himself, speaking slowly, clearly, more loudly than normal.

'Tea?' Madame Dyson asked.

Oh, no no no, thought Beauvoir. The place smelled of liniment and slightly of urine.

'Yes, please. How kind of you. May I help?' Gamache went with her into the kitchen, leaving Beauvoir alone with the puppet. He tried to make small-talk but ran out after commenting on the weather.

'Nice place,' he finally said and was treated to Monsieur Dyson looking at him as though he was an idiot.

Beauvoir scanned the walls. There was a crucifix above the dining table, and a smiling Jesus surrounded by light. But the rest of the walls were taken up with photographs of one person. Their daughter Lillian. Her life radiated out from the smiling Jesus. Her baby pictures closest to Him, then she got older and older as the pictures wrapped around the walls. Sometimes alone, sometimes with others. The parents too aged, from a young, beaming couple holding their first born, their only born, in front of a neat, compact home. To first Christmas, to gooey birthdays.

Beauvoir scanned the walls for a photo of Lillian and Clara then realized if there had been one it would have been taken down long ago.

There were pictures of a gap-toothed little girl with gleaming orange hair holding a huge stuffed dog, and a little later standing beside a bike with a big bow. Toys, gifts, presents. Everything a little girl could want.

And love. No, not just love. Adoration. This child, this woman, was adored.

Beauvoir felt something stir inside. Something that seemed to have crawled into him while he'd lain in his own blood on the floor of that factory.

Sorrow.

Since that moment death had never been the same, and neither, it must be said, had life.

He didn't like it.

He tried to remember Lillian Dyson forty years after this picture was taken. Too much makeup, hair dyed a straw blond. Bright red look-at-me dress. Almost a mockery. A parody of a person.

But try as Beauvoir might it was too late. He saw Lillian Dyson now as a young girl. Adored. Confident. Heading into the world. A world her parents knew needed to be kept out, with chains.

But still, they'd opened the door a crack, and a crack was enough.

If there was something malevolent, malicious, murderous on the other side, a crack was all it needed.

'Bon,' came the Chief's voice behind him and Beauvoir turned to see Gamache carrying a tin tray with a teapot, some milk, sugar and fine china cups. 'Where would you like me to put this?'

He sounded warm, friendly. But not jovial. The Chief wouldn't want to trick them. Would not want to give the impression they were there with riotous good news.

'Just here, please.' Madame Dyson hurried to clear the TV guide and remote off a faux-wood table by the sofa, but Beauvoir got there first, scooping them up and handing them to her.

She met his eyes and smiled. Not a wide smile, but a softer, sadder version of her daughter's. Beauvoir knew now where Lillian had gotten her smile.

And he suspected these two elderly people knew why they were there. Probably not the exact news. Not that their only daughter was dead. Murdered. But the look Madame Dyson had just given him told Jean Guy Beauvoir that she knew something was up. Amiss.

And she was being kind anyway. Or was she just trying to keep whatever news they had at bay? Keep them silent for one more precious minute.

'A bit of milk and sugar?' she asked the puppet.

Monsieur Dyson sat forward.

'This is a special occasion,' he pretended to confide in their visitors. 'Normally she doesn't offer milk.'

It broke Beauvoir's heart to think these two pensioners probably couldn't afford much milk. That what little they had was being offered now, to their guests.

'Gives me gas,' explained the old man.

'Now, Papa,' said Madame Dyson, handing the cup and saucer to the Chief to hand to her husband. She too pretended to confide in their company. 'It is true. I figure you have about twenty minutes from the first sip.'

Once they all had their cups and were seated Chief Inspector Gamache took a sip and placed the delicate bone china cup on its saucer and leaned toward the elderly couple. Madame Dyson reached out and took her husband's hand.

Would she still call him 'Papa' after today, Beauvoir wondered. Or was that the very last time? Would it be too painful? That must have been what Lillian called him.

Would he still be a father, even if there were no more children?

'I have some very bad news,' said the Chief. 'It's about your daughter, Lillian.'

He looked them in the eyes as he spoke, and saw their lives change. It would forever be dated from this moment. Before the news and after the news. Two completely different lives.

'I'm afraid she's dead.'

He spoke in short, declarative sentences. His voice calm, deep. Absolute. He needed to tell them quickly, not drag it out. And clearly. There could be no doubt.

'I don't understand,' said Madame Dyson, but her eyes said she understood fully. She was terrified. The monster every mother feared had squirmed in through that crack. It had taken her child, and was now sitting in her living room.

Madame Dyson turned to her husband, who was struggling to sit further forward. Perhaps to stand up. To confront this news, these words. To beat them back, out of his living room, out of his home, away from his door. To beat those words until they were lies.

But he couldn't.

'There's more,' said the Chief Inspector, still holding their eyes. 'Lillian was murdered.'

'Oh, God, no,' said Lillian's mother, her hand flying to her mouth. Then it slipped to her chest. Her breast. And rested there, limp.

Both of them stared at Gamache, and he looked at them.

'I'm very sorry to have to bring you this news,' he said, knowing how weak it sounded but also knowing to not say it would be even worse.

Madame and Monsieur Dyson were gone now. They'd crossed over to that continent where grieving parents lived. It looked the same as the rest of the world, but wasn't. Colors bled pale. Music was just notes. Books no longer transported or comforted, not fully. Never again. Food was nutrition, little more. Breaths were sighs.

And they knew something the rest didn't. They knew how lucky the rest of the world was.

'How?' Madame Dyson whispered. Beside her her husband was enraged, so angry he couldn't speak. But his face was contorted and his eyes blazed. At Gamache.

'Her neck was broken,' said the Chief. 'It was very fast. She didn't even see it coming.'

'Why?' she asked. 'Why would anyone kill Lillian?'

'We don't know. But we'll find out who did this.'

Armand Gamache cupped his large hands toward her. An offering.

Jean Guy Beauvoir noticed the tremble in the Chief's right hand. Very slight.

This too was new, since the factory.

Madame Dyson dropped her tiny hand from her breast into Gamache's hands and he closed them, holding hers like a sparrow.

He said nothing then. And neither did she.

They sat in silence, and would sit there for as long as it took.

Beauvoir looked at Monsieur Dyson. His rage had turned to confusion. A man of action in his younger days now imprisoned in an easy chair. Unable to save his daughter. Unable to comfort his wife.

Beauvoir got up and offered the elderly man his own arms. Monsieur Dyson stared at them, then swung both hands to Beauvoir's arm and grabbed on. Beauvoir lifted him to a standing position and supported him while the old man turned to his wife. And put out his arms.

She stood and walked into them.

They held each other and held each other up. And wept. Eventually they parted.

Beauvoir had found tissues and gave each a handful. When they were able Chief Inspector Gamache asked them some questions.

'Lillian lived in New York for many years. Can you tell us anything about her life there?'

'She was an artist,' her father said. 'Wonderful. We didn't visit her often but she came home every couple of years or so.'

It sounded vague, to Gamache. An exaggeration.

'She made a living as an artist?' he asked.

'Absolutely,' Madame Dyson said. 'She was a big success.'

'She was married once?' the Chief asked.

'Morgan was his name,' said Madame Dyson.

'No, not Morgan,' said her husband. 'But close. Madison.'

'Yes, that's it. It was a long time ago and they weren't married long. We never met him but he wasn't a nice man. Drank. Poor Lillian was taken in by him completely. Very charming, but they so often are.'

Gamache noticed Beauvoir taking out his notebook.

'You say he drank?' asked the Chief. 'How do you know?'

'Lillian told us. She finally kicked him out. But that was long ago.'

'Do you know if he ever stopped drinking?' asked Gamache. 'Perhaps joined Alcoholics Anonymous?'

They looked lost. 'We never met him, Chief Inspector,' she repeated. 'I suppose he might have, before he died.'

'He died?' asked Beauvoir. 'Do you know when?'

'Oh, a few years ago now. Lillian told us. Probably drank himself to death.'

'Did your daughter talk about any particular friends?'

'She had a lot of friends. We spoke once a week and she was always off to parties or *vernissages*.'

'Did she talk about any by name?' Gamache asked. They shook their heads. 'Did she ever mention a friend named Clara, back here in Québec?'

'Clara? She was Lillian's best friend. Inseparable. She used to come by for supper when we lived in the house.'

'But they didn't stay close?'

'Clara stole some of Lillian's ideas. Then she dropped Lillian as a friend. Used her and threw her away as soon as she had what she wanted. Hurt Lillian terribly.'

'Why did your daughter go to New York?' asked Gamache.

'She felt the art scene here in Montréal wasn't very supportive. They didn't like it when she criticized their work, but that was her job, after all, as a critic. She wanted to go someplace where artists were more sophisticated.'

'Did she talk about anyone in particular? Someone who might have wished her ill?'

'Back then? She said everyone did.'

'And more recently? When did she come back to Montréal?'

'October sixteenth,' said Monsieur Dyson.

'You know the exact date?' Gamache turned to him.

'You would too, if you had a daughter.'

The Chief nodded. 'You're right. I do have a daughter and I'd remember the day she returned home.'

The two men looked at each other for a moment.

'Did Lillian tell you why she returned?' Gamache did a quick calculation. It would have been about eight months earlier. Shortly after that she'd bought her car and begun going to art shows around town.

'She just said she was missing home,' said Madame Dyson. 'We thought we were the luckiest people alive.'

Gamache paused to let her gather herself. Both Sûreté officers knew there was a small window after telling loved ones the news before they were completely overcome. Before the shock wore off and the pain began.

That moment was fast approaching. The window was slamming shut. They had to make each question count.

'Was she happy in Montréal this time?' Gamache asked.

'I've never seen her happier,' said her father. 'I think she might've found a man. We asked but she always laughed and denied it. But I'm not so sure.'

'Why do you say that?' Gamache asked.

'When she came for dinner she'd always leave early,' said Madame Dyson. 'By seven thirty. We kidded her that she was off on a date.'

'And what did she say to that?'

'She just laughed. But,' she hesitated, 'there was something.'

'What do you mean?'

Madame Dyson took another deep breath as though trying to keep herself going, long enough to help this police officer. To help him find whoever had killed their daughter.

'I don't know what I mean, but she never used to leave early, then suddenly she did. But she wouldn't tell us why.'

'Did your daughter drink?'

'Drink?' asked Monsieur Dyson. 'I don't understand the question. Drink what?'

'Alcohol. We found something at the site that might have come from Alcoholics Anonymous. Do you know if your daughter belonged to AA?'

'Lillian?' Madame Dyson looked astonished. 'I've never seen her drunk in my life. She used to be the designated driver at parties. She'd have a few drinks sometimes, but never many.'

'We don't even keep alcohol in the house,' said Monsieur Dyson.

'Why not?' Gamache asked.

'We just lost interest, I suppose,' said Madame Dyson. 'There were other things to spend our pensions on.'

Gamache nodded and got up. 'May I?' He indicated the pictures on the walls.

'Please.' Madame Dyson joined him.

'Very pretty,' he said as they gazed at the photographs. Lillian aged as they walked around the modest room. From cherished newborn to adored teen and into a lovely young woman, with hair the color of a sunset.

'Your daughter was found in a garden,' he said, trying to make it sound not too gruesome. 'It belonged to her friend Clara.'

Madame Dyson stopped and stared at the Chief Inspector. 'Clara? But that's not possible. Lillian would never have gone there. She'd meet the devil before she'd meet that woman.'

'Did you say Lillian was killed at Clara's home?' demanded Monsieur Dyson.

'*Oui.* In her backyard.'

'Then you know who killed Lillian,' said Monsieur Dyson. 'Have you arrested her?'

'I haven't,' said Gamache. 'There are other possibilities. Is there anyone else your daughter talked about since her return to Montréal? Anyone who might wish her harm?'

'No one as obvious as Clara,' snapped Monsieur Dyson.

'I know this is difficult,' said Gamache quietly, calmly. He waited a moment before speaking again. 'But you need to think about my question. It's vital. Did she talk about anyone else? Anyone she'd had an upset with recently?'

'No one,' said Madame Dyson, eventually. 'As we said, she never seemed happier.'

Chief Inspector Gamache and Beauvoir thanked the Dysons for their help and gave them their cards.

'Please call,' said the Chief, standing at the door. 'If you remember anything, or if you need anything.'

'Who do we speak to about—' Madame Dyson began.

'I'll have someone come over and talk with you about arrangements. Is that all right?'

They nodded. Monsieur Dyson had fought to his feet and stood beside his wife, staring at Gamache. Two men, two fathers. But standing now a continent apart.

As they walked down the stairs, their steps echoing against the walls, Gamache wondered how two such people could produce the woman Clara had described.

Wretched, jealous, bitter, mean.

But then, the Dysons thought the same about Clara.

There was a lot to wonder about.

Madame Dyson had been certain her daughter would never go to Clara Morrow's home. Not knowingly.

Had Lillian Dyson been tricked into it? Lured there not realizing it was Clara's place? But if so, why was she killed, and why there?

TEN

After having rid the garden of all evil spirits, Myrna, Dominique and Ruth sat down for beers in Myrna's loft.

'So what do you think that coin was about?' Dominique asked, relaxing back into the sofa.

'More evil,' said Ruth and the other women looked at her.

'What do you mean?' Myrna asked.

'AA?' demanded Ruth. 'Bunch of devil worshipers. It's a cult. Mind control. Demons. Turning people away from the natural path.'

'Of being alcoholics?' asked Myrna with a laugh.

Ruth eyed her suspiciously. 'I wouldn't expect the witch gardener to understand.'

'You'd be surprised what you can learn in a garden,' said Myrna. 'And from a witch.'

Just then Clara arrived, looking distracted.

'You OK?' asked Dominique.

'Just fine. Peter had put a bottle of champagne in the fridge to celebrate. This was the first chance we had to toast the *vernissage.*' Clara poured herself an iced tea from Myrna's fridge and came over to join them.

'That was nice,' said Dominique.

'Uh-huh,' agreed Clara. Myrna looked at her closely, but said nothing.

'What were you talking about?' Clara asked.

'The body in your garden,' said Ruth. 'Did you kill her or not?'

'OK,' said Clara. 'I'm only going to say this once so I hope you remember. Are you paying attention?'

They nodded, except Ruth.

'Ruth?'

'What?'

'You asked a question. I'm about to answer it.'

'Too late. I've lost interest. Aren't we getting anything to eat?'

'Pay attention.' Clara looked at all of them and spoke clearly and slowly. 'I. Did. Not. Kill. Lillian.'

'Do you have a piece of paper?' Dominique asked. 'I'm not sure I can remember all that.'

Ruth laughed.

'So,' said Myrna. 'Let's just assume we believe you. For the moment. Who did?'

'It had to be someone else at the party,' said Clara.

'But who, Sherlock?' Myrna asked.

'Who hated her enough to kill her?' Dominique asked.

'Anyone who met her,' said Clara.

'But that's not fair,' said Myrna. 'You hadn't seen her in more than twenty years. And it's possible she was simply mean to you. It happens sometimes. We trigger something in someone else, bring out the worst in each other.'

'Not Lillian,' said Clara. 'She was generous in her disdain. She hated everyone and everyone eventually hated her. Like you said before. The frog in the frying pan. She'd turn up the heat.'

'I hope that isn't a dinner suggestion,' said Ruth, 'because that's what I had for breakfast.'

They looked at her and she grinned. 'Well, maybe it was an egg.'

They turned back to Myrna.

'Maybe it wasn't a frying pan,' Ruth continued. 'But a glass. And now that I think of it, it wasn't an egg at all.'

They turned back to Ruth.

'It was Scotch.'

They focused back on Myrna, who explained the psychological phenomenon.

'I think I always hated myself for staying so long, for letting Lillian hurt me so much before I actually left. Never again.'

Clara was surprised when Myrna said nothing.

'Gamache probably thinks I did it.' Clara finally broke the silence. 'I'm screwed.'

'I'd have to agree,' said Ruth.

'Of course you're not,' said Dominique. 'In fact, just the opposite.'

'What d'you mean?'

'You have something the Chief Inspector doesn't,' said Dominique. 'You know the art world and you know most of the people at your party. What's the biggest question you have?'

'Besides who killed her? Well, what was Lillian doing here?'

'Excellent,' said Dominique, getting up. 'Good question. Why don't we ask?'

'Who?'

'The guests still here in Three Pines.'

Clara thought for a moment. 'Worth a try.'

'Waste of time,' said Ruth. 'I still think you did it.'

'Watch it, old woman,' said Clara. 'You're next.'

The forensics team met Chief Inspector Gamache and Inspector Beauvoir at Lillian Dyson's apartment in Montréal. While they took prints and collected specimens, Gamache and Beauvoir looked around.

It was a modest apartment on the top floor of a triplex. None of the buildings were tall in the Plateau Mont Royal district so while petite, Lillian's apartment was bright.

Beauvoir walked briskly into the main room and got to work but Gamache paused. To get a feel for the place. It smelled stale. Of oil paint and unopened windows. The furniture was old without being vintage. The kind you found in the Sally Ann, or on the side of the road.

The floors were parquet with dull area rugs. Unlike some artists who cared about the aesthetics of their home, Lillian Dyson appeared indifferent to what was within these walls. What she was not indifferent to was what was on the walls.

Paintings. Luminous, dazzling paintings. Not bright or splashy, but dazzling in their images. Had she collected them? Perhaps from an artist friend in New York?

He leaned in to read the signature.

Lillian Dyson.

Chief Inspector Gamache stepped back and stared, astonished. The dead woman had painted these. He moved from painting to painting, reading the signatures and the dates, just to be sure. But he knew there was no doubt. The style was so strong, so singular.

They were all created by Lillian Dyson, and all within the last seven months.

These were like nothing he'd ever seen before.

Her paintings were lush and bold. Cityscapes, Montréal, made to look and feel like a forest. The buildings were tall and wonky, like strong trees growing this way and that. Adjusting to nature, rather than the other way around. She managed to make the buildings into living things, as though they'd been planted and watered and nurtured, and had sprung from the concrete. Attractive, the way all vital things were attractive.

It was not a relaxing world she painted. But neither was it threatening.

He liked them. A lot.

'More in here, Chief,' called Beauvoir, when he noticed Gamache staring at the paintings. 'Looks like she turned her bedroom into a studio.'

Chief Inspector Gamache walked by the forensics team, lifting fingerprints and taking samples, and joined Beauvoir in the small bedroom. A single bed, made up nicely, was shoved against the wall and there was a chest of drawers, but the rest of the modest room was taken up with brushes soaking in tins, canvases leaning against the walls. The floor was covered in a tarpaulin and the room smelled of oil and cleaner.

Gamache walked over to the canvas sitting on the easel.

It was unfinished. It showed a church, in bright red, almost as though it was on fire. But it wasn't. It simply glowed. And beside it swirled roads like rivers and people like reeds. No other artist he knew was painting in this style. It was as though Lillian Dyson had invented a whole new art movement, like the Cubists or the Impressionists, like the post-modernists and Abstract Expressionists.

And now there was this.

Armand Gamache could barely look away. Lillian was painting Montréal as though it was a work of nature, not man. With all the force, the power, the energy and beauty of nature. And the savagery too.

It seemed clear she'd been experimenting with this style, growing into it. The earliest works, from seven months ago, showed some promise but were tentative. And then, sometime around Christmas, there seemed to have been a breakthrough and the flowing, audacious style took hold.

'Chief, look at this.'

Inspector Beauvoir was standing next to the nightstand. There was a large blue book on it. The Chief Inspector brought a pen from his pocket and opened the book to the bookmark.

There was a sentence highlighted in yellow and underlined. Almost violently.

'*The alcoholic is like a tornado,*' read Chief Inspector Gamache, '*roaring his way through the lives of others. Hearts are broken. Sweet relationships are dead.*'

He let the book fall closed. On its royal blue cover in bold white print was *Alcoholics Anonymous.*

'I guess we know who belonged to AA,' said Beauvoir.

'I guess so,' said Gamache. 'I think we need to ask these people some questions.'

After everything had been gone over by the forensics team the Chief Inspector handed Beauvoir one of the booklets from the drawer. It was dog-eared, dirty, well used. Inspector Beauvoir flipped through it then read the front.

Alcoholics Anonymous Meeting List.

Inside a meeting for Sunday night was circled. Beauvoir could guess what they'd be doing at eight that night.

The four women paired up, figuring they'd be safer in twos.

'You obviously haven't watched many horror films,' said Dominique. 'Women are always in pairs. One to die horribly and the other to shriek.'

'Dibs on the shrieking,' said Ruth.

'I'm afraid, dear one, that you're the horror,' said Clara.

'Well, that's a relief. Are you coming?' Ruth asked Dominique, who stared back with mock-loathing at Myrna and Clara.

Myrna watched them go then turned to Clara.

'How's Peter?'

'Peter? Why'd you ask?'

'I was just wondering.'

Clara studied her friend. 'You never just wonder. What is it?'

'You didn't exactly look happy when you arrived. You said the two of you toasted your *vernissage*. Is that all that happened?'

Clara remembered Peter standing in their kitchen, drinking sour champagne. Toasting her solo show with rancid wine, and a smile.

But she wasn't yet ready to talk about it. Besides, Clara thought as she looked at her friend, she was afraid of what Myrna might say.

'It's just a difficult time for Peter,' she said instead. 'I think we all know that.'

And she watched Myrna's gaze intensify, then relent.

'He's doing his best,' said Myrna.

It was, thought Clara, a diplomatic answer.

Across the village green they could see Gabri and Olivier sitting on the porch of their B and B, sipping beer. Relaxing before the late afternoon rush at the bistro.

'Mutt and Jeff.' Gabri waved the two women over.

'Bert and Ernie,' said Myrna as she and Clara climbed the steps onto the verandah.

'Your artist friends are still here,' said Olivier, rising and kissing the women on both cheeks.

'Staying on for a few more days, apparently.' Gabri was none too pleased. His idea of a perfect B and B was an empty B and B. 'Gamache's people said the others could leave, so they did. I think they found it boring. Apparently only one murder isn't enough to hold their attention.'

Myrna and Clara left them to monitor the village, and walked into the B and B.

'So what have you been working on?' Clara asked Paulette. They'd been chatting for a few minutes. About the weather, of course. And Clara's show. Given equal weight by Paulette and Normand. 'Still doing that wonderful series on flight?'

'Yes, in fact a gallery in Drummondville is interested and there's a juried show in Boston we might enter.'

'That's terrific.' Clara turned to Myrna. 'Their series on wings is stunning.'

Myrna almost gagged. If she heard the word 'stunning' once more she really would vomit. She wondered what it was code for. Crappy? Hideous? So far Normand had described Clara's works, which he clearly didn't like, as stunning. Paulette had said Normand was planning some powerful pieces which, she assured them, they'd find stunning.

And, of course, they were both simply stunned by Clara's success.

But then, they'd admitted to being stunned by Lillian's murder.

'So,' said Clara, nonchalantly picking at a bowl of licorice allsorts on the table in the sitting room, 'I was just sort of wondering how Lillian came to be here yesterday. Do you know who invited her?'

'Didn't you?' asked Paulette.

Clara shook her head.

Myrna leaned back and listened closely as they speculated about who might have been in contact with Lillian.

'She'd been back in Montréal for a few months, you know,' said Paulette.

Clara hadn't known.

'Yeah,' said Normand. 'Even came up to us at a *vernissage* and apologized for being such a bitch years ago.'

'Really?' asked Clara. 'Lillian did that?'

'We figure she was just sucking up,' said Paulette. 'When she left we were nobodies but now we're pretty well established.'

'Now, she needs us,' said Normand. 'Needed us.'

'For what?' asked Clara.

'She said she'd gone back to doing some art. Wanted to show us her portfolio,' said Normand.

'And what did you say?'

They looked at each other. 'We told her we didn't have time. We weren't rude, but we didn't want anything to do with her.'

Clara nodded. She'd have done the same thing, she hoped. Been polite, but distant. It was one thing to forgive, it was another to climb back into the cage with that bear, even if it was wearing a tutu and smiling. Or, what was the analogy Myrna had used?

The frying pan.

'Maybe she crashed the party. Lots of people did,' said Normand. 'Like Denis Fortin.'

Normand said the gallery owner's name lightly, slipping it into the conversation, like a sharp word thrust between bones. A word meant to wound. He watched Clara. And Myrna watched him.

She sat forward, curious to see how Clara would handle this attack. Because that was what it was. Civil and subtle and said with a smile. A sort of social neutron bomb. Meant to keep the structures of polite conversation standing, while slaying the person.

Having listened to this couple for half an hour now, Myrna could say she wasn't exactly stunned by this attack. And neither was Clara.

'But he was invited,' Clara said, matching Normand's light tone. 'I personally asked Denis to come.'

Myrna almost smiled. Clara's *coup de grâce* was calling Fortin by his first name, as though she and the prominent gallery owner were buddies. And, yes, yes, there it was.

Both Normand and Paulette were stunned.

Still, two very troubling questions remained unanswered.

Who did invite Lillian to Clara's party?

And why did she accept?

ELEVEN

— ⁓ —

'Honestly, you're the worst investigator in history,' said Dominique.
'At least I was asking questions,' snapped Ruth.

'Only because I couldn't get a word in.'

Myrna and Clara had joined the other two women in the bistro and were now sitting in front of a fire, lit more for effect than necessity.

'She asked André Castonguay how big his dick was.'

'I did not. I asked how big a dick he was. There's a difference.'

Ruth brought up her thumb and forefinger to indicate about two inches.

Despite herself, Clara smirked. She'd often wanted to ask gallery owners the same question.

Dominique shook her head. 'Then she asked the other one—'

'François Marois?' asked Clara. She'd been tempted to give the artists to Dominique and Ruth and take the dealers for herself, but she didn't feel like seeing Castonguay just yet. Not after his phone call, and her conversation with Peter.

'Yes, François Marois. She asked what his favorite color was.'

'I thought it might be helpful,' said Ruth.

'And was it?' Dominique demanded.

'Not as much as you'd think,' admitted Ruth.

'So despite this grilling neither confessed to killing Lillian Dyson?' asked Myrna.

'They held up surprisingly well,' said Dominique. 'Though Castonguay did let it slip that his first car was a Gremlin.'

'Tell me that's not psychotic,' said Ruth.

'How'd you two do?' asked Dominique, reaching for her lemonade.

'I'm not sure how we did,' said Myrna, almost emptying the bowl of cashews with one handful. 'I liked the way you disarmed that Normand fellow when he brought up Denis Fortin.'

'What do you mean?' Clara asked.

'Well, when you told him you'd invited Fortin yourself. Actually, that's another mystery, now that I think of it. What was Denis Fortin doing here?'

'I hate to break it to you,' said Clara, 'but I really did invite him.'

'Why in the world would you do that, child?' asked Myrna. 'After what he did?'

'Well, if I kept out every gallery owner and dealer who turned me down, the place would've been empty.'

Not for the first time Myrna marveled at her friend, who could forgive so much. And who had so much to forgive. She considered herself fairly stable, but Myrna doubted she'd last long in the wine and cheese and cutthroat world of art.

She also wondered who else had been forgiven and invited who shouldn't have been.

Gamache had called ahead and now he pulled into the parking spot at the back of the gallery on rue St-Denis in Montréal. The lot was reserved for staff, but it was five thirty on a Sunday and most had gone home.

Getting out of his car he looked around. St-Denis was a cosmopolitan Montréal street. But the alley that ran behind it was squalid, with used condoms and empty needles littering the ground.

The glorious front hid what was foul.

And which was the real St-Denis? he wondered as he locked the car and walked toward the vibrant street.

The glass front door of the Galerie Fortin was locked. Gamache looked for a doorbell, but Denis Fortin appeared, all smiles, and unlocked it for him.

'Monsieur Gamache,' he said, holding out his hand and shaking the Chief Inspector's. 'A pleasure to see you again.'

'*Mais, non,*' said the Chief, bowing slightly. 'The pleasure is mine. Thank you for seeing me so late.'

'Gave me a chance to catch up on some work. You know what it's like.' Fortin carefully locked the door and waved the Chief deeper into the gallery. 'My office is upstairs.'

Gamache followed the younger man. They'd met a few times before, when Fortin had been in Three Pines considering Clara for a show. Fortin was perhaps forty, with a bright and attractive manner. He wore a finely tailored jacket, open-collar ironed shirt and black jeans. Smart and stylish.

Up the stairs they walked and Gamache listened while Fortin described with great animation some of the works on his walls. The Chief, while listening closely, also scanned the gallery for a painting by Lillian Dyson. Her style was so singular it would declare itself. But the walls, while containing some clearly brilliant works, didn't proclaim a Dyson.

'*Café?*' Fortin indicated a cappuccino maker just outside his office.

'*Non, merci.*'

'A beer, perhaps? It's turned into a warm day.'

'That would be nice,' said the Chief, and made himself comfortable in Fortin's office. Once Fortin was out of sight, Gamache leaned over his desk and scanned the papers. Contracts for artists. Some publicity mock-ups for upcoming shows. One for a famous Québec artist, one for someone Gamache had not heard of. An up-and-comer, presumably.

But no mention, in his quick scan, of Lillian Dyson. Or Clara Morrow.

Gamache heard the soft tread and took his seat just as Fortin walked through his office door.

'Here we go.' The gallery owner was carrying a tray with two beers and some cheese. 'We always have a stock of wine and beer and cheese. The tools of the trade.'

'Not canvas and brushes?' asked the Chief Inspector, taking the cold beer in the frosted glass.

'Those are for the creative ones. I'm just a lowly businessman. A bridge between talent and money.'

'À votre santé.' The Chief raised his glass, as did Fortin, then both men took a satisfying sip.

'Creative,' said Gamache, lowering his glass and accepting a piece of fragrant Stilton. 'But artists are also emotional, unstable at times, I imagine.'

'Artists?' asked Fortin. 'What could you possibly mean?'

He laughed. It was easy and light. Gamache couldn't help but smile back. It was hard not to like him.

Charm was also a tool, he knew, of the art gallery trade. Fortin offered cheese and charm. When he chose.

'I suppose,' Fortin continued, 'it depends what you compare them to. Now, compared to a rabid hyena or, say, a hungry cobra an artist comes off pretty well.'

'Doesn't sound like you much like artists.'

'Actually, I do. I like them, but more importantly, I understand them. Their egos, their fears, their insecurities. There're very few artists who are comfortable among other people. Most prefer to work away quietly in their studios. Whoever said, "Hell is other people" must have been an artist.'

'It was Sartre,' said Gamache. 'A writer.'

'I suspect if you speak with a publisher their experiences with writers would be the same. Here you have, in my case, artists who manage to capture on a small flat canvas not just the reality of life, but the mysteries, the spirit, the deep and conflicting emotions of being human. And yet most of them hate and fear other people. I understand that.'

'Do you? How?'

There was a slight strained silence then. Denis Fortin, for all his bonhomie, didn't like penetrating questions. He preferred to lead the conversation rather than be led. He was used, Gamache realized, to being listened to, acquiesced to, fawned over. He was used to having his decisions and statements simply accepted. Denis Fortin was a powerful man in a world of vulnerable people.

'I have a theory, Chief Inspector,' said Fortin, crossing his legs and smoothing the material of his jeans. 'That most jobs are self-selecting. We might grow into them, but for the most part we fall into a career because it suits what we're good at. I love art. Can't paint worth a damn. I know because I tried. I actually thought I wanted to be an artist, but that miserable failure led me to what I was always meant to do. Recognize talent in others. It's a perfect match. I make a very good living and am surrounded by great art. And great artists. I get to be part of this culture of creativity without all the angst of actually creating it.'

'I expect your world isn't without its angst.'

'True. If I choose to represent an artist and the show's a bust, it can reflect badly on me. But then I just make sure word spreads that it simply means I'm daring and willing to take risks. Avant-garde. That plays well.'

'But the artist ...' said Gamache, letting it hang there.

'Ah, there you have it. He gets it in the neck.'

Gamache looked at Fortin and tried not to let his distaste show. Like the street his gallery was on, Fortin had an attractive front, hiding quite a foul interior. He was opportunistic. He fed on the talent of others. Got rich on the talent of others. While most of the artists themselves barely scraped by, and took all the risks.

'Do you protect them?' Gamache asked. 'Try to defend them against the critics?'

Fortin looked both astonished and amused. 'They're adults, Monsieur Gamache. They take the accolades when they come and they must take the criticism when it comes. Treating artists like children is never a good idea.'

'Not as children, perhaps,' said Gamache, 'but as respected partners. Would you not stand by a respected partner if he was being attacked?'

'I have no partners,' said Fortin. The smile was still in place, but perhaps just a little too fixed. 'It gets too messy. As you would know. Best not to have anyone to defend. It can throw off your judgment.'

'An interesting perspective,' said Gamache. He knew then that Fortin had seen the video of the attack in the factory. This was a veiled allusion to what had happened. Fortin, along with the rest of the world, had seen his failure to defend his own people. To save them.

'As you know, I wasn't able to protect my own people,' said Gamache. 'But at least I tried. You don't?'

It was clear Fortin hadn't expected the Chief Inspector to confront the event directly. It threw him off center.

Not quite as stable, Gamache thought, *as you pretend to be. Perhaps you're more like an artist than you like to believe.*

'Fortunately people aren't actually shooting at my artists,' said Fortin finally.

'No, but there're other forms of attack. Of hurting. Even of killing. You can murder a person's reputation. You can kill their drive and their desire, even their creativity, if you try hard enough.'

Fortin laughed. 'If an artist is that fragile he should either find something else to do or not venture beyond his door. Just toss the canvases out and lock up quick. But most artists I know have huge egos. And huge ambition. They want that praise, they want that recognition. That's their problem. That's what makes them vulnerable. Not their talent, but their egos.'

'But you agree they're vulnerable, for whatever reason?'

'I do. I've already said that.'

'And do you agree that being so vulnerable can make some artists fearful?'

Fortin hesitated a moment, sensing a trap but not sure where it lay. He nodded.

'And that fearful people can lash out?'

'I suppose so. What're we talking about? I'm guessing this isn't just a pleasant Sunday afternoon chat. And I guess you aren't in the market for one of my paintings.'

Suddenly they'd become 'my' paintings, Gamache noticed.

'*Non, monsieur.* I'll tell you in a moment, if you'll indulge me.'

Fortin looked at his watch. All subtlety, all charm, gone.

'I'm wondering why you went to Clara Morrow's celebration yesterday.'

Far from being the last shove to throw Fortin completely off, Gamache's question made the art dealer first gape then laugh.

'Is that what this is about? I don't understand. I can't have broken any law. Besides, Clara herself invited me.'

'*Vraiment?* But you weren't on the guest list.'

'No, I know. I'd heard of course about her *vernissage* at the Musée and decided to go.'

'Why? You'd dropped her as an artist and split under not very good conditions. In fact you quite humiliated her.'

'Did she tell you that?'

Gamache was silent, staring at the other man.

'Of course she did. Where else would you have heard it? I remember now. You two are friends. Is that why you're here? To threaten me?'

'Am I being threatening? I think you might find it difficult to convince anyone of that.' Gamache tilted his beer glass toward the still astonished gallery owner.

'There are other ways of threatening besides putting a gun in my face,' snapped Fortin.

'Quite so. My point earlier. There're different forms of violence. Different ways to kill while keeping the body alive. But I'm not here to threaten you.'

Was he really so easily threatened? Gamache wondered. Was Fortin himself so vulnerable that a simple conversation with a police officer would feel like an attack? Perhaps Fortin really was more like the artists he represented than he believed. And perhaps he lived in more fear than he admitted.

'I'm almost finished and then I'll leave you to what's left of your Sunday,' said Gamache, his voice pleasant. 'Why, if you'd decided Clara Morrow's art wasn't worth your while, did you go to her *vernissage*?'

Fortin took a deep, deep breath, held it for a moment while staring at Gamache, then let it out in a long beer-infused exhale.

'I went because I wanted to apologize to her.'

Now it was Gamache's turn to be surprised. Fortin didn't seem the sort to admit fault easily.

Fortin took another deep breath. This was clearly taking a toll.

'When I was in Three Pines last summer to discuss the show, Clara and I had drinks at that bistro and a large man served us. Anyway, I said something stupid about him when he'd left. Clara later called me on it and I'm afraid I was so annoyed at her doing that I lashed out. Canceled her show. It was a stupid thing to do and I almost immediately regretted it. But by then it was too late. I'd already announced it and I couldn't go back.'

Armand Gamache stared at Denis Fortin, trying to decide if he believed him. But there was an easy way to confirm his story. Just ask Clara.

'So you went to the opening to apologize to Clara? Why bother?'

Now Fortin colored slightly and looked to his right, out the window, into the early evening light. Outside, people would be gathering on the *terrasses* up and down St-Denis for beers and martinis, for wine and pitchers of sangria. Enjoying one of the first really warm, sunny days of spring.

Inside the quiet gallery, though, the atmosphere was neither warm nor sunny.

'I knew she was going to be big. I'd offered her a solo show because her art is like no other out there. Have you seen it?'

Fortin leaned forward, toward Gamache. No longer wrapped up in his own anxiety, no longer defensive. Now he was almost giddy. Excited. Energized talking about great works of art.

Here, Gamache realized, was a man who truly loved art. He might be a businessman, might be opportunistic. Might be a ranting egoist.

But he knew and loved great art. Clara's art.

Lillian Dyson's art?

'I have,' said the Chief Inspector. 'And I agree. She's remarkable.'

Fortin launched into a passionate dissection of Clara's portraits. The nuances, right down to the use of tiny strokes within longer, languid strokes of her brush. It was fascinating for Gamache to hear. And he found himself enjoying this time with Fortin, despite himself.

But he hadn't come to discuss Clara's painting.

'As I remember, you called Gabri a "fucking queer".'

The words had the desired effect. They weren't simply shocking, they were disgusting, disgraceful. Especially in light of what Fortin was just describing. The light and grace and hope Clara had created.

'I did,' Fortin admitted. 'It's something I say often. Said often. I don't anymore.'

'Why would you say it at all?'

'It's what you were saying earlier, about different ways to kill. A lot of my artists are gay. When I'm with a new artist I know is gay, I'd often point someone out and say what you just said. It throws them off. Keeps them afraid, off balance. It's a mind-fuck. And if they don't fight back I know I have them.'

'And do they?'

'Fight back? Clara was the first. That should've also told me she was something special. An artist with a voice, a vision and a backbone. But that backbone can be inconvenient. Much rather have them compliant.'

'So you fired her, and tried to smear her reputation.'

'Didn't work,' he smiled ruefully. 'The Musée scooped her up. I went there to apologize. I knew that pretty soon she'd be the one with all the power, all the influence.'

'Enlightened self-interest on your part?' Gamache asked.

'Better than none at all,' said Fortin.

'What happened when you arrived?'

'I got there early and the first person I saw was that guy, the one I insulted.'

'Gabri.'

'Right. I realized I owed him as well. So I apologized to him first. It was quite a festival of contrition.'

Gamache smiled again. Fortin, finally, seemed sincere. And he could always check out the story. Indeed, it was so easy to check Gamache suspected it was the truth. Denis Fortin had gone to the *vernissage*, uninvited, to apologize.

'And then you approached Clara. What did she say?'

'Actually, she approached me. I guess she heard me saying sorry to Gabri. We got to talking and I said how sorry I was. And congratulated her on a fabulous show. I told her I wished it was at the Galerie Fortin, but that she was much better off at the Musée. She was very nice about it.'

Gamache could hear the relief, and even surprise, in Fortin's voice.

'She invited me down to the party that night in Three Pines. I actually had dinner plans but felt I couldn't really say no. So I ducked out to cancel the plans with my friends and went to the barbecue instead.'

'How long did you stay?'

'Honestly? Not long. It's a long drive down and back. I spoke to a few colleagues, fended off a few mediocre artists—'

Gamache wondered if those included Normand and Paulette and suspected it did.

'—chatted with Clara and Peter so they'd know I was there. Then I left.'

'Did you speak to André Castonguay or François Marois?'

'I spoke to both of them. Castonguay's gallery's just down the road if you're looking for him.'

'I've already talked to him. He's still in Three Pines, as is Monsieur Marois.'

'Is that right?' said Fortin. 'I wonder why.'

Gamache felt in his pocket and brought out the coin. Holding the Baggie up between them he asked, 'Have you ever seen one of these before?'

'A silver dollar?'

'Look more closely, please.'

'May I?' Fortin gestured toward it and Gamache handed it to him. 'It's light.' Fortin looked at one side then the other before handing it back. 'I'm sorry, I have no idea what it is.'

He looked closely at the Chief Inspector.

'I've been patient, I think,' said Fortin. 'But perhaps now you'll tell me what this's about.'

'Do you know a woman named Lillian Dyson?'

Fortin thought, then shook his head. 'Should I? Is she an artist?'

'I have a picture of her, would you mind looking?'

'Not at all.' Fortin reached for it, fixing Gamache with a perplexed glance, then looked down at the photograph. His brows drew together.

'She looks . . .'

Gamache didn't finish Fortin's sentence. Was he going to say 'familiar'? 'Dead'?

'Asleep. Is she?'

'Do you know her?'

'I think I might have seen her at a few *vernissages*, but I see so many people.'

'Did you see her at Clara's show?'

Fortin thought then shook his head. 'She wasn't at the *vernissage* while I was there. But it was early and there weren't many people yet.'

'And the barbecue?'

'It was dark by the time I arrived so she might have been there and I just didn't notice.'

'She was definitely there,' said Gamache, replacing the coin. 'She was killed there.'

Fortin gaped at him. 'Someone was killed at the party? Where? How?'

'Have you ever seen her art, Monsieur Fortin?'

'That woman's?' Fortin asked, nodding toward the photo, now on the table between them. 'Never. I've never seen her and I've never seen her art, not as far as I know, anyway.'

Then another question struck Gamache.

'Suppose she's a great artist. Would she be worth more to a gallery dead or alive?'

'That's a grisly question, Chief Inspector.' But Fortin considered it. 'Alive she would produce more art for the gallery to sell, and presumably for more and more money. But dead?'

'*Oui?*'

'If she was that good? The fewer paintings the better. A bidding war would ignite and the prices ...'

Fortin looked to the ceiling.

Gamache had his answer. But was it the right question?

TWELVE

～

'What's this?'

Clara stood beside the phone in the kitchen. The barbecue was on and Peter was outside poking steaks from the Bresee farm.

'What?' he called through the screen door.

'This.'

Clara walked outside and held up a piece of paper. Peter's face fell.

'Oh, shit. Oh, my God, Clara, I completely forgot. In all the chaos of finding Lillian and all the interruptions—' He waved the prongs, then stopped.

Clara's face, rather than softening as it had so often, had hardened. And in her hand she held his scribbled list of messages, of congratulations. He'd left it by the phone. Under the phone. Pinned there, for safe keeping. He'd been meaning to show it to her.

It had just slipped his mind.

From where she stood Clara could see the police tape, outlining a ragged circle in her garden. A hole. Where a life had ended.

But another hole now opened up, right where Peter stood. And she could almost see the yellow tape around him, encircling him. Swallowing him, as it had Lillian.

Peter stared at her, his eyes imploring her to understand. Begging her.

And then, as Clara watched, Peter seemed to disappear, leaving just an empty space where her husband had been.

Armand Gamache sat in his study at home, taking notes and speaking with Isabelle Lacoste.

'I've spoken to Inspector Beauvoir about this, and he suggested I call you as well, Chief. Most of the guests have been interviewed,' she said, down the phone line from Three Pines. 'We're getting a picture of the evening, but what isn't in the picture is Lillian Dyson. We asked everyone, including the waiters. No one saw her.'

Gamache nodded. He'd been following her written reports all day. They were impressive as always. Clear, thorough. Intuitive. Agent Lacoste wasn't afraid to follow her instinct. She wasn't afraid to be wrong.

And that, the Chief knew, was a great strength.

It meant she'd be willing to explore dim alleys a lesser agent wouldn't even see. Or, if they did, they'd dismiss as unlikely. A waste of time.

Where, he asked his agents, was a murderer likely to hide? Where it was obvious? Perhaps. But most of the time they were found in unexpected places. Inside unexpected personalities and bodies.

Down the dim alleys, most of them with pleasant veneers.

'What do you think it means that no one saw her at the party?' he asked.

Agent Lacoste was quiet for a moment. 'Well, I wondered if she could've been killed somewhere else and her body brought into the Morrow garden. That would explain why no one saw her at either party.'

'And?'

'I spoke with the forensics team and that seems unlikely. They believe she died where she was found.'

'What are the other options?'

'Besides the obvious? That she was teleported there by aliens?'

'Besides that one.'

'I think she arrived and went directly to the Morrows' garden.'

'Why?'

Now Isabelle Lacoste paused, walking slowly through the possibilities. Not being afraid to make a mistake, but not rushing to make one either.

'Why drive an hour and a half to a party then ignore it and make straight for a quiet garden?' she asked, musing out loud.

Gamache waited. He could smell the dinner Reine-Marie had prepared. A favorite pasta dish of fresh asparagus, pine nuts and goat cheese on fettuccini. It was almost ready.

'She was in the garden to meet someone,' said Lacoste at last.

'I wonder,' said Gamache. He had his reading glasses on and was making notes. They'd already been through the facts, all the forensic findings, the preliminary autopsy results, the witness interviews. Now they were on to interpretation.

Entering the dim alley.

This was where a murderer was found. Or lost.

His daughter Annie appeared at the door with a plate in her hand. *Here?* she mouthed.

He shook his head and smiled, putting up his hand to indicate just a minute more and he'd join Annie and her mother. When she left he turned his attention back to Agent Lacoste.

'And what did Inspector Beauvoir say?' asked Gamache.

'He asked similar questions. He wanted to know who I thought Lillian Dyson might be meeting.'

'That's a good question. And what did you tell him?'

'I think she was meeting her killer,' said Isabelle Lacoste.

'Yes, but was it the person she expected to meet?' asked Gamache. 'Or did she think she was meeting one person but someone else showed up?'

'You think she was lured there?'

'I think it's a possibility,' said Gamache.

'So does Inspector Beauvoir. Lillian Dyson was ambitious. She'd just returned to Montréal and needed to jump-start her career. She knew Clara's party would be packed with gallery owners and dealers. Where better to network? Inspector Beauvoir thinks she was tricked into going to the garden, by someone pretending to be a prominent gallery owner. Then murdered.'

Gamache smiled. Jean Guy was taking his role as mentor seriously. And doing a good job.

'And what do you think?' he asked.

'I think she would have to have a very good reason to show up at Clara Morrow's party. By all accounts they hated each other. So what could lure Lillian Dyson there? What could overcome that sort of rancor?'

'It would have to be something she wanted very badly,' said Gamache. 'And what would that be?'

'To meet a prominent gallery owner. Impress him with her art,' said Lacoste without hesitation.

'I wonder,' said the Chief, leaning over his desk and scanning the reports. 'But how'd she find her way down to Three Pines?'

'Someone must have invited her to the party, perhaps lured her there with the promise of a private meeting with one of the big dealers,' said Lacoste, following the Chief's train of thought.

'He'd have had to show her the way there,' Gamache remembered the useless maps on Lillian's front seat, 'then he killed her in Clara's garden.'

'But why?' Now it was Agent Lacoste's turn to ask. 'Did the murderer know it was Clara's garden, or would any place do? Could it just as easily have been Ruth's or Myrna's place?'

Gamache took a deep breath. 'I don't know. Why set up a *rendez-vous* at a party at all? If he was planning murder wouldn't he choose someplace more private? And convenient? Why Three Pines and not Montréal?'

'Maybe Three Pines was convenient, Chief.'

'Maybe,' he agreed. It was something he'd been considering. The murder happened there because the murderer was there. Lived there.

'Besides,' said Lacoste, 'the killer must've known there'd be plenty of suspects. The party was filled with people who knew Lillian Dyson from years ago, and hated her. And it'd be easy to melt back into the crowd.'

'But why the Morrows' garden?' the Chief Inspector pressed. 'Why not in the woods, or anywhere else? Was Clara's garden chosen on purpose?'

No, thought Gamache, getting up from his chair, there was still too much hidden. The alley was still too dim. He liked tossing around ideas, theories, speculation. But he was careful not to run too far ahead of the facts. They were stumbling around now, in danger of getting themselves lost.

'Any progress on the motive?' he asked.

'Between Inspector Beauvoir in Montréal and me here we've interviewed just about everyone at the party and they all agree. Hardly anyone had any contact with Lillian since she'd been back, but anyone who knew her years ago, when she was a critic, hated and feared her.'

'So the motive was revenge?' asked Gamache.

'Either that or to stop her from doing even more damage now that she was back.'

'Good.' He paused for a moment, thinking. 'There's another possibility, though.'

He told her about his interview with Denis Fortin and the gallery owner's certainty that a brilliant dead artist was more valuable than a brilliant living one.

Chief Inspector Gamache had no doubt that Lillian Dyson was both a loathsome person and a brilliant artist.

A brilliant dead artist. So much more sellable. And manageable. Her paintings could now make someone very rich indeed.

He said good night to Agent Lacoste, made a couple more notes, then joined Reine-Marie and Annie in the dining room. They had a quiet dinner of pasta and fresh baguette. He offered them wine but decided not to have a glass himself.

'Keeping a clear head?' Reine-Marie asked.

'Actually, I plan to go to an AA meeting tonight. Thought I shouldn't have alcohol on my breath.'

His wife laughed. 'Though you might not be the only one. You've finally admitted you have a problem?'

'Oh, I have a problem, just not with alcohol.' He smiled at them. Then looked more closely at his daughter, Annie. 'You've been quiet. Is something wrong?'

'I need to speak to the two of you.'

THIRTEEN

⌒

Chief Inspector Gamache stood on rue Sherbrooke, in downtown Montréal, and stared at the heavy, red brick church across the street. It wasn't made with bricks so much as huge, rectangular ox blood stones. He'd passed it hundreds of times while driving and never really looked at it.

But now he did.

It was dark and ugly and uninviting. It didn't shout salvation. Didn't even whisper it. What it did shout was penance and atonement. Guilt and punishment.

It looked like a prison for sinners. Few would enter with an easy step and light heart.

But now another memory stirred. Of the church bright, not quite in flames, but glowing. And the street he was on a river, and the people reeds.

This was the church on Lillian Dyson's easel. Unfinished, but already a work of genius. If he'd had any doubts, seeing the real thing vanquished them. She'd taken a building, a scene, most would find foreboding and made it into something dynamic and alive. And deeply attractive.

As Gamache watched, the cars became a stream of vehicles. And the people entering the church were reeds. Floating in. Drawn in.

As was he.

*

'Hi, welcome to the meeting.'

Chief Inspector Gamache hadn't even entered the church but he'd already found himself in a gauntlet of greetings. People on either side of him had their hands out, smiling. He tried not to think they were smiling maniacally, but one or two of them definitely were.

'Hi, welcome to the meeting,' a young woman said, and led him through the door and down the stairs into the dingy, ill-lit basement. It smelt stale, of old cigarettes and bad coffee, of sour milk and sweat.

The ceiling was low and everything looked like it had a film of dirt on it. Including most of the people.

'Thank you,' he said, shaking the hand she offered.

'Your first time here?' she asked, examining him closely.

'It is. I'm not sure I'm in the right place.'

'I felt like that too, at first. But give it a chance. Why don't I introduce you to someone. Bob!' she bellowed.

An older man with an uneven beard and mismatched clothes came over. He was stirring his coffee with his finger.

'I'll leave you with him,' said his young escort. 'Men should stick with men.'

Leaving the Chief Inspector to wonder further just what he might be getting into.

'Hi. My name's Bob.'

'Armand.'

They shook hands. Bob's seemed sticky. Bob seemed sticky.

'So, you're new?' asked Bob.

Gamache bent down and whispered, 'Is this Alcoholics Anonymous?'

Bob laughed. His breath smelled of coffee and tobacco. Gamache straightened up.

'It sure is. You're in the right place.'

'I'm not actually an alcoholic.'

Bob looked at him with amusement. 'Of course you aren't. Why don't we get a coffee and we can talk. The meeting'll start in a few minutes.'

Bob got Gamache a coffee. Half full.

'In case,' said Bob.

'Of what?'

'The DTs.' Bob cast a critical eye over Gamache and noticed the slight tremor in the hand holding the mug of coffee. 'I had 'em. No fun. When was your last drink?'

'This afternoon. I had a beer.'

'Just one?'

'I'm not an alcoholic.'

Again Bob smiled. His teeth, the few he had left, were stained. 'That means you're a few hours sober. Well done.'

Gamache found he was quite pleased with himself and was glad he hadn't had that glass of wine over dinner.

'Hey, Jim,' Bob shouted across the room to a gray-haired man with very blue eyes. 'Got another newcomer.'

Gamache looked over and saw Jim talking earnestly to a young man who seemed resistant.

It was Beauvoir.

Chief Inspector Gamache smiled and caught Beauvoir's eye. Jean Guy stood up but Jim made him sit back down.

'Come over here,' said Bob, leading Gamache to a long table filled with books and pamphlets, and coins. Gamache picked one up.

'A beginner's chip,' said the Chief, examining it. It was exactly the same as the one found in Clara's garden.

'I thought you said you weren't an alcoholic.'

'I'm not,' said Gamache.

'Then that was a pretty good guess on your part,' said Bob with a guffaw.

'Do many people have one of these?' Gamache asked.

'Sure.'

Bob produced a shiny coin from his pocket, and looked down at it, his face softening. 'Took this at my first meeting. I keep it with me always. It's like a medal, Armand.'

Then he reached out to Gamache's hand and folded it in.

'No, sir,' protested Gamache. 'I really can't.'

'But you must, Armand. I give it to you, and you can give it to someone else one day. Someone who needs it. Please.'

Bob closed Gamache's fingers over the coin. Before Gamache could say anything else, Bob broke away and turned back to the long table.

'You'll also need this.' He held up a thick blue book.

'I already have one.' Gamache opened his satchel and showed him the book in there.

Bob raised his brow. 'You can use one of these, I think.' He gave Gamache a pamphlet called *Living in Denial*.

Gamache brought out the meeting list he found in Lillian's home and got the look from his new friend he'd so quickly come to expect. Amusement.

'Still claim not to be an alcoholic? Not many sober people carry around the AA book, a beginner's chip and a meeting list.' Bob examined the meeting list. 'I see you've marked a bunch of meetings. Including some women's meetings. Honestly, Armand.'

'This doesn't belong to me.'

'I see. Does it belong to a friend?' Bob asked with infinite patience.

Gamache almost smiled. 'Not really. The young woman who introduced us said that men should stick with men. What did she mean?'

'Clearly, you need to be told.' Bob waved the meeting list in front of Gamache. 'This isn't a pick-up joint. Some guys hit on women. Some women want to find a boyfriend. Think that'll save 'em. It won't. In fact, just the opposite. Getting sober's hard enough without that distraction. So men speak mostly to men. Women to women. That way we can concentrate on what's important.'

Bob fixed Gamache with a hard stare. A penetrating look. 'We're friendly, Armand, but we're serious. Our lives are at stake. Your life is at stake. Alcohol'll kill us, if we let it. But I have to tell you, if an old drunk like me can get sober, so can you. If you'd like help, that's what I'm here for.'

And Armand Gamache believed him. This sticky, disheveled little man would save his life, if he could.

'*Merci*,' said Gamache, and meant it.

Behind him a gavel hit wood with several sharp raps. Gamache turned and saw a distinguished older man sitting at the front of the room at a long table, an older woman beside him.

'Meeting's started,' whispered Bob.

Gamache turned back and saw Beauvoir trying to catch his eye, waving him to an empty seat beside him. Vacated, presumably, by Jim, who was now sitting across the room with someone else. Perhaps he'd given up on Beauvoir as a hopeless case, thought Gamache, smiling and making his way past others to take the empty seat.

Bob had stuck with him and was now sitting on Gamache's other side.

'How the mighty have fallen,' Gamache leaned over and whispered to Beauvoir. 'Last night you were the art critic for *Le Monde* and now you're a drunk.'

'I'm in good company,' said Beauvoir. 'I see you've made a friend.'

Beauvoir and Bob smiled and nodded to each other across Gamache.

'I need to speak to you, sir,' whispered Beauvoir.

'After the meeting,' said Gamache.

'We have to stay?' asked Jean Guy, crestfallen.

'You don't have to,' said Gamache. 'But I'm going to.'

'I'll stay,' said Beauvoir.

Chief Inspector Gamache nodded, and handed the beginner's chip over to Beauvoir, who examined it and raised his brow.

Gamache felt a slight pressure on his right arm and looked over to see Bob squeezing it and smiling. 'I'm glad you're staying,' he whispered. 'And you even convinced that young man to stay. And you gave him your chip. That's the spirit. We'll get you sober yet.'

'How very kind,' said Gamache.

The president of Alcoholics Anonymous welcomed everyone and asked for a moment of silence, to be followed by the Serenity Prayer.

'God,' they said in unison. 'Grant me the serenity—'

'It's the same prayer,' said Beauvoir under his breath. 'The one on the coin.'

'It is,' agreed Gamache.

'What is this? A cult?'

'Praying doesn't make something a cult,' whispered the Chief.

'Did you get a load of all the smiling and shaking hands? What was that? You can't tell me these people aren't into mind-control.'

'Happiness isn't a cult either,' whispered Gamache, but Beauvoir looked like he didn't believe it. The Inspector looked around suspiciously.

The room was packed. Filled with men and women of all ages. Some, at the back, shouted out every now and then. Some arguments erupted and were quickly brought under control. The rest smiled as they listened to the president.

They looked, to Beauvoir, demented.

Who could possibly be happy sitting in a disgusting church basement on a Sunday night? Unless they were drunk, stoned, or demented.

'Does he look familiar to you?' Beauvoir indicated the president of AA, one of the few who looked sane.

The Chief had just been wondering the same thing. The man was clean-shaven, handsome. He looked to be in his early sixties. His gray hair was trim, his glasses were both classic and stylish, and he wore a light sweater that looked cashmere.

Casual but expensive.

'A doctor, do you think?' Beauvoir asked.

Gamache considered. Maybe a doctor. More likely a therapist. An addictions counselor who was responsible for this gathering of alcoholics. The Chief wanted to have a word with him when the meeting was over.

The president had just introduced his secretary, who was reading endless announcements, most of which were out-of-date, and trying to find papers she seemed to have lost.

'God,' whispered Beauvoir. 'No wonder people drink. This's about as much fun as drowning.'

'Shhh,' said Bob, and gave Gamache a warning look.

The president introduced the speaker for that evening, mentioning something about 'sponsor'. Beside him Beauvoir groaned and looked at his watch. He seemed fidgety.

A young man slouched to the front of the room. His head was shaved and there were tattoos around his skull. One was a hand with the finger up. 'Fuck You' was tattooed across his forehead.

His entire face was pierced. Nose, brows, lips, tongue, ears. The Chief didn't know if it was fashion or self-mutilation.

He glanced at Bob, who was sitting placidly beside him as though his grandfather had just walked to the front of the room.

Absolutely no alarm.

Perhaps, thought Gamache, he had wet-brain. Gone soft in the head by too much drinking and had lost all judgment. All ability to recognize danger. Because if anyone screamed warning, this young man at the front did.

The Chief looked at the president, sitting at the head table, keenly watching the young man. He at least seemed alert. Taking everything in.

And he would, thought Gamache, if he was sponsoring this boy who looked capable of doing anything.

'My name's Brian and I'm an alcoholic and addict.'

'Hi, Brian,' they all said. Except Gamache and Beauvoir.

Brian spoke for thirty minutes. He told them about growing up in Griffintown, below the tracks in Montréal. Born to a crack-addicted mother and a meth-addicted grandmother. No father. The gang became his father, his brothers, his teachers.

His talk was littered with swear words.

He told them about robbing pharmacies, about robbing homes, about even breaking into his own home one night. And robbing it.

The room erupted into laughter. Indeed, people laughed all the way through. When Brian told them about being in the psych ward and having his doctor ask how much he drank, and he told him a beer a day, the place went hysterical with laughter.

Gamache and Beauvoir exchanged looks. Even the president was amused.

Brian had been given shock treatment, had slept on park benches, had woken up one day and found himself in Denver. He still couldn't explain that one.

More hilarity.

Brian had run a child down with a stolen car.

And fled the scene.

Brian had been fourteen. The child had died. As did the laughter.

'And even then I didn't stop drinking and using,' admitted Brian. 'It was the kid's fault. The mother's fault. But it wasn't my fault.'

There was silence in the room.

'But finally there weren't enough fucking drugs in the world to make me forget what I'd done,' he said.

There was complete silence now.

Brian looked at the president, who held the young man's stare, then nodded slightly.

'Do you know what finally brought me to my knees?' Brian asked the gathering.

No one answered.

'I wish I could say it was guilt, or a conscience, but it wasn't. It was loneliness.'

Beside Gamache, Bob nodded. People in front nodded, slowly. As though bowing their heads under a great weight. And lifting them again.

'I was so fucking lonely. All of my life.'

He lowered his head, showing a huge black swastika tattooed there.

Then he lifted it again and looked at all of them. Looked straight at Gamache, before his gaze moved on.

They were sad eyes. But there was something else there. A gleam. Of madness? Gamache wondered.

'But no more,' said Brian. 'All my life I looked for a family. Who'd have thought it'd be you fuckers?'

The place burst into uproarious laughter. With the exception of Gamache and Beauvoir. Then Brian stopped laughing, and he looked out at the crowd.

'This is where I belong.' He spoke quietly. 'In a shit-hole church basement. With you.'

He bowed slightly, awkwardly, and for a moment he looked like the boy he really was, or could have been. Young, barely twenty. Shy, handsome. Even with the scarring of tattoos and piercing and lone-liness.

There was applause. Finally the president stood and picked up a coin from his desk. Holding it up, he spoke.

'This is a beginner's chip. It has a camel on one side because if a camel can go twenty-four hours without a drink, so can you. We can show you how to stop drinking, one day at a time. Are there any newcomers here who'd like to take one?'

He held it up, as though it was a host, a magic wafer.

And he looked directly at Armand Gamache.

In that instant Gamache knew exactly who the man running the meeting was, and why he looked so familiar. This man wasn't a ther-apist or a doctor. He was Chief Justice Thierry Pineault, of the Québec Supreme Court.

And Mr Justice Pineault had obviously recognized him.

Eventually Mr Justice Pineault put the coin down and the meet-ing was over.

'Would you like to go for coffee?' Bob asked. 'A few of us go to Tim Hortons after the meeting. You're welcome to join us.'

'I might see you there,' said Gamache. 'Thank you. I just need to speak with him.' Gamache indicated the president and they shook hands good-bye.

The president looked up from his papers as they arrived at the long desk.

'Armand.' He stood and met Gamache's eyes. 'Welcome.'

'*Merci, Monsieur le Justice.*'

The Chief Justice smiled and leaned forward. 'This is anonymous, Armand. You might have heard.'

'Including you? But you run the meeting for the alcoholics. They must know who you are.'

Now Mr Justice Pineault laughed and came around from behind the desk. 'My name is Thierry, and I'm an alcoholic.'

Gamache raised his brow. 'I thought—'

'That I was in charge? The sober guy leading the drunks?'

'Well, the one responsible for the meeting,' said Gamache.

'We're all responsible,' said Thierry.

The Chief Inspector glanced over to a man arguing with his chair.

'To varying degrees,' admitted Thierry. 'We take turns running the meetings. A few people here know what I do for a living, but most know me as plain old Thierry P.'

But Gamache knew the jurist and knew there was nothing 'plain old' about him.

Thierry turned his attention to Beauvoir. 'I've seen you in the courthouse too.'

'Jean Guy Beauvoir,' said Beauvoir. 'I'm an inspector in homicide.'

'Of course. I should have recognized you sooner. I just didn't expect to see you here. But then, obviously you didn't expect to see me either. What brings you here?'

He looked from Beauvoir to Gamache.

'A case,' said Gamache. 'Can we speak in private?'

'Absolutely. Come with me.'

Thierry led them through a rear door then down a series of corridors, each dingier than the last. Finally they found themselves in a back stairwell. Mr Chief Justice Pineault indicated a step as though inviting them into an opera stall, then he took one himself.

'Here?' asked Beauvoir.

'It's about as private as this place gets I'm afraid. Now, what's this about?'

'We're investigating the murder of a woman in a village in the Eastern Townships,' said Gamache, sitting on the filthy step beside the Chief Justice. 'A place called Three Pines.'

'I know it,' said Thierry. 'Wonderful bistro and bookstore.'

'That's right.' Gamache was a little taken aback. 'How do you know Three Pines?'

'We have a country place close by. In Knowlton.'

'Well, the woman who was killed lived in Montréal but was visiting the village. We found this near her body,' Gamache handed Thierry the beginner's chip, 'and this was in her apartment, along with a number of pamphlets.' He gave Thierry the meeting list. 'This meeting was circled.'

'Who was she?' asked Thierry, looking at the meeting list and coin.

'Lillian Dyson.'

Thierry looked up, into Gamache's deep brown eyes. 'Are you serious?'

'You knew her.'

Thierry P. nodded. 'I wondered why she wasn't here tonight. She normally is.'

'How long have you known her?'

'Oh, I'd have to think. A few months anyway. Not more than a year.' Thierry trained sharp eyes on Gamache. 'She was murdered, I take it.'

Gamache nodded. 'Her neck was broken.'

'Not a fall? An accident?'

'Definitely not,' said Gamache. He could see that 'plain old' Thierry P. had disappeared and the man sitting beside him on the dirty steps was the Chief Justice of Québec.

'Any suspects?'

'About two hundred. There was a party to celebrate an art show.'

Thierry nodded. 'You know, of course, that Lillian was an artist.'

'I do. How do you know?'

Gamache found himself on guard. This man, while being the Chief Justice, also knew both the victim and the tiny village where she died.

'She talked about it.'

'But I thought this was anonymous,' said Beauvoir.

Thierry smiled. 'Well, some people have bigger mouths than others. Lillian and her sponsor are both artists. I'd hear them talking over coffee. After a while you get to know each other personally. Not just in shares.'

'Shares?' Beauvoir asked. 'Share of what?'

'Sorry. That's AA speak. A share is what you heard from Brian tonight. It's a speech, but we don't like to call it that. Makes it sound too much like a performance. So we call it sharing.'

Chief Justice Pineault's clever eyes picked up Beauvoir's expression. 'You find that funny?'

'No sir,' said Beauvoir quickly. But they all knew it was a lie. He found it both funny and pathetic.

'I did too,' Thierry admitted. 'Before I joined AA. Thought words like "sharing" were laughable. A crutch for stupid people. But I was wrong. It's one of the most difficult things I've ever done. In our AA shares we need to be completely and brutally honest. It's very painful. Like what Brian did tonight.'

'Why do it if it's so painful?' asked Beauvoir.

'Because it's also freeing. No one can hurt us, if we're willing to admit our flaws, our secrets. Very powerful.'

'You tell people your secrets?' asked Gamache.

Thierry nodded. 'Not everyone. We don't take an ad out in the *Gazette*. But we tell people in AA.'

'And that gets you sober?' asked Beauvoir.

'It helps.'

'But some stuff's pretty bad,' said Beauvoir. 'The Brian fellow killed a kid. We could arrest him.'

'You could, but he's already been arrested. Turned himself in actually. Served five years. Came out about three years ago. He's faced his demons. Doesn't mean they don't pop up again.' Thierry Pineault turned to the Chief Inspector. 'As you know.' Gamache held his eyes and said nothing. 'But they have far less power, if they're in the light. That's what this is about, Inspector. Bringing all the terrible stuff up from where it's hiding.'

'Just because you can see it,' Beauvoir persisted, 'doesn't make it go away.'

'True, but until you see it you haven't a hope.'

'Had Lillian shared recently?' Gamache asked.

'Never, as far as I know.'

'So no one knew her secrets?' asked the Chief.

'Only her sponsor.'

'Like you and Brian?' asked Gamache, and Thierry nodded.

'We choose one person in AA, and that person becomes a sort of mentor, a guide. We call it a sponsor. I have one, and Lillian has one. We all have one.'

'And you tell that sponsor everything?' Gamache asked.

'Everything.'

'Who was Lillian's sponsor?'

'A woman named Suzanne.'

The two investigators waited for more. Like a last name. But Thierry simply looked at them, waiting for the next question.

'I wonder if you can be more specific?' asked Gamache. 'Suzanne in Montréal isn't very helpful.'

Thierry smiled. 'I suppose not. I can't tell you her last name, but I can do better. I'll introduce you to her.'

'*Parfait*,' said Gamache, getting up. He tried not to notice that his slacks clung slightly to the stair as he rose.

'But we need to hurry,' said Thierry, walking ahead, his strides long and rapid, almost breaking into a jog. 'She might've left by now.'

The men walked quickly back through the corridors. Then they broke into the large room where the meeting was held. But it was empty. Not just of people, but of chairs and tables and books and coffee. Everything was gone.

'Damn,' said Thierry. 'We've missed her.'

A man was putting mugs away in a cupboard and Thierry spoke with him then returned. 'He says Suzanne's at Tim Hortons.'

'Would you mind?' Gamache indicated the door and Thierry again took the lead, walking with them over to the coffee shop. As they waited for a break in traffic to dart across rue Sherbrooke Gamache asked, 'What did you think of Lillian?'

Thierry turned to examine Gamache. It was a look Gamache knew from seeing him on the bench. Judging others. And he was a good judge.

Then Thierry turned back to watch the traffic, but as he did so he spoke.

'She was very enthusiastic, always happy to help. She often volunteered to make coffee or set up the chairs and tables. It's a big job getting a meeting ready, then cleaning up after. Not everyone wants to help, but Lillian always did.'

The three men, seeing the hole between cars at the same time, ran across the four-lane street together, making it safely to the other side.

Thierry paused, turning to look at Gamache.

'It's so sad, you know. She was getting her life back together. Everyone liked her. I liked her.'

'This woman?' asked Beauvoir, taking the photo from his pocket, his amazement obvious. 'Lillian Dyson?'

Thierry looked at it and nodded. 'That's Lillian. Tragic.'

'And you say everyone liked her?' Beauvoir pressed.

'Yes,' said Thierry. 'Why?'

'Well,' said Gamache. 'Your description doesn't match what others are saying.'

'Really? What're they saying?'

'That she was cruel, manipulative, abusive even.'

Thierry didn't say anything, instead he turned and began walking down a dark side street. The next block over they could see the familiar Tim Hortons sign.

'There she is,' said Thierry as they entered the coffee shop. 'Suzanne,' he called and waved.

A woman with close-cropped black hair looked up. She was in her sixties, Gamache guessed. Wore lots of flashy jewelry, a tight shirt with a light shawl, a skirt about three inches too short on her barrel body. There were six other women, of varying ages, at the table.

'Thierry.' Suzanne jumped up and threw her arms around Thierry, as though she hadn't just seen him. Then she turned bright, inquisitive eyes on Gamache and Beauvoir. 'New blood?'

Beauvoir bristled. He didn't like this bawdy, brassy woman. Loud. And now she seemed to think he was one of them.

'I saw you at the meeting tonight. It's OK, honey,' she laughed as she saw Beauvoir's expression. 'You don't need to like us. You just need to get sober.'

'I'm not an alcoholic.' Even to his ears it sounded like the word was a dead bug or a piece of dirt he couldn't wait to get out of his mouth. But she didn't take offense.

Gamache, though, did. He gave Beauvoir a warning look and put out his hand to Suzanne.

'My name is Armand Gamache.'

'His father?' Suzanne gestured to Beauvoir.

Gamache smiled. 'Mercifully, no. We're not here about AA.'

His somber manner seemed to impress itself on her and Suzanne's smile dimmed. Her eyes, however, remained alert.

Watchful, Beauvoir realized. What he'd first taken to be the shine of an idiot was in fact something far different. This woman paid attention. Behind the laughter and bright shine, a brain was at work. Furiously.

'What is it?' she asked.

'I wonder if we could talk privately?'

Thierry left them and joined Bob and Jim and four other men across the coffee shop.

'Would you like a coffee?' Suzanne asked as they found a quiet table near the toilets.

'*Non, merci*,' said Gamache. 'Bob very kindly got me one, though it was only half full.'

Suzanne laughed. She seemed, to Beauvoir, to laugh a lot. He wondered what that hid. No one, in his experience, was ever that amused.

'The DTs?' she asked and when Gamache nodded she looked over at Bob with great affection. 'He lives at the Salvation Army, you know. Goes to seven meetings a week. He assumes everyone he meets is an alcoholic.'

'There're worse assumptions,' said Gamache.

'How can I help you?'

'I'm with the Sûreté du Québec,' said Gamache. 'Homicide.'

'You're Chief Inspector Gamache?' she asked.

'I am.'

'What can I do for you?'

Beauvoir was happy to see she was a lot less buoyant and more guarded.

'It's about Lillian Dyson.'

Suzanne's eyes opened wide and she whispered, 'Lillian?'

Gamache nodded. 'I'm afraid she was murdered last night.'

'Oh, my God.' Suzanne brought a hand to her mouth. 'Was it a robbery? Did someone break into her apartment?'

'No. It didn't seem to be random. It was at a party. She was found dead in the garden. Her neck was broken.'

Suzanne exhaled deeply and closed her eyes. 'I'm sorry. I'm just shocked. We spoke on the phone yesterday.'

'What about?'

'Oh, it was just a check in. She calls me every few days. Nothing important.'

'Did she mention the party?'

'No, she said nothing about it.'

'You must know her well, though,' said Gamache.

'I do.' Suzanne looked out the window, at the men and women walking by. Lost in their own thoughts, in their own world. But Suzanne's world had just changed. It was a world where murder existed. And Lillian Dyson did not.

'Have you ever had a mentor, Chief Inspector?'

'I have. Still do.'

'Then you know how intimate that relationship can be.' She looked at Beauvoir for a moment, her eyes softening, and she smiled a little.

'I do,' said the Chief.

'And I can see you're married.' Suzanne indicated her own barren ring finger.

'True,' said Gamache. He was watching her with thoughtful eyes.

'Imagine now those relationships combined and deepened. There's nothing on earth like what happens between a sponsor and sponsee.'

Both men stared at her.

'How so?' Gamache finally asked.

'It's intimate without being sexual, it's trusting without being a friendship. I want nothing from my sponsees. Nothing. Except honesty. All I want for them is that they get sober. I'm not their husband or wife, not their best friend or boss. They don't answer to me for anything. I just guide them, and listen.'

'And what do you get out of it?' asked Beauvoir.

'My own sobriety. One drunk helping another. We can bullshit a lot of people, Inspector, and often do. But not each other. We know each other. We're quite insane, you know,' Suzanne said with a small laugh.

This wasn't news to Beauvoir.

'Was Lillian insane when you first met her?' Gamache asked.

'Oh, yes. But only in the sense that her perception of the world was all screwy. She'd made so many bad choices she no longer knew how to make good ones.'

'I understand that as part of this relationship Lillian told you her secrets,' said the Chief.

'She did.'

'And what were Lillian Dyson's secrets?'

'I don't know.'

Gamache stared at this fireplug. 'Don't know, madame? Or won't say?'

FOURTEEN

⁓

Peter lay in bed, clutching the edge of their double mattress. The bed was too small for them, really. But a double had been all they could afford when they were first married and Peter and Clara had grown used to having each other close.

So close they touched. Even on the hottest, stickiest July nights. They'd lie naked in bed, the sheets kicked off, their bodies wet and slick from sweat. And still they'd touch. Not much. Just a hand to her back. A toe to his leg.

Contact.

But tonight he clung to his side of the bed, and she clung to hers, as though to dual cliff faces. Afraid to fall. But fearing they were about to.

They'd gone to bed early so the silence might feel natural.

It didn't.

'Clara?' he whispered.

The silence stretched on. He knew the sound of Clara sleeping, and this wasn't it. Clara asleep was almost as exuberant as Clara awake. She didn't toss and turn, but she snorted and grunted. Sometimes she'd say something ridiculous. Once she mumbled, 'But Kevin Spacey's stuck on the moon.'

She hadn't believed it when he'd told her the next morning, but he'd heard it clearly.

In fact, she didn't believe it when he told her she snorted and hummed and made all manner of noises. Not loudly. But Peter was attuned to Clara. He heard her, even when she herself couldn't.

But tonight she was silent.

'Clara?' he tried again. He knew she was there, and he knew she was awake. 'We need to talk.'

Then he heard her. A long, long inhale. And then a sigh.

'What is it?'

He sat up in bed but didn't turn the light on. He'd rather not see her face.

'I'm sorry.'

She didn't move. He could see her, a dark ridge in the bed, shoved up at the very edge of the world. She couldn't get further from him without falling out.

'You're always sorry.' Her voice was muffled. She was speaking into the bedding, not even raising her head.

What could he say to that? She was right. As he looked back down their relationship it was a series of him doing and saying something stupid and her forgiving him. Until today.

Something had changed. He'd thought the biggest threat to their marriage would be Clara's show. Her success. And his sudden failure. Made all the more spectacular by her triumph.

But he'd been wrong.

'We have to sort this out,' said Peter. 'We have to talk.'

Clara sat up suddenly, fighting with the duvet, trying to get her arms clear. Finally she did, and turned to him.

'Why? So that I can just forgive you again? Is that it? You don't think I know what you've been doing? Hoping my show would fail? Hoping the critics would decide my art sucks and you're the real artist? I know you, Peter. I could see your mind working. You've never understood my art, you've never cared about it. You think it's childish and simplistic. Portraits? How embarrassing,' she lowered her voice to mimic his.

'I never said that.'

'But you thought it.'

'I didn't.'

'Don't fucking lie to me, Peter. Not now.'

The warning in her voice was clear. And new. They'd had their fights before, but never like this.

Peter knew then their marriage was either over or soon would be. Unless he could find the right thing to say. To do.

If 'I'm sorry' didn't work, what would?

'You must've been thrilled when you saw the *Ottawa Star* review. When it called my art *an old and tired parrot mimicking actual artists*. Did that give you pleasure, Peter?'

'How can you think that?' Peter asked. But it had given him pleasure. And relief. It was the first really happy moment he'd had in a very long time. 'It's the *New York Times* review that matters, Clara. That's the one I care about.'

She stared at him. And he felt cold creeping down his fingers and toes and up his legs. As though his heart had weakened and couldn't get the blood that far anymore.

His heart was only now catching up with what the rest of him had known all his life. He was weak.

'Then quote me from the *New York Times* review.'

'Pardon?'

'Go on. If it made that big an impression, if it was that important to you, surely you can remember a single line.'

She waited.

'A word?' she asked, her voice glacial.

Peter scanned his memory, desperate for something, anything from the *New York Times*. Something to prove to himself, never mind Clara, that he'd cared in any way.

But all he remembered, all he saw, was the glorious review in the Ottawa paper.

Her art, while nice, was neither visionary nor bold.

He'd thought it was bad when her paintings were simply embarrassing. But it was worse when they were brilliant. Instead of reflected glory, it just highlighted what a failure he was. His creations dimmed as hers brightened. And so he'd read and re-read the parrot line, applying it to his ego as though it was an antiseptic. And Clara's art was the septic.

But he knew now it wasn't her art that had gone septic.

'I thought not,' snapped Clara. 'Not even a word. Well let me remind you. *Clara Morrow's paintings are not just brilliant, they are luminous. She has, in an audacious and generous stroke, redefined portraiture.* I went back and memorized it. Not because I believe it's true, but so that I have a choice of what to believe, and it doesn't always have to be the worst.'

Imagine, thought Peter, as the cold crept closer to his core, having a choice of things to believe.

'And then the messages,' said Clara.

Peter closed his eyes, slowly. A reptilian blink.

The messages. From all of Clara's supporters. From gallery owners and dealers and curators around the world. From family and friends.

He'd spent most of the morning, after Gamache and Clara and the others had left, after Lillian's body had left, answering the phone.

Ringing, ringing. Tolling. And each ring diminished him. Stripped him, it felt, of his manhood, his dignity, his self-worth. He'd written out the good wishes, and said nice things to people who ran the art world. The titans. Who knew him only as Clara's husband.

The humiliation was complete.

Eventually he'd let the answering machine take over and had hidden in his studio. Where he'd hidden all his life. From the monster.

He could feel it in their bedroom now. He could feel its tail swishing by him. Feel its hot, fetid breath.

All his life he knew if he was quiet enough, small enough, it wouldn't see him. If he didn't make a fuss, didn't speak up, it wouldn't hear him, wouldn't hurt him. If he was beyond criticism and hid his cruelty with a smile and good deeds, it wouldn't devour him.

But now he realized there was no hiding. It would always be there, and always find him.

He was the monster.

'You wanted to see me fail.'

'Never,' said Peter.

'I actually thought deep down you were happy for me. You just needed time to adjust. But this is really who you are, isn't it.'

A denial was again on Peter's lips, almost out his mouth. But it stopped. Something stopped it. Something stood between the words in his head and the words out his mouth.

He stared at her, and finally, nails ripping and bloody from a lifetime clinging on, he lost his grip.

'The portrait of the Three Graces,' the words tumbled from his mouth. 'I saw it, you know, before it was finished. I snuck into your studio and took the sheet off your easel.' He paused to try to compose himself. But it was way too late for that. Peter was plummeting. 'I saw—' He searched for the right word. But finally he realized he wasn't searching for it. He was hiding from it. 'Glory. I saw glory, Clara, and such love it broke my heart.'

He stared at the bed sheets, twisted in his hands. And sighed.

'I knew then that you were a far better artist than I could ever be. Because you don't paint things. You don't even paint people.'

He saw again Clara's portrait of the three elderly friends. The Three Graces. Émilie and Beatrice and Kaye. Their neighbors in Three Pines. How they laughed, and held each other. Old, frail, near death.

With every reason to be afraid.

And yet everyone who looked at Clara's painting felt what those women felt.

Joy.

Looking at the Graces Peter had known at that moment that he was screwed.

And he knew something else. Something people looking at

Clara's extraordinary creations might not consciously realize, but feel. In their bones, in their marrow.

Without a single crucifix, or host, or bible. Without benefit of clergy, or church. Clara's paintings radiated a subtle, private faith. In a single bright dot in an eye. In old hands holding old hands. For dear life.

Clara painted dear life.

While the rest of the cynical art world was painting the worst, Clara painted the best.

She'd been marginalized, mocked, ostracized for it for years. By the artistic establishment and, privately, by Peter.

Peter painted things. Very well. He even claimed to paint God, and some dealers believed it. Made a good story. But he'd never met God so how could he paint Him?

Clara not only met Him, she knew Him. And she painted what she knew.

'You're right. I've always envied you,' he said, looking at her directly. There was no fear now. He was beyond that. 'From the first moment I saw you I envied you. And it's never left. I tried, but it's always there. It's even grown with time. Oh, Clara. I love you and I hate myself for doing all this to you.'

She was silent. Not helping. But not hurting either. He was on his own.

'But it's not your art I've envied. I thought it was, and that's why I ignored it. Pretended to not understand. But I understood per-fectly well what you were doing in your studio. What you were struggling to capture. And I could see you getting closer and closer over the years. And it killed me. Oh, God, Clara. Why couldn't I just be happy for you?'

She was silent.

'And then, when I saw *The Three Graces* I knew you were there. And then that portrait. Ruth. Oh, God.' His shoulders slumped. 'Who else but you would paint Ruth as the Virgin Mary? So full of scorn and bitterness and disappointment.'

He opened his arms, then dropped them and exhaled.

'And then that dot. The tiny bit of white in her eyes. Eyes filled with hatred. Except for that dot. Seeing something coming.'

Peter looked at Clara, so far away across the bed.

'It's not your art I envy. It never was.'

'You're lying, Peter,' whispered Clara.

'No, no, I'm not,' said Peter, his voice rising in desperation.

'You criticized *The Three Graces*. You mocked the one of Ruth,' yelled Clara. 'You wanted me to screw them up, to destroy them.'

'Yes, but it wasn't the paintings,' Peter shouted back.

'Bullshit.'

'It wasn't. It was—'

'Well?' yelled Clara. 'Well? What was it? Let me guess. It was your mother's fault? Your father's? Was it that you had too much money or not enough? That your teachers hurt you, and your grandfather drank? What excuse are you dreaming up now?'

'No, you don't understand.'

'Of course I do, Peter. I understand you too well. As long as I was schlepping along in your shadow we were fine.'

'No.' Peter was out of bed now, backing up until he was against the wall. 'You have to believe me.'

'Not anymore I don't. You don't love me. Love doesn't do this.'

'Clara, no.'

And then the dizzying, disorienting, terrible plummet finally ended. And Peter hit the ground.

'It was your faith,' he shouted, and slumped to the floor. 'It was your beliefs. Your hope,' he choked out, his voice a croak amid gasps. 'It was far worse than your art. I wanted to be able to paint like you, but only because it would mean I'd see the world as you do. Oh, God, Clara. All I've ever envied you was your faith.'

He threw his arms around his legs and drew them violently to his chest, making himself as tiny as he could. A small globe. And he rocked himself.

Back and forth. Back and forth.

On the bed Clara stared. Silenced now not by rage, but by amazement.

Jean Guy Beauvoir picked up an armful of dirty laundry and threw it into a corner.

'There,' he smiled, 'make yourself at home.'

'*Merci*,' said Gamache, sitting down. His knees immediately and alarmingly bounced up almost around his shoulders.

'Watch out for the sofa,' Beauvoir called from the kitchen. 'I think the springs are gone.'

'That is possible,' said Gamache, trying to get comfortable. He wondered if this was what a Turkish prison felt like. While Beauvoir poured them each a drink, the Chief looked around the furnished efficiency apartment right in Montréal's downtown core.

The only personal touches seemed to be the stack of laundry now in the corner, and a stuffed animal, a lion, just visible on the unmade bed. It looked odd, infantile even. He'd not have taken Jean Guy for a man with a stuffed toy.

They'd strolled the three blocks from the coffee shop to his apartment, comparing notes in the clear, cool night air.

'Did you believe her?' Beauvoir had asked.

'When Suzanne said she couldn't remember Lillian's secrets?' Gamache considered. The trees lining the downtown street were in leaf, just turning from bright, young green to a deeper more mature color. 'Did you?'

'Not for a minute.'

'Neither did I,' said the Chief. 'But the question is, did she lie to us intentionally, to hide something, or did she just need time to gather her thoughts?'

'I think it was intentional.'

'You always do.'

That was true. Inspector Beauvoir always thought the worst. It was safer that way.

Suzanne had explained that she had a number of sponsees, that each told her everything about their lives.

'It's step five in the AA program,' she'd said, then quoted. '*Admitted to God, to ourselves, and to another human being the exact nature of our wrongs.* I'm the "other human being."'

She laughed again and made a face.

'You don't enjoy it?' Gamache asked, interpreting the grimace.

'At first I did, with my first few sponsees. I was honestly kinda curious to find out what sort of shenanigans they'd gotten up to in their drinking careers and if they were at all like mine. It was exciting to have someone trust me like that. Hadn't happened much when I was drinking, I'll tell ya. You'd have had to be nuts to trust me then. But it actually gets boring after a while. Everyone thinks their secrets are so horrible, but they're all pretty much the same.'

'Like what?' asked the Chief Inspector.

'Oh, affairs. Being a closeted gay. Stealing. Thinking horrible thoughts. Getting drunk and missing big family events. Letting down loved ones. Hurting loved ones. Sometimes it's abuse. I'm not saying what they did was right. It's clearly not. That's why we buried it for so long. But it's not unique. They're not alone. You know the toughest part of step five?'

'"Admitted to ourselves"?' asked Gamache.

Beauvoir was amazed the Chief had remembered the wording. It seemed just a big whine to him. A bunch of alcoholics feeling sorry for themselves and looking for instant forgiveness.

Beauvoir believed in forgiveness, but only after punishment.

Suzanne smiled. 'That's it. You'd think it'd be easy to admit these things to ourselves. After all, we were there when it happened. But of course, we couldn't admit what we'd done was so bad. We'd spent years justifying and denying our behavior.'

Gamache had nodded, thinking.

'Are the secrets often as bad as Brian's?'

'You mean killing a child? Sometimes.'

'Have any of your sponsees killed someone?'

'I've had some sponsees admit to killing,' she finally said. 'Never intentionally. Never murder. But some accident. Mostly drunk driving.'

'Including Lillian?' Gamache asked quietly.

'I can't remember.'

'I don't believe you.' Gamache's voice was so low it was hard to hear. Or perhaps it was the words Suzanne found so difficult to hear. 'No one listens to a confession like that and forgets.'

'Believe what you want, Chief Inspector.'

Gamache nodded and gave her his card. 'I'll be staying in Montréal tonight but we'll be back in Three Pines after that. We'll be there until we find out who killed Lillian Dyson. Call me when you've remembered.'

'Three Pines?' Suzanne asked, taking the card.

'The village where Lillian was killed.'

He rose, and Beauvoir rose with him.

'You said your lives depend on the truth,' he said. 'I'd hate for you to forget that now.'

Fifteen minutes later they were in Beauvoir's new apartment. While Jean Guy opened and closed cupboards and mumbled, Gamache hauled himself out of the torturous sofa and strolled around the living room, looking out the window to the pizza place across the way advertising the Super Slice, then he turned back into the room, looking at the gray walls and Ikea furniture. His gaze drifted over to the phone and the pad of paper.

'You're not just eating at the pizza place, then,' said Gamache.

'What d'you mean?' Beauvoir called from the kitchen.

'Restaurant Milos,' Gamache read from the pad of paper by the phone. 'Very chic.'

Beauvoir looked into the room, his eyes directly on the desk and the pad, then up to the Chief.

'I was thinking of taking you and Madame Gamache there.'

For a moment, the way the bare light in the room caught his face, Beauvoir looked like Brian. Not the defiant, swaggering young man at the beginning of his share. But the bowed boy. Humbled. Perplexed. Flawed. Human.

Guarded.

'To thank you for all your support,' said Beauvoir. 'This separation from Enid, and the other stuff. It's been a difficult few months.'

Chief Inspector Gamache looked at the younger man, astonished. Milos was one of the finest seafood restaurants in Canada. And certainly one of the most expensive. It was a favorite of his and Reine-Marie's, though they only went on very special occasions.

'*Merci*,' he said at last. 'But you know we'd be just as happy with pizza.'

Jean Guy smiled and taking the pad from the desk he slid it into a drawer. 'So no Milos. But I will spring for the Super Slice, and no arguments.'

'Madame Gamache will be pleased,' laughed Gamache.

Beauvoir walked into the kitchen and returned with their drinks. A micro-brewery beer for the Chief and water for himself.

'No beer?' asked the Chief, raising his glass.

'All this talk of booze turned me off it. Water's fine.'

They sat again, Gamache this time choosing one of the hard chairs around the small glass dining table. He took a sip.

'Does it work, do you think?' Beauvoir asked.

It took a moment for the Chief to figure out what his Inspector was talking about.

'AA?'

Beauvoir nodded. 'Seems pretty self-indulgent to me. And why would spilling their secrets stop them from drinking? Wouldn't it be better to just forget instead of dredging all that stuff up? And none of these people are trained. That Suzanne's a mess. You can't tell me she's much help to anyone.'

The Chief stared at his haggard deputy. 'I think AA works because no one, no matter how well-meaning, understands what an experience is like except someone who's been through the same thing,' Gamache said, quietly. He was careful not to lean forward, not to get into his Inspector's space. 'Like the factory. The raid. No one knows what it was like except those of us who were there. The therapists help, a lot. But it's not the same as talking to one of us.' Gamache looked at Beauvoir. Who seemed to be collapsing into himself. 'Do you often think about what happened in the factory?'

Now it was Beauvoir's turn to pause. 'Sometimes.'

'Do you want to talk about it?'

'What good would it do? I've already told the investigators, the therapists. You and I've been over it. I think it's time to stop talking about it and just get on with it, don't you?'

Gamache cocked his head to one side and examined Jean Guy. 'No, I don't. I think we need to keep talking until it's all out, until there's no unfinished business.'

'What happened in the factory's over,' snapped Beauvoir, then restrained himself. 'I'm sorry. I just think it's self-indulgent. I just want to get on with my life. The only unfinished business, the only thing still bothering me, if you really want to know, is who leaked the video of the raid. How'd it get onto the Internet?'

'The internal investigation said it was a hacker.'

'I know. I read the report. But you don't really believe it, do you?'

'I have no choice,' said Gamache. 'And neither do you.'

There was no mistaking the warning in the Chief's voice. A warning Beauvoir chose not to hear, or to heed.

'It wasn't a hacker,' he said. 'No one even knows those tapes exist except other Sûreté officers. A hacker didn't pirate that recording.'

'That's enough, Jean Guy.' They'd been down this road before. The video of the raid on the factory had been uploaded onto the Internet, where it had gone viral. Millions around the world had watched the edited video.

Seen what had happened.

To them. And to others. Millions had watched as though it was a TV show. Entertainment.

The Sûreté, after months of investigation, had concluded it was a hacker.

'Why didn't they find the guy?' Beauvoir persisted. 'We have an entire department that only investigates cyber crime. And they couldn't find an asshole who, by their own report, just got lucky?'

'Let it be, Jean Guy,' said Gamache, sternly.

'We have to find the truth, sir,' said Beauvoir, leaning forward.

'We know the truth,' said Gamache. 'What we have to do is learn to live with it.'

'You're not going to look further? You're just going to accept it?'

'I am. And so are you. Promise me, Jean Guy. This is someone else's problem. Not ours.'

The two men stared at each other for a moment until Beauvoir gave one curt nod.

'*Bon*,' said Gamache, emptying his glass and walking with it into the kitchen. 'Time to go. We need to be back in Three Pines early.'

Armand Gamache said good night and walked slowly through the night streets. It was chilly and he was glad for his coat. He'd planned to wave down a cab, but found himself walking all the way up Ste-Urbain to avenue Laurier.

And as he walked he thought about AA, and Lillian, and Suzanne. About the Chief Justice. About the artists and dealers, asleep in their beds in Three Pines.

But mostly he thought about the corrosive effect of secrets. Including his own.

He'd lied to Beauvoir. It wasn't over. And he hadn't let it go.

Jean Guy Beauvoir washed the beer glass then headed toward his bedroom.

Keep going, just keep going, he begged himself. *Just a few more steps.*

But he stopped, of course. As he'd done every night since that video had appeared.

Once on the Net it could never, ever be taken off. It was there forever. Forgotten, perhaps, but still there, waiting to be found again. To surface again.

Like a secret. Never really hidden completely. Never totally forgotten.

And this video was far from forgotten. Not yet.

Beauvoir sat heavily into the chair and brought his computer out of sleep. The link was on his favorites list, but intentionally mislabeled.

His eyes heavy with sleep and his body aching, Jean Guy clicked on it.

And up came the video.

He hit play. Then play again. And again.

Over and over he watched the video. The picture was clear, as were the sounds. The explosions, the shooting, the shouting, 'Officer down, officer down.'

And Gamache's voice, steady, commanding. Issuing clear orders, holding them together, keeping the chaos at bay as the tactical team had pressed deeper and deeper into the factory. Cornering the gunmen. So many more gunmen than they'd expected.

And over and over and over Beauvoir watched himself get shot in the abdomen. And over and over and over he watched something worse. Chief Inspector Gamache. Arms thrown out, back arching. Lifting off, then falling. Hitting the ground. Still.

And then the chaos closing in.

Finally exhausted, he pushed himself away from the screen and got ready for bed. Washing, brushing his teeth. Taking out the prescription medication he popped an OxyContin.

Then he slipped the other small bottle of pills under his pillow. In case he needed it in the night. It was safe there. Out of sight. Like a weapon. A last resort.

A bottle of Percocet.

In case the OxyContin wasn't enough.

In his bed, in the dark, he waited for the painkiller to kick in. He could feel the day slip away. The worries, the anxieties, the images receded. As he hugged his stuffed lion and drifted toward oblivion one image drifted along with him. Not of himself being shot. Not even of seeing the Chief hit, and fall.

All that had faded, gobbled up by the OxyContin.

But one thought remained. Followed him to the edge.

Restaurant Milos. The phone number, now hidden in the desk drawer. Every week for the past three months he'd called the Restaurant Milos and made a reservation. For two. For Saturday night. The table at the back, by the whitewashed wall.

And every Saturday afternoon he canceled it. He wondered if they even bothered to take down his name anymore. Maybe they just pretended. As he did.

But tomorrow, he felt certain, would be different.

He'd definitely call her then. And she'd say yes. And he'd take Annie Gamache to Milos, with its crystal and white linen. She'd have the Dover sole, he'd have the lobster.

And she'd listen to him, and look at him with those intense eyes. He'd ask her all about her day, her life, her likes, her feelings. Everything. He wanted to know everything.

Every night he drifted off to sleep with the same image. Annie looking at him across the table. And then, he'd reach out and place his hand on hers. And she'd let him.

As he sank into sleep he placed one hand over the other. That was how it would feel.

And then, the OxyContin took everything. And Jean Guy Beauvoir had no more feelings.

FIFTEEN

⁓

Clara came down to breakfast. The place smelled of coffee and toasted English muffins.

When Clara had woken up, surprised she'd even fallen asleep, the bed was empty. It had taken her a moment to remember what had happened the night before.

Their fight.

How close she'd come to getting dressed and leaving him. Taking the car, driving to Montréal. Checking into a cheap hotel.

And then?

And then, something. The rest of her life, she supposed. She hadn't cared.

But then Peter had finally told her the truth.

They'd talked into the night, and fallen asleep. Not touching, not yet. They were both too bruised for that. It was as though they'd been skinned and dissected. Deboned. Their innards brought out. Examined. And found to be rotten.

They didn't have a marriage, they had a parody of a partnership.

But they'd also found that maybe, maybe, they could put themselves together again.

It would be different. Would it be better?

Clara didn't know.

'Morning,' said Peter when she appeared, her hair sticking up on one side, a crust of sleep on her face.

'Morning,' she said.

He poured her a mug of coffee.

Once Clara had fallen asleep, and he'd heard the heavy breathing and a snort, he'd gone down to the living room. He found the newspaper. He found the glossy catalog for her show.

And he'd sat there all night. Memorizing the *New York Times* review. Memorizing the London *Times* review. So that he knew them by heart.

So that he too would have a choice of what to believe.

And then he'd stared at the reproductions of her paintings in the catalog.

They were brilliant. But then he already knew that. In the past, though, he'd looked at her portraits and seen flaws. Real or imagined. A brush stroke slightly off. The hands that could have been better. He'd deliberately concentrated on the minutiae so that he wouldn't have to see the whole.

Now he looked at the whole.

To say he was happy about it would be a lie, and Peter Morrow was determined not to lie anymore. Not to himself. Not to Clara.

The truth was, it still hurt to see such talent. But for the first time since he'd met Clara he was no longer looking for the flaws.

But there was something else he'd struggled with all night. He'd told her everything. Every stinking thing he'd done and thought. So she'd know it all. So there was nothing hidden, to surprise either of them.

Except one thing.

Lillian. And what he'd said to her at the student art show so many years ago. The number of words he could count on his fingers. But each had been a bullet. And each had hit its target. Clara.

'Thanks,' said Clara, accepting the mug of rich, strong coffee. 'Smells good.'

She too was determined not to lie, not to pretend everything was fine in the hope that fantasy might become reality. The truth was, the coffee did smell good. That at least was safe to say.

Peter sat down, screwing up his courage to tell her about what he'd done. He took a breath, closed his eyes briefly, then opened his mouth to speak.

'They're back early.' Clara nodded out the window, where she'd been staring.

Peter watched as a Volvo pulled up and parked. Chief Inspector Gamache and Jean Guy Beauvoir got out and walked toward the bistro.

He closed his mouth and stepped back, deciding now wasn't the time after all.

Clara smiled as she watched the two men out the window. It amused her that Inspector Beauvoir no longer locked their car. When they'd first come to Three Pines, to investigate Jane's murder, the officers had made sure the car was always locked. But now, several years later, they didn't bother.

They knew, she presumed, that people in Three Pines might occasionally take a life, but not a car.

Clara looked at the kitchen clock. Almost eight. 'They must've left Montréal just after six.'

'Uh-huh,' said Peter, watching Gamache and Beauvoir disappear into the bistro. Then he looked down at Clara's hands. One held the mug, but the other rested on the old pine table, a loose fist.

Did he dare?

He reached out and very slowly, so as not to surprise or frighten her, he placed his large hand on hers. Cupping her fist in his palm. Making it safe there, in the little home his hand created.

And she let him.

It was enough, he told himself.

No need to tell her the rest. No need to upset her.

'I'll have,' said Beauvoir slowly, staring at the menu. He had no appetite, but he knew he had to order something. There were blueberry pancakes, crêpes, eggs Benedict, bacon and sausages and fresh, warm croissants on the menu.

He'd been up since five. Had picked up the Chief at quarter to six. And now it was almost seven thirty. He waited for his hunger to kick in.

Chief Inspector Gamache lowered the menu and looked at the waiter. 'While he's trying to decide, I'll have a bowl of *café au lait* and some blueberry pancakes with sausages.'

'*Merci*,' said the waiter, taking Gamache's menu and looking at Beauvoir. 'And you, monsieur?'

'It all looks so good,' said Beauvoir. 'I'll have the same thing as the Chief Inspector, thank you.'

'I thought for sure you'd have the eggs Benedict,' smiled Gamache, as the waiter left them. 'I thought it was your favorite.'

'I made it for myself just yesterday,' said Beauvoir, and Gamache laughed. They both knew it was more likely he'd had a Super Slice for breakfast. In fact, just lately, Beauvoir had had just coffee and perhaps a bagel.

Through the window they could see Three Pines in the early morning sun. Not many were out yet. A few villagers walked dogs. A few sat on porches, sipping coffee and reading the morning paper. But most still slept.

'How's Agent Lacoste doing, do you think?' the Chief Inspector asked once their *cafés* had arrived.

'Not bad. Did you speak with her last night? I asked her to run a few things by you.'

The two men sipped their coffees and compared notes.

Beauvoir looked at his watch as their breakfast arrived. 'I asked her to meet us here at eight.' It was ten to, and he looked up to see Lacoste walking across the village green, a dossier in her hand.

'I like being a mentor,' said Beauvoir.

'You do it well,' said Gamache. 'Of course, you had a good teacher. Benevolent, just. Yet firm.'

Beauvoir looked at the Chief Inspector with exaggerated

puzzlement. 'You? You mean you've been mentoring me all these years? That sure explains the need for therapy.'

Gamache looked down at his meal, and smiled.

Agent Lacoste joined them and ordered a cappuccino. 'And a croissant, *s'il vous plaît*,' she called after the waiter. Then she placed her dossier on the table. 'I read your report of the meeting last night, Chief, and did some digging.'

'Already?' asked Beauvoir.

'Well, I got up early and frankly I didn't want to hang around the B and B with those artists.'

'Why not?' asked Gamache.

'I'm afraid I found them boring. I had dinner with Normand and Paulette last night, to see if I could get anything else out of them about Lillian Dyson but they seem to have lost interest.'

'What did you talk about?' asked Beauvoir.

'They spent most of dinner laughing about the *Ottawa Star* review of Clara's show. They said it would put paid to her career.'

'But who cares what the *Ottawa Star* thinks?' asked Beauvoir.

'Ten years ago nobody, but now with the Internet it can be read around the world,' said Lacoste. 'Insignificant opinions suddenly become significant. As Normand said, people only remember the bad reviews.'

'I wonder if that's true,' said Gamache.

'Have you gotten anywhere tracing that review Lillian Dyson did?' asked Beauvoir.

'*He's a natural, producing art like it's a bodily function?*' Lacoste quoted, and wished it had been written about Normand or Paulette. Though, she thought for the first time, maybe it had. Maybe the 'he' in the review was Normand. That might explain his bitterness, and his delight when someone else got a bad review.

Isabelle Lacoste shook her head. 'No luck tracing that review. It was so long ago now, more than twenty years. I've sent an agent along to the archives at *La Presse*. We'll have to go through the microfiche one at a time.'

'*Bon.*' Inspector Beauvoir nodded his approval.

Lacoste tore her warm and flaky croissant in half. 'I looked into Lillian Dyson's sponsor, as you asked, Chief,' she said, then took a bite of her croissant before putting it down and picking up the dossier. 'Suzanne Coates, age sixty-two. She's a waitress over at Nick's on Greene Avenue. Do you know it?'

Beauvoir shook his head, but Gamache nodded. 'A Westmount institution.'

'As is Suzanne, apparently. I called this morning before coming here. Spoke to one of the other waitresses. A Lorraine. She confirmed that Suzanne had worked there for twenty years. But she got a little cagey when I asked what her hours were. Finally this Lorraine admitted they all cover for each other when they pick up extra cash working private parties. Suzanne's supposed to be on the lunch shift, but wasn't in Saturday. She worked yesterday, though, as usual. Her shift starts at eleven.'

'By "working private parties", that doesn't mean—?' asked Beauvoir.

'Prostitution?' asked Lacoste. 'The woman's sixty-two. Though she was in the profession years ago. Two arrests for prostitution and one for break and enter. This was back in the early eighties. She was also charged with theft.'

Both Gamache and Beauvoir raised their brows. Still, it was a long time ago and a long way from those crimes to murder.

'I also found her tax information. Her declared income last year was twenty-three thousand dollars. But she's heavily in debt. Credit card. She has three of them, all maxed out. She seems to consider it not so much a credit limit as a goal. Like most people in debt she's juggling creditors, but it's all about to come crashing down.'

'Does she realize it?' Gamache asked.

'Hard not to, unless she's completely delusional.'

'You haven't met her,' said Beauvoir. 'Delusional is one of her better qualities.'

*

André Castonguay could smell the coffee.

He lay in bed, on the comfortable mattress, under the 600-thread-count sheets and goose down duvet. And he wished he was dead.

He felt like he'd been dropped from a great height. And somehow survived, but was bruised and flattened. Reaching out a shaky hand for the glass of water he gulped down what was left. That felt better.

Slowly he sat up, letting himself adjust to each new position. Finally he stood and pulled the bathrobe around his soft body. Never again, he said as he trudged to the bathroom and stared at his reflection. Never again.

But he'd said that yesterday. And the day before. And the day before that.

The Sûreté team spent the morning in the Incident Room, set up in the Canadian National Railway station. The low brick building, a century old, sat across the Rivière Bella Bella from Three Pines. The building was abandoned, the trains having simply stopped stopping there decades earlier. No explanation.

For a while the trains still chugged by, winding through the valley and between the mountains. And disappearing around a bend.

And then, one day, even they stopped. No twelve o'clock express. No three P.M. milk run into Vermont.

Nothing for the villagers to set their clocks by.

And so both the trains and time stopped in Three Pines.

The station sat empty until one day Ruth Zardo had a thought that didn't include olives or ice cubes. The Three Pines Volunteer Fire Department would take over the space. And so, with Ruth in the vanguard, they'd descended on the lovely old brick building and made themselves at home.

As the homicide team did now. In one half of the open room sat firefighting equipment, axes, hoses, helmets. A truck. In the other half were desks, computers, printers, scanners. The walls held posters with fire safety tips, detailed maps of the region, photos of past winners of the Governor General's Award for Poetry, including Ruth, and several large boards with headings like: *Suspects*, *Evidence*, *Victim*, and *Questions*.

There were a lot of questions, and the team spent the morning trying to answer them. The detailed coroner's report came in and Inspector Beauvoir handled that, as well as the forensic evidence. He was looking into how she died while Agent Lacoste tried to figure out how she'd lived. Her time in New York City, her marriage, any friends, any colleagues. What she did, what she thought. What others thought of her.

And Chief Inspector Gamache put them all together.

He started out at his desk, with a cup of coffee, reading all the reports from the day and night before. From that morning.

Then picking up the large blue book on his desk he went for a walk. Instinctively he made for the village, but paused on the stone bridge that arched over the river.

Ruth was sitting on the bench on the village green. Not doing much of anything, apparently, though the Chief Inspector knew differently. She was doing the most difficult thing in the world.

She was waiting and she was hoping.

As he watched she tilted her gray head to the skies. And listened. For a distant sound, like a train. Someone coming home. Then her head dropped back down.

How long, he wondered, would she wait? It was already almost mid-June. How many others, mothers and fathers, had sat right where Ruth was, waiting, hoping? Listening for the train. Wondering if it would stop and a familiar young man would step down, having been spewed back from places with pretty names, like Vimy Ridge or Flanders Fields or Passchendaele? By Dieppe and Arnhem.

How long did hope live?

Ruth tilted her head to the sky and listened again, for some far cry. And then she lowered it again.

An eternity, thought Gamache.

And if hope lasted forever, how long did hate last?

He turned around, not wanting to disturb her. But neither did he want to be disturbed. He needed quiet time, to read and think. And so he walked back, past the old railway station and down the dirt road, one of the spokes that radiated out from the village green. He'd taken a lot of walks around Three Pines but never down this particular road.

Huge maples lined the road, their branches meeting overhead. Their leaves almost blocking out the sun. But not quite. It filtered through and hit the dirt, and hit him and hit the book in his hand in soft dots of light.

Gamache found a large gray rock, an outcropping by the side of the road. Sitting down he put on his reading glasses, crossed his legs and opened the book.

An hour later he closed it and stared ahead. Then he got up and walked some more, further down the tunnel of shade and light. In the woods he could see dried leaves and tight little fiddlehead ferns and hear the scrambling of chipmunks and birds. He was aware of all that, though his mind was somewhere else.

Finally he stopped, turned around and walked back, his steps slow but deliberate.

SIXTEEN

‘Right,’ said Gamache settling into his chair at the makeshift conference table. ‘Tell me what you know.’

‘Dr Harris’s full report arrived this morning,’ said Beauvoir, standing by the sheets of paper attached to the wall. He wafted an uncapped Magic Marker under his nose. ‘Lillian Dyson’s neck was snapped, twisted in a single move.’ He mimicked wringing a neck. ‘There was no bruising on her face or arms. Nowhere except a small spot on her neck, where it broke.’

‘Which tells us what?’ asked the Chief.

‘That death was fast,’ said Beauvoir, writing it down in bold letters. He loved this part. Putting down facts, evidence. Writing them in ink so that fact became truth. ‘As we thought, she was taken by surprise. Dr Harris says the killer could have been either a man or woman. Probably not elderly. Some strength and leverage was necessary. The murderer was probably no shorter than Madame Dyson,’ said Beauvoir, consulting the notes in his hand. ‘But since she was five foot five most people would have been taller.’

‘How tall is Clara Morrow?’ Lacoste asked.

The men looked at each other. ‘About that size, I’d say,’ said Beauvoir and Gamache nodded.

It was, sadly, a pertinent question.

‘There was no other violation,’ Beauvoir continued. ‘No sexual assault. No evidence of recent sexual activity at all. She was slightly overweight but not by much. She'd had dinner a couple of hours earlier. McDonald's.'

Beauvoir tried not to think of the Happy Meal the coroner had found.

'Any other food in her stomach?' asked Lacoste. 'The catered food at the party?'

'None.'

'Was there any alcohol or drugs in her system?' Gamache asked.

'None.'

The Chief turned to Agent Lacoste. She looked down at her notes, and read.

'Lillian Dyson's former husband was a jazz trumpeter in New York. He met Lillian at an art show. He was performing at a cocktail party and she was one of the guests. They gravitated to each other. Both alcoholics, apparently. They got married and for a while both seemed to straighten out. Then it all fell apart. For both of them. He got into crack and meth. Got fired from gigs. They were evicted from their apartment. It was a mess. Eventually she left him and hooked up with a few other men. I've found two of them, but not the rest. It seemed casual, not actual relationships. And, it seems, increasingly desperate.'

'Was she also addicted to crack or methamphetamines?' Gamache asked.

'No evidence of that,' said Lacoste.

'How'd she make a living?' the Chief asked. 'As an artist or critic?'

'Neither. Looks like she lived on the margins of the art world,' said Lacoste, going back to her notes.

'So what did she do?' asked Beauvoir.

'Well, she was illegal. No work permit for the States. From what I can piece together she worked under the table at art supply shops. She picked up odd jobs here and there.'

Gamache thought about that. For a twenty-year-old it would've been an exciting life. For a woman nearing fifty it would've been exhausting, discouraging.

'She might not have been an addict, but could she have dealt drugs?' he asked. 'Or been a prostitute?'

'Possibly both for a while, but not recently,' said Lacoste.

'Coroner says there's no evidence of sexually transmitted disease. No needle tracks or scarring,' said Beauvoir, consulting the printout. 'As you know, most low-level dealers are also addicts.'

'Lillian's parents thought her husband might have died,' said the Chief.

'He did,' said Lacoste. 'Three years ago. OD'd.'

Beauvoir put a stroke through the man's name.

'Canada Customs records show she crossed the border on a bus from New York City on October sixteenth of last year,' said Lacoste. 'Nine months ago. She applied for welfare and got it.'

'When did she join Alcoholics Anonymous?' asked Gamache.

'I don't know,' said Lacoste. 'I tried to reach her sponsor, Suzanne Coates, but there was no answer and Chez Nick says she's on a couple of days off.'

'Scheduled?' asked Gamache, sitting forward.

'I didn't ask.'

'Ask, please,' said the Chief, getting to his feet. 'When you find her let me know. I have some questions for her as well.'

He went to his desk and placed a call. He could have given the name and number to Agent Lacoste or Inspector Beauvoir, but he preferred to do this himself.

'Chief Justice's office,' said the efficient voice.

'May I speak with Mr Justice Pineault, please? This is Chief Inspector Gamache, of the Sûreté.'

'I'm afraid Justice Pineault isn't in today, Chief Inspector.'

Gamache paused, surprised. 'Is that right? Is he ill? I saw him just last night and he didn't mention anything.'

Now it was Mr Justice Pineault's secretary's turn to pause. 'He called in this morning and said he'd be working from home for the next few days.'

'Was this unexpected?'

'The Chief Justice is free to do as he likes, Monsieur Gamache.' She sounded tolerant of what was clearly an inappropriate question on his part.

'I'll try him at home. *Merci.*'

He tried the next number in his notebook. Chez Nick, the restaurant.

No, the harried woman who answered said, Suzanne wasn't there. She called to say she wouldn't be in.

The woman didn't sound pleased.

'Did she say why not?' asked Gamache.

'Wasn't feeling well.'

Gamache thanked her and hung up. Then he tried Suzanne's cell phone. It had been disconnected. Hanging up, he tapped his glasses on his hand, softly.

It seemed the Sunday night meeting of Alcoholics Anonymous had gone missing.

No Suzanne Coates, no Thierry Pineault.

Was this cause for concern? Armand Gamache knew anyone missing in a murder investigation was cause for concern. But not panic.

He got up and walked over to the window. From there he could see across the Rivière Bella Bella and into Three Pines. As he watched a car drove up and stopped. It was a two-seater, sleek and new and expensive. A contrast to the older cars in front of the homes.

A man got out and looked around. He seemed uncertain, but not lost.

Then he walked confidently into the bistro.

Gamache's eyes narrowed as he watched.

'Huh,' he grunted. Turning around he looked at the clock. Almost noon.

The Chief picked up the big book on his desk.

'I'll be in the bistro,' he said and saw knowing smiles on Lacoste's and Beauvoir's faces.

Couldn't say he blamed them.

*

Gamache's eyes adjusted to the dim interior of the bistro. It was warming up outside but still a fire burned in both stone hearths.

It was like walking into another world, with its own atmosphere and season. It was never too hot or cold in the bistro. It was the middle bear.

'*Salut, patron,*' said Gabri, waving from behind the long, polished wooden bar. 'Back so soon? Did you miss me?'

'We must never speak of our feelings, Gabri,' said Gamache. 'It would crush Olivier and Reine-Marie.'

'Too true,' laughed Gabri and coming around from the bar he offered the Chief Inspector a licorice pipe. 'And I hear it's always best to suppress emotions.'

Gamache put the licorice pipe in his mouth as though he was smoking it.

'Very continental,' said Gabri, nodding approval. 'Very Maigret.'

'*Merci.* The look I was going for.'

'Not sitting outside?' asked Gabri, gesturing toward the *terrasse*, with its round tables and cheery umbrellas. A few villagers were sipping coffees, a few had *apéritifs*.

'No, I'm looking for someone.'

Armand Gamache pointed deeper into the bistro, to the table beside the fireplace. Sitting comfortably, looking perfectly at ease and at home was Denis Fortin, the gallery owner.

'I have a question for you first, though,' said Gamache. 'Did Monsieur Fortin speak to you at Clara's *vernissage*?'

'In Montréal? Yes,' laughed Gabri. 'He sure did. He apologized.'

'What did he say?'

'He said, and I quote, "I'm very sorry for calling you a fucking queer." End quote.' Gabri gave Gamache a searching look. 'I am one, you know.'

'I'd heard the rumors. But not nice to be called one.'

Gabri shook his head. 'Not the first time, and probably not the last. But you're right. It never gets old. Always feels like a fresh wound.'

The two men were looking at the casual art dealer. Languid, relaxed.

'How do you feel about him now?' asked Gamache. 'Should I have his drink tested?'

Gabri smiled. 'Actually, I like him. Not many people who call me a fucking queer actually apologize. He gets marks for that. He also apologized to Clara for treating her so badly.'

So the gallery owner had been telling the truth, thought Gamache.

'He was at the party Saturday night down here too. Clara invited him,' said Gabri, following the Chief's gaze. 'I didn't realize he stayed.'

'He didn't.'

'So what's he doing back?'

Gamache was wondering the same thing. He'd watched Denis Fortin arrive a few minutes earlier, and had come over to ask just that.

'I didn't expect to see you here,' said Gamache, approaching Fortin, who'd risen from his seat.

They shook hands.

'I didn't expect to come down, but Monday the gallery's closed and I got to thinking.'

'About what?'

The two men sat in the armchairs. Gabri brought Gamache a lemonade.

'You were saying that you got to thinking?' said Gamache.

'About what you'd said when you came to visit me yesterday.'

'About the murder?'

Denis Fortin actually reddened. 'Well, no. About François Marois and André Castonguay still being here.'

Gamache knew what the gallery owner meant, but needed him to say it out loud. 'Go on.'

Fortin grinned. It was boyish and disarming. 'We in the art

world like to think we're rebels, non-conformists. Free spirits. An intellectual and intuitive cut above the rest. But they don't call it the "art establishment" for nothing. Fact is, most are followers. If one dealer is sniffing around an artist it won't be long before others join him. We follow the buzz. That's how phenomenons are created. Not because the artist is better than anyone else, but because the dealers have a pack mentality. Suddenly they all decide they want one particular artist.'

'They?'

'We,' he said, reluctantly, and Gamache noticed again that flush of annoyance never far from Fortin's skin.

'And that artist becomes the next big thing?'

'Can do. If it was just Castonguay I wouldn't worry. Or even just Marois. But both of them?'

'And why do you think they're still here?' Gamache asked. He knew why. Marois had told him. But again, he wanted to hear Fortin's interpretation.

'The Morrows, of course.'

'Is that why you're here?'

'Why else?'

Fear and greed, Monsieur Marois had said. That was what roiled behind the glittery exterior of the art world. And that was what had taken a seat in the calm bistro.

Jean Guy Beauvoir picked up the ringing phone.

'Inspector Beauvoir? It's Clara Morrow.'

Her voice was low. A whisper.

'What is it?' Beauvoir also, instinctively, lowered his voice. Agent Lacoste, at her own desk, looked over.

'There's someone in our back garden. A stranger.'

Beauvoir got to his feet. 'What're they doing?'

'Staring,' whispered Clara. 'At the place Lillian was killed.'

*

Agent Lacoste stood on the edge of the village green. Alert.

To her left, Inspector Beauvoir was quietly making his way around the Morrows' cottage. To her right, Chief Inspector Gamache was walking softly on the lawn. Careful not to disturb whoever was back there.

Villagers paused as they walked their dogs. Conversations grew hushed and petered out, and soon Three Pines was standing still. Waiting and watching as well.

Lacoste's job, she knew, was to save the villagers, if it came to that. If whoever was back there got past the Chief. Got past Beauvoir. Isabelle Lacoste was the last line of defense.

She could feel her gun in the holster on her hip, hidden beneath the stylish jacket. But she didn't take it out. Not yet. Chief Inspector Gamache had drilled into them time and again, never, ever draw your gun unless you mean to use it.

And shoot to stop. Don't aim for a leg, or arm. Aim for the body.

You don't necessarily want to kill, but you sure as hell don't want to miss. Because if a weapon was drawn it meant all else had failed. All hell had broken loose.

And again, unbidden, an image came to mind. Of leaning in as the Chief lay on the floor, trying to speak. His eyes glazed. Trying to focus. Of holding his hand, sticky with blood, and looking at his wedding ring, covered in it. So much blood on his hands.

She dragged her mind back, and focused.

Beauvoir and Gamache had disappeared. All she could see was the quiet little cottage in the sunshine. And all she could hear was her heart thudding, thudding.

Chief Inspector Gamache rounded the corner of the cottage, and stopped.

Standing with her back to him was a woman. He was pretty sure he knew who it was, but wanted to be certain. He was also pretty sure she was harmless, but also wanted to be certain, before he dropped his guard.

Gamache glanced to his left and saw Beauvoir standing there, also alert. But no longer alarmed. The Chief raised his left hand, a signal to Beauvoir to stay where he was.

'*Bonjour*,' said Gamache, and the woman leapt and yelped and spun around.

'Holy shit,' said Suzanne, 'you scared the crap out of me.'

Gamache grinned slightly. '*Désolé*, but you scared the crap out of Clara Morrow.'

Suzanne looked over to the cottage and saw Clara standing in the kitchen window. Suzanne gave a little wave and an apologetic smile. Clara gave a hesitant wave back.

'Sorry,' said Suzanne. Just then she noticed Beauvoir, standing a few feet away, at the other side of the garden. 'I really am harmless, you know. Foolish, perhaps. But harmless.'

Inspector Beauvoir glared at her. In his experience foolish people were never harmless. They were the worst. Stupidity accounted for as many crimes as anger and greed. But he relented, walking toward them and whispering to the Chief.

'I'll let Lacoste know it's all right.'

'*Bon*,' said the Chief. 'I'll take it from here.'

Beauvoir looked over his shoulder at Suzanne and shook his head.

Foolish woman.

'So,' said Gamache when they were alone. 'Why are you here?'

'To see where Lillian died. I couldn't sleep last night, the reality of it just kept getting stronger and stronger. Lillian was killed. Murdered.'

But she still looked as though she barely believed it.

'I had to come down. To see where it'd happened. You said you'd be here and I wanted to offer my help.'

'Help? How?'

Now it was Suzanne's turn to look surprised. 'Unless it was a mistake or a random attack, someone killed Lillian on purpose. Don't you think?'

Gamache nodded, watching this woman closely.

'Someone wanted Lillian dead. But who?'

'And why?' said the Chief.

'Exactly. I might be able to help with the "why".'

'How?'

'When?' asked Suzanne and smiled. Then her smile drifted away as she turned to look back at the hole in the garden, surrounded by yellow, fluttering tape. 'I knew Lillian better than anyone. Better than her parents. Probably better than she knew herself. I can help you.'

She stared into his deep brown eyes. She was defiant, prepared for battle. What she wasn't prepared for was what she saw there. Consideration.

He was considering her words. Not dismissing them, not marshaling arguments. Armand Gamache was thinking about what she'd said, and he'd heard.

The Chief Inspector studied the energetic woman in front of him. Her clothing was too tight, and mismatched. Was this creative, or just clumsy dressing? Did she not see herself, or not care how she looked?

She looked foolish. Even declared herself to be that.

But she wasn't. Her eyes were shrewd. Her words even shrewder.

She knew the victim better than anyone. She was uniquely placed to help. But was that the real reason she was there?

'Hello,' said Clara, tentatively. She was walking toward them from the kitchen door.

Suzanne immediately turned and stared, then she walked toward Clara, her hands out.

'Oh, I am sorry. I should have knocked on your door and asked permission instead of just barging into your garden. I don't know why I didn't. My name's Suzanne Coates.'

As the two women exchanged greetings and were talking Gamache looked from Suzanne back to the garden. To the prayer stick stuck in the ground. And he remembered what Myrna had found beneath that stick.

A beginner's chip. From AA.

He'd assumed it belonged to the victim, but now he wondered. Did it in fact belong to the murderer? And did that explain why Suzanne was in the garden, unannounced?

Was she looking for the missing coin, her missing coin? Not realizing they already had it?

Clara and Suzanne had joined him and Clara was describing finding Lillian's body.

'Were you a friend of Lillian's?' asked Clara, when she'd finished.

'Sort of. We had mutual friends.'

'Are you an artist?' asked Clara, eyeing the older woman and her getup.

'Of sorts,' laughed Suzanne. 'Not in your league at all. I like to think of my work as intuitive, but critics have called them something else.'

Both women laughed.

Behind them, seen only by Gamache, the ribbons of the prayer stick fluttered, as though catching their laughter.

'Well, mine have been called "something else" for years,' admitted Clara. 'But mostly they were called nothing at all. Not even noticed. This was my first show in living memory.'

The women compared artistic notes while Gamache listened. It was a chronicle of life as an artist. Of balancing ego and creation. Of battling ego and creation.

Of trying not to care. And caring too deeply.

'I wasn't at your *vernissage*,' said Suzanne. 'Too rarified for me. I'm more likely to be the one serving the sandwiches than eating them, but I hear it was magnificent. Congratulations. I plan to get to the show as soon as I can.'

'We can go together,' Clara offered. 'If you're interested.'

'Thank you,' said Suzanne. 'Had I known you were this nice I'd have trespassed years ago.'

She looked around and fell silent.

'What're you thinking about?' Clara asked.

Suzanne smiled. 'I was actually thinking about contrasts. About violence in such a peaceful place. Something so ugly happening here.'

They all looked around then, at the quiet garden. Their eyes finally resting on the spot circled by yellow tape.

'What's that?'

'It's a prayer stick,' said Clara.

All three stared at the ribbons, intertwined. Then Clara had an idea. She explained about the ritual then asked, 'Would you like to attach a ribbon?'

Suzanne considered for a moment. 'I'd like that very much. Thank you.'

'I'll be back in a few minutes.' Clara nodded to both of them then walked toward the village.

'Nice woman,' said Suzanne, watching her go. 'Hope she manages to stay that way.'

'You have doubts?' asked Gamache.

'Success can mess with you. But then so can failure,' she laughed again, then grew quiet.

'Why do you think Lillian Dyson was murdered?' he asked.

'Why do you think I'd know?'

'Because I agree with you. You knew her better than anyone. Better than she knew herself. You knew her secrets, and now you're going to tell me.'

SEVENTEEN

—

'Helloooo,' called Clara. *'Bonjour.'*
She could hear voices, shouts. But they seemed tinny, far away. As though on TV. Then they stopped and there was silence. The place felt empty, though she knew it probably wasn't.

She advanced a little further into the old railway station, past the shiny red fire truck, past their equipment. Clara saw her own helmet and boots. Everyone in Three Pines was a member of the volunteer fire department. And Ruth Zardo was the chief, since she alone was more terrifying than any conflagration. Given a choice between Ruth and a burning building, most would choose the building.

'Oui, âllo?'

A man's voice echoed through the large room and Clara, coming around the truck, saw Inspector Beauvoir at a desk looking in her direction.

He smiled and greeted her with a kiss on both cheeks.

'Come, sit. What can I do for you?' he asked.

His manner was cheery, energetic. But Clara had still been shocked to see him at the *vernissage*, and now. Haggard, tired. Thin even for the always wiry man. Like everyone else, she knew what he'd been through. At least, like everyone else, she knew the words, the story. But Clara realized she didn't really 'know'. Could never know.

'I came for advice,' she said, sitting in the swivel chair beside Beauvoir's.

'From me?' His surprise was obvious, as was his delight.

'From you.' She saw this and was happy she hadn't told him the reason she wasn't asking Gamache was because he wasn't alone. And Beauvoir was.

'Coffee?' Jean Guy gestured toward a full pot already brewed.

'I'd love one, thanks.'

They got up and poured coffees into chipped white mugs, and each got a couple of Fig Newtons, then sat back down.

'So, what's the story?' Beauvoir leaned back and looked at her. In a way that was all his own yet reminiscent of Gamache.

It was very comforting, and Clara was glad she'd decided to speak with this young Inspector.

'It's about Lillian's parents. Mr and Mrs Dyson. I knew them, you know. Quite well at one stage. I was wondering if they're still alive.'

'They are. We went to see them yesterday. To tell them about their daughter.'

Clara paused, trying to imagine what that was like, for both parties.

'It must have been horrible. They adored her. She was their only child.'

'It's always horrible,' admitted Beauvoir.

'I liked them a lot. Even when Lillian and I fell out I tried to keep in touch but they weren't interested. They believed what Lillian told them about me. It's understandable, I guess.' She sounded, though, less than convinced.

Beauvoir said nothing, but remembered the venom in Mr Dyson's voice when he all but accused Clara of their daughter's murder.

'I was thinking of visiting them,' said Clara. 'Of telling them how sorry I am. What is it?'

The look on Beauvoir's face had stopped her.

'I wouldn't do that,' he said, putting his mug down and leaning forward. 'They're very upset. I think a visit from you wouldn't help.'

'But why? I know they believed the terrible things Lillian said, but maybe my going could ease some of that. Lillian and I were best friends growing up, don't you think they'd like to talk about her with someone who loved her?' Clara paused. 'Once.'

'Maybe, eventually. But not now. Give them time.'

It was, more or less, the advice Myrna had given her. Clara had gone to the bookstore for ribbon and the dried sage and sweetgrass cigar. But she'd also gone for advice. Should she drive into Montréal to visit the Dysons?

When Myrna had asked why she'd want to do such a thing, Clara had explained.

'They're old and alone,' Clara had said, shocked her friend needed to be told. 'This is the worst thing that could happen. I just want to offer them some comfort. Believe me, the last thing I want to do is drive in to Montréal and do this, but it just seems the right thing to do. To put all the hard feelings behind.'

The ribbon was twisted tight around Clara's fingers, strangling them.

'For you, maybe,' Myrna had said. 'But what about them?'

'How do you know they haven't let all that go?' Clara unwound the ribbon, then fidgeted with it. Winding it. Worrying it. 'Maybe they're sitting there all alone, devastated. And I'm not going because I'm afraid?'

'Go if you have to,' said Myrna. 'But just make sure you're doing it for them and not for you.'

With that ringing in her ears Clara had crossed the village green and made for the Incident Room, to speak with Beauvoir. But also to get something else.

Their address.

Now, after listening to the Inspector, Clara nodded. Two people had given her the same advice. To wait. Clara realized she was staring at the wall of the old railway station. At the photos of Lillian, dead. In her garden.

Where that strange woman and Chief Inspector Gamache were waiting for her.

'I've remembered most of Lillian's secrets, I think.'

'You think?' asked Gamache. They were strolling around Clara's garden, stopping now and then to admire it.

'I wasn't lying to you last night, you know. Don't tell my sponsees, but I get their secrets all mixed up. After a while it's hard to separate one from the other. All a bit of a blur, really.'

Gamache smiled. He too was the safe in which many secrets were stored. Things he'd learned in investigations that had no relevance to the case. That never needed to come to light. And so he'd locked them away.

If someone suddenly demanded Monsieur C's secrets he'd balk. At spilling them, certainly, but also, frankly, he'd need time to separate them from the rest.

'Lillian's secrets were no worse than anyone's,' said Suzanne. 'At least, not the ones she told me about. Some shoplifting, some bad debts. Stealing money from her mother's purse. She'd dabbled in drugs and cheated on her husband. When she was in New York she'd steal from her boss's till and not share some tips.'

'Nothing huge,' said Gamache.

'It never is. Most of us are brought down by a bunch of tiny transgressions. Little things that add up until we collapse under them. It's fairly easy to avoid doing the big bad things, but it's the hundred mean little things that'll get you eventually. If you listen to people long enough you realize it's not the slap or the punch, but the whispered gossip, the dismissive look. The turned back. That's what people with any conscience are ashamed of. That's what they drink to forget.'

'And people without a conscience?'

'They don't end up in AA. They don't think there's anything wrong with them.'

Gamache thought about that for a moment. 'You said "at least, not the ones she told me about." Does that mean she kept some secrets from you?'

He wasn't looking at his companion. He found people opened up more if given the conceit of their own space. Instead, Chief Inspector Gamache stared straight ahead at the honeysuckle and roses growing up an arbor and warming in the early afternoon sun.

'Some manage to flush it all out in one go,' said Suzanne. 'But most need time. It's not that they're intentionally hiding anything. Sometimes they've buried it so deep they don't even know it's there anymore.'

'Until?'

'Until it claws its way back up. By then something tiny has turned into something almost unrecognizable. Something big and stinky.'

'What happens then?' asked the Chief Inspector.

'Then we have a choice,' said Suzanne. 'We can look the truth square in the face. Or we can bury it again. Or, at least try.'

To a casual observer they would appear to be two old friends discussing literature or the latest concert at the village hall. But someone more astute might notice their expressions. Not grave, but perhaps a little somber on this lovely, sunny day.

'What happens if people try to bury it again?' Gamache asked.

'I don't know about normal human beings, but for alcoholics it's lethal. A secret that rotten will drive you to drink. And the drink will drive you to your grave. But not before it steals everything from you. Your loved ones, your job, your home. Your dignity. And finally, your life.'

'All because of a secret?'

'Because of a secret, and the decision to hide from the truth. The choice to chicken out.' She looked at him closely. 'Sobriety isn't for cowards, Chief Inspector. Whatever you might think of an alcoholic, to get sober, really sober demands great honesty, and that demands great courage. Stopping drinking's the easy part. Then we have to face ourselves. Our demons. How many people are willing to do that?'

'Not many,' Gamache admitted. 'But what happens if the demons win?'

Clara Morrow walked slowly across the bridge, pausing to glance into the Rivière Bella Bella below. It burbled past, catching the sun in silver and gold highlights. She could see the rocks, rubbed smooth at the bottom of the stream, and every now and then a rainbow trout glided past.

Should she go into Montréal? The truth was, she'd already looked up the Dysons' address, she'd just wanted to confirm it with Beauvoir. It sat in her pocket, and now she glanced over at their car, sitting. Waiting.

Should she go into Montréal?

What was she waiting for? What was she afraid of?

That they would hate her. Blame her. Tell her to go away. That Mr and Mrs Dyson, who had once been second parents to Clara, would disown her.

But she knew she had to do it. Despite what Myrna said. Despite what Beauvoir said. She hadn't asked Peter. Didn't yet trust him enough with something this important. But she suspected he'd say the same thing.

Don't go.

Don't risk it.

Clara turned away from the river and walked off the bridge.

'It's true,' said Suzanne, 'sometimes the demon wins. Sometimes we can't face the truth. It's just too painful.'

'What happens then?'

Suzanne was swishing the grass with her feet, no longer looking at the pretty garden.

'Have you ever heard of "Humpty Dumpty", Chief Inspector?'

'The nursery rhyme? I used to read it to my children.'

Daniel, as he remembered, had loved it. Wanted it read over and over again. Never tired of the illustrations of the silly old egg and the noble King's horses and men, rushing to the rescue.

But Annie? She'd howled. The tears had gone on and on, staining his shirt where he'd held her to him. Rocking her. Trying to comfort her. It had taken Gamache a while to calm her down and work out what the problem was. And then it was clear. Little Annie, all of four, couldn't stand the thought of Humpty Dumpty so shattered. Never able to heal. Hurt too badly.

'It's an allegory, of course,' said Suzanne.

'You mean Mr Dumpty never existed?' asked Gamache.

'I mean exactly that, Chief Inspector.' Suzanne's smile faded and she walked in silence for a few paces. 'Like Humpty Dumpty, some people are just too damaged to heal.'

'Was Lillian?'

'She was healing. I think she might have done all right. She was sure working hard at it.'

'But?' said Gamache.

Suzanne took a few more steps. 'Lillian was damaged, very messed up. But she was putting her life back together again, slowly. That wasn't the problem.'

The Chief Inspector considered what this woman, so loud and yet so loyal, was trying to tell him. And then he thought he had it.

'She wasn't Humpty Dumpty,' he said. 'She hadn't fallen off the wall. She pushed others. Others had had great falls, thanks to Lillian.'

Beside him Suzanne Coates's head bobbed up and down very subtly with each footstep.

'Sorry it took so long,' said Clara, coming around the old lilac bush at the corner of her home. 'I got these from Myrna.'

She held up the ribbon and the cigar and was treated to both the Chief Inspector and Suzanne looking disconcerted.

'What sort of a ritual is this exactly?' asked Gamache, with an uncertain smile.

'It's a ritual of cleansing. Would you like to join us?'

Gamache hesitated, then nodded. He was familiar with this sort of ritual. Some of the villagers had done it at the scenes of earlier murders. But he'd never been asked to join before. Though, God knew, he'd had enough incense wafted over him in his Catholic youth, this couldn't be any worse.

For the second time in two days Clara lit the sage and sweetgrass. She gently pushed the fragrant smoke toward the intense artist, smoothing it over the woman's head and down her body. Releasing, Clara explained, any negative thoughts, any bad energy.

Then it was Gamache's turn. She looked at him. His expression was slightly bemused, but mostly relaxed, attentive. She moved the smoke over him, until it hung like a sweet cloud around him and then dissipated in the breeze.

'All the negative energy taken away,' said Clara, doing it to herself. 'Gone.'

If only, they all quietly thought, it was that easy.

Then Clara gave them each a ribbon and invited them to say a silent prayer for Lillian, then tie it to the stick.

'What about the tape?' asked Suzanne.

'Oh, it doesn't matter,' said Clara. 'More of a suggestion than a command. Besides, I know the fellow who put it up.'

'Incompetent,' said Gamache, holding the tape down for Suzanne, then stepping through himself. 'But well meaning.'

Agent Isabelle Lacoste slowed her car almost to a stop. She was heading out of Three Pines and into Montréal to help search the archives of *La Presse* for Lillian Dyson's reviews. To try to find out who that one particularly vicious critique was written about.

As she drove past the Morrow house she saw something she never thought she'd see. A senior Sûreté du Québec officer apparently praying to a stick.

She smiled, wishing she could join him. She'd often said silent prayers at a crime scene. When everyone else had left, Isabelle Lacoste returned. To let the dead know they were not forgotten.

This time, though, it seemed the Chief's turn. She wondered what he was praying for. She remembered holding that bloody hand, and thought maybe she could guess.

Chief Inspector Gamache placed his right hand on the stick and cleared his mind. After a moment he tied his ribbon to it and stepped back.

'I said the Serenity Prayer,' said Suzanne. 'You?'

But Gamache chose not to tell them what he'd prayed for.

'And you?' Suzanne turned to Clara.

She was bossy and inquisitive, Gamache noticed. He wondered if those were good qualities in a sponsor.

Like Gamache, Clara kept quiet.

But she had her answer.

'I need to leave for a little while. I'll see you later.' Clara hurried into her home. She was now in a rush. Too much time had already been wasted.

EIGHTEEN

⌐

'Are you sure I can't come with you?' Peter followed Clara down their front path, to the car parked just outside their gate.

'I won't be long. Just one quick thing I need to do in Montréal.'

'What? Can't I help?'

He was desperate to prove to Clara he'd changed. But while she was civil with him it was clear. His wife, who had so much faith, had finally lost all faith in him.

'No. Enjoy yourself here.'

'Call when you get there,' he yelled after the car, but he wasn't sure she'd heard.

'Where's she gone?'

Peter turned round to see Inspector Beauvoir standing beside him.

'Montréal.'

Beauvoir raised his brows but said nothing. Then he walked away, toward the bistro and its *terrasse*.

Peter watched Inspector Beauvoir take a seat under one of the yellow and blue Campari umbrellas, all by himself. Olivier came out immediately, like the Inspector's private butler.

Beauvoir accepted two menus, ordered a drink, and relaxed.

Peter envied that. To sit alone. All alone. And be company enough. He envied that almost as much as he envied the people sitting in groups of two or three or four. Enjoying each other's company. For Peter, the only thing worse than company was being alone. Unless he was alone in his studio. Or with Clara. Just the two of them.

But now she'd left him standing by the side of the road.

And Peter Morrow didn't know what to do.

'Your man is going to be pissed off that you're keeping him from his lunch.' Suzanne nodded toward the bistro.

They'd left Clara's garden and decided to walk around the village green. Ruth sat on the bench at the very center of the little park. The source of all gravity in Three Pines.

She was staring into the sky and Gamache wondered if prayers really were answered. He glanced up as well, as he had when his hand had rested on the stick.

But the sky remained empty, and silent.

Then his gaze fell to earth and Beauvoir sitting at a bistro table, watching them.

'He doesn't look happy,' said Suzanne.

'He's never happy when he's hungry.'

'And I bet he's often hungry,' said Suzanne. The Chief looked at her, expecting to see the omnipresent smile, and was surprised to find her looking very serious.

They resumed their walk.

'Why do you think Lillian Dyson came to Three Pines?' Gamache asked.

'I've been wondering that.'

'And have you come to a conclusion?'

'I think it's one of two things. She was here to either repair damage done,' Suzanne stopped to look at Gamache directly. 'Or to do more.'

The Chief Inspector nodded. He'd thought the same thing. But what a world between the two. In one Lillian was sober and healthy, and in the other she was cruel, unchanged, unrepentant. Was she one of the King's men, or had she come to Three Pines to push someone else off the wall?

Gamache put on his reading glasses and opened the large book he'd left at the bistro and retrieved.

'*The alcoholic is like a tornado, roaring his way through the lives of others,*' he read in a deep, quiet voice. He looked at Suzanne over his half-moon glasses. 'We found this on her bedside table. Those words were highlighted.'

He held the book up. In bright white letters on a dark background were the words 'Alcoholics Anonymous'.

Suzanne grinned. 'Not very discreet. Ironic really.'

Gamache smiled and looked back down at the book. 'There's more. *Hearts are broken. Sweet relationships are dead.*'

He slowly closed the book and took off his glasses.

'Does that tell you anything?'

Suzanne held out her hand and Gamache gave her the book. Opening it to the bookmark she scanned the page, and smiled.

'It tells me she was on step nine.' She gave the book back to Gamache. 'She must've been reading that section of the book. It's the step where we make amends to people we've harmed. I guess she was here for that.'

'What is step nine?'

'*Made direct amends to such people except when to do so would injure them or others,*' she quoted.

'Such people?'

'The ones we've damaged by our actions. I think she came here to say she was sorry.'

'*Sweet relationships are dead,*' said Gamache. 'Do you think she came to speak to Clara Morrow? To, what did you call it? Make amends?'

'Maybe. Sounds like there were lots of art people here. She might've come down to apologize to any of them. God knows, she owed a lot of amends.'

'But would someone really do that?'

'What d'you mean?'

'If I wanted to sincerely apologize I don't think I'd choose to do it at a party.'

'That's a good point.' She gave a big sigh. 'There's another thing, something I think I didn't want to really admit. I'm not sure she'd actually reached step nine. I don't think she'd done all the steps leading up to it.'

'Does it matter? Do you have to do them in order?'

'You don't have to do anything, but it sure helps. What would happen if you took first year university then skipped to the final year?'

'You'd probably fail.'

'Exactly.'

'But what would failing mean, in this case? You wouldn't get kicked out of AA?'

Suzanne laughed, but without real amusement. 'No. Listen, all the steps are important, but step nine is perhaps the most delicate, the most fraught. It's really the first time we reach out to others. Take responsibility for what we've done. If it's not done right . . . '

'What happens?'

'We can do more damage. To them and to ourselves.'

She paused to sniff a lilac in full bloom on the edge of the quiet road. And, Gamache suspected, to give herself time to think.

'It's beautiful,' she said, raising her nose from the fragrant flower and looking around, as if seeing the pretty little village for the first time. 'I could see living here. It would make a nice home.'

Gamache didn't say anything, judging she was working herself up to something.

'Our lives, when we were drinking, were pretty complicated. Pretty chaotic. We got into all sorts of trouble. It was a mess. And this is all we ever wanted. A quiet place in the bright sunshine. But every day we drank we got further from it.'

Suzanne looked at the little cottages around the village green. Most homes had porches and front gardens with peonies and lupins and roses in bloom. And cats and dogs lounging in the sun.

'We long to find home. After years and years of making war on everyone around us, on ourselves, we just want peace.'

'And how do you find it?' Gamache asked. He more than most knew that peace, like Three Pines, could be very hard to find.

'Well, first we have to find ourselves. Somewhere along the way we got lost. Ended up wandering around in a confusion of drugs and alcohol. Getting further and further away from who we really are.' She turned to him, a smile on her face again. 'But some of us find our way back. From the wilderness.' Suzanne looked up from Gamache's deep brown eyes, from the village green and homes and shops, to the forest and mountains surrounding them. 'Getting sloshed was only part of the problem. This is a disease of the emotions. Of perception.' She tapped her temple a few times. 'We get all screwy in how we see things, how we think. We call it stinking thinking. And that affects how we feel. And I can tell you, Chief Inspector, that it's very hard and very scary to change our perceptions. Most can't do it. But a lucky few do. And in doing that, we find ourselves and,' she looked around, 'we find home.'

'You have to change your head to change your heart?' Gamache asked.

Suzanne didn't answer. Instead she continued to gaze at the village. 'How interesting that no cell phones work here. And not a car has come by since we've been walking. I wonder if the outside world even knows it's here.'

'It's an anonymous village,' said Gamache. 'Not on any map. You have to find your own way here.' He turned to his companion. 'Are you sure Lillian had actually stopped drinking?'

'Oh, yes, from her first meeting.'

'And when was that?'

Suzanne considered for a moment. 'About eight months ago.'

Gamache did the calculation. 'So she arrived in AA in October. Do you know why?'

'You mean, did anything happen? No. For some, like Brian, something terrible happens. The world falls apart. They shatter. For others it's quieter, almost imperceptible. More a crumble. Inside. That's what happened to Lillian.'

Gamache nodded. 'Had you ever been to her home?'

'No. We always met in a café or at my place.'

'Had you seen her art?'

'No. She told me she'd started painting again but I didn't see it. Didn't want to.'

'Why not? As an artist yourself I'd have thought you'd be interested.'

'I was, actually. I'm afraid I'm pretty nosy. But it seemed a no-win. If it was great I might become jealous, and that wouldn't be good. And if it sucked, what would I say? So no, I hadn't seen her art.'

'Would you really have been jealous of your sponsee? That doesn't sound like the relationship you described.'

'That was an ideal. I'm close to perfection, as you've no doubt noticed, but not quite there yet,' Suzanne laughed at herself. 'It's my only flaw. Jealousy.'

'And nosiness.'

'My two flaws. Jealousy and nosiness. And I'm bossy. Oh, God. I really am fucked up.'

She laughed.

'And I understand you're in debt.'

That stopped Suzanne in her tracks. 'How'd you know that?' She stared at him and when Gamache didn't respond she gave a resigned nod. 'Of course you'd find out. Yes, I'm in debt. Never was good with money and now that apparently I'm not allowed to steal, life is much more difficult.'

She gave him a disarming smile. 'Another flaw to add to the growing list.'

A growing list indeed, thought Gamache. What else was she not telling him? It struck him as strange that two artists wouldn't compare work. That Lillian wouldn't show her paintings to her sponsor. For approval, for feedback.

And what would Suzanne do? She'd see their brilliance, and then what? Kill Lillian in a jealous rage?

It seemed unlikely.

But it did seem strange that in eight months of an intimate relationship Suzanne had never once visited Lillian's place. Never seen her art.

Then something else occurred to Gamache. 'Was AA the first time you met, or did you know each other before that?'

He could tell he'd hit on something. The smile never wavered, but her eyes grew sharper.

'As a matter of fact, we did know each other. Though "know" isn't quite right. We'd bump into each other at shows years ago. Before she left for New York. But we were never friends.'

'Were you friendly?'

'After a few drinks? I was more than friendly, Chief Inspector.' And Suzanne laughed.

'But not, presumably, with Lillian.'

'Well, not in that way,' agreed Suzanne. 'Look, the truth is, I wasn't worth her while. She was the big, important critic for *La Presse* and I was just another drunken artist. And between us? That was just fine with me. She was such a bitch. Famous for it. No amount of booze would make approaching Lillian a good idea.'

Gamache thought for a moment, then resumed walking.

'How long have you been in AA?' he asked.

'Twenty-three years last March eighteenth.'

'Twenty-three years?' He was astonished, and it showed.

'You should have seen me when I first came in,' she laughed. 'Cuckoo for Cocoa Puffs. What you see is the result of twenty-three years of hard labor.'

They passed the front of the *terrasse*. Beauvoir gestured toward his beer and Gamache nodded.

'Twenty-three years,' repeated Gamache when they resumed their walk. 'You stopped drinking about the time Lillian left for New York.'

'I guess I did.'

'Was that just coincidence?'

'She wasn't part of my life. Lillian had nothing to do with me getting drunk or getting sober.'

Suzanne's voice had developed an edge. A slight annoyance.

'Do you still paint?' Gamache asked.

'Some. Mostly I dabble. Take some courses, teach some courses, go to *vernissages* where there's free food and drink.'

'Did Lillian mention Clara or her show?'

'She never mentioned Clara, not by name anyway. But she did say she needed to make amends to a lot of artists and dealers and gallery owners. Clara might have been among them.'

'And were they among them, do you think?' With a small movement of his head Gamache indicated the two people sitting on the porch of the B and B, watching them.

'Paulette and Normand? No, she didn't talk about them either. But I wouldn't be surprised if she owed them an apology. She wasn't very nice when she was drinking.'

'Or writing. *He's a natural, producing art like it's a bodily function,*' quoted Gamache.

'Oh, you know about that, do you?'

'Obviously you do too.'

'Every artist in Québec knows that. It was Lillian's finest moment. As a critic, that is. Her *pièce de résistance*. A near perfect assassination.'

'Do you know who it was about?'

'Don't you?'

'Would I be asking?'

Suzanne studied Gamache for a moment. 'You might. You're very tricky, I think. But no, I don't know.'

A near perfect assassination. And that was what it had been. Lillian had delivered a mortal blow with that line. Had the victim waited decades and then returned the favor?

*

'Mind if I join you?'

But it was too late. Myrna had taken a seat, and once down she was not ever going to be easy to shift.

Beauvoir looked at her. His expression was not very inviting.

'Fine. No problem.'

He scanned the *terrasse*. A few others were sitting at tables in the sunshine, nursing beers or lemonades or iced tea. But there were some empty tables. Why had Myrna decided to sit with him?

The only possible answer was the only one he dreaded.

'How are you?' she asked.

That she wanted to talk. He took a long sip of beer.

'I'm doing well, thank you.'

Myrna nodded, playing with the moisture on her own beer glass.

'Nice day,' she finally said.

Beauvoir continued to stare ahead, judging this wasn't worth responding to. Perhaps she'd get the point. He wanted to be alone with his thoughts.

'What're you thinking about?'

Now he did look at her. There was a mild expression on her face. Interested, but not piercing. Not searching.

A pleasant look.

'The case,' he lied.

'I see.'

They both looked over to the village green. There wasn't much activity. Ruth was trying to stone the birds, a few villagers were working in their gardens. One was walking a dog. And the Chief Inspector and some strange woman were walking along the dirt road.

'Who's she?'

'Someone who knew the dead woman,' said Beauvoir. No need to say too much.

Myrna nodded and took a few plump cashews from the bowl of mixed nuts.

'It's good to see the Chief Inspector looking so much better. Has he recovered do you think?'

'Of course he has. Long ago.'

'Well, it could hardly be long ago,' she said, reasonably. 'Since it only happened just before Christmas.'

Was that all it was, Beauvoir asked himself, amazed. Only six months? It seemed ages ago.

'Well, he's fine, as am I.'

'Fucked up, insecure, neurotic and egotistical? Ruth's definition of fine?'

This brought an involuntary smile to his lips. He tried to turn it into a grimace, but couldn't quite.

'I can't speak for the Chief, but I think that's just about right for me.'

Myrna smiled and took a sip of her beer. She followed Beauvoir, who was following Gamache.

'It wasn't your fault, you know.'

Beauvoir tensed, an involuntary spasm. 'What d'you mean?'

'What happened, in the factory. To him. There was nothing you could have done.'

'I know that,' he snapped.

'I wonder if you do. It must've been horrible, what you saw.'

'Why're you saying this?' Beauvoir demanded, his head in a whirl. Everything was suddenly topsy-turvy.

'Because I think you need to hear it. You can't always save him.' Myrna looked at the tired young man across from her. He was suffering, she knew. And she also knew only two things could produce such pain so long after the event.

Love. And guilt.

'Things are strongest where they're broken,' she said.

'Where did you hear that?' He glared at her.

'I read it in an interview the Chief Inspector gave, after the raid. And he's right. But it takes a long time, and a lot of help, to mend. You probably thought he was dead.'

Beauvoir had. He'd seen the Chief shot. Fall. And lie still.

Dead or dying. Beauvoir had been sure of it.

And he'd done nothing to help him.

'There was nothing you could do,' said Myrna, rightly interpreting his thoughts. 'Nothing.'

'How do you know?' demanded Beauvoir. 'How can you know?'

'Because I saw it. On the video.'

'And you think that tells you everything?' he demanded.

'Do you really believe there was more you could've done?'

Beauvoir turned away, feeling the familiar ache in his belly turn into jabs of pain. He knew Myrna was trying to be kind but he just wished she'd go away.

She hadn't been there. He had, and he'd never believe there was nothing more he could have done.

The Chief had saved his life. Dragged him to safety. Bandaged him. But when Gamache himself had been hurt it had been Agent Lacoste who'd fought her way to him. Saved the Chief's life.

While he himself had done nothing. Just lay there. Watching.

'You liked her?' Gamache asked.

They'd come full circle and were now standing on the village green, just across from the *terrasse*. He could see André Castonguay and François Marois sitting at a table, enjoying lunch. Or at least, enjoying the food if not the company. They didn't seem to be talking much.

'I did,' said Suzanne. 'She'd become kind. Thoughtful even. Happy. I didn't expect to like her when she first dragged her sorry ass into the church basement. We weren't exactly best friends before she'd left for New York. But we were both younger then, and drunker. And I suspect neither of us was very nice. But people change.'

'Are you so sure Lillian had?'

'Are you so sure I have?' Suzanne laughed.

It was, Gamache had to admit, a good question.

And then another question occurred to him. One he was surprised he hadn't thought of earlier.

'How did you find Three Pines?'

'What do you mean?'

'The village. It's almost impossible to find. And yet, here you are.'

'He drove me down.'

Gamache turned and looked to where she was pointing. Past the *terrasse* and into a window, where a man stood, his back to them. A book in his hand.

Though the Chief Inspector couldn't see his face Gamache did recognize the rest of the man. Thierry Pineault was standing at the window of Myrna's bookstore.

NINETEEN

⌒

Clara Morrow sat in the car, staring at the decrepit old apartment building. It was a far cry from the pretty little home the Dysons had lived in when Clara knew them.

For the whole drive in she'd been remembering her friendship with Lillian. The mind-numbing Christmas job they got together sorting mail. Then later, as lifeguards. That'd been Lillian's idea. They'd taken the lifesaving courses and passed their swim exams together. Helping each other. Sneaking out behind the life preserver shed for smokes, and tokes.

They'd been on the school volleyball and track teams together. They'd spotted each other at gymnastics.

There was barely a good memory from Clara's childhood that didn't include Lillian.

And Mr and Mrs Dyson were always there too. As kindly supporting characters. In the background, like the *Peanuts* parents. Rarely seen, but somehow there were always egg salad sandwiches, and fruit salad and warm chocolate chip cookies. There was always a pitcher of bright pink lemonade.

Mrs Dyson had been short, rotund, with thinning hair always in place. She'd seemed old but Clara realized she was younger than Clara was now. And Mr Dyson had been tall, wiry, with curly red hair. That looked, in the bright sunshine, like rust on his head.

No. There was no doubt, and Clara was appalled at herself for ever questioning it. This was the right thing to do.

After giving up on an elevator she climbed the three flights, trying not to notice the stale smells of tobacco and dope and urine.

She stood in front of their closed door. Staring. Catching her breath from an exertion not wholly physical.

Clara closed her eyes and conjured up little Lillian, standing in green shorts and a T-shirt, framed by her door. Smiling. Inviting little Clara in.

Then Clara Morrow knocked on the door.

'Chief Justice,' said Gamache, offering his hand.

'Chief Inspector,' said Thierry Pineault, taking it and shaking.

'There can be too many chiefs after all,' said Suzanne. 'Let's grab a table.'

'We can join Inspector Beauvoir,' said Gamache, ushering them toward his Inspector, who'd gotten up and was indicating his table.

'I'd rather we sat over here,' said Chief Justice Pineault. Suzanne and Gamache paused. Pineault was indicating a table shoved up against the brick building, in the least attractive area.

'More discreet,' Pineault explained, seeing their puzzled expressions. Gamache raised a brow but agreed, waving Beauvoir over. Chief Justice Pineault sat first, his back to the village. Gabri took their orders.

'Will this bother you?' Gamache asked, pointing to the beers Beauvoir had brought over.

'Not at all,' said Suzanne.

'I tried to call you this morning,' said Gamache.

Gabri put their drinks on the table and whispered to Beauvoir, 'Who's this other guy?'

'The Chief Justice of Québec.'

'Of course he is.' Gabri shot Beauvoir an annoyed look and left.

'And what did my secretary say?' asked Pineault, taking a sip of his Perrier and lime.

'Only that you were working from home,' said Gamache.

Pineault smiled. 'I am, sort of. I'm afraid I didn't specify which home.'

'You've decided to come down to the one in Knowlton?'

'Is this an interrogation, Chief Inspector? Should I get a lawyer?'

The smile was still in place but neither man was under any illusion. Close questioning the Chief Justice of Québec was a risky thing to do.

Gamache smiled back. 'This is a friendly conversation, Mr Justice. I'm hoping you can help.'

'Oh, for Christ's sake, Thierry. Just tell the man what he wants to know. Isn't that why we're here?'

Gamache regarded Suzanne across the table. Their lunches had arrived and she was shoveling terrine of duck into her mouth. It was a gesture not of greed, but of fear. She all but had her arm around her plate. Suzanne didn't want someone else's food. She wanted just her own. And she was willing to defend it, if need be.

But, between mouthfuls, Suzanne had asked an interesting question.

Why, if not to help his investigation, was Thierry Pineault there?

'Oh, I'm here to help,' Pineault said, casually. 'It was an instinctive reaction, I'm afraid, Chief Inspector. A lawyer's reaction. My apologies.'

Gamache noticed something else. While the Chief Justice seemed happy to challenge him, the head of homicide for the Sûreté du Québec, he never challenged Suzanne, the sometime artist and full-time waitress. In fact he took her little mocking jabs, her criticisms, her flamboyant gestures, all with great equilibrium. Was it manners?

The Chief didn't think so. He had the impression the Chief Justice was somehow cowed by Suzanne. As though she had something on him.

'I asked him to bring me down,' said Suzanne. 'I knew he'd want to help.'

'Why? I know Suzanne here cared about Lillian. Did you too, sir?'

The Chief Justice turned clear, cool eyes on Gamache. 'Not in the manner you're imagining.'

'I'm not imagining anything. Just asking.'

'I'm trying to help,' said Pineault. His voice was stern, his eyes hard. Gamache was used to this, from court appearances. From high-level Sûreté conferences.

And he recognized it for what it was. Chief Justice Thierry Pineault was pissing on him. It was delicate, sophisticated, genteel, mannerly. But it was still piss.

The problem with a pissing contest, as Gamache knew, was that what should have remained private became public. Chief Justice Pineault's privates were on display.

'And how do you think you can help, sir? Do you know something I don't?'

'I'm here because Suzanne asked me, and because I know where Three Pines is. I drove her down. That's my help.'

Gamache looked from Thierry to Suzanne, now ripping up a piece of fresh baguette, smearing it with butter and popping it in her mouth. Could she really command the Chief Justice like that? Treat him like a chauffeur?

'I asked Thierry for help because I knew he'd be calm. Sensible.'

'And he's the Chief Justice?' asked Beauvoir.

'I'm an alcoholic, not an idiot,' said Suzanne with a smile. 'It seemed an advantage.'

It was an advantage, thought Gamache. But why did she feel she needed one? And why had Chief Justice Pineault chosen this table, away from the others? The worst table on the terrace, and then quickly taken the seat facing the wall.

Gamache glanced around. Was the Chief Justice hiding? He'd arrived and gone straight into the bookstore, coming out only when

Suzanne returned. And now he sat with his back to everyone. Where he couldn't see anything, but neither could he be seen.

Gamache's eyes swept around the village, taking in what Chief Justice Pineault was missing.

Ruth on the bench, feeding the birds and every now and then glancing into the sky. Normand and Paulette, the middling artists, on the verandah of the B and B. A few villagers were carrying string bags of groceries home from Monsieur Béliveau's general store. And then there were the other bistro patrons, including André Castonguay and François Marois.

Clara stood in the hallway, staring at the door, slammed in her face. The sound still echoed off the walls, along the corridors, down the stairwell, and finally out the door. Spilling into the bright sunshine.

Her eyes wide, her heart pounding. Her stomach sour.

Clara thought she might throw up.

'Ah, there you are,' said Denis Fortin, standing in the doorway of the bistro. He had the great pleasure of seeing André Castonguay jump and almost knock over his white wine.

François Marois, however, did not jump. He barely reacted.

Like a lizard, thought Fortin, sunning himself on a rock.

'Tabernac,' exclaimed Castonguay. 'What the hell are you doing here?'

'May I?' asked Fortin, and took a seat at their table before either man could deny him.

They'd always denied him a seat at their table. For decades. The cabal of art dealers and gallery owners. Old men now. As soon as Fortin had decided to stop being an artist and had opened his own gallery they'd closed ranks. Against the interloper, the new-comer.

Well, he was there now. More successful than any of them.

Except, maybe, these two men. Of all the members of the art establishment in Québec, the only two whose opinion he cared about were Castonguay and Marois.

Well, one day they'd have to acknowledge him. And it might as well be today.

'I'd heard you were here,' he said, signaling to the waiter for another round.

Castonguay, he saw, was well into the white wine. Marois, though, was sipping an iced tea. Austere, cultured, restrained. Cool. Like the man.

He himself had switched to a micro-brewery beer. McAuslan. Young, golden, impertinent.

'What're you doing here?' Castonguay repeated, the emphasis on 'you', as though Fortin had to explain himself. And he almost did, in an instinctive reaction. A need to appease these men.

But Fortin stopped himself and smiled charmingly.

'I'm here for the same reason you are. To sign the Morrows.'

That brought a reaction from Marois. Slowly, so slowly, the art dealer turned his head and, looking directly at Fortin, he slowly, so slowly lifted his brows. In anyone else it might have been comical. But from Marois, the results were terrifying.

Fortin felt himself grow cold, as though he'd looked at the Gorgon's Head.

He swallowed hard and continued to stare, hoping if he'd been turned to stone it was at least with a look of casual disdain on his face. He feared, though, his face had a whole other expression.

Castonguay sputtered with laughter.

'You? Sign the Morrows? You had your shot and you blew it.' Castonguay grabbed his glass and took a great draught.

The waiter brought more drinks and Marois put out his hand to stop him. 'I think we've had enough.' He turned to Castonguay. 'Perhaps time for a little walk, don't you think?'

But Castonguay didn't think. He took the glass. 'You'll never sign the Morrows, and do you know why?'

Fortin shook his head and could have kicked himself for even reacting.

'Because they know you for what you are.' He was speaking loudly now. So loudly conversation around them died.

At the back table everyone looked around, except Thierry Pineault. He kept his face to the wall.

'That's enough, André,' said Marois, laying a hand on the other man's arm.

'No, it's not enough.' Castonguay turned to François Marois. 'You and I worked hard for what we have. Studied art, know technique. We might disagree, but it's at least an intelligent discussion. But this one,' his arm jerked in Fortin's direction, 'all he wants is a quick buck.'

'And all you want, sir,' said Fortin, getting to his feet, 'is a bottle. Who is worse?'

Fortin gave a stiff little bow and walked away. He didn't know where he was going. Just away. From the table. From the art establishment. From the two men staring at him. And probably laughing.

'People don't change,' said Beauvoir, squashing his burger and watching the juices ooze out.

Chief Justice Pineault and Suzanne had left, walking over to the B and B. And now, finally, Inspector Beauvoir could discuss murder, in peace.

'You think not?' asked Gamache. On his plate were grilled garlic shrimp and quinoa mango salad. The barbecue was working overtime for the hungry lunch crowd, producing chargrilled steaks and burgers, shrimp and salmon.

'They might seem to,' said Beauvoir, picking his burger up, 'but if you were a nasty piece of work growing up, you'll be an asshole as an adult and you'll die pissed off.'

He took a bite. Where once this burger, with bacon and mushrooms, caramelized onions and melting blue cheese, would have sent him into raptures, now it left him feeling slightly queasy. Still, he forced himself to eat, to appease Gamache.

Beauvoir noticed the Chief watching him eat and felt a slight annoyance, but that quickly faded. Mostly he didn't care. After his conversation with Myrna he'd taken himself off to the bathroom and popped a Percocet, staying there, his head in his hands, until he could feel the warmth spread, and the pain ebb and drift away.

Across the table Chief Inspector Gamache took a forkful of grilled garlic shrimp and the quinoa mango salad with genuine enjoyment.

They'd both looked up when André Castonguay had raised his voice.

Beauvoir had even gone to get up, but the Chief had stopped him. Wanting to see how this would play out. Like the rest of the patrons, they watched Denis Fortin walk stiffly away, his back straight, his arms at his side.

Like a little soldier, Gamache had thought, reminded of his son Daniel as a child, marching around the park. Either into or away from a battle. Resolute.

Pretending.

Denis Fortin was retreating, Gamache knew. To nurse his wounds.

'I suspect you don't agree?' said Beauvoir.

'That people don't change?' asked Gamache, looking up from his plate. 'No, I don't agree. I believe people can and do.'

'But not as much as the victim appeared to change,' said Beauvoir. 'That would be very chiaroscuro.'

'Very what?' Gamache lowered his knife and fork and stared at his second in command.

'It means a bold contrast. The play of light and dark.'

'Is that so? And did you make up that word?'

'I did not. Heard it at Clara's *vernissage* and even used it a few times. Such a snooty crowd. All I had to do was say "chiaroscuro" a few times and they were convinced I was the critic for *Le Monde*.'

Gamache picked his knife and fork back up and shook his head. 'So it could've meant anything and you still used it?'

'Didn't you notice? The more ridiculous the statement the more it was accepted. Did you see their faces when they realized I wasn't with *Le Monde*?'

'Very schadenfreude of you,' said Gamache and wasn't surprised to see the suspicious look on Beauvoir's face. 'So you looked up "chiaroscuro" this morning. Is that what you do when I'm not around?'

'That and Free Cell. And porn, of course, but we only do that on your computer.'

Beauvoir grinned and took a bite of his burger.

'You think the victim was very chiaroscuro?' asked Gamache.

'I don't actually. Just said that to show off. I think it's all bullshit. One moment she's a bitch, the next she's this wonderful person? Come on. That's crap.'

'I can see how they'd mistake you for a formidable critic,' said Gamache.

'Fucking right. Listen, people don't change. You think the trout in the Bella Bella are there because they love Three Pines? But maybe next year they'll go somewhere else?' Beauvoir jerked his head toward the river.

Gamache looked at his Inspector. 'What do you think?'

'I think the trout have no choice. They return because they're trout. That's what trout do. Life is that simple. Ducks return to the same place every year. Geese do it. Salmon and butterflies and deer. Jeez, deer are such creatures of habit they wear a trail through the woods and never deviate. That's why so many are shot, as we know. They never change. People are the same. We are what we are. We are who we are.'

'We don't change?' Gamache took a piece of fresh asparagus.

'Exactly. You taught me that people, that cases, are basically very simple. We're the ones who complicate it.'

'And the Dyson case? Are we complicating it?'

'I think so. I think she was killed by someone she screwed. End of story. A sad story, but a simple one.'

'Someone from her past?' Gamache asked.

'No, that's where I think you're wrong. The people who knew the new Lillian after she stopped drinking say she'd become a decent person. And the people who knew the old one, before she stopped drinking, say she was a bitch.'

Beauvoir was holding up both hands, one was clutching the massive burger, the other held a french fry. Between them was space, a divide.

'And I'm saying the old and new are the same person.' He brought his hands together. 'There's only one Lillian. Just as there's only one me. Only one you. She might have gotten better at hiding it after she joined AA, but believe me, that bitter, nasty, horrible woman was still there.'

'And still hurting people?' the Chief asked.

Beauvoir ate the fry and nodded. This was his favorite part of an investigation. Not the food, though in Three Pines that was never a hardship. He could remember other cases, in other places, when he and the Chief had gone days with barely anything to eat, or shared cold canned peas and Spam. Even that, he had to admit, had been fun. In retrospect. But this little village produced bodies and gourmet meals in equal proportion.

He liked the food, but what he mostly loved were the conversations with the Chief. Just the two of them.

'One theory is that Lillian Dyson came here to make amends to someone,' said Gamache. 'To apologize.'

'If she did I bet she wasn't sincere.'

'So why would she have been here, if she wasn't sincere?'

'To do what it was in her nature to do. To screw someone.'

'Clara?' Gamache asked.

'Maybe. Or someone else. She had lots to choose from.'

'And it went wrong,' said Gamache.

'Well, it sure didn't go right, for her anyway.'

Was the answer so simple? Gamache wondered. Was Lillian Dyson just being true to who she really was?

A selfish, destructive, hurtful person. Drunk or sober.

The same person, with the same instincts and nature.

To hurt.

'But,' said Gamache, 'how'd she know about this party? It was a private party. By invitation only. And we all know Three Pines is hard to find. How did Lillian know about the party, and how'd she find it? And how did the murderer know she'd even be here?'

Beauvoir took a deep breath, trying to think, then shook his head. 'I got us this far, Chief. It's your turn to do something useful.'

Gamache sipped his beer and grew quiet. So quiet, in fact, that Beauvoir became concerned. Maybe he'd upset the Chief with his flippant remark.

'What is it?' Beauvoir asked. 'Something wrong?'

'No, not really.' Gamache looked at Beauvoir, as though trying to make up his mind about something. 'You say people don't change, but you and Enid loved each other once, right?'

Beauvoir nodded.

'But now you're separated, on your way to a divorce. So what happened?' Gamache asked. 'Did you change? Did Enid? Something changed.'

Beauvoir looked at Gamache with surprise. The Chief was genuinely perturbed.

'You're right,' admitted Beauvoir. 'Something changed. But I don't think it was us really. I think we just realized that we weren't the people we pretended to be.'

'I'm sorry?' asked Gamache, leaning forward.

Beauvoir collected his scattered thoughts. 'I mean, we were young. I think we didn't know what we wanted. Everyone was getting married and it seemed like fun. I liked her. She liked me. But I don't think it was ever really love. And I think I was pretending, really. Trying to be someone I wasn't. The man Enid wanted.'

'So what happened?'

'After the shootings, I realized I had to be the man I was. And that man didn't love Enid enough to stay.'

Gamache was quiet for a few moments, immobile, thinking.

'You spoke to Annie Saturday night, before the *vernissage*,' said Gamache finally.

Beauvoir froze. The Chief went on, not needing a reply.

'And you saw her and David together at the party.'

Beauvoir willed himself to blink. To breathe. But he couldn't. He wondered how long before he passed out.

'You know Annie well.'

Beauvoir's brain was shrieking. Wanting this to be over, for the Chief to just say what was on his mind. Gamache finally looked up, directly at Beauvoir. His eyes, far from angry, were imploring.

'Did she tell you about her marriage?'

'*Pardon?*' Beauvoir barely whispered.

'I thought she might have said something to you, asked your advice or something. Knowing about you and Enid.'

Beauvoir's head swam. None of this was making sense.

Gamache leaned back and exhaled deeply, throwing his balled-up napkin onto his plate. 'I feel such a fool. We'd had little signs that things weren't well. David canceling dinners together, showing up late, like on Saturday night. Leaving early. They weren't as demonstrative as before. Madame Gamache and I had talked about it, but thought it might just be their relationship evolving. Less in each other's pockets. And couples grow apart, then come back together again.'

Beauvoir felt his heart start again. With a mighty thump.

'Are Annie and David growing apart?'

'She didn't say anything to you?'

Beauvoir shook his head. His brain sloshing about in there. With only one thought now. Annie and David were growing apart.

'Had you noticed anything?'

Had he? How much was real and how much was imagined, exaggerated? He remembered Annie's hand on David's arm. And David not caring. Not listening. Distracted.

Beauvoir had seen all that, but had been afraid to believe it was anything other than a shame. Affection wasted on a man who didn't care. His own jealousy speaking, and not the truth. But now . . .

'What're you saying, sir?'

'Annie came over last night for dinner and to talk. She and David are having a difficult time.' Gamache sighed. 'I'd hoped she'd said something to you. For all your arguing, I know Annie's like a little sister to you. You've known her since she was, what?'

'Fifteen.'

'Has it been that long?' asked Gamache, with amazement. 'Not a happy year for Annie. Her first crush, and it had to be on you.'

'She had a crush on me?'

'Didn't you know? Oh yes. Madame Gamache and I had to hear about it every time you visited. Jean Guy this and Jean Guy that. We tried to tell her what a degenerate you were but that just seemed to add to the attraction.'

'Why didn't you tell me?'

Gamache looked at him with amusement. 'You'd have wanted to know? You were already teasing her, it would've been intolerable. Besides, she begged us not to tell you.'

'But now you have.'

'A confidence broken. I trust you not to tell her.'

'I'll do my best. What's the problem with David?' Beauvoir looked down at his half-eaten burger, as though it had suddenly done something fascinating.

'She won't be specific.'

'Are they separating?' he asked, hoping he sounded politely disinterested.

'I'm not sure,' said Gamache. 'There's so much happening in her life, so many changes. She's taken another job, as you know. In the Family Court office.'

'But Annie hates children.'

'Well, she's not very good with them, but I don't think she hates them. She adores Florence and Zora.'

'She has to,' said Beauvoir. 'They're family. She's probably depending on them, in her old age. She'll be bitter Auntie Annie, with the stale chocolates and the doorknob collection. And they'll have to look after her. So she can't drop them on their heads now.'

Gamache laughed while Beauvoir remembered Annie with the Chief's first granddaughter, Florence. Three years ago. When Florence had been an infant. It might have been the first time his feelings for Annie had breached the surface. Shocking him with their size and ferocity. Crashing down. Swamping in. Capsizing him.

But the moment itself had been so tiny, so delicate.

There was Annie. Smiling, cradling her niece. Whispering to the tiny little girl.

And Beauvoir had suddenly realized he wanted children. And he wanted them with Annie. No one else.

Annie. Holding their own daughter or son.

Annie. Holding him.

He felt his heart tug, as tethers he never knew existed were released.

'We suggested she try to work it out with David.'

'What?' asked Beauvoir, shocked back to the present.

'We just don't want to see her make a mistake.'

'But,' said Beauvoir, his mind racing. 'Maybe she's already made the mistake. Maybe David's the mistake.'

'Maybe. But she has to be sure.'

'So what did you suggest?'

'We told her we'd support whatever she decided, but we did gently suggest couple's counseling,' said the Chief, putting his large, expressive hands on the wooden table and trying to hold Beauvoir's eyes. But all he saw was his daughter, his little girl, in their living room Sunday night.

She'd swung from sobbing to raging. From hating David, to hating herself, to hating her parents for suggesting counseling.

'Is there something you're not telling us?' Gamache had finally asked.

'Like what?' Annie had demanded.

Her father had been quiet for a moment. Reine-Marie sat beside him on the sofa, looking from him to their daughter.

'Has he hurt you?' Gamache had asked. Clearly. His eyes firmly on his daughter. Searching for the truth.

'Physically?' Annie asked. 'Has he hit me, do you mean?'

'I do.'

'Never. David would never do that.'

'Has he hurt you in other ways? Emotionally? Is he abusive?'

Annie shook her head. Gamache held his daughter's eyes. He'd peered into the faces of so many suspects trying to glean the truth. But never did anything feel so important.

If David had abused his daughter—

He could feel the rage roil up, just at the thought. What would he do if he found out the man had actually—

Gamache had pulled himself back from that precipice and nodded. Accepting her answer. He'd sat beside her then, and folded her into his arms. Rocking her. Feeling her head in the hollow by his shoulder. Her tears through his shirt. Just as he'd done when she'd cried for Humpty Dumpty. But this time she was the one who'd had a great fall.

Eventually Annie pulled away and Reine-Marie handed her some tissues.

'Would you like me to shoot David?' Gamache had asked as she blew her nose with a mighty honk.

Annie laughed, catching her breath in snags. 'Maybe just knee cap him.'

'I'll move it to the very top of my to-do list,' said her father. Then he bent down so that they were eye to eye, his face serious now. 'Whatever you decide to do, we're behind you. Understand?'

She nodded, and wiped her face. 'I know.'

Like Reine-Marie, he wasn't necessarily shocked, but he was perplexed. There seemed something Annie wasn't telling them. Something that didn't quite add up. Every couple had difficult periods. He and Reine-Marie argued at times. Hurt each other's feelings, at times. Never intentionally, but when people lived that close it was bound to happen.

'Suppose you and Dad had been married to different people when you met,' Annie finally asked, looking them square in the face. 'What would you have done?'

They were silent, staring at their daughter. It had been, thought Gamache, exactly the same question Beauvoir had recently asked.

'Are you saying you've met someone else?' Reine-Marie asked.

'No,' Annie shook her head. 'I'm saying the right person is out there for David and for me. And holding on to something wrong isn't going to fix it. This will never be right.'

Later, when he and Reine-Marie were alone, she'd asked him the same question.

'Armand,' she'd asked, taking off her reading glasses as they lay in bed, each with their own books. 'What would you have done if you'd been married when we met?'

Gamache lowered his book and stared ahead. Trying to imagine it. His love for Reine-Marie had been so immediate and so complete it was difficult seeing himself with anyone else, never mind married.

'God help me,' he finally said, turning to her. 'I'd have left her. A terrible, selfish decision, but I'd have made a rotten husband after that. All your fault, you hussy.'

Reine-Marie had nodded. 'I'd have done the same thing. Brought little Julio Jr. and Francesca with me, of course.'

'Julio and Francesca?'

'My children by Julio Iglesias.'

'Poor man, no wonder he sings so many sad songs. You broke his heart.'

'He's never recovered.' She smiled.

'Perhaps we can introduce him to my ex,' said Gamache. 'Isabella Rossellini.'

Reine-Marie snorted and picked up her book, but lowered it again.

'Not still thinking about Julio, I hope.'

'No,' she'd said. 'I was thinking about Annie and David.'

'Do you think it's over?' he'd asked.

She'd nodded. 'I think she's found someone else but doesn't want to tell us.'

'Really?' She'd surprised him, but now he thought it might be true.

Reine-Marie nodded. 'I think he might be married. Maybe someone at her law firm. That might explain why she's changing jobs.'

'God, I hope not.'

But he also knew there was nothing he could do either way. Except be there to help pick up the pieces. But that image reminded him of something.

'Well, gotta get back to work,' said Beauvoir, rising. 'The porn doesn't look itself up.'

'Wait,' said Gamache. And seeing his Chief's face Beauvoir sank back into his chair.

Gamache sat silently, his forehead furrowed. Thinking. Beauvoir had seen that look many times. He knew Chief Inspector Gamache was following a lead in his head. A thought, that led to another, that led to another. Into the darkness, not so much an alley as a shaft. Trying to find the thing most deeply hidden. The secret. The truth.

'You said the raid on the factory was what finally made you decide to separate from Enid.'

Beauvoir nodded. That much was the truth.

'I wonder if it had the same effect on Annie.'

'How so?'

'It was a shattering experience, for everyone,' said the Chief. 'Not just us. But our families too. Maybe, like you, it made Annie reexamine her life.'

'Then why wouldn't she tell you that?'

'Maybe she didn't want me to feel responsible. Maybe she doesn't even realize it herself, not consciously.'

Then Beauvoir remembered his conversation with Annie, before the *vernissage*. How she'd asked him about his separation. And made a vague allusion to the raid, and the fall-out.

She'd been right of course. It was the final push he'd needed.

He'd shut her down, refused to discuss it out of fear he'd say too much. But had she really been wanting to talk about her own turmoil?

'How would you feel if that's what happened?' Beauvoir asked his Chief.

Chief Inspector Gamache sat back, his face slightly troubled.

'It might be a good thing,' suggested Beauvoir, quietly. 'It would be good, wouldn't it, if something positive came out of what happened? Maybe Annie can find real love now.'

Gamache looked at Jean Guy. Drawn, tired, too thin. He nodded.

'*Oui.* It would be good if something positive came out of what happened. But I'm not sure the end of my daughter's marriage could be considered a good thing.'

But Jean Guy Beauvoir disagreed.

'Would you like me to stay?' he asked.

Gamache roused himself from his reverie. 'I'd like you to actually do some work.'

'Well, I do have to look up "schnaugendender".'

'Look up what?'

'That word you used.'

'"Schadenfreude",' smiled Gamache. 'Don't bother. It means being happy for the misfortunes of others.'

Beauvoir paused at the table. 'I think that describes the victim pretty well. But Lillian Dyson took it to the next step. She actually created the misfortune. She must've been a very happy person.'

But Gamache thought differently. Happy people didn't drink themselves to sleep every night.

Beauvoir left and the Chief Inspector sipped his coffee and read from the AA book, noting passages underlined and comments in the margins, losing himself in the archaic but beautiful language of this book that so gently described the descent into hell and the long climb back out. Eventually he closed the book over his finger and stared into space.

'May I join you?'

Gamache was startled. He got to his feet, bowing slightly, and pulled out a chair. 'Please do.'

Myrna Landers sat, putting her éclair and *café au lait* on the bistro table. 'You looked lost in thought.'

Gamache nodded. 'I was thinking about Humpty Dumpty.'

'So the case is almost solved.'

The Chief smiled. 'We're getting closer.' He looked at her for a moment. 'May I ask you a question?'

'Always.'

'Do you think people change?'

Myrna, the éclair on its way to her mouth, paused. Lowering the pastry she looked at the Chief Inspector with clear, searching eyes.

'Where did that come from?'

'There's some debate over whether the dead woman had changed, whether she was the same person everyone knew twenty years ago, or if she was different.'

'What makes you think she'd changed?' Myrna asked, then took a bite.

'That coin you found in the garden? You were right, it's from AA and it belonged to the dead woman. She'd stopped drinking for eight months now,' said the Chief. 'People who knew her in AA describe a completely different person than Clara does. Not just slightly different, but completely. One is kind and generous, the other is cruel and manipulative.'

Myrna frowned and thought, taking a sip of her *café au lait*.

'We all change. Only psychotics remain the same.'

'But isn't that more growth than change? Like harmonics, but the note remains the same.'

'Just a variation on a theme?' asked Myrna, interested. 'Not really change?' She considered. 'I think that's often the case. Most people grow but they don't become totally different people.'

'Most. But some do?'

'Some, Chief Inspector.' She watched him closely. Saw the familiar face, clean-shaven. The graying hair curling slightly around his ears. And the deep scar by his temple. Below that scar his eyes were kindly. She'd been afraid they might have changed. That when she next looked into them they'd have hardened.

They hadn't. Nor had he.

But she didn't kid herself. He might not look it, but he'd changed. Anyone who came out of that factory alive came out different.

'People change when they have no choice. It's change or die. You mentioned AA. Alcoholics only stop drinking when they hit bottom.'

'What happens then?'

'What you'd expect after a great fall.' She looked at him now, understanding dawning. A great fall. 'Like Humpty Dumpty.'

He nodded his head slightly.

'When people hit bottom,' she continued, 'they can lie there and die, most do. Or they can try to pick themselves up.'

'Put the pieces back together,' said Gamache. 'Like our friend Mr Dumpty.'

'Well he had the help of all the King's horses and all the King's men,' said Myrna, with mock earnestness. 'And even they couldn't put Mr Dumpty together again.'

'I've read the reports,' agreed the Chief.

'Besides, even if they succeeded, he'd just fall again.' Now she really did look serious. 'The same person will just keep doing the same stupid thing, over and over. So if you put all the pieces back exactly as they were, why would you expect your life to be different?'

'Is there another option?'

Myrna smiled at him. 'You know there is. But it's the hardest. Not many have the stomach for it.'

'Change,' said Gamache.

Maybe, he thought, that was the point of Humpty Dumpty. He wasn't meant to be put together again. He was meant to be different. After all, an egg on a wall would always be in peril.

Maybe Humpty Dumpty had to fall. And maybe all the King's men had to fail.

Myrna drained her mug and rose. He rose too.

'People do change, Chief Inspector. But you need to know something.' She lowered her voice. 'It's not always for the better.'

'Why don't you go and say something to him?' Gabri asked, as he put the tray of empty glasses on the counter.

'I'm busy,' said Olivier.

'You're cleaning glasses, one of the waiters can do that. Speak to him.'

Both men looked out the leaded glass window, at the large man sitting alone at the table. A coffee and a book in front of him.

'I will,' said Olivier. 'Just don't push me.'

Gabri took the dishtowel and started drying the glasses as his partner washed the suds off. 'He made a mistake,' said Gabri. 'He apologized.'

Olivier looked at his partner, with his cheery white and red heart-shaped apron. The one he'd begged Gabri not to buy for Valentine's Day two years ago. Had begged him not to wear. Had been ashamed of, and prayed no one they knew from Montréal visited and saw Gabri in such a ridiculous outfit.

But now Olivier loved it. Didn't want him to change it.

Didn't want him to change anything.

As he washed the glasses he saw Armand Gamache take a sip of his coffee and get to his feet.

Beauvoir walked over to the sheets of paper tacked to the walls of the old railway station. Uncapping the Magic Marker he waved it under his nose as he read what was written. It was all in neat, black columns.

Very soothing. Legible, orderly.

He read and reread their lists of evidence, of clues, of questions. Adding some gathered by their investigations so far that day.

They'd interviewed most of the guests at the party. Not surprisingly, none had admitted to wringing Lillian Dyson's neck.

But now, staring at the sheets, something occurred to him.

All other thoughts left his mind.

Was it possible?

There were others at the party. Villagers, members of the art community, friends and family.

But someone else was there. Someone mentioned a number of times but never remarked upon. And never interviewed, at least not in depth.

Inspector Beauvoir picked up the phone and dialed a Montréal number.

TWENTY

—

Clara closed the door and leaned against it. Listening for Peter. Hoping, hoping. Hoping she'd hear nothing. Hoping she was alone.

And she was.

Oh, no no no, she thought. *Still the dead one lay moaning.*

Lillian wasn't dead. She was alive in Mr Dyson's face.

Clara had raced home, barely able to keep her car on the road, her view obscured by that face. Those faces.

Mr and Mrs Dyson. Lillian's mom and dad. Old, infirm. Almost unrecognizable as the robust, cheery people she'd known.

But their voices had been strong. Their language stronger.

There was no doubt. Clara had made a terrible mistake. And instead of making things better, she'd made them worse.

How could she have been so wrong?

'Fucking little asshole.' André Castonguay shoved the table away and got up, unsteadily. 'I have a thing or two to say to him.'

François Marois also got up. 'Not now, my friend.'

They both watched as Denis Fortin walked back down the hill and into the village. He didn't hesitate, didn't look in their direction. Didn't deviate from a course he'd clearly chosen.

Denis Fortin was making for the Morrow house. That much was clear to Castonguay, to Marois, and to Chief Inspector Gamache, who was also watching.

'But we can't let him speak to them,' said Castonguay, trying to pull himself away from Marois.

'He won't be successful, André. You know that. Let him have his try. Besides, I saw Peter Morrow leave a few minutes ago. He's not even there.'

Castonguay turned unsteadily toward Marois. *'Vraiment?'* There was a slightly stupid smile on his face.

'Vraiment,' Marois confirmed. 'Really. Why don't you go back to the inn and relax.'

'Good idea.'

André Castonguay walked slowly, deliberately across the village green.

Gamache had watched all this, and now his gaze shifted to François Marois. There was a look of weary sophistication on the art dealer's face. He seemed almost bemused.

The Chief Inspector stepped off the *terrasse* and joined Marois, whose eyes hadn't left the Morrow cottage, as though he expected it to do something worth witnessing. Then his look shifted to Castonguay, trudging up the dirt road.

'Poor André,' said Marois to Gamache. 'That really wasn't very nice of Fortin.'

'What wasn't?' asked Gamache, also watching the gallery owner. Castonguay had stopped at the top of the hill, swayed a bit, then carried on. 'It seemed to me Monsieur Castonguay was the one being abusive.'

'But he was provoked,' said Marois. 'Fortin knew how André would react as soon as he sat at the table. And then . . .'

'Yes?'

'Well, ordering more drinks. Getting André drunk.'

'Did he know Monsieur Castonguay has a problem?'

'Daddy's little problem?' Marois smiled, then shook his head. 'It's become an open secret. Most of the time he has it under control. Has to. But sometimes . . .'

He made an eloquent gesture with his hands.

Yes, thought Gamache. Sometimes . . .

'And then to actually tell André he was here to try to sign the Morrows. Fortin was just asking for trouble. Smug little man.'

'Aren't you being a bit disingenuous?' Gamache asked. 'After all, that's the reason you're here.'

Marois laughed. '*Touché*. But we were here first.'

'Are you telling me there's a dibs system? There's so much about the art world I didn't know.'

'What I meant is that no one needs to tell me what great art is. I see it, I know it. Clara's art is brilliant. I don't need the *Times*, or Denis Fortin, or André Castonguay to tell me. But some people buy art with their ears and some with their eyes.'

'Does Denis Fortin need to be told?'

'In my opinion, yes.'

'And do you spread your opinion around? Is that why Fortin hates you?'

François Marois turned his complete attention to the Chief Inspector. His face was no longer a cipher. His astonishment was obvious.

'Hate me? I'm sure he doesn't. We're competitors, yes, often going after the same artists and buyers, and it can get pretty gruesome, but I think there's a respect, a collegiality. And I keep my opinions to myself.'

'You told me,' said Gamache.

Marois hesitated. 'You asked. Otherwise I would never have said anything.'

'Is Clara likely to sign with Fortin?'

'She might. Everyone loves a repentant sinner. And I'm sure he's doing his mea culpas right now.'

'He already has,' said Gamache. 'That's how he got invited to the *vernissage*.'

'Ahhh,' nodded Marois. 'I was wondering about that.' He looked troubled for the first time. Then, with an effort, his handsome face cleared. 'Clara's no fool. She'll see through him. He didn't know what he had with her before, and he still doesn't understand her paintings. He's worked hard to build up a reputation as cutting edge, but he isn't. One false move, one bad show, and the whole thing will come crashing down. A reputation's a fragile thing, as Fortin knows better than most.'

Marois motioned toward André Castonguay, almost at the inn. 'Now, he's less vulnerable. He has a number of clients and one big corporate account. Kelley Foods.'

'The baby food manufacturer?'

'Exactly. Huge corporate buyer. They invest heavily in art for their offices worldwide. Makes them seem less money grubbing and more sophisticated. And guess who finds them the art?'

It needed no answer. André Castonguay had plunged headlong into the doorway of the inn and spa. And disappeared.

'They're fairly conservative, of course,' continued the dealer. 'But then, so's André.'

'If he's so conservative why's he interested in Clara Morrow's work?'

'He's not.'

'Peter?'

'I think so. This way he gets two for one. A painter whose work he can sell to Kelley Foods. Safe, conventional, respected. Nothing too daring or suggestive. But he'll also get all sorts of publicity and legitimacy in picking up someone truly avante-garde. Clara Morrow. Never underestimate the power of greed, Chief Inspector. Or ego.'

'I'll make a note of that, *merci.*' Gamache smiled and watched Marois follow Castonguay up the hill.

'Not with a club the heart is broken.'

Gamache turned toward the voice. Ruth was sitting on the bench, her back to him.

'Nor with a stone,' she said, apparently to thin air. '*A whip so small you could not see it I have known.*'

Gamache sat next to her.

'Emily Dickinson,' said Ruth, staring ahead of her.

'Armand Gamache,' said the Chief Inspector.

'Not me, you idiot. The poem.'

She turned angry eyes on him, only to find the Chief smiling. She gave one large guffaw.

'*Not with a club the heart is broken,*' repeated Gamache. It was familiar. Reminded him of something someone had recently said.

'A lot of drama today,' said Ruth. 'Too much noise. Scares away the birds.'

And sure enough, there wasn't a bird in sight, though Gamache knew she was thinking of one bird, not many.

Rosa, her duck, who had flown south last fall. And had not returned with the rest. Had not returned to the nest.

But Ruth hadn't given up hope.

Sitting quietly on the bench, Gamache remembered why that phrase from the Dickinson poem was so familiar. Opening the book still in his hands he looked down at the words highlighted by a dead woman.

Hearts are broken. Sweet relationships are dead.

Then he noticed someone watching them from the bistro. Olivier.

'How's he doing?' Gamache asked, gesturing slightly toward the bistro.

'Who?'

'Olivier.'

'I don't know. Who cares?'

Gamache was quiet for a moment. 'He's a good friend of yours, as I remember,' said the Chief Inspector.

Ruth was silent, her face immobile.

'People make mistakes,' said Gamache. 'He's a good man, you know. And I know he loves you.'

Ruth made a rude noise. 'Look, all he cares about is money. Not me, not Clara or Peter. Not even Gabri. Not really. He'd sell us all for a few bucks. You should know that better than most.'

'I'll tell you what I know,' said Gamache. 'I know he made a mistake. And I know he's sorry. And I know he's trying to make it up.'

'But not to you. He barely looks at you.'

'Would you? If I arrested you for a crime you hadn't committed, would you forgive?'

'Olivier lied to us. To me.'

'Everyone lies,' said Gamache. 'Everyone hides things. His were pretty bad, but I've seen worse. Much worse.'

Ruth's already thin lips all but disappeared.

'I'll tell you who did lie,' she said. 'That man you were just speaking to.'

'François Marois?'

'Well, I don't know his fucking name. How many men were you just talking to? Whatever his name was, he wasn't telling you the truth.'

'How so?'

'The young fellow wasn't ordering all the drinks. He was. Long before the young guy showed up the other fellow was drunk.'

'Are you sure?'

'I have a nose for booze, and an eye for drunks.'

'And an ear for lies, apparently.'

Ruth cracked a smile that surprised even her.

Gamache got up and cast a look toward Olivier, before bowing slightly to Ruth and whispering so that only she could hear,

'Now here's a good one:
you're lying on your deathbed.
You have one hour to live.'

'Enough,' she interrupted him, her bony hand up and in his face. Not quite touching it, but close enough to block the words. 'I know how it ends. And I wonder if you really know the answer to the question?' She looked at him hard. *'Who is it, exactly, you have needed all these years to forgive,* Chief Inspector?'

He straightened up and left her, walking toward the bridge over the Rivière Bella Bella, lost in thought.

'Chief.'

He turned to see Inspector Beauvoir striding toward him from the Incident Room.

He knew that look. Jean Guy had news.

TWENTY-ONE

—

All Clara Morrow wanted was to be left alone. But instead she found herself in her kitchen, listening to Denis Fortin. Looking more boyish than ever. More contrite.

'Coffee?' she asked, then wondered why she'd offered. All she wanted was for Fortin to leave.

'No, *merci*,' he smiled. 'I really don't want to disturb you.'

But you already are, thought Clara, and knew it was uncharitable. She was the one who'd opened the door. She was beginning to dislike doors. Closed or open.

If someone had said a year ago that she'd long for this prestigious gallery owner to leave her home, she'd never have believed it. Her whole effort, the efforts of every artist she knew, including Peter, was to get Fortin's attention.

But all she could think about was getting rid of him.

'I suspect you know why I'm here,' said Fortin, with a grin. 'I'd actually hoped to speak with both you and Peter. Is he home?'

'No, he's not. Do you want to come back when he's here?'

'I don't want to waste your time,' he said, getting up. 'I realize we got off to a terrible start. All my fault. I wish I could change all that. I was very, very stupid.'

She started to say something and he put up his hand and smiled.

'You don't have to be nice, I know what an ass I was. But I've learned, and I won't be like that again. To you or to anyone else, I hope. I'd like to just say this once, and leave. Let you and maybe your husband think about it. Is that OK?'

Clara nodded.

'I'd like to represent both you and Peter. I'm young and we can all grow together. I'll be around a long time to help guide your careers. I think that's important. My thought is to build toward a solo show for each of you and then a combined exhibition. Take advantage of both your talents. It would be thrilling. The show of the year, of the decade. Please consider it, that's all I ask.'

Clara nodded and watched Fortin leave.

Inspector Beauvoir joined the Chief Inspector on the bridge.

'Look at this.' Beauvoir gave him a printout.

Gamache noticed the heading then quickly read down the page. Stopping, as though hitting a wall, three quarters of the way down. He lifted his eyes and met Beauvoir's, who was waiting. Smiling.

The Chief went back to the sheet, reading more slowly this time. Reading right to the end.

He didn't want to miss anything, the way they almost had.

'Well done,' he said, handing the page back to Inspector Beauvoir. 'How did you find that?'

'I was going over the interviews and realized we might not have talked to everyone at the party down here.'

Gamache was nodding. 'Good. Excellent.'

He looked toward the B and B, his arm extended. 'Shall we?'

A few moments later they stepped from the bright, warm sunshine onto the cooler verandah. Normand and Paulette had watched their progress across the village green. Indeed, Gamache suspected everyone in the village had.

It might look sleepy, but Three Pines was in fact keenly aware of everything.

The two artists looked up as they approached.

'I wonder if I might ask you a very great favor?' Gamache said, smiling.

'Of course,' said Paulette.

'Could you perhaps go for a walk around the village, or have a drink at the bistro? On me?'

They looked at him, uncomprehending at first, then it clicked with Paulette. Gathering up her book and a magazine she nodded. 'I think a walk would be a great idea, don't you, Normand?'

Normand looked like he'd just as soon stay where he was, in the comfortable swing on the cool porch, with an old *Paris Match* and a lemonade. Gamache couldn't say he blamed him. But he did need them gone.

The two men waited until the artists were well out of ear-shot. Then they turned to the third occupant of the verandah.

Suzanne Coates sat in a rocking chair with a lemonade. But instead of a magazine she had her sketch pad on her lap.

'Hello,' she said, though she didn't get up.

'*Bonjour,*' said Beauvoir. 'Where's the Chief Justice?'

'He went off to his home in Knowlton. I've checked in here for the night.'

'Why?' asked Beauvoir. He pulled up a seat, while Gamache sat in a nearby rocking chair, and crossed his legs.

'I plan to stay until you find out who killed Lillian. I figure that's pretty big incentive for you to get the job done quickly.'

She smiled, as did Beauvoir.

'It would move a lot faster if you told us the truth.'

That wiped the smile off her face.

'About what?'

Beauvoir handed her the sheet of paper. Suzanne took it and read, then handed it back. Her considerable energy didn't so much wane as contract, like an implosion. She looked from Beauvoir to his boss. Gamache was giving her nothing. He simply continued to watch with interest.

'You were here the night of the murder,' said Beauvoir.

Suzanne paused and Gamache was surprised to see that even at this late date, when there was no hope of escape, she still seemed to be considering a lie.

'I was,' she finally admitted, darting looks from one man to the other.

'Why didn't you tell us that?'

'You asked if I was at the *vernissage* at the Musée, and I wasn't. You didn't actually ask about the party here.'

'Are you saying you didn't lie?' demanded Beauvoir, glancing at Gamache as if to say, See? Another deer on the same old path. People don't change.

'Look,' said Suzanne, squirming in her chair, 'I go to lots of *vernissages*, but I'm mostly on the business end of a cocktail wiener. I told you that. It's how I pick up extra cash. I don't hide it. Well, I mean, I hide it from Revenue Canada. But I told you all about it.'

She implored Gamache, who nodded.

'You didn't tell us all about it,' said Beauvoir. 'You failed to mention you were here when your friend was murdered.'

'I wasn't a guest. I was working the party. And not even as a waiter. I was in the kitchen all night. I didn't see Lillian. Didn't even know she was here. Why would I? Look, this party was planned long ago. I was hired weeks ago.'

'Did you mention it to Lillian?' asked Beauvoir.

'Of course not. I don't tell her about every party I'm working.'

'Did you know who it was for?'

'Not a clue. I knew it was an artist, but most of them are. The caterers I work for do mostly *vernissages*. I didn't decide to come here, it was the party I was assigned. I had no idea who it was for, and I didn't care. All I cared about was that no one complained, and that I got paid.'

'When we told you that Lillian had died at a party in Three Pines you must have known then,' Beauvoir pressed. 'Why didn't you tell us then?'

'I should have,' she admitted. 'I know that. In fact, that was one of the reasons I came down. I knew I had to tell you the truth. I was just getting my courage up.'

Beauvoir looked at her with a mixture of disgust and admiration.

It was a masterful display of deceit. He glanced over to the Chief, who was also pondering the woman. But his face was indecipherable.

'Why didn't you tell us this last night?' Beauvoir demanded again. 'Why lie?'

'I was shocked. When you said Three Pines at first I thought I must have heard wrong. It was only after you left it really sank in. I was here that night. Maybe even here when she died.'

'And why didn't you tell us as soon as you arrived today?' asked Beauvoir.

She shook her head. 'I know. It was stupid. But the longer it went on the more I realized how bad it looked. And then I convinced myself it didn't matter since I hadn't been out of the bistro kitchen all night. I hadn't seen anything. Really.'

'Do you have a beginner's chip?' Gamache asked.

'Pardon?'

'An AA beginner's chip. Bob told me everyone takes one. Do you have one?'

Suzanne nodded.

'May I see it?'

'I forgot. I gave it away.'

The two men stared and her color rose.

'To who?' Gamache asked.

Suzanne hesitated.

'To who?' Beauvoir demanded, leaning forward.

'I don't know, I can't think.'

'What you can't think of is a lie. We want the truth. Now,' snapped Beauvoir.

'Where is your beginner's chip?' asked Gamache.

'I don't know. I gave it to one of my sponsees, years ago. We do that.'

But the Chief Inspector thought the chip was much closer than that. He suspected it was in an evidence bag, having been found caked in dirt where Lillian fell. He suspected that was one of the many reasons Suzanne Coates had come to Three Pines. To try to find her missing chip. To see how the investigation was going. To perhaps try to derail it.

But not, certainly, to tell them the truth.

Peter walked down the dirt road and noticed their car parked a little askew, on the grass border.

Clara was home.

He'd sat in St. Thomas's Anglican Church for much of the afternoon. Repeating the prayers he remembered as a child, which pretty much boiled down to the Lord's Prayer, the dinner prayer, 'Bless, oh Lord, this food to our use ...', and Vespers, but then he remembered that was Christopher Robin and not one of the apostles.

He'd prayed. He'd sat quietly. He'd even sung something from the hymnal.

His bottom hurt and he felt neither joyful nor triumphant.

And so he left. If God was in St. Thomas's He was hiding from Peter.

God and Clara both avoiding him. It was not, by most standards, a good day. Though as he walked down into the village he had to think Lillian would have traded places with him.

There were worse things than not meeting God. Meeting Him, for instance.

As he approached their home he noticed Denis Fortin just leaving. The two men waved to each other as Peter walked up the path.

He found Clara in the kitchen, staring at a wall.

'I just saw Fortin,' said Peter, coming up behind her. 'What did he want?'

Clara turned around and the smile froze on Peter's face.

'What is it? What's the matter?'

'I've done something terrible,' she said. 'I need to speak to Myrna.'

Clara went to walk around him, making for the door.

'No, wait, Clara. Talk to me. Tell me about it.'

'Did you see her face?' Beauvoir asked, as he hurried to catch up with Gamache.

The two men were walking across the village green, having left Suzanne sitting on the verandah. The rocking chair stilled. The watercolor on her lap, of Gabri's exuberant garden, crunched and ruined. By her own hand. The hand that made it had destroyed it.

But Beauvoir had also seen Gamache's face. The hardening, the chill in his eyes.

'Do you think that beginner's chip was hers?' asked Beauvoir, falling into step beside the Chief.

Gamache slowed. They were almost on the bridge once again.

'I don't know.' His face was set. 'Thanks to you we know she lied about being in Three Pines on the night Lillian died.'

'She says she never left the kitchen,' said Beauvoir, surveying the village. 'But it would've been easy for her to sneak around back of the shops and into Clara's garden.'

'And meet Lillian there,' said Gamache. He turned and looked toward the Morrow home. They were standing on the bridge. A few trees and lilac bushes had been planted, to give Clara and Peter's garden privacy. Even guests on the bridge wouldn't have seen Lillian there. Or Suzanne.

'She must have told Lillian about Clara's party, knowing that Clara was on Lillian's apology list,' said Beauvoir. 'I bet she even encouraged Lillian to come down. And arranged to meet her in the garden.' Beauvoir looked around again. 'It's the closest garden to the bistro, the most convenient. That explains why Lillian was found there. It could've been anyone's, it just happened to be Clara's.'

'So she lied about telling Lillian about the party,' said Gamache. 'And she lied about not knowing who the party was for.'

'I can guarantee you, sir. Everything that woman says is a lie.'

Gamache nodded. It was certainly beginning to look like that.

'Lillian might have even gotten a lift with Suzanne—' said Beauvoir.

'That won't work,' said Gamache. 'She had her own car.'

'Right,' said Beauvoir, thinking, trying to see the sequence of events. 'But she might have followed Suzanne down.'

Gamache considered that, nodding. 'That would explain how she found Three Pines. She followed Suzanne.'

'But no one saw Lillian at the party,' said Beauvoir. 'And in that red dress, if she was here someone would have seen her.'

Gamache considered that. 'Maybe Lillian didn't want to be seen, until she was ready.'

'For what?'

'To make an amend to Clara. Maybe she stayed in her car until an appointed hour, when she'd arranged to meet her sponsor in the garden. Perhaps with the promise of a final word of support before going out to make a difficult amend. She must have thought Suzanne was doing her a great favor.'

'Some favor. Suzanne killed her.'

Gamache stood there and thought, then shook his head. It fit, maybe. But did it make sense? Why would Suzanne kill her sponsee? Kill Lillian? And in a way that was so premeditated. And so personal. To wrap her hands around Lillian's neck, and break it?

What could have driven Suzanne to do that?

Was the victim not quite the woman Suzanne described? Was Beauvoir right again? Maybe Lillian hadn't changed, but was the same cruel, taunting, manipulative woman Clara had known. Had she pushed Suzanne over the edge?

Did Suzanne have a great fall, but this time did she reach up and take Lillian with her? By the throat.

Whoever killed Lillian had hated her. This was not a dispassionate crime. This was thought out and deliberate. As was the weapon. The murderer's own hands.

'I made such a terrible mistake, Peter.'

Gamache turned toward the voice, as did Beauvoir. It was Clara, and it came from behind the lush screen of leaves and lilacs.

'Tell me, you can tell me,' said Peter, his voice low and reassuring, as though trying to coax a cat from under the sofa.

'Oh, God,' said Clara, taking rapid, shallow breaths. 'What've I done?'

'What did you do?'

Gamache and Beauvoir exchanged looks and both edged quietly closer to the stone wall of the bridge.

'I went to visit Lillian's parents.'

Neither Sûreté officer could see Peter's face, or Clara's for that matter, but they could imagine it.

There was a long pause.

'That was kind,' said Peter, but his voice was uncertain.

'It wasn't kind,' snapped Clara. 'You should've seen their faces. It was like I'd found two people almost dead and then decided to skin them. Oh, God, Peter, what've I done?'

'Are you sure you don't want a beer?'

'No, I don't want a beer. I want Myrna. I want . . .'

Anybody but you.

It wasn't said, but everyone heard it. The man in the garden and the men on the bridge. And Beauvoir found his heart aching for Peter. Poor Peter. So at a loss.

'No wait, Clara,' Peter's voice called. It was clear Clara was walking away from him. 'Just tell me, please. I knew Lillian too. I know that you were once good friends. You must've loved the Dysons too.'

'I did,' said Clara, stopping. 'I do.' Her voice was clearer. She'd turned to face Peter, to face the officers hidden behind the trees. 'They were only ever kind to me. And now I've done this.'

'Tell me,' said Peter.

'I asked a bunch of people before I went and they all said the same thing,' said Clara, walking back toward Peter. 'Not to go. That the Dysons would be too hurt to see me. But I went anyway.'

'Why?'

'Because I wanted to say how sorry I was. About Lillian. But also about our falling out. I wanted to give them the chance to talk about old times, about Lillian as a kid. To exchange stories maybe, with someone who knew and loved her.'

'But they didn't want to?'

'It was horrible. I knocked on the door and Mrs Dyson answered. She'd obviously been crying for a long time. She looked all collapsed. It took her a moment to recognize me but when she did . . .'

Peter waited. They all waited. Imagining the elderly woman at the door.

'. . . I've never seen such hate. Never. If she could've killed me right there she would've. Mr Dyson joined her. He's tiny, barely there, barely alive. I remember when he was huge. He used to pick us up and carry us on his shoulders. But now he's all stooped over and,' she paused, obviously searching for words, 'tiny. Just tiny.'

There were no words. Or hardly any more.

'"You killed our daughter," he said. "You killed our daughter." And then he tried to swing his cane at me but it got all caught in the door and he just ended up crying in frustration.'

Beauvoir and Gamache could see it now. Frail, grieving, gentlemanly Mr Dyson reduced to a murderous rage.

'You tried, Clara,' said Peter, in a calming, comforting voice. 'You tried to help them. You couldn't have known.'

'But everyone else did. Why didn't I?' demanded Clara with a sob. And once again Peter was wise enough to stay quiet. 'I thought about it all the way back here and you know what I realized?'

Again Peter waited, though Beauvoir, hidden fifteen feet away, almost spoke, almost asked, 'What?'

'I convinced myself it was somehow courageous, saintly even, to go and comfort the Dysons. But I really did it for myself. And now look what I've done. If they weren't so old I think Mr Dyson would've killed me.'

Gamache and Beauvoir could hear muffled sobs, as Peter hugged his wife.

The Chief Inspector turned away from the bridge, and started walking toward the Incident Room, on the other side of the Rivière Bella Bella.

At the Incident Room they separated, Beauvoir to follow up the now promising leads and Gamache to head in to Montréal.

'I'll be back by dinner,' he said, slipping behind the wheel of his Volvo. 'I need to speak with Superintendent Brunel about Lillian Dyson's art. About what it might be worth.'

'Good idea.'

Beauvoir, like Gamache, had seen the art on the victim's walls. They just looked like weird, distorted images of Montréal streets. Familiar, recognizable, but where the streets and buildings in real life were angular, the ones in the paintings were rounded, flowing.

They made Beauvoir slightly nauseous. He wondered what Superintendent Brunel would make of them.

So did Chief Inspector Gamache.

It was late afternoon by the time he arrived in Montréal and made his way through rush hour traffic to Thérèse Brunel's Outremont apartment.

He'd called ahead, making sure the Brunels were home, and as he climbed the stairs Jérôme opened the door. He was an almost perfect square, and was certainly a perfect host.

'Armand.' He extended his hand and grasped the Chief Inspector's. 'Thérèse is in the kitchen, preparing a little tray. Why don't we sit on the balcony. What can I get you to drink?'

'Just a Perrier, *s'il te plaît*, Jérôme,' said Gamache, following his host through the familiar living room, past the piles of open reference books and Jérôme's puzzles and ciphers. They walked onto the front balcony, which looked across the street and onto a leafy, green park. It was hard to believe that just around the corner was avenue Laurier, filled with bistros and brasseries and boutiques.

He and Reine-Marie lived just a few streets over and had been to this home many times, for dinner or for cocktails. And the Brunels had been to their home many times as well.

While this wasn't exactly a social call the Brunels managed to make everything feel comfortable. If it was necessary to talk about crime, about murder, why not do it over drinks and cheese and spiced sausage and olives?

Armand Gamache's feelings exactly.

'*Merci*, Jérôme,' said Thérèse Brunel, handing the tray of food to her husband and accepting a white wine.

They stood on the balcony in the afternoon sun, looking out over the park.

'Lovely time of year, isn't it?' said Thérèse. 'So fresh.'

Then she turned her attention to the man beside her. And he to her.

Armand Gamache saw a woman he'd known for more than ten years. Had trained, in fact. Had taught at the academy. She'd stood out from the rest of the cadets, not only for her obvious intelligence but because she was old enough to be their mother. She was, in fact, a full decade older than Gamache himself.

She'd joined the Sûreté after a distinguished career as the chief curator at the Musée des Beaux Arts in Montréal. A celebrated art historian and advocate, she'd been consulted by the Sûreté on the appearance of a mysterious painting. Not the disappearance, mind, but the sudden appearance of one.

In that instance, in that crime, she'd discovered a love of puzzles. After helping on a few cases she'd realized it was what she really wanted to do, was meant to do.

So she'd taken herself off to a quite astonished recruiting officer and signed up.

That had been twelve years ago. And now she was one of the

senior officers in the Sûreté, outstripping her teacher and mentor. But only, they both knew, because he'd chosen, and been given, a different path.

'How can I help, Armand?' she asked, indicating one of their balcony chairs with an elegant, slender hand.

'Shall I leave you?' Jérôme asked, struggling out of his seat.

'No, no,' Gamache waved him down, 'please stay if you'd like.'

Jérôme always liked. A retired emergency room doctor, he'd loved puzzles all his life and was more than amused that his wife, always gently poking fun at his endless ciphers, was now neck deep in puzzles herself. Of a more serious nature, to be sure.

Chief Inspector Gamache put his Perrier down and brought the dossier out of his satchel. 'I'd like you to look at these and tell me what you think.'

Superintendent Brunel spread the photographs on the wrought iron table, using their glasses and food platter to pin them down against the slight breeze.

The men waited quietly as she studied them. She took her time. Cars drove by. Across the way, in the park, children kicked around a soccer ball and played on the swings.

Armand Gamache sipped his sparkling water, stirring the bubbly wedge of lime with his finger, and watched as she examined the paintings from Lillian Dyson's apartment. Thérèse looked stern, a seasoned investigator handed an element in a murder case. Her eyes darted here and there, scanning the paintings. And then they slowed and rested first on one image then another. She moved the paintings about on the table, tilting her coiffured head to the side.

Her eyes never softened, but her expression did, as she began to lose herself in the paintings and the puzzle.

Armand hadn't told her anything about them. About who'd done them, about what he wanted to know. He'd given her no information, except that they were from a murder investigation.

He wanted her to form her own opinion, unsullied by his questions or comments.

The Chief Inspector had taught her at the academy that a crime scene wasn't simply on the ground. It was in people's heads. Their memories and perceptions. Their feelings. And you don't want to contaminate those with leading questions.

Finally she leaned away from the table and looked up, first as always at Jérôme, then to Gamache.

'Well, Superintendent?'

'Well, Chief Inspector, I can tell you I've never seen these works or this artist before. The style is singular. Like nothing else out there. Deceptively simple. Not primitive, but not self-conscious either. They're beautiful.'

'Would they be valuable?'

'Now there's a question.' She considered the images again. 'Beautiful isn't in fashion. Edgy, dark, stark, cynical, that's what galleries and curators want. They seem to think they're more complex, more challenging, but I can tell you, they're not. Light is every bit as challenging as dark. We can discover a great deal about ourselves by looking at beauty.'

'And what do these,' Gamache indicated the paintings on the table, 'tell you?'

'About myself?' she asked with a smile.

'If you'd like, but I was thinking more about the artist.'

'Who is he, Armand?'

He hesitated. 'I'll tell you in a moment, but I'd like to hear what you think.'

'Whoever painted these is a wonderful artist. Not, I think, a young artist. There's too much nuance. As I said, they're deceptively simple, but if you look closely they're made up of grace notes. Like here.' She pointed to where a road swept around a building, like a river around a rock. 'That slight play of light. And over here, in the distance, where sky and building and road all meet and become difficult to distinguish.'

Thérèse looked at the paintings, almost wistfully. 'They're magnificent. I'd like to meet the artist.' She looked into Gamache's eyes and held them for a moment longer than necessary. 'But I suspect I won't. He's dead, isn't he? He's the victim?'

'Why do you say that?'

'Besides the fact you're the head of homicide?' She smiled and beside her Jérôme gave a harrumph of amusement. 'Because for you to bring these to me the artist would have to be either a suspect or the victim, and whoever painted these would not kill.'

'Why not?'

'Artists tend to paint what they know. A painting is a feeling. The best artists reveal themselves in their works,' said Superintendent Brunel, glancing again at the art. 'Whoever painted this was content. Not, perhaps, perfect, but a content man.'

'Or woman,' said the Chief Inspector. 'And you're right, she's dead.'

He told them about Lillian Dyson, her life and her death.

'Do you know who killed her?' Jérôme asked.

'I'm getting closer,' said Gamache, gathering up the photographs. 'What can you tell me about François Marois and André Castonguay?'

Thérèse raised a finely shaped brow. 'The art dealers? Are they involved?'

'Along with Denis Fortin, yes.'

'Well,' said Thérèse, sipping her white wine. 'Castonguay has his own gallery, but most of his income comes from the Kelley contract. He landed it decades ago and has managed to hold on to it.'

'You make it sound tenuous.'

'I'm actually amazed he still has it. He's lost a lot of his influence in recent years, with new, more contemporary galleries opening.'

'Like Fortin's?'

'Exactly like Fortin. Very aggressive. Fortin's taken a real run at the gentlemen's club. Can't say I blame him. They shut him out so he had no choice but to pound down the doors.'

'Denis Fortin doesn't seem content with pounding down just the doors,' said Gamache, taking a thin slice of cured Italian sausage and a black olive. 'I get the impression he wants everything to come crashing down around Castonguay's ears. Fortin wants it all, and means to get it.'

'Van Gogh's ear,' said Thérèse, and smiled as Gamache paused before putting the sliced sausage in his mouth. 'Not the cold cut, Armand. You're safe. Though I can't vouch for the olives.'

She gave him a wicked look.

'Did you just say, "Van Gogh's ear"?' asked the Chief Inspector. 'Someone else used the same expression earlier in the investigation. Can't remember who now. What does it mean?'

'It means scooping up everything for fear of missing something important. Like they missed Van Gogh's genius in another era. Denis Fortin is doing just that. Grabbing up all the promising artists, in case one of them turns out to be the new Van Gogh, or Damien Hirst or Anish Kapoor.'

'The next big thing. He missed it with Clara Morrow.'

'He sure did,' agreed Superintendent Brunel. 'Which must make him desperate not to do it again.'

'So he'd want this artist?' Gamache indicated the now closed dossier on the table.

She nodded. 'I think so. As I said, beautiful isn't in, but then if you're going to find the next big thing it won't be among all the people doing what everyone else's doing. You need to find someone creating their own form. Like her.'

She tapped the dossier with a manicured finger.

'And François Marois?' asked Gamache. 'How does he fit in?'

'Ah, now there's a good question. He gives every appearance of urbane disinterest, certainly in the infighting. Seems to live above the fray. Claims to only want to promote great art and the artists. And he certainly knows it. Of all the dealers in Canada, and certainly in this city, I'd say he's most likely to recognize talent.'

'And then what?'

Thérèse Brunel looked at Gamache closely. 'You've obviously spent time with him, Armand. What do you think?'

Gamache thought for a moment. 'I think of all the dealers he's the most likely to get what he wants.'

Brunel nodded slowly. 'He's a predator,' she finally said. 'Patient, ruthless. As charming as can be, as you've probably noticed, until he spots what he wants. And then? Best to hide somewhere until the slaughter is over.'

'That bad?'

'That bad. I've never known François Marois not to get his way.'

'Has he ever broken the law?'

She shook her head. 'Not the laws of man, anyway.'

The three friends sat quietly for a moment. Until finally Gamache spoke.

'I've come across a quote in this case and wonder if you know it. *He's a natural, producing art like it's a bodily function.*'

He sat back and watched their reactions. Thérèse, so serious a moment before, smiled a bit while her husband guffawed.

'I know that quote. From a critique, I believe. But many years ago,' said Thérèse.

'It was. A review in *La Presse*. Written by the dead woman.'

'By her or about her?'

'The review mentions a "he", Thérèse,' said her husband with amusement.

'That's true, but Armand might have misquoted. He's famous for shoddy work, you know,' she said with a smile, and Gamache laughed.

'Well, this time, by dumb luck, I got it right,' he said. 'Do you remember who the line was written about?'

Thérèse Brunel thought, then shook her head. 'I'm sorry, Armand. As I say, it's become a famous line, but I suspect whoever it was written about didn't become a famous artist.'

'Are reviews that important?'

'To Kapoor or Twombly, no. To someone just starting out, a first show, they're crucial. Which reminds me, I saw the wonderful reviews of Clara's show. We couldn't make the *vernissage*, but I'm not surprised. Her works are genius. I called to congratulate her but couldn't get through. I'm sure she's busy.'

'Are Clara's paintings better than these?' Gamache indicated the dossier.

'They're different.'

'*Oui*. But if you were still the chief curator at the Musée, which artist would you buy, Clara Morrow or Lillian Dyson?'

Thérèse considered for a moment. 'You know, I say they're different, but they have one big thing in common. They're both quite joyous, in their own way. How lovely if that's where art's heading.'

'Why?'

'Because it might mean that's where the human spirit's heading. Out of a period of darkness.'

'That would be good,' agreed Gamache, picking up his dossier. But before he rose he looked at Thérèse, then made up his mind.

'What do you know about Chief Justice Thierry Pineault?'

'Oh, God, Armand, don't tell me he's involved?'

'He is.'

Superintendent Brunel took a deep breath. 'I don't know him personally, only as a jurist. He seems very straight, upstanding. No blemishes on his judicial record. Everyone has their stumbles, but I haven't heard anything against him as a sitting judge.'

'And off the bench?' pressed Gamache.

'I'd heard he liked his drink and could get pretty nasty at times. But then, he had reason to. Lost a grandson, or was it a little girl? A DUI. He quit drinking after that.'

Gamache got up and helped clear the table, carrying the tray into their kitchen. Then he made for the door. But there he paused.

He'd been debating saying anything to Thérèse and Jérôme. But if there was ever a time, it was now. And if there was ever a couple, it was them.

As they stood on the threshold, Gamache slowly closed the door and looked at them. 'I have another question for you,' he said quietly. 'Nothing to do with the case. It's about something else.'

'*Oui?*'

'The video of the attack,' he said, watching them closely. 'Who do you really think released it onto the Internet?'

Jérôme looked perplexed, but Superintendent Brunel didn't.

She looked angry.

TWENTY-TWO

Thérèse led them back into the apartment, away from the door, and away from the open French windows. Into the dim center of the room.

'There was an internal investigation,' she said, her voice low and angry. 'You know that, Armand. They discovered it was a hacker. Some kid who found the file and probably didn't even know what it was. That's all.'

'If it was some kid with dumb luck why haven't they found him?' Gamache asked.

'Leave it for the investigators,' she said, her voice softer now.

Gamache considered the two people in front of him. An older man and woman. Creased, worn.

But then, so was he.

Which was why he'd warned Beauvoir away from looking further. Why he hadn't quietly assigned this to any of his other hundred agents. Any one of them would have gladly dug deeper.

But what would they find buried there?

No, best to do it himself. With the help of two people he trusted. And the Brunels had one other, outstanding, qualification. They were nearer the end than the beginning. As was he. The end of all their careers. The end of all their lives. If they lost either now, they'd still have lived fully.

Gamache would not put a young agent on this case. He would not lose another one, not if he had a choice.

'I waited for the report of the internal investigation,' he said. 'I read it, and spent two months studying it, thinking about it.'

Superintendent Brunel considered carefully before asking the question she really didn't want the answer to. 'And what did you conclude?'

'That the investigation was flawed, perhaps even intentionally. In fact, almost certainly intentionally. Someone inside the Sûreté is trying to cover up the truth.'

There was no use pretending otherwise. That was what he believed.

'What makes you say that?' Jérôme asked.

'Because it would be nearly impossible for a hacker to find the video file. And if one had, the investigators would have found him. That's what they do. There's a whole department that only investigates cyber crime. They'd have found him.'

Thérèse and Jérôme were quiet. Then Jérôme turned to his wife.

'What do you think?' he asked.

She looked from her husband to her guest.

'You say someone inside the Sûreté is trying to cover up the truth. What do you think is the truth?'

'That it was an internal leak,' said Gamache. 'Someone inside the Sûreté released the video, deliberately.'

Even as he spoke he realized he wasn't telling her anything she didn't already know, or suspect.

'But why?' she asked. It was clearly a question she'd been asking herself.

'I think the "why" depends on the "who",' said the Chief. He watched her closely. 'This is no surprise to you, is it?'

Thérèse Brunel hesitated then shook her head. 'I also read the report, as did all the other superintendents. I don't know what they thought, but I came to the same conclusion you did. Not necessarily that it was an inside job,' she looked at him with warning, 'but that for some strange reason, the investigation was inconclusive. Given that it involved the deaths of four officers and the betrayal of their families and the service, I'd have expected the investigation to be rigorous. I'd have thought they'd throw everything they had at it. And they claimed to. And yet the conclusion, under all the rhetoric, was shockingly thin. The tape was stolen by an unknown hacker.'

She shook her head and took a deep breath, exhaling before she spoke again.

'We have a problem, Armand.'

He nodded, looking at both of them. 'We have a big problem.'

Superintendent Brunel sat and indicated chairs for the other two, who joined her. She paused, about to cross the Rubicon. 'Who do you think did it?'

Gamache held her intelligent, bright eyes. 'You know who I think.'

'I do, but I need you to say it.'

'Chief Superintendent Sylvain Francoeur.'

Outside they could hear the shrieks of children chasing each other, running and laughing.

'This'll be fun,' Jérôme Brunel said, rubbing his hands together at the thought of a thorny puzzle.

'Jérôme!' said his wife. 'Haven't you been listening? The head of the Sûreté du Québec may very well have done something not only illegal, but deeply cruel. An attack on officers dead and alive. And their families. For his own ends.'

Thérèse turned back to Gamache. 'If it was Francoeur, why would he do it?'

'I don't know. But I know he's been trying to get rid of me for years. He might have thought this would be the final shove.'

'But the video didn't make you look bad, Armand,' said Jérôme. 'Just the opposite. It made you look very good.'

'And what would cripple you, Jérôme?' Gamache looked with affection at the man across from him. 'Being falsely accused or being falsely praised? Especially when there was so much pain and so little to praise.'

'It wasn't your fault,' said Jérôme, looking his friend square in the face.

'*Merci*,' Gamache inclined his head, 'but it wasn't my finest hour either.'

Jérôme nodded. The spotlight could be a tricky thing. It could send a person rushing for someplace dim to hide. Away from the crippling glare of public approval.

Gamache hadn't run, but both Jérôme and Thérèse knew he'd been sorely tempted. Had come within a breath of handing in his warrant and retiring. And no one would have blamed him. Just as no one blamed him for the deaths of those young agents. No one, except Gamache himself.

But instead of retiring, retreating, the Chief Inspector had stayed.

And Jérôme wondered if this was why. If there was one more thing Chief Inspector Gamache needed to do. His final duty, to both the living and the dead.

To find the truth.

Agent Isabelle Lacoste wiped her face with her hands and looked at her watch.

Seven thirty-five in the evening.

The Chief had called earlier with what seemed a strange request. A suggestion really. It had meant extra work, but she'd assigned another agent to the search. Now five of them were going over the files in the morgue of the Montréal daily *La Presse*.

It was going much more quickly, but not knowing when the review had been published, not the year, not even the decade, was difficult. And Chief Inspector Gamache had just made it more difficult still.

'Look at this,' one of the junior agents said, turning to Lacoste. 'I think I've found it.'

'Oh, thank God,' moaned another.

The other three agents crowded around the microfiche.

'Can you magnify it?' Lacoste asked and the agent clicked a dial. The screen leapt closer, and clearer.

There, in bold type, were the words 'A Deeply Moving Exhibit'. And what followed was not so much a review or critique but a comedy routine, a riff on the word 'move', as in 'movement'. As in 'bodily function'.

Even the drained agents chuckled as they read.

It was juvenile, immature. But still, quite funny. Like watching someone slip on a banana peel. And fall. Nothing subtle about it. But for some reason laughable.

Isabelle Lacoste did not laugh.

Unlike the others, she'd seen how this review concluded. Not with the period on the page, but with the body sprawled in the late spring garden.

It started with a joke, and it ended in murder.

Agent Lacoste had copies of the review printed out, making sure the date was clear. Then she thanked and dismissed the other agents and got into her car for the drive back to Three Pines. Convinced that in her car she carried a conviction.

TWENTY-THREE

Peter sat in Clara's studio.

She'd gone off right after a fairly silent supper to speak with Myrna. He hadn't been enough after all. He'd been tested, he knew. And found wanting.

He was always wanting. But up until now he hadn't really known what he wanted, so he'd gone after everything.

Now, at least, he knew.

He sat in Clara's studio and waited. God, he knew, lived here too. Not just in St. Thomas's on the hill. But here, in the cluttered space, with the dried-up apple cores, the tins with oil-hardened brushes shoved into them. The paintings.

The big fiberglass feet and the uteruses rampant.

Across the hall in his pristine studio he'd made space for inspiration. All clean and tidy. But inspiration had mistaken the address, and landed here instead.

No, thought Peter, it wasn't just inspiration he was looking for, it was more.

That had been the problem. All his life he'd mistaken the one for the other. Thinking inspiration was enough. Mistaking the created for the Creator.

He'd brought a bible with him into Clara's studio, in case that would help. In case God needed proof he was sincere. He flipped through it, finding the apostles.

Thomas. Like their church. Doubting Thomas.

How odd that Three Pines would have a church named after a doubter.

And his own name? Peter. He was the rock.

To pass the time until God found him Peter skimmed the bible for any references to his name.

He found lots of very satisfying ones.

Peter the rock, Peter the apostle, Peter the saint. A martyr even.

But then Peter was something else too. Something Jesus had said to Peter when the apostle had been faced with an obvious miracle. A man walking on water. And Peter, though he himself was also walking on water, hadn't believed it.

Hadn't believed all the evidence, all the proof.

'O, ye of little faith.'

It had been said of Peter.

He closed the book.

It was twilight by the time Agent Isabelle Lacoste parked the car and entered the Incident Room. She'd called ahead and Chief Inspector Gamache and Inspector Beauvoir were waiting for her.

She'd read them the review over the phone, but still both men met her, anxious to actually see it.

She handed a copy to each of them and watched.

'Holy shit,' said Beauvoir, having raced through it. They both turned to Gamache, who had his reading glasses on and was taking his time. Finally he lowered the paper and removed his glasses.

'Well done.' He nodded gravely to Agent Lacoste. To say what she found was surprising was an understatement.

'Well, that just about does it, don't you think?' said Beauvoir. *'He's a natural, producing art like it's a bodily function,'* he quoted without looking at the review. 'How'd so many get it wrong, though?'

'Over time things can get a little warped,' said Gamache, 'we all know that from interviewing witnesses. People remember things differently. Fill in the blanks.'

'So, what now?' asked Beauvoir. It was clear what he thought should happen. Gamache considered for a moment then turned to Agent Lacoste.

'Would you do the honors? Inspector, perhaps you could go with her.'

Agent Lacoste laughed. 'You don't expect trouble, surely.'

But she instantly regretted it.

The Chief, though, smiled. 'I always expect trouble.'

'So do I,' said Beauvoir, checking his gun, as did Lacoste. The two headed out into the night while Chief Inspector Gamache sat down, and waited.

Monday being a quiet night at the bistro it was only half full.

As Lacoste entered she scanned the room, not taking anything for granted. Just because it was familiar, and comfortable, didn't mean it was safe. Most accidents happen close to home, most murders happen in the home.

No, this was not the time, or place, to let her guard down.

Myrna and Dominique and Clara were having tisane and dessert, talking quietly at a table by the mullioned window. In the far corner, by the stone fireplace, she could see the artists, Normand and Paulette. And at a table across from them sat Suzanne and her dinner companions, Chief Justice Thierry Pineault and Brian, dressed in torn jeans and a worn leather jacket.

Denis Fortin and François Marois shared a table, Fortin telling some anecdote that amused him. Marois looked polite and slightly bored. There was no sign of André Castonguay.

'Après toi,' Beauvoir murmured to Lacoste as they moved into the bistro. By now most had noticed the two Sûreté officers. At first the patrons looked, some smiled, then went back to their conversations.

But after a moment some looked up again, sensing something different.

Myrna, Clara, Dominique grew quiet and watched as the officers walked between the tables, leaving silence in their wake.

Past the three women.

Past the art dealers.

At Normand and Paulette's table they stopped. And turned.

'May I have a word?' Agent Lacoste asked.

'Here? Now?'

'No. I think perhaps someplace more private, don't you?' And Agent Lacoste quietly placed the photocopied article on the round wooden table.

Then that table too fell silent.

Except for Suzanne's groan, 'Oh, no.'

Chief Inspector Gamache rose as they entered and greeted them as though it was his home and they honored guests.

No one was fooled. Nor were they meant to be. It was a courtesy, nothing more.

'Would you have a seat, please?' He motioned to the conference table.

'What's all this about?' Chief Justice Thierry Pineault asked.

'Madame,' said Gamache, ignoring Pineault and concentrating on Suzanne, pointing to a chair.

'Messieurs.' The Chief then turned to Thierry and Brian. The Chief Justice and his tattooed, pierced, shaved companion took chairs across from Gamache. Beauvoir and Lacoste sat on either side of the Chief.

'Can you explain that, please?' Chief Inspector Gamache's voice was conversational. He pointed to the old *La Presse* article in the middle of the table, an island between their sparring continents.

'In what way?' Suzanne asked.

'In any way you choose,' said Gamache. He sat quietly, one hand cupped in the other.

'Is this an interrogation, Monsieur Gamache?' the Chief Justice demanded.

'If it was, neither of you would be sitting with us.' Gamache looked from Thierry to Brian. 'This is a conversation, Monsieur Pineault. An attempt to understand an inconsistency.'

'He means a lie,' said Beauvoir.

'You've gone too far.' Pineault turned to Suzanne. 'I'm going to advise you to stop answering questions.'

'Are you her lawyer?' Beauvoir asked.

'I'm a lawyer,' snapped Pineault. 'And good thing too. You can call this what you like, but using a soothing voice and nice words doesn't disguise what you're trying to do.'

'And what's that?' demanded Beauvoir, matching the Chief Justice's tone.

'Trap her. Confuse her.'

'We could have waited until she was alone and questioned her then,' said Beauvoir. 'You should be glad you're even allowed in here.'

'All right,' said Gamache, raising his hand, though his voice was still reasonable. Both men paused, mouths open, ready to attack. 'Enough. I'd like to speak with you, Mr Justice Pineault. I think my Inspector has a good point.'

But before speaking with the Chief Justice, Gamache took Beauvoir aside and whispered, 'Keep yourself in check, Inspector. No more of that.'

He held Beauvoir's gaze.

'Yessir.'

Beauvoir took himself off to the bathroom and sat once again in a stall. Quietly. Gathering himself up. Then he washed his face and hands, and taking half a pill he looked at his reflection.

'Annie and David are having difficulties,' he whispered and felt himself calm down. *Annie and David are having difficulties.* The pain in his gut began to slip away.

Outside in the Incident Room, Chief Inspector Gamache and Chief Justice Pineault had walked a distance from the others and now stood beside the large red fire truck.

'Your man is treading too close to the line, Chief Inspector.'

'But he's right. You need to decide. Are you here as Suzanne Coates's advocate or her AA . . .' he paused, not sure what word to use, '. . . friend.'

'I can be both.'

'You can't, and you know it. You're the Chief Justice. Decide, sir. Now.'

Armand Gamache faced Chief Justice Pineault, waiting for an answer. The Chief Justice was taken aback, clearly not thinking he'd be challenged.

'I'm here as her AA friend. As Thierry P.'

The answer surprised Gamache and he showed it.

'You think that's the weaker role, Chief Inspector?'

Gamache didn't say anything, but he obviously did.

Thierry smiled briefly, then looked very serious. 'Anyone can make sure her rights aren't violated. I think you can. But what you can't do is guard her sobriety. Only another alcoholic can help her stay sober through this. If she loses that she loses everything.'

'Is it that fragile?' asked Gamache.

'It's not that sobriety is so fragile, it's that addiction is so cunning. I'm here to guard her against her addiction. You can guard her rights.'

'You trust me to do that?'

'You I do. But your Inspector?' The Chief Justice nodded toward Beauvoir, who was just leaving the restrooms. 'You need to watch him.'

'He's a senior homicide officer,' said Gamache, his voice cold. 'He needs no watching.'

'Every human needs watching.'

That sent chills down Gamache, and he wondered at this man who had such power. Who had so many gifts, and so many flaws.

And he wondered, once again, who was Chief Justice Pineault's sponsor. What was he whispering into that powerful ear?

'Monsieur Pineault has agreed to be Madame Coates's AA friend and to help her in that role,' said the Chief Inspector as they took their seats.

Both Lacoste and Beauvoir looked surprised but didn't say anything. It made their job easier.

'You lied to us,' Beauvoir repeated, and held the review up to Suzanne's face. 'Everyone quoted it wrong, didn't they? Remembered it as being written about some guy no one could remember. But it wasn't about a man, it was about a woman. You.'

'Suzanne,' warned Thierry, then looked at Gamache. 'I'm sorry. I can't just stop being a jurist.'

'You'll have to try harder, monsieur,' said Gamache.

'Besides,' said Suzanne, 'it's a little late for caution, don't you think?' She turned back to the Sûreté officers. 'A Chief Justice, a Chief Inspector, and now it appears I've become the chief suspect.'

'Too many chiefs again?' asked Gamache with a rueful smile.

'Way too many for my comfort,' said Suzanne. She waved at the sheet of paper and snorted. 'Goddamned review. Bad enough to be insulted like that, but then to have it misquoted. The least they could do is get the insult right.'

She seemed more amused than angry.

'It threw us off,' admitted Gamache, leaning his elbows on the table. 'Everyone quoted it as "He's a natural ..." when in fact the review says, "She's a natural. ..."'

'How'd you finally realize that?' asked Suzanne.

'Reading the AA book helped,' said Gamache, nodding toward the large book still on his desk. 'It talks about the alcoholic as "he", but clearly many are "she's". All the way through this investigation people did it. Where a gender was in question there was an assumption it was "he" and not "she". I realized it's a sort of automatic position. When people couldn't remember who the review was written about they just said, "He's a natural …", when in fact Lillian wrote it about you. Agent Lacoste here finally found it in the clippings morgue of La Presse.'

They all looked at the photocopied article. Something dragged up from a morgue. Buried in the files, but far from dead.

There was a picture of Suzanne, unmistakable even twenty-five years younger. She was grinning and standing in front of one of her paintings. Proud. Excited. Her dream finally coming true. Her art finally noticed. After all, the reviewer for *La Presse* was there.

Suzanne's smile in the photograph was permanent, but in person it faded, to be replaced by something else. A look of almost whimsy.

'I remember that moment. The photographer asking me to stand beside one of my works and smile. But smiling wasn't a problem. Had he asked me to stop, that might've been difficult. The *vernissage* was at a local café. Lots of people there. And then Lillian introduced herself. I'd seen her at shows but always avoided her. She seemed so sour. But this time she was really sweet. Asked me some questions and said she was going to do a review of my show in *La Presse*. That photograph,' she gestured toward the paper on the table, 'was taken about thirty seconds after she said that.'

They all looked again.

It showed a young Suzanne with a smile that burst out of the old photograph. It lit up the room even now. A young woman, though, who didn't yet realize the ground had just fallen out from underneath her. Who didn't yet appreciate she'd been tossed into mid-air. Into thin air. By the sweet woman beside her, taking notes. Also smiling.

It was a chilling image. Like seeing a person just as the truck enters the frame. Milliseconds before the disaster.

'*She's a natural,*' said Suzanne, not needing to read the review, '*producing art like it's a bodily function.*' She looked up from the table, and smiled. 'Never had another solo show. Too humiliated. Even if gallery owners had forgotten I hadn't. I didn't think I could survive another review like that.'

She looked at Chief Inspector Gamache.

'All the King's horses, and all the King's men,' he said quietly. And she nodded.

'I'd had a great fall.'

'You lied to us,' said the Chief.

'I did.' She looked directly into his eyes.

'Suzanne.' The Chief Justice placed a hand on her arm.

'It's OK,' she said. 'I was always going to tell them the truth, you know that. It's just a shame they came for me first, before I had a chance to volunteer it.'

'You had plenty of chances,' said Beauvoir.

Pineault jerked, springing to her defense, but contained himself.

'You're right,' said Suzanne.

'She's telling the truth,' said Brian.

Everyone turned to him, surprised by the words, but also the voice. It was shockingly young, reminding them that beneath the ink and torn skin was a boy.

'Suzanne asked Thierry and me to join her for dinner. To talk,' said Brian. 'She told us all about that.' He gestured an inked hand casually toward the article. 'And said she was going to speak to you first thing in the morning.'

It was also shocking to hear this tattooed, pierced kid call the Chief Justice by his first name. Gamache looked at Pineault and couldn't decide if he admired him for helping such a damaged young man, or felt he'd lost all sense.

What other mistakes in judgment was the distinguished jurist making?

The Chief Inspector turned experienced eyes on Brian. The young man was relaxed, comfortable even. Was he high? Gamache wondered. He certainly seemed removed from the situation. Not amused, but not upset either. Sort of floating above it.

'And what did you tell her?' asked Beauvoir, keeping his eye on Brian. He'd met punks like this before, and it rarely ended well.

'I was torn,' admitted Pineault. 'The jurist in me thought she should get a lawyer, who'd probably tell her to keep quiet. Not volunteer information. The AA member thought she should tell the truth immediately.'

'And who won?' asked Beauvoir.

'Your people arrived before I could say anything.'

'You must have known, though, that this was improper,' said Gamache.

'The Chief Justice giving advice to a murder suspect?' Thierry asked. 'Of course I knew it was improper, perhaps even unethical. But if your daughter or son were suspected of murder and came to you, would you send them off to someone else?'

'Of course not. But you're not saying Suzanne is a blood relative?'

'I'm saying I know Suzanne better than most, and she knows me. Better than any parent, sibling, child. Just as we know Brian, and he us.'

'I appreciate that you understand each other's addiction to alcohol,' said Gamache. 'But you can't claim to know what's in each other's hearts. You can't be saying that just by virtue of being sober and belonging to AA Suzanne is innocent. You can't possibly know if she's even telling the truth now. And you can't possibly know if she's guilty of murder.'

Thierry bristled at that and the two powerful men stared at each other.

'We owe each other our lives,' said Brian.

Gamache leaned forward, fixing sharp eyes on the young man. 'And one of you is dead.'

Still staring at Brian he pointed to the wall behind him. Filled with photographs of Lillian, sprawled in the Morrows' garden. Gamache had deliberately placed all three facing the wall. And facing the pictures. So that none could forget why they were there.

'You don't understand,' said Suzanne, her voice rising, an edge of desperation in it now. 'When Lillian did that to me,' she pointed to the review, 'we were different. Two drunks. I was nearing the end of my drinking and she was just starting. And yes, I hated her for it. I was already fragile and it pushed me right over the edge. After that I spent all day getting pissed and high. Whoring for my next drink. It was disgusting. I was disgusting. And finally I hit bottom and came into AA. And started to put my life together again.'

'And when Lillian walked through the doors of AA twenty years later?' Gamache asked.

'I was surprised how much I still hated her—'

'Suzanne,' the Chief Justice cautioned again.

'Look, Thierry, I'm either going to tell it all, or why bother. Right?'

He looked unhappy, but agreed.

'But then she asked me to be her sponsor,' said Suzanne, turning back to the investigators, 'and something weird happened.'

'What?' asked Beauvoir.

'I forgave her.'

This was met with silence, broken eventually by Beauvoir.

'Just like that?'

'Not quite just like that, Inspector. I first had to agree. There's something freeing, when you help your enemy.'

'Did she ever apologize for that review?' the Chief asked.

'She did. About a month ago.'

'Was she sincere, do you think?' Agent Lacoste asked.

Suzanne paused to think, then nodded. 'I wouldn't have accepted it if I thought it wasn't. I really believe she was sorry she'd done that to me.'

'And to others?' asked Lacoste.

'And to others,' agreed Suzanne.

'So, if she apologized to you for that review,' Chief Inspector Gamache nodded to the page on the table, 'presumably she was also going around apologizing to other people she reviewed.'

'I think that's probably true. She didn't tell me about it if she was. I thought her apology to me was just because we were sponsor–sponsee and she needed to clear it up. But now that I think about it I think you're right. I'm not the only one she apologized to.'

'And not the only artist whose career she destroyed?' asked Gamache.

'Probably not. Not every review was as spectacularly cruel as mine. I take some pride in that. But they'd have been no less effective.'

Suzanne smiled but the officers facing her had caught the sharp edge that sliced toward them on the words 'spectacularly cruel'.

She hasn't forgiven, thought Gamache. At least, not completely.

When Suzanne and the others had left, the three officers sat around the conference table.

'Do we have enough to make an arrest?' asked Lacoste. 'She admits to harboring a long-standing hatred of the victim and to being here. She had motive and opportunity.'

'But there's no proof,' said Gamache, leaning back in his chair. It was frustrating. They were so close to making a case against Suzanne Coates, but they couldn't quite nail it. 'It's all suggestive. Very suggestive.' He picked up the review and stared at it, then lowered it and looked at Lacoste.

'You need to go back to *La Presse.*'

Isabelle Lacoste's face fell. 'Anything but that, *patron*. Can't you just shoot me?'

'I'm sorry,' he smiled a little wearily. 'I think that morgue has more bodies in it.'

'How so?' asked Beauvoir.

'The other artists whose careers Lillian killed.'

'The other people she was apologizing to,' said Lacoste, resigned, getting to her feet. 'Maybe she came down to Clara's party not to say sorry to Clara, but to apologize to someone else.'

'You don't think Suzanne Coates killed Lillian?' asked Beauvoir.

'I don't know,' admitted the Chief. 'But I suspect if Suzanne wanted to kill her she'd have done it sooner. And yet ...' Gamache paused. 'Did you notice her reaction when talking about the review?'

'She's still angry,' said Lacoste.

Gamache nodded. 'She's spent twenty-three years in AA trying to get over her resentments, and she's still angry. Can you imagine someone who hasn't been trying? How angry they must be?'

Beauvoir picked up the review and stared at the joyous young woman.

What happened when not only hopes were dashed, but dreams and careers. A whole life? But of course, he knew the answer to that. They all did.

It was tacked on the wall behind them.

Jean Guy Beauvoir splashed water on his face and felt the stubble beneath his hands. It was two thirty in the morning and he couldn't sleep. He'd woken with an ache, had lain in bed hoping it would go. But of course, it didn't.

So he'd dragged himself up, and to the bathroom.

Now he turned his face this way and that. Staring at his reflection. The man in the mirror was drawn. With lines. Bold strokes of lines not created by laughter, around his eyes and mouth. Between his brows. On his forehead. He brought his hand up and stroked his cheeks, trying to iron out the wrinkles. But they wouldn't go.

And now he bent closer. The stubble, in the bright glare of the B and B bathroom, was gray.

He turned his head to the side. There was gray at his temples. His whole head was shot through with gray. When had that happened?

My God, he thought. *Is this what Annie sees? An old man? Worn and gray? Oh, God*, he thought.

Annie and David are having difficulties. But too late.

Beauvoir walked back into the bedroom and sat on the side of the bed, staring into space. Then he slid his hand beneath the pillow and taking the top off the bottle he shook out a pill. It sat in the palm of his hand. Staring at it, slightly bleary, he closed his fist over it. Then he swiftly opened his hand and tossed the pill into his mouth, then chased it down with a gulp of water from the glass on the nightstand. Beauvoir waited. For the now familiar sensation. Slowly he began to feel the ache subside. But another, deeper hurt remained.

Jean Guy Beauvoir got dressed and quietly left the B and B, disappearing into the night.

Why hadn't he seen it before?

Beauvoir leaned closer to the screen, shocked by what he saw. He'd watched the video hundreds of times. Over and over. He'd seen it all, every wretched frame, filmed by the cameras on the headgear.

Then how could he have missed this?

He hit replay, and watched again. Then hit replay, and watched again.

There he was, on the screen. Weapon out, aiming at a gunman. Suddenly he was shoved backward. His legs buckled. As Jean Guy watched, he saw himself fall to his knees. Then pitch forward face first onto the floor. He remembered that.

He could still see the filthy concrete floor rushing toward him. Still see the dirt, as his face smashed into it.

And then the pain. Indescribable pain. He'd clutched at his abdomen, but the pain was beyond his reach.

On the screen he heard a shout, 'Jean Guy!' And then Gamache, assault rifle in hand, ran across the open factory floor. Grabbing him by the back of the tactical vest, he'd dragged Beauvoir behind a wall.

And then the intimate close-up. Of Beauvoir drifting in and out of consciousness. Of Gamache speaking to him, commanding him to stay awake. Bandaging him and holding his hand over the wound, to stanch the blood.

Of seeing the blood on the Chief's hand. So much blood on his hands.

And then Gamache had leaned forward. And done something not meant to be seen by anyone else. He'd kissed Jean Guy on the forehead in a gesture so tender it was as shocking as the gunfire.

Then he left.

It wasn't the kiss that stunned Beauvoir. It was what came after. Why hadn't he ever seen it before? Of course, he'd seen it, but he'd never really recognized it for what it was.

Gamache had left him.

Alone.

To die.

He'd abandoned him, to die alone on a filthy factory floor.

Beauvoir hit replay, replay, replay. And in each, of course, the same thing happened.

Myrna was wrong. He wasn't upset because he'd failed to save Gamache. He was angry because Gamache had failed to save him.

And the bottom dropped out from beneath Jean Guy Beauvoir.

Armand Gamache groaned and looked at the clock.

Three twelve.

His bed at the B and B was comfortable, the duvet warm around him as the cool night air drifted through the open window, bringing with it the hooting of an owl in the distance.

He lay in bed, pretending he was about to fall asleep.

Three eighteen.

It was rare now for him to wake in the middle of the night, but it still happened.

Three twenty-two.

Three twenty-seven.

Gamache resigned himself to the situation. Getting up, he threw on some clothes and tiptoed downstairs. Putting on his Barbour coat and a cap he left the B and B. The air was fresh and cool and now even the owl was quiet.

Nothing stirred. Except a homicide detective.

Gamache walked slowly, counter-clockwise, around the village green. The homes were still and dark. People asleep inside.

The three tall pines rustled slightly in the breeze.

Chief Inspector Gamache walked, his pace measured, his hands clasped behind his back. Clearing his mind. Not thinking about the case, trying, in fact, to not think about anything. Trying to just take in the fresh night air and the peace and quiet.

A few paces past Peter and Clara's home he stopped and looked over the bridge, to the Incident Room. A light was on. Not bright. Barely even visible.

It wasn't so much light he saw at the window as not dark.

Lacoste? he wondered. Had she found something and returned? Surely she'd wait until morning.

He walked across the bridge, toward the old railway station.

Looking through the window he could see that the light was a glow from one of their terminals. Someone was sitting in the dark in front of a computer.

He couldn't quite see who. It looked like a man, but it was too far away and the person was in too much shadow.

Gamache didn't have a gun. Never carried one, if he could help it. Instead, he'd automatically taken his reading glasses from the bedside table. He never went anywhere without tucking them into his pocket. In his opinion they were far more help, and more powerful, than any gun. Though he had to admit, they didn't seem all that helpful right now. He briefly considered going back and rousing Beauvoir, but thought better of it. Whoever this was might be gone by then.

Chief Inspector Gamache tried the door. It was unlocked.

Slowly, slowly, he opened it. The door creaked and he held his breath, but the figure in front of the screen didn't move. He seemed transfixed.

Finally Gamache had the door open enough to enter. Standing just inside he took everything in. Was the intruder alone, or were there more?

He scanned the dark corners, but saw no movement.

The Chief took a few more steps into the Incident Room, preparing to confront the person in front of the screen.

Then he saw what was on the monitor. Images flickered in the dark. Of Sûreté agents carrying automatic weapons, moving through a factory. As Gamache watched he saw Beauvoir hit. Beauvoir fall. And he saw himself racing across the cavernous room to get to him.

Whoever was at the screen was watching the pirated video. From the back the Chief could see the intruder had short hair and was slender. That much, and only that, Gamache could see.

More images flashed on the screen. Gamache saw himself bending over Beauvoir. Bandaging him.

Gamache could barely watch. And yet whoever was sitting in front of it was mesmerized. Unmoving. Until now. Just as the Gamache on the video left Beauvoir, the intruder's right hand moved, and the picture skipped.

Back to the beginning.

And the raid started all over again.

Gamache edged closer and as he did his vision and his certainty increased. Until finally, with a sick feeling in his stomach, he knew.

'Jean Guy?'

Beauvoir almost fell out of the chair. He grabbed for the mouse, madly trying to click. To pause, to stop, to close the images. But it was too late. Way too late.

'What're you doing?' Gamache asked, approaching.

'Nothing.'

'You're watching the video,' the Chief said.

'No.'

'Of course you are.'

Gamache strode over to his own desk and turned on the lamp. Jean Guy Beauvoir was sitting at his computer, staring at the Chief, his eyes red and bleary.

'Why're you here?' asked Gamache.

Beauvoir got up. 'I just needed to look at it again. Our talk yesterday about the internal investigation brought it all back, and I needed to see.'

And Beauvoir had the satisfaction of seeing the look of both pain and concern in Gamache's eyes.

But Jean Guy Beauvoir now knew it was a fake. An act. This man standing there looking so concerned wasn't at all. He was pretending. If he cared he'd never have left him. To die. Alone.

Behind him now the video, unseen by either man, had moved on. Past the place Beauvoir had hit replay. Chief Inspector Gamache, in tactical vest and carrying an assault rifle, was racing up a flight of stairs after a gunman.

'You need to let it go, Jean Guy,' said the Chief.

'And forget?' snapped Beauvoir. 'You'd like that, wouldn't you?'

'What do you mean?'

'You'd like me to forget, you'd like us all to forget what happened.'

'Are you all right?' Gamache approached him but Beauvoir backed away. 'What's the matter?'

'You don't even care who released the tape. Maybe you wanted it released. Maybe you wanted everyone to see how heroic you were. But we both know the truth.'

Behind them on the screen dim figures were struggling, scrambling.

'You recruited every one of us,' said Beauvoir, his voice rising. 'You mentored all of us, and then chose to take us into the factory. We followed you, trusted you, and what happened? They died. And now you can't even be bothered to find out who released the

tape of their deaths.' Beauvoir was shouting now, almost screaming. 'You don't believe it was some dumb-ass kid any more than I
do. You're no better than that hacker. You don't care about us,
about any of us.'

Gamache stared at him, his jaw clamped so tight Beauvoir could
see the muscles bunched and taut. Gamache's eyes narrowed and his
breathing became sharp. On the screen the Chief, his face bloody,
dragged the unconscious and cuffed gunman down the stairs and
threw him at his feet. Then, weapon in hand, he scanned the room
as shots rang out in rapid succession.

'Don't you ever say that again,' Gamache rasped through a mouth
barely open.

'You're no better than the hacker,' Beauvoir repeated, leaning into
his Chief, enunciating each word. Feeling reckless and powerful and
invincible. He wanted to hurt. Wanted to push him, push him. Away.
Wanted to close his hands tight into cannonballs and pound
Gamache's chest. Hit him. Hurt him. Punish him.

'You've gone too far.' Gamache's voice was low with warning.
Beauvoir saw the Chief close his hands tight against the tremor of
rage.

'And you haven't gone far enough. Sir.'

On the screen the Chief Inspector turned quickly but too late.
His head snapped back, his arms opened wide, his gun was thrown.
His back arched as Gamache was lifted off his feet.

Then he hit the floor. Deeply, gravely wounded.

Armand Gamache slumped into his chair. His legs weak, his hand
trembling.

Beauvoir had left, the slammed door still echoing through the
Incident Room.

From Beauvoir's monitor Gamache could hear the video though
he couldn't see it. He could hear his people calling each other. Hear
Lacoste calling for medics. Hear shouts and gunfire.

He didn't have to see it. He knew. Each and every young agent. Knew when and how they'd died in that raid he'd led.

The Chief Inspector continued to stare ahead. Breathing deeply. Hearing the gunfire behind him. Hearing the cries for help.

Hearing them die.

He'd spent the past six months trying to get beyond this. He knew he had to let them go. And he was trying. And it was happening, slowly. But he hadn't realized how long it took to bury four healthy young men and women.

Behind him the gunshots and shouts moved in and out. He recognized voices now gone.

He'd come close, so close it shocked him, to striking Jean Guy.

Gamache had been angry before. Had certainly been taunted and tested. By yellow journalists, by suspects, by defense lawyers and even colleagues. But he'd rarely come this close to actually lashing out physically.

He'd pulled himself back. But with an effort so great it left him winded and exhausted. And hurt.

He knew that. Knew the reason suspects and even colleagues, while frustrating and maddening, hadn't brought him this close to physical violence was because they couldn't hurt him deeply.

But someone he cared about could. And did.

You're no better than the hacker.

Was that true?

Of course it wasn't, thought Gamache, impatiently. That was just Beauvoir lashing out.

But that didn't make him wrong.

Gamache sighed again, feeling as though he couldn't quite get enough air.

Perhaps he should tell Beauvoir he was in fact investigating the leak. Should trust him. But it wasn't an issue of trust. It was one of protection. He wouldn't expose Beauvoir to this. If he'd ever been tempted, the events of the last quarter hour cured Gamache of that. Beauvoir was too vulnerable, too wounded still. Whoever had leaked the video was both powerful and vindictive. And Beauvoir, in his weakened condition, was no match for that.

No, this was a task for those who were expendable. In their careers and otherwise.

Gamache got up and went to turn the computer off. The video had restarted and before the Chief could turn it off he saw again Jean Guy Beauvoir gunned down. Falling. Hitting the concrete floor.

Until this moment Chief Inspector Gamache hadn't realized that Jean Guy Beauvoir never really got up.

TWENTY-FOUR

~

C hief Inspector Gamache made himself a pot of coffee and settled in.

It was no use trying to get back to sleep now. He looked at the clock on his desk. Four forty-three. Not all that long until he'd get up anyway. Really.

Placing his mug on a stack of paper he tapped the keyboard. Waited for the information to come up, then tapped some more. He clicked and scrolled. Read. And read some more.

The glasses had proved useful after all. He wondered what he might have done had he had a gun. But that didn't bear thinking of.

Gamache tapped and read. And read some more.

It had proven easy to get the broad strokes of Chief Justice Thierry Pineault's life. Canadians enjoyed an open society. Trumpeted it. Reveled in being the very model of transparency, where decisions were made in full view. Where public and powerful figures were accountable and their lives open to examination.

Such was the conceit.

And, like most open societies, few bothered to test the limits, to see where and when open became closed. But there was always a limit. Chief Inspector Gamache had found it a few minutes earlier.

Gamache had examined the public records of Chief Justice Pineault's professional life. His rise as a prosecutor, his term as professor of law at the Université Laval. His ascent to the bench. And then to Chief Justice.

He was widowed with three children and four grandchildren. Three surviving. One not.

Gamache knew the story. Superintendent Brunel had told him. How the child had been killed by a drunk driver. Gamache wanted to find out who that driver was, and whether it was, as he suspected, Pineault himself.

What else could have shattered the man so much he'd hit bottom? Stopped drinking? Turned his life around. Had the dead grandchild given Thierry Pineault a second chance at life?

That could also explain the strange connection between the Chief Justice and young Brian. Both knew what it felt like to hear the soft thud. The hesitation of the car.

And to know what it was.

Gamache sat at his desk and tried to imagine what that would be like. Tried to imagine being behind the wheel of his Volvo, knowing what had just happened. Getting out.

But his mind stopped there. Some things were beyond imagining.

To clear his mind, Gamache went back to the keyboard and renewed the search for information on the accident. But there was none.

The door of the open society had slowly swung shut. And locked.

But in the quiet Incident Room, in the first glow of a new day, Chief Inspector Gamache slipped below the surface of the public face of Québec. The public face of the Chief Justice. Into the place secrets were kept. Or at least, confidences were kept. The private files of public people.

There he found information about Thierry Pineault's drinking, his at times erratic behavior, his run-ins with other justices. And then a gap. A three-month leave.

And his return.

The private files also showed that systematically, over the past two years, Thierry Pineault had been calling up all his judgments from the bench. And at least one case had been officially reviewed. And reversed.

And there was another case. Not a Supreme Court case, not one he'd attended, at least not as a judge. But one Chief Justice Pineault had gone back to, over and over and over again. The file described an open-and-shut case, of a child killed by a drunk driver.

But there was no more information. The file had been locked away, in an area even Gamache couldn't get to.

He sat back in his chair and took his glasses off, tapping them rhythmically on his knee.

Agent Isabelle Lacoste wondered if anyone had ever actually died of boredom, or if she would be the first.

She now knew more than she ever wanted to about the art scene in Québec. The artists, the curators, the shows. The critiques. The themes, the theories, the history.

Famous Québec artists like Riopelle and Lemieux and Molinari. And a whole lot she hadn't heard of and never would again. Artists Lillian Dyson had reviewed into obscurity.

She rubbed her eyes. With each new review she had to remind herself why she was there. Had to remember Lillian Dyson lying on the soft green grass in Peter and Clara's garden. A woman who would grow no older. A woman who had stopped, there. In the pretty, peaceful garden. Because someone had taken her life.

Though, after reading all these repulsive reviews Lacoste was tempted to take a club to the woman herself. She felt dirty, as though someone had thrown a pile of *merde* all over her.

But someone had killed Lillian Dyson, hideous human being or not, and Lacoste was determined to find out who. The more she read the more she was convinced that someone was hiding here. In the newspaper morgue. In the microfiche. The beginning of this murder was so old it existed only on plastic files seen through a dusty viewer. An outdated technology that recorded a murder. Or at least, the birth of a death. The beginning of an end. An old event still fresh and alive in someone's mind.

No, not fresh. It was rotten. Old and rotten, the flesh falling off it.

And Agent Lacoste knew if she looked long enough, and hard enough, the murderer would be revealed.

For the next hour, as the sun rose and the people rose, Chief Inspector Gamache worked. When he got tired he took off his reading glasses, wiped his face with his hands, leaned back in the chair and looked at the sheets of paper pinned to the walls of the old railway station.

Sheets of paper with answers to their questions in bold red Magic Marker, like trails of blood, leading to a murderer.

And he looked at the photographs. Two in particular. The one given him by Mr and Mrs Dyson, of Lillian alive. Smiling.

And one taken by the crime scene photographer. Of Lillian dead.

He thought of the two Lillians. Alive and dead. But more than that. The happy, sober Lillian. The one Suzanne claimed to know. A far cry from the embittered woman Clara knew.

Did people change?

Chief Inspector Gamache pushed himself away from the computer. The time for gathering was over. Now was the time to put it all together.

Agent Isabel Lacoste stared at the screen. Reading and rereading. There was even a photo accompanying the review. Something, Lacoste had come to appreciate, Lillian Dyson reserved for her most vicious attacks. It showed a very young artist standing with a young Lillian on either side of a painting. The artist was smiling. Beaming. Pointing to the work as though to a trophy fish. As though to something extraordinary.

And Lillian?

Lacoste turned the knob and the image leapt closer.

Lillian was also smiling. Smug. Inviting the reader into the joke.

And the review?

Lacoste read it and felt her skin crawl. As though she was watching a snuff film. Watching someone die. For that's what the review was meant to do. Kill a career. To kill the artist inside the person.

Agent Isabelle Lacoste hit the key and the printer began to growl, as though it had a foul taste in its mouth, before it spat out the copies.

TWENTY-FIVE

‘ J ean Guy?’ Gamache knocked.

There was no answer.

He waited a moment then turned the handle. It was unlocked and he walked in.

Beauvoir lay in the brass bed, covers around him, sleeping soundly. Even snoring slightly.

Gamache stared down at him, then looked into the open door of the bathroom. Keeping an eye on Beauvoir he walked over, and into the bathroom, quickly scanning the washstand. There, beside the deodorant and toothpaste, was a pill bottle.

Glancing into the mirror and seeing Beauvoir still asleep, the Chief picked it up. There was Beauvoir's name, and the prescription for fifteen OxyContin.

It called for Beauvoir to take a pill each night, as needed. Gamache opened the bottle and dumped the pills into his palm. There were seven left.

But when was the prescription filled? The Chief replaced the pills, put the cap back on and looked at the bottom of the label. The date was typed in very small numerals. Gamache reached into his pocket for his reading glasses, and putting them on he picked up the pill bottle again.

Beauvoir groaned.

Gamache froze, and stared into the mirror. Very slowly he lowered the bottle, and removed his glasses.

Beauvoir, in the mirror, shifted in bed.

Gamache backed out of the bathroom. One pace, two. Then he stopped at the foot of the bed.

'Jean Guy?'

More moaning, clearer, stronger this time.

A chilly, damp breeze was blowing into Beauvoir's room, fluttering the white cotton curtains. It had begun to drizzle and the Chief could hear the muffled tap of rain on leaves, and smell the familiar scent of wood fires from the village homes.

He closed the window then turned back to the bed. Beauvoir had burrowed into his pillow.

It was just after seven A.M. and Agent Lacoste had called. She was in her car, turning off the autoroute. She'd found something in the archives.

Gamache wanted his Inspector part of the discussion when she arrived.

He himself had returned to the B and B, showered, shaved and changed.

'Jean Guy?' he whispered again, lowering his head so that he was face-to-face with his slightly drooling Inspector.

Beauvoir pried his heavy lids open and looked through slits at Gamache, a goofy smile on Beauvoir's face. Then his eyes flew open and the smile turned into a gasp as he jerked his head away from the Chief's.

'Don't worry,' said Gamache, standing up. 'You were a perfect gentleman.'

It took a moment for the bleary Beauvoir to grasp what the Chief meant and then he chuckled.

'Did I at least buy you champagne?' he asked, wiping the crusty sleep from his eyes.

'Well, you made a nice pot of coffee.'

'Last night?' Beauvoir asked, sitting up in bed. 'Here?'

'No, at the Incident Room.' Gamache looked at him, searching. 'Remember?'

Beauvoir looked blank, then shook his head. 'Sorry. I'm still half asleep.'

He rubbed his face, trying to remember.

Gamache dragged a chair up to the side of the bed and sat.

'What time is it?' Beauvoir asked, looking around.

'Just past seven.'

'I'll get up.' And Jean Guy grabbed at the duvet.

'No. Not yet.' Gamache's voice was soft, but certain, and Beauvoir's hand stopped then fell back to the bedding.

'We need to talk about last night,' said the Chief.

Gamache watched Beauvoir, still exhausted. There was a puzzled look on the Inspector's face.

'Did you mean what you said?' asked Gamache. 'Is that how you feel? Because if it is you need to tell me now, in the light of day. We need to talk about it.'

'Do I believe what?'

'What you said last night. That I wanted the video released, that in your opinion I'm as bad as the hacker.'

Beauvoir's eyes widened. 'Did I say that? Last night?'

'You don't remember?'

'I remember watching the video, getting upset. But I can't remember why. Did I really say that?'

'You did.' The Chief peered at Beauvoir. He seemed sincerely shocked.

But was this better? It meant Beauvoir might not believe what he'd said, but it would also mean his Inspector couldn't remember. Was in a sort of blackout.

Chief Inspector Gamache studied Beauvoir for a moment. Beauvoir, feeling the scrutiny, reddened.

'I'm so sorry,' he said again. 'Of course I don't think that. I can't believe I said it. I'm sorry.'

And he looked it.

Gamache held up his hand, 'I know you are. I'm not here to punish you. I'm here because I think you need help—'

'I don't. I'm fine, I really am.'

'You're not. You're losing weight, you're stressed. You're testy. You let your anger show last night in the interrogation of Madame Coates. Lashing out at the Chief Justice was reckless.'

'He started it.'

'This isn't a school yard. Suspects push us all the time. We need to stay calm. You let yourself be thrown off balance.'

'Fortunately, you were there to right me,' said Beauvoir.

Gamache regarded him again, not missing the slight acid in the words. 'What's wrong, Jean Guy? You need to tell me.'

'I'm just tired.' He rubbed his face. 'But I am getting better. Stronger.'

'You're not. You were for a while but now you're getting worse. You need more help. You need to go back to the Sûreté counselors.'

'I'll consider it.'

'You'll more than consider it,' said Gamache. 'How many OxyContin pills do you take?'

Beauvoir had a protest on his lips, but silenced it.

'What the prescription says.'

'And what's that?' The Chief's face was stern, his eyes sharp.

'One pill every night.'

'Do you take more?'

'No.'

The two men stared at each other, Gamache's deep brown eyes unyielding.

'Do you?' he repeated.

'No,' said Beauvoir, adamant. 'Listen, we deal with enough junkies, I don't want to turn into that.'

'And you think that's what the junkies wanted?' demanded Gamache. 'You think that's what Suzanne and Brian and Pineault expected to happen? No one starts out with that as the goal.'

'I'm just tired, a little stressed. That's all. I need the pills to take the edge off the pain, to sleep, but nothing more. I promise.'

'You'll go back to counseling, and I'll be monitoring it. Understand?' Gamache got up and carried the chair back to the corner of the room. 'If there's really nothing wrong the counselor will tell me. But if there is, you need more help.'

'Like what?' Beauvoir looked shocked.

'Whatever the counselor and I decide. This isn't a punishment, Jean Guy.' Gamache's voice softened. 'I still go to counseling myself. And still I have bad days. I know what you're going through. But no two of us were hurt the same way, and no two of us will get better the same way.'

Gamache regarded Beauvoir for a moment. 'I know how horrible this is for you. You're a private man, a good man. A strong man. Why else would I have chosen you, of the hundreds of agents? You're my second in command because I trust you. I know how smart and brave you are. And you need to be brave now, Jean Guy. For me, for the department. For yourself. You need to get help to get better. Please.'

Beauvoir closed his eyes. And then he did remember. Last night. Seeing the video over and over, as though for the first time. Seeing himself hit.

And Gamache leaving. Turning his back. Leaving him to die alone.

He opened his eyes and saw the Chief looking at him, with much the same expression as in the factory.

'I'll do it,' said Beauvoir.

Gamache nodded. '*Bon.*'

And he left. As he had that dreadful day. As he always would, Beauvoir knew.

Gamache would always leave him.

Jean Guy Beauvoir reached under his pillow and removing the tiny bottle, he shook a pill into the palm of his hand. By the time he was shaved and dressed and downstairs he was feeling just fine.

*

W hat did you find?' asked Chief Inspector Gamache.

They were having breakfast at the bistro, since they needed to talk and didn't want to share the B and B dining room, or their information, with the other guests.

The waiter had brought them frothy bowls of *café au lait*.

'I found this.' Agent Lacoste placed the photocopies of the article on the wooden table and stared out the window while Chief Inspector Gamache and Inspector Beauvoir read.

The drizzle had turned into a Scotch mist and clung to the hills surrounding the village so that Three Pines felt particularly intimate. As though the rest of the world didn't exist. Only here. Quiet and peaceful.

A log fire crackled in the grate. Just enough to take the chill off.

Agent Lacoste was exhausted. She wished she could take her bowl of *café au lait* and a croissant, and curl up on the large sofa by the fireplace. And read one of the well-worn paperbacks from Myrna's shop. An old Maigret. Read and nap. Read and nap. In front of the fireplace. While the outside world and worries receded into the mist.

But the worries were in here, she knew. Trapped in the village with them.

Inspector Beauvoir was the first to look up, meeting her eyes.

'Well done,' he said, tapping the article with his fingers. 'Must have taken all night.'

'Just about,' she admitted.

They looked over to the Chief, who seemed to be taking an unusually long time to read what was a short, sharp review.

Finally he lowered the page and took off his reading glasses just as the waiter arrived with their food. Toast and home-made *confiture* for Beauvoir. Pear and spiced blueberry crêpes for Lacoste. She'd kept herself awake on the drive down from Montréal by imagining what breakfast she'd have. This won. A bowl of porridge with raisins, cream and brown sugar was placed in front of the Chief.

He poured the brown sugar and cream on top then picked up the photocopy again.

Lacoste, seeing this, also laid her knife and fork down. 'Is that it, do you think, Chief? Why Lillian Dyson was murdered?'

He took a deep breath. 'I do. We need to confirm, to backfill some of the dates and information, but I think we have a motive. And we know there was opportunity.'

When they'd finished breakfast Beauvoir and Lacoste went back to the Incident Room. But Gamache had something he still needed to do in the bistro.

Pushing open the swinging door to the kitchen he found Olivier standing by the counter, chopping strawberries and cantaloupe.

'Olivier?'

Olivier startled and dropped the knife. 'For God's sake, don't you know enough not to do that to someone with a sharp knife?'

'I came in to talk to you.'

The Chief Inspector closed the door behind him.

'I'm busy.'

'So am I, Olivier. But we still need to talk.'

The knife sliced through the strawberries, leaving thin wafers of fruit and a small stain of red juice on the chopping block.

'I know you're angry at me, and I know you have every right to be. What happened was unforgivable, and my only defense is that it wasn't malicious, it wasn't done to harm you—'

'But it did.' Olivier slammed the knife down. 'Do you think prison is less horrible because you didn't do it maliciously? Do you think, when those men surrounded me in the yard that I thought, *Oh, well, this'll be OK because that nice Chief Inspector Gamache didn't wish me harm?*'

Olivier's hands shook so badly he had to grip the edges of the counter.

'You have no idea what it feels like to know the truth will come out. To trust the lawyers, the judges. You. That I'll be let go. And then to hear the verdict. Guilty.'

For a moment Olivier's rage disappeared, to be replaced by wonder, shock. That single word, that judgment. 'I was guilty, of course, of many things. I know that. I've tried to make it up to people. But—'

'Give them time,' said Gamache quietly. He stood across the counter from Olivier, his shoulders square, his back straight. But he too grasped the wooden counter. His knuckles white. 'They love you. It would be a shame not to see that.'

'Don't lecture me about shame, Chief Inspector,' snarled Olivier.

Gamache stared at Olivier, then nodded. 'I am sorry. I just wanted you to know that.'

'So that I could forgive you? Let you off the hook? Well, maybe this is your prison, Chief Inspector. Your punishment.'

Gamache considered. 'Perhaps.'

'Is that it?' Olivier asked. 'Are you finished?'

Gamache took a deep breath and exhaled. 'Not quite. I have another question, about Clara's party.'

Olivier picked up his knife, but his hand was still shaking too hard to use it.

'When did you and Gabri hire the caterers?'

'As soon as we decided to throw the party, three months ago I guess.'

'Was the party your idea?'

'It was Peter's.'

'Who made up the guest list?'

'We all did.'

'Including Clara?' Gamache asked.

Olivier gave a curt nod.

'So a lot of people would've known about it weeks in advance,' said the Chief.

Olivier nodded again, no longer looking at Gamache.

'*Merci*, Olivier,' he said, and lingered a moment, looking at the blond head, bowed over the chopping block. 'Do you think, maybe, we've ended up in the same cell?' asked Gamache.

When Olivier didn't respond Gamache walked toward the door then hesitated. 'But I wonder who the guards are. And who has the key.'

Gamache watched him for a moment, then left.

All morning and into the afternoon Armand Gamache and his team gathered information.

At one o'clock the phone rang. It was Clara Morrow.

'Are you and your people free for dinner?' she asked. 'It's so miserable we thought we'd poach a salmon and see who can come over.'

'Isn't poaching illegal?' asked Gamache, confused as to why she'd be telling him this.

Clara laughed. 'Not poached like that. Poached as in cooked.'

'Frankly, either way would've been fine,' admitted Gamache.

'Great. It'll be very relaxed. *En famille.*'

Gamache smiled at the French phrase. It was one Reine-Marie often used. It meant 'come as you are', but it meant more than that. She didn't use it for every relaxed occasion and with every guest. It was reserved for special guests, who were considered family. It was a particular position, a compliment. An intimacy offered.

'I accept,' he said. 'And I'm sure the other two will be delighted as well. *Merci,* Clara.'

Armand Gamache called Reine-Marie then showered and looked longingly at his bed.

The room, like all the others in Gabri and Olivier's B and B, was surprisingly simple. But not Spartan. It was elegant and luxurious, in its way. With crisp white bed linen, and a duvet filled with goose down. Hand-stitched Oriental carpets were thrown onto wide plank pine floors, which were original from when the B and B had been a coaching inn. Gamache wondered how many fellow travelers had rested in that very room. A pause in their difficult and dangerous journey. He wondered, briefly, where they'd come from and where they were going.

And if they made it.

The B and B was far less magnificent than the inn and spa on the hill. And he supposed he could have stayed there. But as he got older he yearned for less and less. Family, friends. Books. Walks with Reine-Marie and Henri, their dog.

And a full night's sleep in a simple bedroom.

Now, as he sat on the edge of the bed and put his socks on, he longed to just flop back, to feel his body hit the soft duvet, and sink in. To close his heavy lids, and let go.

Sleep.

But there was still a distance to go in his journey.

The Sûreté officers walked through mist and drizzle across the village green and arrived at Clara and Peter's home.

'Come on in,' said Peter with a smile. 'No keep your shoes on. Ruth's here and I think she walked through every mud puddle on her way over.'

They looked at the floor and sure enough, there were muddy shoe prints.

Beauvoir was shaking his head. 'I expected to see a cloven hoof.'

'Perhaps that's why she keeps her shoes on,' said Peter. The Sûreté officers rubbed their shoes as clean as they could on the welcome mat.

The home smelled of salmon and fresh bread, with slight hints of lemon and dill.

'Dinner won't be long,' said their host as he led them through the kitchen and into the living room.

Within minutes Beauvoir and Lacoste had glasses of wine. Gamache, already tired, asked for water. Lacoste wandered over to the two artists, Normand and Paulette. Beauvoir chatted with

Myrna and Gabri. Mostly, Gamache suspected, because they were as far from Ruth as possible.

Gamache's eyes swept the room. It was habit now. Noticing where everyone was, and what they were doing.

Olivier was by the bookcases, his back to the room. Apparently fascinated by the books, but Gamache suspected he'd seen those shelves many times.

François Marois and Denis Fortin were standing together, though not talking. Gamache wondered where the other one was. André Castonguay.

And then he found him. In a corner of the room, talking with Chief Justice Pineault while a few steps away young Brian was watching.

What was the look on Brian's face, Gamache wondered. It took an effort to dig below the tattoos, the swastika, the raised finger, the 'fuck you'. And see other expressions. Brian was certainly alert, watchful. Not the detached youth of the evening before.

'You must be kidding,' said Castonguay, his voice raised. 'You can't tell me you like it.'

Gamache wandered a little closer, while everyone else glanced over, then wandered a little further away. Except Brian. He stood his ground.

'I don't just like it, I think it's amazing,' Pineault was saying.

'Waste of time,' said the art dealer, his voice thick. He clutched an almost empty glass of red wine.

Gamache maneuvered closer and noticed the two men were standing in front of one of Clara's paintings. A study, really, of hands. Some clutching, some fists, some just opening, or closing, depending on your perception.

'It's all just bullshit,' said Castonguay, and Pineault made a subtle gesture to try to get the art dealer to lower his voice. 'Everyone says it's so great, but you know what?'

Castonguay leaned toward Pineault, and Gamache focused on Castonguay's lips, hoping to make out what the art dealer was about to whisper.

'People who think that are idiots. Morons. Wet brains.'

Gamache needn't have worried about hearing. Everyone heard. Castonguay shouted his opinion.

Again the circle around the dealer grew. Pineault scanned the room, looking for Clara, Gamache supposed. Hoping she wasn't hearing what one of her guests was saying about her work.

Then the Chief Justice's gaze settled back on Castonguay, his eyes hard. Gamache had seen that look often in court. Rarely directed at him, mostly directed at some poor trial lawyer who'd transgressed.

Had Castonguay been a Death Star, his head would have exploded.

'I'm sorry to hear that, André,' said Pineault, his voice polar. 'Maybe one day you'll feel as I do.'

The Chief Justice turned and walked away.

'Feel?' demanded Castonguay to Pineault's retreating back. 'Feel? Jeez, maybe you should try using your brains.'

Pineault hesitated, his back to Castonguay. The entire room was quiet now, watching. Then the Chief Justice continued walking away.

And André Castonguay was left all alone.

'He needs to hit bottom,' said Suzanne.

'I've hit many bottoms,' said Gabri. 'And I find it helps.'

Gamache looked around the room for Clara, but fortunately she wasn't there. Almost certainly in the kitchen preparing dinner. Wonderful aromas drifted through the open door, almost masking the stink of Castonguay's words.

'So,' said Ruth, turning her back on the swaying art dealer and focusing on Suzanne. 'I hear you're a drunk.'

'Very true,' said Suzanne. 'In fact, I come from a long line of drunks. They'd drink anything. Lighter fluid, pond scum, one of my uncles swore he could turn urine into wine.'

'Really?' said Ruth, perking up. 'I can turn wine into urine. Did he perfect the process?'

'Not surprisingly, he died before I was born but my mother had a still and would ferment everything. Peas, roses. Lamps.'

Ruth looked disbelieving. 'Come on. Peas?'

Still, she looked ready to try. She took a swig of her drink and inclined it toward Suzanne. 'Bet your mother never tried this.'

'What is it?' asked Suzanne. 'If it's a distilled Oriental carpet, she did that too. Tasted like my grandfather, but got the job done.'

Ruth looked impressed, but shook her head. 'It's my special blend. Gin, bitters, and the tears of little children.'

Suzanne didn't seem surprised.

Armand Gamache decided not to join that conversation.

Just then Peter called, 'Dinner!' and the guests filed into the kitchen.

Clara had lit candles around the large room, and vases of flowers had been placed along the center of the long pine table.

As Gamache took his seat he noticed that while the three art dealers seemed to travel together, so did the three AA members. Suzanne, Thierry and Brian.

'What're you thinking?' Myrna asked, taking a seat on his right. She handed him a basket of warm baguettes.

'Groups of threes.'

'Really? Last time we were together you were thinking of Humpty Dumpty.'

'Christ,' muttered Ruth, on his other side, 'this murder'll never be solved.'

Gamache looked at the old poet. 'Guess what I'm thinking now.'

She stared back at him, her cold blue eyes narrowing, her face flint. Then she laughed. 'Quite right too,' she said, grabbing some bread. 'I'm all that, and more.'

The platter, with the whole poached salmon, was being passed in one direction, while spring vegetables and salad were going in the other. Everyone helped themselves.

'So, groups of threes,' Ruth nodded to the art dealers. 'Like Curly, Larry and Moe over there?'

François Marois laughed but André Castonguay looked bleary and peeved.

'There's a long tradition of groups of threes,' said Myrna. 'Everyone thinks in terms of couples, but actually threes are very common. Mystical even. The holy trinity.'

'Three Graces,' said Gabri, helping himself to vegetables. 'Like in your painting, Clara.'

'The Three Fates,' said Paulette.

'There's "three on a match",' said Denis Fortin. 'Ready. Aim.' He looked at Marois. 'Fire. But we're not the only ones to move in threes,' said Fortin.

Gamache looked at him inquiringly.

'You do too,' said Fortin, looking from Gamache, to Beauvoir to Lacoste.

Gamache laughed. 'I hadn't thought of that, but it's true.'

'Three blind mice,' said Ruth.

'Three pines,' said Clara. 'Maybe you're the three pines. Keeping us safe.'

'Sure made a balls-up of that,' said Ruth.

'Stupid conversation,' muttered Castonguay, and knocked his fork to the floor. He glared at it, a stupid look on his face. The room grew quiet.

'Never mind,' said Clara cheerfully. 'We have plenty.'

She got up but Castonguay reached out to grab her as she passed. 'I'm not hungry,' he said, his voice loud and querulous.

Missing Clara, his hand hit Agent Lacoste beside him. 'Sorry,' he mumbled.

Peter, Gabri and Paulette began speaking at once. Loudly, cheerfully.

'Don't want any,' snapped Castonguay as Brian offered him the salmon. Then the gallery owner seemed to focus on the young man. 'Jeez, who invited you?'

'The same person who invited you,' said Brian.

Peter, Gabri and Paulette spoke even more loudly. More cheerfully.

'What're you?' slurred Castonguay, trying to focus on Brian.

'Christ, don't tell me you're an artist too. You look fucked up enough to be one.'

'I am,' said Brian. 'I'm a tattoo artist.'

'What?' demanded Castonguay.

'It's all right, André,' said François Marois, in a soothing voice, and it seemed to work. Castonguay swayed a bit in his chair and stared down at his plate, mesmerized.

'Who wants seconds?' asked Peter, brightly.

No one put their hand up.

TWENTY-SIX

'So,' said Denis Fortin, as they stood on the covered porch with their coffees and cognacs. 'Have you two had a chance to talk?'

'About what?' asked Peter, turning from surveying the wet village to surveying the gallery owner. It was still raining, a fine drizzle.

Fortin looked at Clara. 'You haven't discussed it with him?'

'Not yet,' said Clara, feeling guilty. 'But I will.'

'What?' asked Peter again.

'I came by today to see if you and Clara might be interested in being represented by me. I know I screwed up the first time, and I really am sorry. I'm just ...' he paused to collect his thoughts, then looked from Peter back to Clara. 'I'm asking for another chance. Please let me prove that I'm sincere. I really think we'd make a great team, the three of us.'

'What do you think?' Chief Inspector Gamache nodded out the window toward Peter, Clara and Fortin standing on the porch.

'About them?' asked Myrna. They couldn't hear what the three were talking about, but it was easy enough to guess.

'Will Fortin convince Clara to give him another shot?' asked the Chief, taking a sip of his double espresso.

'It's not Fortin who needs another shot,' said Myrna.

Gamache turned to her. 'Peter?'

But Myrna lapsed into silence and Gamache wondered if Peter had told Clara about his part in the scathing review years ago.

I think we need time to consider it,' said Clara.

'I understand,' said Fortin, with a charming smile. 'No pressure. The only thing I'll say is that you might want to consider signing with a younger, growing gallery. Someone who won't retire in a few years. Just a thought.'

'It's a good point,' said Peter.

Not long ago that would have been enough for Clara to go with Fortin. Peter's obvious enthusiasm. She'd trusted him completely to know what was best for them. For both of them. To have her best interests at heart.

Now she realized, looking at this man she'd spent the past twenty-five years with, that she had no idea what he kept in his heart. But she was pretty sure it wasn't her best interests.

Clara didn't know what to do. But she did know that something had to change.

Peter was trying, she knew that. He was trying so hard to change. And now, maybe, it was her turn to try too.

He's still suffering, you know,' said Myrna.

'Peter?' asked Gamache, then he followed her look. She was no longer watching the three people on the verandah. Her gaze was closer to home. She was staring at Jean Guy Beauvoir, who was standing with Ruth and Suzanne.

Ruth seemed to have quite lost her heart to the odd former drunk, who apparently had endless recipes for distilling furniture.

'I know,' said Gamache, quietly. 'I spoke with Jean Guy about it this morning.'

'And what did he say?'

'That he was fine, getting better. But of course, he isn't.'

Myrna was quiet for a moment. 'No. He isn't. Did he tell you why he's suffering?'

Gamache studied her for a moment. 'I asked, but he didn't say. I presumed it was the combination of his wounds and losing so many colleagues.'

'It is, but I think it's more specific than that. In fact, I know it is. He told me.'

Gamache turned his full attention to her. In the background Castonguay raised his voice. Vexed, whining, petulant. But nothing would get Gamache to look away from Myrna now.

'What did Jean Guy tell you?'

Myrna examined Gamache for a moment. 'You're not going to like it.'

'There's nothing about what happened in that factory I like. But I need to hear it.'

'Yes,' said Myrna, making up her mind. 'He feels guilty.'

'About what?' asked Gamache, astonished. This wasn't the answer he'd expected.

'About not being able to help you. He can't get beyond seeing you fall, and not being able to help. As you helped him.'

'But that's ridiculous. He couldn't.'

'You know that, and I know that. He even knows that. But what we know and what we feel can be two different things.'

Gamache's heart dropped. Remembering the sallow young man early that morning in the Incident Room, his face made all the paler by the harsh light from the computer screen. Watching that damned video, over and over.

But not the scene of Gamache himself being gunned down. Jean Guy was watching himself being shot. He told Myrna what he'd found the night before.

Myrna exhaled. 'I think he's punishing himself. Like self-mutilation. Taking a knife to himself, only the video is the blade.'

The video, thought Gamache, feeling his fury rise. The goddamned

371

video. It had already done so much damage, and now it was killing a young man he loved.

'I've ordered him back to counseling—'

'Ordered?'

'It started as a suggestion,' said the Chief, 'but ended up an order.'

'He was resistant?'

'Very.'

'He loves you,' said Myrna. 'That's his road home.'

Gamache looked over at Jean Guy and waved across the crowded room. Once again the Chief saw him fall. And hit the ground.

And Jean Guy, across the living room, smiled and waved back.

He saw Gamache looking down at him, eyes filled with concern. And then leaving.

'Christ,' said Castonguay in disgust, and gestured to the room in general. 'That's it. The end of the world. The end of civilization.' He slurped his drink toward Brian. 'He tattoos "Mother" on bikers and calls himself an artist. *Maudit tabernac.*'

'Come on,' said Thierry Pineault. 'Let's get some fresh air.'

He took Castonguay by the elbow and tried to lead him to the front door but Castonguay shook him off.

'I haven't seen a good artist in years. Not her.' He gestured toward Clara, just coming in from the porch. 'She's been circling the drain for years. Stuff's trite. Sentimental. Portraits.' He almost spat the word.

People were stepping away, leaving Castonguay alone in the void.

'And him,' said Castonguay, choosing his next victim. It was Peter. 'His stuff's OK. Conventional, but I could sell it to Kelley Foods. Bury it in their Guatemalan office. Depends how drunk I can get their buyers. Though fucking Kelley's won't allow drinking. Ruins the corporate image. So I guess I won't be able to sell you after all, Morrow. But neither will he.'

Castonguay fixed a belligerent look on Denis Fortin. 'What's he been promising you? Solo shows? A joint show? Or maybe just a joint? He could be selling lawn furniture, for all he knows about art. Stank at it himself, and now he stinks as a gallery owner. The only thing he's good at is mind-fucks.'

Gamache caught Beauvoir's eye, who signaled subtly to Lacoste. The three officers positioned themselves around Castonguay, but let him continue.

François Marois appeared at Gamache's elbow.

'Stop this,' he whispered.

'He's done nothing wrong,' said the Chief.

'He's humiliating himself,' said Marois, looking agitated. 'He doesn't deserve this. He's sick.'

'Now, you two.' Castonguay swirled and lost his balance, stumbling against the sofa.

'Jeez,' said Ruth, 'don't you just hate a drunk?'

Castonguay righted himself and turned to, and on, Normand and Paulette. 'Don't think we don't know why you're here.'

'We came down for Clara's party,' said Paulette.

'Shhh,' hissed Normand. 'Don't encourage him.' But it was too late. Castonguay had her in his sights.

'But why'd you stay? Not to support Clara,' he sputtered with laughter. 'The only thing worse than poets for hating each other is artists.' He turned to Ruth and bowed exaggeratedly. 'Madame.'

'Fucking idiot,' said Ruth, then she turned to Gabri. 'Can't say he isn't right, though.'

'You hate Clara, you hate her art, you hate all artists,' Castonguay closed in on Normand and Paulette. 'Probably even hate each other. And yourselves. And you sure hated the dead woman, and with good reason.'

'All right,' said Marois, breaking into the void and approaching Castonguay. 'Time to say good night to these nice people and go to bed.'

'I'm not going anywhere,' shouted Castonguay, twisting away from Marois.

Gamache, Beauvoir and Lacoste moved a step closer as everyone else took a step back.

'You'd like that. You'd like me to just go away. But I found her first. She was going to sign with me. And then you stole her.'

His voice rose, and with a jerk Castonguay pitched his glass at Marois. It whizzed by him, shattering against the wall.

And then Castonguay launched himself at the elderly dealer, clasping his strong hands around Marois's throat, propelling the two of them backward.

The Sûreté officers leapt after them, Gamache and Beauvoir grabbing Castonguay, and Lacoste trying to get her body between the struggling art dealers. Finally Castonguay was pried off Marois.

François Marois held his throat and stared, shocked, at his colleague. And he wasn't alone. Everyone in the room stared at Castonguay, as he was arrested and led away.

Armand Gamache and Jean Guy Beauvoir returned to Peter and Clara's home an hour later. This time Gamache did accept a drink, and subsided into the large armchair Gabri offered.

Everyone was still there, as he expected they would be. Too wired from the events, and with too many questions still to be answered to be able to go to bed. They couldn't rest yet.

And neither could he.

'Ahh,' he said, taking a sip of cognac. 'This tastes good.'

'What a day,' said Peter.

'And it's not over yet. Agent Lacoste is looking after Monsieur Castonguay and the paperwork.'

'By herself?' asked Myrna, looking from Gamache to Beauvoir.

'She knows what she's doing,' said the Chief Inspector. Myrna's look said she sure hoped he knew what he was doing.

'So what happened?' asked Clara. 'I'm all confused.'

Gamache sat forward in the chair. Everyone took seats or perched on the arms of the easy chairs. Only Beauvoir and Peter remained standing. Peter as a good host, and Beauvoir as a good officer.

Outside the rain had picked up and they could hear it tapping against the windowpanes. The door to the porch was still open, to let in fresh air, and they could hear rain hitting the leaves outside.

'This murder is about contrasts,' said Gamache, his voice low, soft. 'About sober and drunk. About appearance and reality. About change for the better, or for the worse. The play of light and dark.'

He looked at their attentive faces.

'A word was used at your *vernissage*.' He turned to Clara. 'To describe your paintings.'

'I'm almost afraid to ask,' she said, with a weary smile.

'Chiaroscuro. It means the contrast between light and dark. Their juxtaposition. You do it in your portraits, Clara. In the colors you use, the shading, but also in the emotions your works evoke. Especially in the portrait of Ruth—'

'There's one of me?'

'—there's a clear contrast. The dark hues, the trees in the background. Her face partly in shadow. Her expression thunderous. Except for one tiny dot. The smallest hint of light, in her eyes.'

'Hope,' said Myrna.

'Hope. Or maybe not.' Gamache turned to François Marois. 'You said something curious, when we were standing in front of that portrait. Do you remember?'

The art dealer looked perplexed. 'I said something useful?'

'You don't remember?'

Marois was quiet for a moment, one of those rare people who could keep others waiting without distress. Finally he smiled.

'I asked if you thought it was real,' said Marois.

'You did,' nodded the Chief Inspector. 'Was it real, or just a trick of the light? Hope offered, then denied. A particular cruelty.'

He looked around the gathering. 'That's what this crime, this murder was about. The question of just how genuine the light actually was. Was the person really happy, or just pretending to be?'

'Not waving but drowning,' said Clara. She noticed again Gamache's kindly eyes beneath the deep scar.

'Nobody heard him,' Clara quoted, 'the dead man,

'But still he lay moaning:
I was much further out than you thought
And not waving but drowning.'

But this time, as Clara recited the poem, Peter didn't come to mind. This time Clara thought of someone else.

Herself. Pretending, for a lifetime. Looking on the bright side, but not always feeling it. But no more. Things were going to change.

The room fell silent, except for the gentle tip-tapping of the rain.

'C'est ça,' said Gamache. 'How often have we mistaken the one for the other? Too afraid, or in too much of a hurry to see what was really happening? To see someone sinking?'

'But drowning men are sometimes saved.'

They swung their eyes from Gamache to the man who'd spoken. The young man. Brian.

Gamache regarded him for a few moments in silence, taking in the tattoos, the piercing, the studs on the clothing, and through the skin. Slowly the Chief Inspector nodded, then shifted his glance to the others.

'The question that we struggled with was whether Lillian Dyson was saved. Had she changed? Or was it just a false hope? She was an alcoholic. A cruel, bitter, self-absorbed woman. She hurt everyone who ever knew her.'

'But she wasn't always like that,' said Clara. 'She was nice once. A good friend, once.'

'Most people are,' said Suzanne, 'at first. Most people aren't born in prison or under a bridge or in a crack house. They become like that.'

'People can change for the worse,' said Gamache. 'But how often do people really change for the better?'

'I believe we do,' said Suzanne.

'Had Lillian changed?' Gamache asked her.

'I think so. At least, she was trying.'

'Have you?' he asked.

'Have I what?' asked Suzanne, though she must have known what he meant.

'Changed.'

There was a long pause. 'I hope so,' said Suzanne.

Gamache lowered his voice so that they had to strain to hear. 'But is it real hope? Or just a trick of the light?'

TWENTY-SEVEN

~

'You lied to us at every turn, then dismissed it as simply habit.' Gamache continued to stare at Suzanne. 'That doesn't sound like real change to me. It sounds like situational ethics. Change, as long as it's convenient. And a lot about what's happened in the last few days has been extremely inconvenient. But some was very convenient. For instance, your sponsee coming to Clara's party.'

'I didn't know Lillian was even here,' said Suzanne. 'I told you that.'

'True. But then you told us a lot of things. For instance, that you didn't know who the famous line *He's a natural, producing art like it's a bodily function* was about. It was you.'

'You?' said Clara, turning to the lively woman beside her.

'That review was the last shove,' said Gamache. 'After that you went into free-fall. And landed in AA, where you may or may not have changed. But you weren't the only one of your group to lie.'

Gamache shifted his gaze to the man sitting beside Suzanne on the sofa. 'You also lied, sir.'

Chief Justice Pineault looked amazed. 'I lied? How?'

'It was, to be sure, more a sin of omission, but it was still a lie. You know André Castonguay, don't you?'

'I can't say.'

'Well, let me save you the trouble. Monsieur Castonguay had to stop drinking if he had any hope of keeping the Kelley Foods contract. As he himself said, they're a notoriously sober company. And he was becoming notoriously inebriated. So he tried AA.'

'If you say,' said Thierry.

'When you arrived in Three Pines yesterday you spent an hour in Myrna's bookstore. It's a lovely store, but an hour seemed excessive. And then, when we sat outside you insisted on a table by the wall and sat with your back to the village.'

'It was a courtesy, Chief Inspector, to take the worst seat for myself.'

'It was also a convenience. You were hiding from someone. But then, at the end of our talk you got up and happily walked over to the B and B with Suzanne.'

Thierry Pineault and Suzanne exchanged looks.

'You were no longer hiding. I looked around and tried to figure out what had changed. And only one thing had. André Castonguay had left. He was making his drunken way back to the inn and spa.'

Chief Justice Pineault was giving nothing away. He stared, stone-faced, at Gamache.

'I made a small mistake tonight,' admitted Gamache. 'When we arrived you and Castonguay were talking in the corner. You appeared to be arguing and I assumed it was about Clara's art.'

He looked, and they followed his gaze, into the corner where the study of the hands was hanging.

'*Désolé,*' he said to Clara, who smiled.

'People argue about my art all the time. No harm done.'

But Gamache didn't believe that. Harm had been done. A great deal of it.

'I was wrong, though,' the Chief continued. 'You weren't arguing about whether Clara's art was any good, you were arguing about AA.'

'We weren't arguing,' said Pineault. He took a deep breath. 'We were discussing. It's no use arguing with a drunk. And no use trying to sell someone on AA.'

'Besides,' said Gamache, 'he'd already tried it.'

The two men stared at each other and finally Pineault nodded.

'He came in about a year ago, desperate to get sober,' Pineault admitted. 'It didn't work.'

'You knew him there,' said Gamache. 'And I suspect you more than knew him.'

Again Pineault nodded. 'He was my sponsee. I tried to help, but he couldn't stop drinking.'

'When did he stop going to AA?' Gamache asked.

Pineault thought. 'About three months ago. I tried calling him but he never returned my calls. Eventually I stopped, figuring he'd come back when he'd bottomed.'

'When you saw him here yesterday, drunk, you immediately appreciated the problem,' said Gamache.

'What problem?' asked Suzanne.

'When André joined our group he met a lot of people,' said Pineault. 'Including Lillian. And she, of course, met him. And knew who he was right away. She told him about her art, and even showed him her portfolio. He told me about it, and I advised him not to pursue it. That men needed to stick with men, and besides, this wasn't a networking opportunity.'

'Was talking about her art against the rules?' asked Gamache.

'There aren't any rules,' said Thierry. 'It's just not a great idea. It's hard enough getting sober without mixing in business.'

'But Lillian did,' said Gamache.

'I didn't know about this,' said Suzanne. 'If she'd told me I'd have told her to stop. Probably why she never told me.'

'Then André quit AA,' said Gamache, and Pineault nodded. 'But there was a problem.'

'As you said, André had one big client,' said Thierry. 'Kelley Foods. He lived in terror someone was going to tell them about his drinking.'

'But he couldn't keep it secret for long,' said Myrna. 'If his time here is anything to go by, he was drunk more than he was sober.'

'True,' said Thierry. 'It was just a matter of time before André lost everything.'

'As soon as you saw him here you realized what might have happened,' said Gamache. 'You listen to trials all the time, often murder trials. You put things together.'

Pineault seemed to be considering what to say next. Everyone naturally leaned forward, toward the Chief Justice. Drawn to the silence, and the promise of a story.

'I was afraid that Lillian had come to the party to confront him. That she'd met him in Clara's garden and threatened to tell the Kelley people about his drinking unless André represented her,' said Pineault. 'You saw him tonight. There's no control left, of his drinking or his anger.'

When Pineault was silent for a few moments Gamache gently prodded.

'Go on.'

Still they waited. Their eyes wide, their breathing shallow.

'I was afraid Lillian had pushed him over the edge. Threatening blackmail.'

Pineault stopped again, and again, after an excruciating pause, Gamache prodded.

'Go on.'

'I was afraid he killed her. In a blackout probably. Probably couldn't even remember doing it.'

Gamache wondered if a jury, or a judge, would believe that. And whether it would matter. He also wondered if anyone else had caught what he had.

The Chief Inspector waited.

'But,' said Clara, perplexed. 'Didn't Monsieur Castonguay just accuse you of stealing Lillian from him?'

She turned to François Marois. The elderly art dealer was silent. Clara's brows were drawn together in concentration. As she tried to figure it out. Her gaze shifted to Gamache.

'Have you seen Lillian's art?'

He nodded.

'Was it that good? Worth fighting over?'

He nodded again.

Clara looked surprised, but accepted Gamache's judgment. 'So she wouldn't have had to blackmail Castonguay. In fact, it sounds like Castonguay was desperate to sign Lillian. There'd be no need for her to confront him. He was sold, he wanted her art. Unless,' said Clara, making the connections, 'that's what pushed him over the edge.'

She looked at Gamache, but his face told her nothing. He was listening, attentive, but nothing more.

'Castonguay knew he'd lose Kelley,' said Clara, walking carefully through the facts. 'Once he quit AA that was inevitable. His only hope was to find something to replace Kelley Foods. An artist. But not just anyone. They had to be brilliant. They'd save his gallery. His career. But it had to be someone no one else knew about. His own find.'

Around her there was silence. Even the rain had stopped, perhaps to better listen.

'Lillian and her art would save him,' Clara continued. 'But Lillian did something Castonguay never expected. She did what she always did. She looked after herself. She spoke to Castonguay, but she also approached Monsieur Marois, the more powerful dealer.' Clara turned to Marois. 'And you took her on.'

François Marois's face had slid from a benign, kindly smile to a sneer.

'Lillian Dyson was a grown woman. She wasn't indentured to André,' said Marois. 'She was free to choose whoever she wanted.'

'Castonguay saw her at the party here,' Clara continued, trying not to be intimidated by Marois's glare. 'He probably wanted a quiet word with her. He must have led her into our garden for privacy.'

They all imagined the scene. The fiddlers, the dancing and laughing.

Castonguay spots Lillian just arriving, coming down du Moulin from where she'd parked the car. He's had a few drinks and hurries to intercept her. Anxious to pin down their deal before she gets a chance to speak to others at the party. All the dealers and curators and gallery owners.

He steers her into the nearest garden.

'He probably didn't even realize it was ours,' said Clara. Still watching Gamache. And still he revealed nothing. Just listened.

They breathed silence. It felt as though the world had stopped, the world had shrunk. To this instant, and this place. And these words.

'Then Lillian told him that she'd signed with François Marois.'

Clara stopped, seeing in her mind the stricken gallery owner. Well into his sixties, and ruined. A broken, drunken man. Given the final blow. And what does he do?

'She was his last hope,' said Clara softly. 'And now it's gone.'

'He'll plead to diminished capacity or manslaughter,' said Chief Justice Pineault. 'He must have been drunk at the time.'

'At the time of what?' asked Gamache.

'At the time he killed Lillian,' said Thierry.

'Oh, André Castonguay didn't kill her. One of you did.'

TWENTY-EIGHT

～

Even Ruth was paying attention now. Outside, the rain had begun again, falling from the dark sky and hitting the windows in great lashes, the water streaming down the old glass. Peter walked over to the door onto the porch and closed it.

They were sealed in now.

He rejoined the group, huddled together in a ragged circle. Staring at each other.

'Castonguay didn't kill Lillian?' Clara repeated. 'Then who did?'

They shot glances at each other, careful not to lock eyes. And then all eyes arrived back at Gamache. The center of the circle.

The lights flickered and even through the sealed windows they could hear a rumble of thunder. And see a flash as the dark forest around them was illuminated. Briefly. Then fell back to darkness.

Gamache spoke quietly. Barely heard above the rain and the rumble.

'One of the first things to strike us about this case was the contrast between the two Lillians. The vile woman you knew.' He looked at Clara. 'And the kind, happy woman you knew.' He turned to Suzanne.

'Chiaroscuro,' said Denis Fortin.

Gamache nodded. 'Exactly. The dark and the light. Who was she really? Which was the real Lillian?'

'Do people change?' asked Myrna.

'Do people change,' repeated Gamache. 'Or do they revert to type, eventually? There seemed little doubt Lillian Dyson was once a dreadful person, hurting anyone unfortunate enough to come close. She was filled with bitterness and self-pity. She expected everything would just be given to her, and when it wasn't she couldn't cope. It took forty years but finally her life spiraled out of control, hurried along by alcohol.'

'She hit bottom,' said Suzanne.

'And she shattered,' said Gamache. 'And while it was clear to us she was once a horrendous mess, it was equally clear she was trying to heal. To pick herself up with the help of AA and find,' he looked at Suzanne, 'what did you call it?'

She looked puzzled for a moment then smiled slightly. 'A quiet place in the bright sunshine.'

Gamache nodded, thoughtful. '*Oui. C'est ça.* But how to find it?'

The Chief scanned their faces and stopped, briefly, on Beauvoir, who looked as though he might weep.

'The only way was to stop drinking. But as I've found out in the last few days, for alcoholics stopping drinking is just the beginning. They have to change. Their perceptions, attitudes. And they have to clean up the mess they left behind. *The alcoholic is like a tornado, roaring his way through the lives of others,*' Gamache quoted. 'Lillian underlined those words in her AA book. She underlined another passage. *Hearts are broken. Sweet relationships are dead.*'

His eyes fell on Clara now. She looked stricken.

'I think she was genuinely sorry about what she did to you and your friendship. By not only failing to be supportive, but actually trying to destroy your career. It was one of the things she was sincerely ashamed of. I don't know for sure, of course,' said Gamache, and it seemed to Clara as though everyone else had disappeared, and they were alone in the room. 'But I believe that beginner's chip you found in the garden was hers. I think she brought it with her and was holding it, trying to get up the courage to speak with you. To say she was sorry.'

Gamache brought a coin out of his pocket and held it in his open palm. It was Bob's beginner's chip. The one he'd given Gamache at the AA meeting. He hesitated just an instant, then offered it to Clara.

'*Who is it, exactly, you have needed,*' Ruth whispered, '*all these years to forgive?*'

She looked across the room, but Olivier wasn't looking at her. Like everyone else, his eyes were firmly on Clara, and Gamache.

Clara reached out and took the coin, closing her fist around it.

'But Lillian never got the chance to apologize,' Gamache continued. 'She made a terrible mistake. In her rush to get better she skipped over some of the steps of AA. Instead of doing them slowly and carefully, in order, Lillian jumped ahead to step nine. Can you remember the exact wording?' he asked the three AA members.

'*Made direct amends to such people wherever possible,*' said Suzanne.

'But there's a second part to it, isn't there?' asked Gamache. 'Everyone seems to concentrate on the amends part. But there's more.'

'*Except when to do so would injure them or others,*' said Brian.

'But how can an apology ever hurt someone?' asked Paulette.

'By reopening old wounds,' said Suzanne.

'In trying to put her own demons to rest,' said Gamache, 'Lillian unexpectedly raised someone else's. Something that had been dormant sprang back to life.'

'Do you think she approached someone with an amend who didn't want to hear it?' Thierry asked.

'Lillian wasn't a tornado,' said Gamache. 'A tornado is a destructive but natural phenomenon. Without a will or intent. Lillian deliberately, maliciously hurt people. Set out to ruin them. And for an artist it wasn't just a job or career. Creating their works is who they are. Destroy that and you destroy them.'

'It's a form of murder,' said Brian.

Gamache regarded the young man for a moment, then nodded. 'It's exactly that. Lillian Dyson murdered, or tried to murder, many people. Not physically, but just as cruelly. By taking away their dreams. Their creations.'

'Her weapon was her reviews,' said Normand.

'They weren't just reviews,' agreed Gamache. 'Creative people know being reviewed, and sometimes badly, is part of the package. Not pleasant, but a reality. But Lillian's words were vitriolic. Designed to push sensitive people over the edge. And they did. More than one person gave up being an artist in the face of such judgment and humiliation.'

'She had a lot to apologize for,' said Fortin.

Gamache turned to the gallery owner. 'She did. And she got an early start. But she hadn't taken in the second part of that step. About the possibility of doing damage. Or, perhaps she had.'

'What d'you mean?' Suzanne asked.

'I think some of her amends, while early, were sincere. But I think some weren't. I think while she was healing she wasn't yet healthy. Old habits slipped in, disguised as noble deeds. After all, as many of you just asked, how could an apology ever be wrong? But sometimes it is. One amend gave the murderer a motive. Another gave that murderer an opportunity.'

They glanced at each other again. In the shadows Gamache noticed Beauvoir ease himself around until he was standing in front of the door to the kitchen. The only way out of the room.

They were close. Gamache knew it. Beauvoir knew it. And someone else in the dim room knew it too. The murderer must have felt their hot breaths.

Gamache turned to Clara.

'Lillian came down here to apologize to you. I honestly believe a big part of her was sincere. But a part wasn't. She didn't need to come on the night of your big celebration. She didn't need to wear a dress designed to get attention. Lillian knew she was probably the last person you'd want to see as you celebrated your success.'

'So why did she come?' asked Clara.

'Because the part of her that was still sick wanted to hurt you. Wanted to ruin your big night.'

Clara closed her hand tighter around the coin, feeling it a hard circle in her palm.

'But how'd she know about the party?' asked Myrna. 'It was private. And how'd she find the place? Three Pines isn't exactly a destination.'

'Someone told her,' said Gamache. 'The murderer told her. About the party and how to find it.'

'Why?' asked Peter.

'Because the murderer wanted to hurt Lillian. Kill Lillian. But he also wanted to hurt Clara.'

'Me?' asked Clara, dumbfounded. 'Why? Who?'

She looked around the room, searching for someone who could hate her so much. And her eyes came to rest on one person.

TWENTY-NINE

~

All eyes turned to look.

The murderer smiled tentatively, then his eyes darted around the room, resting finally on Jean Guy Beauvoir, standing in the doorway to the kitchen. The only way out. Blocked.

'You?' said Clara, barely above a whisper. 'You killed Lillian?'

Denis Fortin turned to face Clara.

'Lillian Dyson deserved what she got. The only surprise is that someone hadn't wrung her neck sooner.'

Olivier, Gabri and Suzanne moved away from him, getting over to the other side of the room. The gallery owner stood up, and looked at them, across a great divide.

Only Gamache seemed at ease. Unlike the rest, he hadn't scrambled to safety, but remained seated across from Fortin.

'Lillian had gone to apologize to you, hadn't she,' said the Chief Inspector, as though having a friendly chat with an excitable guest.

Fortin stared at him and finally nodded, then sat back down.

'She didn't even make an appointment. Just showed up at the gallery. Said she was sorry she'd been so horrible in her review.'

Fortin had to pause, to gather himself.

"I'm sorry," he said, lifting a finger for each word, "I was cruel in my review of your art."

He looked at his fingers. 'Eleven words, and she thinks that makes us even. Have you seen the review?'

Gamache nodded. 'I have it here. But I won't read it.'

Fortin met his eyes. 'Well, thank you for that, at least. I can't even remember the exact wording, but I know it was as though she'd strapped a bomb to my chest and set it off. All the worse because at my show she was gushing. Couldn't have been friendlier. Said how much she loved the works. Convinced me I could expect a glowing review in *La Presse* that Saturday. I waited all week, barely able to sleep. I told all my family and friends.'

Fortin stopped to gather himself again. The lights flickered, staying off longer. Peter and Clara got candles from the sideboard and placed them around the room, ready in case they lost power.

Outside lightning flashed and forked behind the mountains. Closing in on Three Pines.

Rain pelted against the windowpanes.

'And then the review appeared. It wasn't just bad, it was a catastrophe. Malicious. Mocking. She made fun of what I'd created. My paintings may not have been brilliant, but I was just starting, doing my best. And she dug her heels into them and ground. It was more than just humiliating. I might've recovered from that, it was that she convinced even me that I had no talent. She killed the best part of me.'

Denis Fortin stopped trembling. He stopped moving. He seemed to stop breathing. He just ground to a halt. Staring blankly ahead.

A giant flash lit up the village green followed immediately by a bang so loud it shook the little house. Everyone leapt, including Gamache. The rain now pounded against the windows, demanding to be let in. Outside they could hear the wild wind in the trees. Twisting them, shaking them. In the next flash of lightning they could see young leaves torn from maples and poplars and whipping across the village green. They could hear the aspens, quaking.

And in the center of the village they could see the three great pines, twirling at their tops. Catching the whirlwind.

The guests looked at each other, wide eyed. Waiting. Listening. Expecting a rending, a tearing, a crashing.

'I stopped painting,' said Fortin, raising his voice above the din. The only one who seemed not to care or notice the storm.

'But you made a career for yourself as a gallery owner,' said Clara, trying to ignore what was happening outside. 'You were a huge success.'

'And you ruined that,' said Fortin.

The storm was now directly overhead. Peter lit the candles and the oil lamps as the lights flickered on and off. On and off.

Clara, though, was frozen in her chair. Staring at Denis Fortin.

'I'd told everyone I'd dropped you because you were crap, and they believed me. Until the Musée decided to give you a solo show. A solo show, for chrissake. It made me look like a fool. I lost all credibility. I have nothing except my reputation, and you took that away.'

'Is that why you killed Lillian here?' asked Clara. 'In our garden?'

'When people remember your show,' he said, staring at her, 'I want them to remember a corpse in your garden. I want you to remember that. To think of your solo show, and to see Lillian, dead.'

He glared at the semi-circle of faces. They looked as though he was something fetid, something fecal.

The lights flickered, then dimmed. A brown-out. They could feel the strain as the light fought to stay on.

And then it left.

And they were left with the wavering candle-light.

No one spoke. Instead they waited, to see if something else would happen. Something worse. They could hear the furious lashing of the wind in the trees, and the rain against the windows and the roof.

Gamache, though, never took his eyes off Denis Fortin.

'If you hated me that much, why'd you come to my *vernissage* at the Musée?' Clara asked.

Fortin turned back to Gamache. 'Can you guess?'

'To apologize,' said Gamache.

Fortin smiled. 'Once Lillian left and the howl in my head settled down, I got to thinking.'

'How to kill twice,' said Gamache.

'A *coup de grâce*,' said Fortin.

'Grace had nothing to do with it,' said Gamache. 'It was a plan filled with hatred.'

'If it was, it was put there by Lillian,' said Fortin. 'She made the monster. She shouldn't have been surprised when it turned on her. And yet, you know, she was.'

'How did you know Lillian even knew me?' asked Clara.

'She told me. Told me what she was doing. Going around and apologizing to people. She said she'd tried to find you in the Montréal phone book, but you weren't there. She wondered if I'd ever heard of you.'

'And what did you tell her?'

He smiled then. Slowly.

'At first I said no, but after she left I got to thinking. I called and told her about your show. Her reaction to the news was almost pay-back enough. She wasn't altogether happy to hear it.'

His vile smile spread to his eyes.

'The Québec art world is a small place, and I'd heard about the after-party down here, though I hadn't, of course, been invited. I told Lillian and suggested it would be a good place for her to talk to you. Took her a few days, but she called back. Wanted the details.'

'But you had a problem,' said the Chief Inspector. 'You'd been to Three Pines before, so giving Lillian directions was no problem. And you knew she was happy to crash the party. But you needed to be here too. And for that you needed a legitimate invitation. But you and Clara weren't exactly on good terms.'

'True, but Lillian had given me an idea.' Fortin looked at Clara. 'I knew if I apologized you'd accept. Which is why you'll never make it in the art world. No guts. No backbone. I knew if I asked to come to the party here, begged, you'd agree. But I didn't have to. You invited me.'

Fortin shook his head. 'I mean, honestly. I treat you like crap and you not only forgive me, but invite me down to your home? You've got to have more sense than that, Clara. People'll take advantage of you, if you're not careful.'

Clara glared at him, but kept her mouth shut.

Another great blast of thunder shook the home, as the storm bounced and magnified, trapped in the valley.

The living room felt intimate. Ancient. As an old sin was revealed. The light from the candles faltered, catching people and furniture. Turning them into something grotesque on the walls, as though there was another range of dark listeners behind them.

'How did you know I killed Lillian?' Fortin asked Gamache.

'It was, finally, quite simple,' said Gamache. 'It had to be someone who'd been to the village before. Knew not only how to find Three Pines but which home was Clara's. It seemed too much of a coincidence that Lillian would be killed just by chance in Clara's garden. No, it must have been planned. And if it was planned, then what was the purpose? Killing Lillian in the garden hurt two people. Lillian, of course. But also Clara. And the party gave you a village filled with suspects. Other people who have known Lillian. Might have wanted her dead. That also explained the timing. The murderer had to be someone in the artistic community, who knew Clara and Lillian, and Three Pines.'

The Chief Inspector held Fortin's gleaming eyes.

'You.'

'If you're expecting remorse you won't find it. She was a hateful, vindictive bitch.'

Gamache nodded. 'I know. But she was trying to get better. She might not have said it as you'd have liked, but I think she really was sorry for what she'd done.'

'You try forgiving someone who ruined your life, you smug bastard, then come and lecture me about forgiveness.'

'If that's the criteria, then let me lecture you.'

Everyone turned to a dark corner, where there was just the suggestion of an outline. Of an odd woman, with mismatched clothing.

'*She's a natural*,' said Suzanne in a whisper, still heard amid the din outside. *'Producing art like it's a bodily function.* I managed to forgive that. And you know why?'

No one answered.

'God forgive me, not for Lillian's sake but my own. I'd held on to that hurt, coddled it, fed it, grew it. Until it had all but consumed me. But finally I wanted something even more than I wanted my pain.'

The storm seemed to have slipped out of the valley and was slowly lumbering away, to another destination.

'A quiet place,' said Chief Inspector Gamache, 'in the bright sunshine.'

Suzanne smiled and nodded. 'Peace.'

THIRTY

⌒

The next morning dawned overcast but fresh, the rain and heavy humidity of the day before had vanished. As the morning progressed breaks appeared in the clouds.

'Chiaroscuro,' said Thierry Pineault, falling into step beside Gamache as he took his morning walk. Leaves and small branches were scattered around the village green and front gardens, but no trees were down from the storm.

'*Pardon?*'

'The sky.' Pineault pointed. 'A contrast of dark and light.'

Gamache smiled.

They strolled together in silence. As they walked they noticed Ruth leaving her home, shutting her little gate and limping along a well-worn path to the bench. Giving a cursory wipe of her hand on the wet wood she sat, staring into the distance.

'Poor Ruth,' said Pineault. 'Sitting all day on that bench feeding the birds.'

'Poor birds,' said Gamache and Pineault laughed. As they watched, Brian came out of the B and B. He waved to the Chief Justice, nodded to Gamache, then walked across the green to sit beside Ruth.

'Does he have a death wish?' asked Gamache. 'Or is he drawn to wounded things?'

'Neither. He's drawn to healing things.'

'He'd fit in well here,' said the Chief Inspector, looking around the village.

'You like it here, don't you,' said Thierry, watching the large man beside him.

'I do.'

The two men stopped and watched Brian and Ruth sitting side-by-side, apparently in their own worlds.

'You must be very proud of him,' said Gamache. 'It's incredible that a boy with such a background could get clean and sober.'

'I'm happy for him,' said Thierry. 'But not proud. Not my place to be proud of him.'

'I think you're being modest, sir. Not every sponsor has such success, I imagine.'

'His sponsor?' said Thierry. 'I'm not his sponsor.'

'Then what are you?' Gamache asked, trying not to show his surprise. He looked from the Chief Justice to the pierced young man on the bench.

'I'm his sponsee. He's my sponsor.'

'I beg your pardon?' said Gamache.

'Brian's my sponsor. He's eight years sober, I'm only two.'

Gamache looked from the elegant Thierry Pineault, in gray flannels and light cashmere sweater, to the skinhead.

'I know what you're thinking, Chief Inspector, and you're right. Brian is pretty tolerant of me. He gets a lot of grief from his friends when he's seen with me in public. My suits and ties and all. Very embarrassing,' Thierry smiled.

'That wasn't exactly what I was thinking,' said Gamache. 'But close enough.'

'You didn't really think I sponsored him, did you?'

'Well I certainly didn't think it was the other way around,' said Gamache. 'Isn't there—'

'Anyone else?' asked Thierry P. 'Lots of others, but I have my reasons for choosing Brian. I'm very grateful he agreed to sponsor me. He saved my life.'

'In that case, I'm grateful to him as well,' said Gamache. 'My apologies.'

'Is that an amend, Chief Inspector?' Thierry asked with a grin.

'It is.'

'Then I accept.'

They continued their walk. It was worse than Gamache had feared. He'd wondered who the Chief Justice's sponsor might be. Someone in AA, obviously. Another alcoholic, with great influence over a greatly influential man. But it never occurred to Gamache that Thierry Pineault would choose a skinhead as a sponsor.

He must have been drunk.

'I realize I'm over-stepping my bounds—'

'Then don't do it, Chief Inspector.'

'—but this is no ordinary situation. You're an important man.'

'And Brian isn't?'

'Of course he is. But he's also a convicted felon. A young man with a record of drug abuse and alcoholism, who killed a little girl while driving drunk.'

'What do you know of that case?'

'I know he admits it. I heard his share. And I know he went to prison for it.'

They walked in silence around the village green, the rain from the day before rose in a mist as the morning warmed up. It was early yet. Few had risen. Just the mist, and the two men, walking around and around the tall pine trees. And Ruth and Brian on the bench.

'The little girl he killed was my granddaughter.'

Gamache stopped.

'Your granddaughter?'

Thierry stopped too and nodded. 'Aimée. She was four years old. She'd be twelve now. If it hadn't happened. Brian went to prison for five years. The day he got out he came over to our house. And apologized. We didn't accept, of course. Told him to go away. But he kept coming back. Mowing my daughter's lawn, washing their car. I'm afraid a lot of the chores had sort of fallen by the wayside. I was drinking heavily and wasn't much help. But then Brian started doing all those things. Once a week he showed up and did chores, for her and for us. He never spoke. Just did them and left.'

Thierry began walking again, and Gamache caught up with him.

'One day, after about a year, he started talking to me about his drinking. About why he drank and how he felt. It was exactly how I felt. I didn't admit it of course. Didn't want to admit I had anything in common with this horrible creature. But Brian knew. Then one day he told me we were going for a drive. And he took me to my first AA meeting.'

They were back at the bench.

'He saved my life. I'd gladly trade that life for Aimée. I know Brian would too. When I was a few months sober he came to me again and asked my forgiveness.'

Thierry stopped on the road.

'And I gave it.'

'Clara, no. Please.'

Peter stood in their bedroom, wearing just his pajama bottoms.

Clara looked at him. There wasn't a single spot on that beautiful body she hadn't touched. Stroked. Loved.

And didn't, she knew, love still. His body wasn't the issue. His mind wasn't the issue. It was his heart.

'You have to go,' she said.

'But why? I'm doing my best, I really am.'

'I know you are, Peter. But we need time apart. We both have to figure out what's important. I know I do. Maybe this'll make us appreciate what we have.'

'But I already do,' Peter pleaded. He looked around in panic. The thought of leaving terrified him. Leaving this room, this home. Their friends. The village. Clara.

Going up that road and over that hill. Out of Three Pines.

Where to? What place could be better than this?

'*Oh, no no no,*' he moaned.

But he knew if Clara wanted this, then he had to go. Had to leave.

'Just for a year,' said Clara.

'Promise?' he said, his eyes bright and holding hers. Afraid to blink in case she broke contact.

'Next year, on exactly this date,' Clara said.

'I'll come home,' said Peter.

'And I'll be waiting for you. We'll have a barbecue, just the two of us. Steaks. And young asparagus. And baguettes from Sarah's boulangerie.'

'I'll bring a bottle of red wine,' he said. 'And we won't invite Ruth.'

'We won't invite anyone,' agreed Clara.

'Just us.'

'Just us,' she said.

Then Peter Morrow dressed, and packed a single suitcase.

From his bedroom window Jean Guy Beauvoir could see the Chief walking slowly to their car. He knew he should hurry, shouldn't keep the man waiting, but there was something he needed to do first.

Something he knew he could finally do.

After getting up, and taking a pill, and having breakfast Jean Guy Beauvoir knew this was the day.

Peter tossed the suitcase into their car. Clara was standing beside him.

Peter could feel himself teetering on the verge of the truth. 'There's something I need to tell you.'

'Haven't we said enough?' she asked, exhausted. She hadn't slept all night. The power had finally come back on at two thirty, and she'd still been awake. After shutting off the lights and going to the bathroom she'd crawled back to bed.

And watched Peter sleep. Watched him breathe, his cheek smushed into the pillow. His long lashes resting together. His hands relaxed.

She studied that face. That lovely body, beautiful into its fifties.

And now the moment had come to let it go.

'No, I need to tell you something,' he said.

She looked at him, and waited.

'I'm sorry that Lillian wrote that terrible review back at school.'

'Why are you telling me this now?' Clara asked, puzzled.

'It's just that I was standing close to her when they were looking at your work and I think I—'

'Yes?' Clara asked, guarded.

'I should have told her how great I thought it was. I mean, I told her I loved your art, but I think I could have been clearer.'

Clara smiled. 'Lillian was Lillian. You couldn't have changed her mind. Don't worry about it.'

She took Peter's hands and rubbed them softly, then she kissed him on his lips.

And left. Walking through their gate, down their path, and through her door.

Just before it closed Peter remembered something else. '*Arisen*,' he called. '*Hope takes its place among the modern masters.*' He stared at the closed door, sure he'd called out in time. Sure she'd heard. 'I memorized the reviews, Clara. All the good ones. I know them by heart.'

But Clara was inside her home. Leaning against her door.

Her eyes closed, she fished in her pocket and brought out the coin. The beginner's chip.

She grasped it so tightly a prayer became printed on her palm.

Jean Guy picked up the phone, and began dialing. Two, three, four numbers. Further than he'd ever been before hanging up. Six, seven numbers.

Sweat sprung to his palms and he felt light-headed.

Out the window he watched the Chief Inspector toss his bag into the back of the car.

Chief Inspector Gamache closed the back door to the car and turned round, watching Ruth and Brian.

Then someone else came into his field of vision.

Olivier walked slowly as though approaching a landmine. He paused just once, then kept going, stopping only when he reached the bench, and Ruth.

She didn't move, but continued to stare into the sky.

'She'll sit there forever, of course,' said Peter, coming up beside Gamache. 'Waiting for something that won't happen.'

Gamache turned to him. 'You don't think Rosa will come back?'

'No, I don't. And neither do you. There's no kindness in false hope.' His voice was hard.

'You aren't expecting a miracle today?' Gamache asked.

'Are you?'

'Always. And I'm never disappointed. I'm about to go home to the woman I love, who loves me. I do a job I believe in with people I admire. Every morning when I swing my legs out of bed I feel like I walk on water.' Gamache looked Peter in the eyes. 'As Brian said last night, sometimes drowning men are saved.'

As they watched, Olivier sat on the bench and joined Ruth and Brian staring up at the sky. Then he took off his blue cardigan and draped it over Ruth's shoulders. The old poet didn't move. But after a moment she spoke.

'Thank you,' she said. 'Numb nuts.'

Eleven numbers.

The phone was ringing. Jean Guy almost hung up. His heart was beating so hard he thought for sure he'd never hear if anyone answered. And probably pass out if they did.

'Oui, âllo?' came the cheerful voice.

'Hello?' he managed. 'Annie?'

Armand Gamache watched Peter Morrow drive slowly along du Moulin, and out of Three Pines.

As he turned back to the village he saw Ruth get to her feet. She was staring into the distance. And then he heard it. A far cry. A familiar cry.

Ruth searched the skies, a veined and bony hand at her throat clutching the blue cardigan.

The sun broke through a small crack in the clouds. The embittered old poet turned her face to the sound and the light. Straining to see into the distance, something not quite there, not quite visible.

And in her weary eyes there was a tiny dot. A glint, a gleam.

ACKNOWLEDGEMENTS

Many people were whispering in my ear as I wrote *A Trick of the Light*. Some still in my life, some now gone but always remembered.

I won't go on at length, except to say I'm deeply grateful I got a chance to write this book. But much more than that, I'm deeply grateful, after many years as a resistor, I now completely believe that sometimes drowning men (and women) are saved. And, when coughed back, might even find some measure of peace in a small village. In the sunshine.

Thank you to my husband and partner and soulmate, Michael. For also believing those things. And believing in me. As I believe in him.

Thank you to Hope Dellon, my brilliant editor at Minotaur Books, who is perfectly named. Her remarkable gifts as an editor are only surpassed by her gifts as a person. For Dan Mallory, my dazzling editor at Little, Brown, who has jets on his heels and has taken me along on a giddy and thrilling ride with one of the bright lights of publishing. I have him in my death-grip.

Thank you to Teresa Chris, my amazing agent, who has crossed that border and become a friend. For guiding this book, and my career, with such a sure and gracious hand.

One thing that has surprised me about a writing career is the mountain of detail involved. Permissions, mailings, accounting, ordering supplies, and simply organizing everything so important things, like the tour schedule, don't get lost. I'm frankly terrible at those sorts of things. Happily the fabulous Lise Desrosiers is as disciplined and organized as I am slothful. In looking after those elements of my life Lise has freed me up to write. We make a great team and I want to thank Lise deeply not only for her hard work but her unfailing optimism and good humor.

I hope you enjoyed reading *A Trick of the Light*. It took several lifetimes to write.